Lucky Numbers

GG CARVER

CHAPTER ONE

'Get your apples! Juicy apples!' bellowed the market trader just as Lucy passed by, almost deafening her. The Saturday market was always busy, but even more so today as the amiable summer sun was proudly displaying its power, bringing out the brilliance of every colour. Oranges, cherries, raspberries, and tomatoes, seemed almost fluorescent as they bathed in the sunshine waiting to be purchased.

Lucy wandered along at a leisurely pace, the crowds of people not allowing for anything more. Soaking up the atmosphere under the shade of her blue and white striped hat, the wide floppy brim allowed her shoulders some protection from the burning heat. You could buy almost anything at the market, from shoelaces to ancient Chinese fertility treatments.

The eclectic mix of sights, sounds and smells was a feast for the senses. Burgers sizzled as they cooked on the grill; paper bags rustled as they were filled with various produce. The distinctive smell of incense drifted through the crowds from the New Age stall, annoying two old ladies that tottered along the cobbled street, waving their hands in front of their faces.

An ambiguous cacophony of voices, laughter, and general hum of people, swarmed in the air. While the relaxed beat of reggae music serenaded the crowds and seemed the perfect compliment to the sunny day.

Lucy stopped to browse the sunglasses stall, which was crowded with young girls wearing skirts that were far too short, and young men with naked torsos covered in far too many tattoos.

After switching between a light-blue pair and a brown-tinted pair several times, Lucy eventually decided to treat herself to the brown pair which matched her chestnut curls. She paid the shirtless vendor and headed down to the end of the market past the briny smell of the fishmongers, with the catch of the day artistically presented on a bed of ice that was melting faster than the Polarice-caps. She stopped to buy some plump strawberries, that looked too delicious to pass by, when her phone rang. She prised it out of her tight white denim shorts.

'Hello, Suzie.'

'I need a man!'

'Oh do you now? Well, I'm at the market, and they sell pretty much everything, but I don't think they sell men.'

'Don't they? Bugger.'

Lucy pointed with a smile to the punnet of strawberries she wanted. 'No, I'm afraid not, although there's an abundance of half naked males parading around this morning.'

The stall owner placed Lucy's choice into a bag and

handed it to her.

'Really? I might have to get my arse in gear and get down there then.'

Wedging the phone between her cheek and her shoulder Lucy paid for the goods, mouthing, *thank you,* as she took the bag.

'I'll warn you though Suzie, there are quite a few with more tattoos than teeth.'

'Mmm, I like a tattooed man, but I also like teeth. Why can I never have my cake and eat it?'

Suzie deserved to find a decent man, especially after her last relationship with a rock climbing instructor called André. He got his kicks from hanging off a cliff face hundreds of feet in the air, and from making Suzie feel worthless with his constant criticism and mental torture.

Like all cowards, he was a perfect gentleman in public and a total bastard in private.

'I thought you had a few dates lined up?'

'Humph, it's been a disaster. I'm finished with internet dating. The last guy I met had lost about six inches in height from his profile description, and it had taken half his hair with it. He was hobbit-like.'

Lucy chuckled into her phone and headed through the market, twisting her shoulders left and right like a salsa dancer, as she dodged the oncoming crowds.

'You may laugh, missy; it was bloody awful. I'm only five foot six, so you can tell how small he was. So, I'm determined to meet a man the old-fashioned way, which leads me to the reason for my call. I was wondering if you fancied putting your glad rags on and hitting the town?'

'Oh, I'm sorry, Suzie, I can't. Mark's coming over tonight. What about Claire?'

'Claire's busy servicing her husband: he's back from the oil rig for the weekend. Are you and Mark back together then?'

Lucy was beckoned towards a waiting stool that sat in front of the artist's easel, surrounded by cartoon sketches of celebrities and past customers. She respectfully declined with a faint smile and a slight wave of her hand.

'No, but I'm sure that's why he wants to come over. He's been texting and calling me all week, and I've finally given in.'

'Third time lucky maybe?'

'Huh, it's definitely three strikes and he's out.'

'So it looks like I'm spending Saturday night with Simon Cowell then,' Suzie sighed.

'You know you love him,' Lucy said playfully.

'Yes, there is something about him, although I'm not sure I could love a man that wears higher heels than me.'

Lucy had come to the end of the market, and she stood and stared at an old gypsy caravan that sat alongside the last stall.

'Yeah, that is a little off-putting, especially if he kept nicking your stilettos.'

'Exactly. Okay, Lu, I'll let you go. Call me in the week, and good luck with tonight.'

'Thanks, Suzie, we'll go out next week, yeah?'

'Deal, speak to you later, babe.'

'Bye.'

Lucy slipped her phone back into her pocket while she contemplated the old wagon, which looked like something from the Wild West. The cab was blood-red and decorated with intricate carvings, which appeared to be sheathed in gold leaf. A canvas roof, the colour of oxidised copper, was stretched over the wooden bow-top. Four spoked, pale-yellow wooden wheels transported the antique wagon.

A collection of A-boards were positioned each side of the small timber staircase that led to the entrance, which was covered from the inside with a crimson curtain. It was there every week; Lucy had always been intrigued by it – or, rather, by the promise it offered. She read one of the A-boards, as she did nearly every week.

Do you want to know your future?

Do you have questions that need answering?

Maybe you need guidance but are unsure who to turn to.

If the answer is yes, then step inside and let Lady Lavinia help and advise you.

The answer was yes to all of the above. She eased through the crowd to take a closer look at the black-and-white photos that hung around the entrance.

Z-list celebrities from long ago, all with a startled expression on their faces as if they had been photobombed, stood next to a rather exotic-looking woman with mysterious dark eyes, wearing a headscarf.

Lucy had always wanted to give it a try, but felt a bit silly. It was all fake, wasn't it? She was about to head back into the market when a raspy, smoke-worn voice called to her from behind the curtain of the old wagon. 'Come in, child.Don't be shy.'

Lucy was thrown somewhat: there were no windows; the voice was ownerless.

'Oh, no, sorry I've… I've got to get back…'

An emaciated hand appeared from behind the curtain. 'You of all people have nothing to be afraid of.' A bony finger pointed at her, and then slowly retreated.

Lucy stood rooted to the spot. *Why me of all people?* she

thought, while she waited for another teaser. The theatrics had worked. Lucy stepped closer to the caravan with a growing feeling of apprehension, and paused at the stairs.

'What are you waiting for, child?'the witch like-voice croaked from behind the curtain, and despite the heat, Lucy's body prickled with goose bumps, half-scared, half excited. She glanced around to see if anyone was watching before slowly stepping up to the mysterious doorway.

She didn't dare touch the opulent curtain without permission. 'May I come in?' Her voice was laced with unease.

'Enter.'

With the palms of her hands together, Lucy slid them between the soft velvet curtains and parted them. The daylight seized its chance and darted into the small space.

'Come in, come in.' The command was spoken with mild annoyance. Lucy stepped inside, and the curtains gracefully fell back together, banishing all natural light.

The interior was lit by a scattering of scented candles that suffused the air with the gentle scent of jasmine and mint.

The exotic lady in the photographs was sitting at a small round table with a crystal ball upon it. Like the wax of the candles, her mysterious beauty had melted away with the years. Two deep ravine-like creases ran along each side of her wide nose, down to thin lips that looked permanently pursed.

Her black headscarf helped to conceal a brow that indicated a troubled life. Even with the heat of the day, and candles, it was surprisingly cool inside the wagon.

'Sit down, child.

Lucy placed her bags down and sat in the old Windsor chair opposite Lady Lavinia. The crystal ball took full advantage of the candlelight as it sat between the two women, glistening like a giant snow globe. Lucy glanced over to a pack of tarot cards that were fanned out on the padded bench seat opposite. Next to the cards was a ouija board with a pack of cigarettes and the morning newspaper placed on top of it. 'Do you use the tarot cards or—'

'Twenty pounds.' Lucy was startled and slightly offended by the blunt demand. 'Oh, okay.' She leaned over and took her purse out from her woven straw bag. She peeled out a £20 note and handed it over. The bony hand made another appearance from under a black shawl, and took the requested payment without thanks.

Lucy was beginning to wish she had walked away, but it was too late now. She looked into Lady Lavinia's eyes, which were heavily bordered with black eyeliner, and together with her matt black frizzy hair that flanked her time-worn face, she looked like an evil pirate queen. Lucy half expected her to shout, *your money or your life!* But instead she asked for her hands. She was more than a little frightened of her by now and immediately placed her hands each side of the crystal ball, palms up. Her cold blue eyes never left Lucy's, and her skeletal hands turned Lucy's over, not wishing to see her palms.

'Hold my hands, child.' Lucy reluctantly wrapped her sunshine brown fingers around the pale scrawny hands of the pirate queen. The tissue-like skin wrinkled under Lucy's gentle grip. Her eyes diverted to the crystal ball then back up to the uncomfortable glare of the old face.

She suddenly realised that there were no sounds coming from the busy market outside. All was perfectly quiet, including the old lady, who had just plundered her for £20. *Okay, I'm freaked out now!* Lucy was just drawing breath to say something when the old lady's voice cracked out, like a rake over hot coals. 'I see that you don't like facing up to the hard work that a relationship entails.'

That's not true. Is this about Mark? Tell me more.

'I see you like to have fun, but life isn't always about fun, and won't always go your way.'

Hmm, that's a bit vague. Lucy didn't react, not wanting to give anything away.

'Good friends will come and go, bad friends will come and stay.'

Can I have that one the other way around please?

'The tree of life grows many branches, some reach for the sky, and others break and fall.'

Okay, crazy lady, this sounds like random babbling. Lucy was beginning to wish she had spent the £20 on the pale blue sunglasses. They may not have shown her the future, but like this reading, she could see straight through them.

'A sister's love is unconditional, from others it is not.'

Hello, I don't have a bloody sister. Lucy resisted the urge to roll her eyes, as the old lady's gaze hadn't faltered. The reading continued under a veil of generality. Lucy began to suspect she was picking out random lines from the horoscope of the morning paper. She had got the horror part right anyway: she'd scared the hell out of her so far.

She found herself thinking about the fruit salad she would be making for this evening, when without warning Lady Lavinia's grip suddenly tightened and her chest wheezed like an old cat as her breathing deepened. Her eyes dropped from Lucy's face for the first time, down to the crystal ball.

The melodramatics certainly worked, she had Lucy's full attention once again.

'I see a man . . .'

Here we go, tall, dark and handsome is he?

'A good man.' She shook her head, her face creased in concentration. 'It's not clear . . . troubled heart . . . difficulty, great sorrow.' She tilted her head to one side and her wrinkled face contorted further, like she had a terrible headache. The deadpan performance had turned into a very animated one, and Lucy's scepticism was quickly vanishing.

'I see numbers... 3, 2, 9... 7, 4... 6,1,5.'

Lucy repeated the numbers in her head, several times, making a mental note.

'These numbers will be lucky for you.' Her head straightened, her eyes still closed, the look of concentration remained etched onto her face. The sudden hiss of air being sucked in through the desert-dry lips startled Lucy. The old lady's hand shot up to her face, covering her mouth.

Her head shook quickly from side to side.

'What! What do you see?' Panic edged its way into Lucy's thoughts; the face she was looking at didn't evoke good news. 'Tell me, please.'

The pirate queen's heavy eyelids raised slowly like a portcullis, to reveal her cold blue eyes bathing in a well of tears. If this was an act, she was very good.

'What did you see?' She repeated her question, feeling a growing sense of unease at what the answer might be.

'Deep scars, torment... a battle lies ahead, but together,

together you can make a difference.'

She let go of Lucy's other hand and exhaled slowly, like a smoker enjoying their first cigarette of the day.

'Make a difference to what? What battle lies ahead? I don't understand.'

'The reading is over.' The old lady's reply was just as frustrating as her predictions. The legs of her chair screeched as they scraped over the floor. She stood and made her way to the comfort of the padded bench.

Lucy remained in her seat, still in the moment, her mind racing. 'Can you tell me what the man looked like? Is he a friend or a stranger?'

'The reading is over.' The deadpan replies returned.

Lucy watched her unwelcoming host for a second before jumping to a conclusion.

'Oh, I understand.' She reached down for her purse and rose to find Lady Lavinia gesturing to the exit with an open hand.

The reading is over. She gave the old lady a nod of understanding, collected her bags and thanked her. Lady Lavinia nodded wearily from her crumpled position in the corner. Lucy slipped back through the curtain, taking her frustration and disappointment with her.

The bright daylight pained her eyes; she carefully stepped down the staircase before delving into her bag and pulling out her sunglasses and a pen. The welcome shades were slipped over her aching eyes, then she quickly wrote the numbers Lady Lavinia had quoted onto the back of her hand, before she forgot them.

3,2,9,7,4,6,1,5. What the hell could they be? A phone number, or a bank account maybe? Going over everything she'd been told, Lucy dissected every sentence, but none of it made any sense. The noise from the market faded back in as she headed into the crowds. Lucy turned to take another look at the old wagon that had tempted her curiosity for so long. Her attempt to satisfy it had only served to inflame it even more.

CHAPTER TWO

6.30. Mark would be arriving any minute. The morning's escapade with the pirate queen hadn't relinquished its grip on Lucy's imagination. She saved the mysterious numbers in her phone as *Gold And Treasure*.

Lucy laid a table in her postage stamp-sized garden; it was such a lovely evening it seemed criminal to be sat inside. She wasn't sure what the night would bring or what she wanted it to bring, for that matter.

The last time she had seen Mark was five weeks ago, when he had said he needed to get his head straight, and used that tired old line, "it's not you, it's me." It was the second time they had separated, and both instances it had been Mark's decision.

He was a real man's man: he loved sport, especially golf, and his Friday nights out with the boys playing pool. He had a big personality, but he also had a distant side. His mood could drop for no apparent reason and it was difficult to deal with sometimes. Work pressure was usually the given reason.

The bell rang and Lucy smoothed out her white cotton dress before opening the door.

'Hello, Lucy.'

Mark stood there holding a large bunch of pink and white carnations and displaying his best version of puppy eyes.

'Come on in.'

Mark stepped into the hall and kissed Lucy on the cheek.

'Mmm, you smell nice. I got you these.' He handed over the flowers with an air of guilt.

'Thank you, they're lovely.'

For two people that had been intimately involved only a short time ago, their greetings had the awkwardness of a couple meeting for the first time. Lucy dipped her nose into the blossoms and drew in their subtle scent.

'I'll put these in some water.'

She closed the front door and led the way into the lounge, then through to the cramped kitchen. Taking out a clear glass vase from under the sink, she filled it with water.

'Haven't we been having fantastic weather?' said Mark, leaning against the doorframe with his hands in his pockets.

'Mmm, we have. I don't think it will last though.' The weather was the saviour of many stilted conversations. 'What would you like to drink?' She dropped the flowers into the vase; they fanned themselves around the rim perfectly. 'There's beer in the fridge or wine on the table.'

'I'll have a beer, thanks.'

Lucy grabbed a cold bottle from the fridge and took the opener from the drawer.

'Let me do that.'

Mark stepped alongside her and grabbed the neck of the bottle, trapping Lucy's fingers. She briefly glanced up, meeting his gaze, before turning away.

'I'll… er… I'll have wine,' she said, wiggling her hand free, then reaching up to the wall unit and taking down a glass for herself.

'How's your work?'

The innocent question was really code for: have you got your shit together now?

'Work's good, it's good… Lu… thanks for inviting me over tonight'

Lucy half-filled her glass and turned around slowly, her chin pointing to the floor and her eyebrows reaching for the ceiling. 'Er, have you forgotten about the twenty text messages, and seven e-mails you sent me asking if you could come over?' There was a facetious tone to her voice.

'Well, I may have suggested it, yes.' He shrugged innocently, his mouth curling up slightly at the corners.

'Borderline harassment, I'd call it.'

'My next step was to send you my underwear doused in cologne; I read somewhere that women love that sort of thing.'

Her semi-serious expression gave way to a sneaky smile that crept onto her face.

'I miss you, Lucy.'

Her smile withered like a flower in the desert.

'I know I've treated you badly… but I intend to make up for that.'

'Mark…' Lucy paused. She held her breath for a few moments, before letting out a sigh. 'I'm not sure if I want that – this. I never know where I stand with you.'

He placed his beer on the side and stepped over to Lucy. Taking her wine glass, he held her fingers tightly.

'It will be different this time.'

'Why will it?' She looked up into his imploring eyes.

'Because I'm different, and I need you in my life, Lucy – simple as that.'

If only it was as simple as that. She wanted to believe him, as much for his sake as hers, but giving Mark another chance seemed like giving in somehow; like saying, you've treated me like dirt, but don't worry, it's okay, take another shot at it.

'What do you say Lucy?' She looked at his clean-shaven handsome face. His wavy blond hair flopped down each side of his sage-green eyes.

Lady Lavinia's mystic words floated around in her thoughts. *A battle lies ahead…* She didn't want to fight, but didn't all relationships have to be worked at?

'I think we should take one step at a time, and not get ahead of ourselves.'

Her diplomatic answer had obviously been converted into another meaning by the display of teeth Mark gave her.

'Now if you don't give me that glass of alcohol back, I won't be responsible for my actions.'

The ice hadn't been broken, so much as melted by the balmy heat of the evening. Now the awkward moment was out of the way, they both relaxed with the help of the beer and wine. Dining alfresco, making the most of the tropical weather that the UK was experiencing, they enjoyed a chorizo and tomato salad that Lucy had prepared for them.

Mark was in good spirits, boosted no doubt by the prospect of a possible reunion. He told her how he felt like a new man, as the pressure at work had eased with the arrival of a new manager.

That was good news. His role as an assistant sales manager at Ford had served to create two very different personalities in Mark, and seemed to be the root of all their problems.

'Lu, that was gorgeous,' Mark commented, as he popped the last bit of fresh focaccia bread into his mouth. 'You always were good with food.' He sagged back in his chair and took a sip of his beer.

'Thank you.' She smiled, accepting the compliment.

'The garden's looking good.'

'Yeah, I just wished I had more room: I'd like to have a little veggie patch.'

'I don't know where you get the patience from.'

Lucy looked at the small square space, admiring her cultivation skills.

'Gardening is very therapeutic; you should try it. It does you good to get your hands dirty every now and again.'

'Really? Well, I think I'll take your word for it. I'm not one for digging around in the dirt.'

The table they were sitting at occupied most of the perfectly clipped lawn. A sweeping border encircled them with an abundance of colour. Each and every flower, being a natural exhibitionist, was competing to be the brightest and the biggest.

'I hope you're hungry for more. I've made a fruit salad.'

'I'm always hungry for more from you.'

Lucy rose from her chair. 'In that case, I'd better try and fill you up, hadn't I?' She collected their empty plates and cutlery.

'Let me help you with that.'

Mark placed his hands on the arms of the chair and began to lift himself.

'No, no, you stay there. I'll only be a minute.'

He was happy to oblige and lowered himself back into his seat, linking his hands behind his head, as carefree as the fluttering butterfly that was spoilt for choice in the small patch of lusciousness.

Lucy's voice resounded from the kitchen.

'Damn it.'

'What's wrong?' Mark called out over his head.

Lucy appeared at the open door, holding her purse and car keys. 'I forgot to pick up the bloody cream, I'll pop down to the shop and get some.'

'No, I'll go,' Mark sprang out of his chair. 'You've done enough. Is there anything else you want?'

Lucy shook her head.

'Just cream. I must have cream on my fruit salad.'

'Whatever the lady wants, she shall have; although you will have to pay for it yourself, as I didn't bring any cash with me. Sorry.'

Lucy handed him a ten-pound note from her purse. He kissed her on the forehead and made his way to the front door.

'I'll get us a lottery ticket, it's a 20-million jackpot tonight. You never know, we may be able to get you that bigger garden.'

Lucy wandered back into the kitchen, then stopped for a moment. Staring into space with her hand pressed against her cheek, she felt as though she had forgotten something. Her hand dropped from her face and her eyes focused as a thought surfaced.

Lottery numbers. What if the fortune teller has given me the winning lottery numbers? She told herself not to be silly: what were the chances of that happening? But there was always achance. Lucy's body jolted into action like a sprinter out of the starting blocks. She grabbed her phone and ran to the front door. Mark's car was just pulling away.

'Mark! Hang on a minute!' She waved her hands in the air as she raced into the street.

He stopped the car with the bonnet already half in the road.

'What's wrong?' he asked, his head poking through the open window.

'Do you have a pen?'

She bent down to look into the car and tucked her falling locks behind her ears.

'Yeah, why?'

'I want you to put these numbers on for me.' She reeled off the numbers from memory, then checked them against the ones she had saved in her phone.

Mark scribbled them down onto one of his business cards. 'Why these particular numbers?'

'I... er... I had a weird dream last night, and these numbers came to me.' She didn't want to divulge that she had visited Lady Lavinia, guessing that he would probably ridicule her for it.

Mark's eyebrows raised in interest.

'A premonition, eh?' And then sank, weighed down with scepticism. 'You don't believe in that rubbish do you?' he said. Just as she suspected.

'Promise you'll put them on for me.'

'Of course I will.' He glanced at the card for a moment. 'You've got eight numbers here, Lu. Lotteries only have six.'

'Bugger... erm... cross the last two off.' She decided to stick with the order in which they had been given to her. Lucy bit her thumbnail, instantly doubting her decision.

'Sure?'

'Yes.' She nodded confidently, although she felt anything but.

'Right, if I don't hurry up I'll be too late. Be back in a moment.' Mark pulled the car out and sped away, a little too fast for the narrow road that was lined on each side with vehicles. Lucy headed back into the house, still wondering if she had chosen the right combination.

She busied herself refreshing their drinks, still dwelling on Mark's comments about it all being 'a load of rubbish.' She felt silly for chasing after the dangling carrot. Opening the fridge door, she stood staring into the chilled space, asking herself if she thought it could work with Mark. She certainly loved him once, and when they first met three years ago it had been exciting; he had been funny and adventurous then, but as time had ushered them along, the fun and adventure had transformed into responsibility and routine. Mark seemed like he had evolved into another man at times, and like a stranger you pass in the street, they had nothing to say to each other, or rather, she had nothing he wanted to hear. But Lucy hated to be alone. The human race was not created to live alone, and every living creature's existence is driven by the need to share life.

Maybe she could find what was once there? It wasn't like she was over the hill at thirty, and desperately needed to bag a man before it all went south. But there was safety in familiarity, or at least the illusion of it.

The fridge was too busy keeping the food cool to divulge any words of wisdom. So she decided to do the thing that most people rarely did: take her own advice, and take it one step at a time.

Snapping out of her daze, she took the two glass bowls containing perfectly constructed fruit salads out of the fridge and placed them on the side. A rhythmic knock at the door signalled Mark's return. Lucy wandered over and let him in.

'One tub of double cream and one lottery ticket.'

'Thank you, sir.' Taking the cream from his raised hands, she went to adorn her desserts with it.

Mark clicked on the TV and followed her into the kitchen. 'They'll be drawing the numbers soon,' he paused. 'Am I not driving home tonight, then?' Lucy turned. Mark was holding the fresh beer she had opened for him.

'Oh, yes, sorry, Mark. I didn't give it a second thought.'

She returned to whipping the cream, trying to ignore what he had said.

'I'd like to stay tonight.' There was a humble hopefulness to his words.

Looking for a suitable answer, Lucy's mind whirred around like the rotary whisk she was using. She stopped what she was doing and lifted her gaze from the bowl.

'Mark... I'm not sure that's such a good idea.' She didn't turn to face him, leaving him staring at her long chestnut-brown hair; the caramel-coloured bouncy curls, bleached by the sun, rested on her golden shoulders.

'I just want to wake up in the morning and you're there.'

'What happened to one step at a time?' she asked, but she knew Mark didn't do things by half; it was all or nothing.

'I'll sleep in the spare room.'

Lucy turned to him and counteracted with the answer that usually pacified.

'we'll see.'

She returned to her whisking. Mark stepped over, brushed her hair to one side and tenderly kissed her shoulder.

'That looks good,' he reached over and dipped his finger into the thickening cream.

'Hey, naughty!' She playfully slapped his hand. 'You'll have to wait.'

'I'll wait as long as it takes.' Mark sucked the cream from his fingers and kissed her on the back of the head. He didn't push the moment any further, and Lucy was grateful for that, although he was certainly making all the right noises.

Mark sat on the couch with his elbows on his knees, watching the TV.

'They're about to draw the numbers.'

Lucy placed an indulgently large dollop of cream onto each of their desserts, then carried them into the lounge.

'Let's sit in the garden. It's too nice to be indoors,' she said.

'Yeah, I'll just watch the draw; your premonitions have got me intrigued now.'

Lucy rolled her eyes like she was agreeing with his earlier sceptical comment and went into the garden with both glass bowls. She wanted to watch it also, but didn't like the effect the fortune teller was having on her; she absolutely refused to surrender to curiosity again that day.

The evening sun was up past its bedtime, and had now

slid down the sky somewhat, creating a blanket of shade that had put one half of the garden to bed.

Lucy sat enjoying the fruits of her labour listening to the distant sounds of neighbours entertaining friends. The faint smell of barbecued food drifted through the windless air.

'We're off to a good start: that's the first number in the bag... That's two now; it's looking good so far,' he shouted playfully.

'I'll hand in my notice at work, shall I?' Lucy called back to him over her shoulder, before taking a bite of kiwi fruit.

'Bloody hell, we've got three now.'

Lucy's attention was taken from her food for a moment. *Three numbers, that's about £25, not quite enough to retire on.* She skewered one half of a plump strawberry with her fork, and delayed its fate as she held it to her lips waiting for Mark's running commentary to continue... Silence. It had all obviously fallen apart with ball number four.

'Oh well,' she shrugged, taking the juicy red diamond from her fork.

'Holy shit! Lu, we've got all five numbers so far!'

Lucy froze for a second. 'What?' she asked, although she'd clearly heard what he had said. Jumping up from her seat, she put her bowl down on the table and flip-flopped into the lounge to find Mark clutching his hair with both hands, his eyes transfixed on the television in wide-eyed bewilderment.

'What?' she repeated.

Mark's saucer-like eyes crawled slowly from the TV and up to Lucy's face.

'We've just won the fucking lottery…'

They both stared at each other, motionless, like two mannequins in a shop window.

'What?' Her stunned brain had crashed and repeated its last command once again.

'We've got all six numbers. We've just won 20 fucking million pounds!' He sprang to his feet, screaming like a teenager at a Beatles concert.

'Oh… my… God!' Lucy joined in with the hysteria, as her brain finally comprehended the words. She jogged on the spot, screaming along with Mark, and they both flung their arms around each other.

They spun around and their minds whirled around with them in an adrenaline-fuelled state of euphoria.

'You're going to get that big garden you always wanted, Lu.'

He held her by the shoulders at arm's length.

'Would Madame like one acre, or two?'

She laughed in giddy excitement at all the possibilities that lay ahead. 'It's all changes for us now, Lu.'

Lucy's gaze lowered to the floor, her thoughts turned to her reading. *Oh my god, she was right!* A shiver ran through her body at the thought of her supernatural experience. *Everything the fortune-teller had predicted had come true.* Mark was now wandering around the house, gesticulating and rambling away to himself like a lost vagrant.

Lucy picked over the parts of the fortune teller's message that applied to her and Mark, and the sting of emotion began to build. They were destined to be together. It was meant to be. Fate had decided.

Her palms were held together, cupping her mouth; she

was truly astonished by the fact that life was not what she thought it was.

'Don't you think, Lu?' Having completing a circuit of the house and garden, Mark had stopped to interrupt her contemplation.

'What, sorry?'

'I said, I'm not even going to take the car back to work. They can come and get it. I'm not wasting another minute of my life in that place. Oh, by the way, I don't think much of your psychic abilities.'

'What do you mean?' Her jubilant expression faltered.

'You didn't get any numbers, I'm afraid. It was my numbers that came up.'

She paused for a moment, shaking her head in disbelief. 'That can't be right. Are you sure?'

'Positive, not one number. Does it really matter?' He tipped his head back and let out a long sigh. '*We* are millionaires.'

Lucy watched him closely, waiting for him to say that he was joking, and it really was her numbers that had won. 'No more deadlines or targets for me.' Mark began another lap of honour, chatting away, mainly to himself.

Lucy flopped down onto the couch. Unbelievably, a feeling of disappointment had found the tiniest opening and crept in. Disappointment spawned guilt, and one fuelled the other. How could she be so ungrateful? So what if it wasn't her numbers? Like Mark had said: did it really matter? Yes, it seemed it did.

She so wanted Lady Lavinia's predictions to come true: there had been a certain comfort in the thought that everything was mapped out for her. Mark had just smashed it all to pieces: the numbers didn't mean anything

– none of it did.

Doubt began to surface. *I'll bet he's bought a ticket for the mid-week draw, or he's mixed it up with an old ticket from his wallet. There must be a mistake somewhere; how can we have won twenty million?*

'Mark… Mark!'

Mark came back into the house, red-eyed, the money already having a powerful effect on him.

'Yeah,'

'Are you absolutely sure you've got the right ticket? Something doesn't seem right.'

His eyebrows lowered in concern. 'Of course I checked every number.'

'Let's double check it.' She held out her hand for the ticket, still not convinced.

Mark stuffed his hand into his jeans and took out his wallet.

'Be careful with it.' He delicately handed over the £20,000,000 piece of paper.

Lucy picked up her phone and pulled up the winning numbers for that evening on Google.

She cautiously inspected each number on the ticket, matching them to the ones on her phone with the speed of a five-year-old. Mark stood over her, rubbing his palms together nervously, reliving it all over again. At times like this, doubt was very contagious.

'Well?' Mark asked impatiently.

She looked up into his angst-riddled face. 'It's right.'

'Yes!' He punched the air triumphantly. 'I knew it! I told you it was right. Give me that, Lu.' He took the ticket from her hand, gently, as though it was made of antique crystal and she might break it.

'I'll keep it safe.'

As he had pointed out more than once, he was indeed correct. He was also correct in the fact that not one of Lucy's numbers had been drawn, but the realisation of what had just happened soon chased away her disappointment.

They decided to savour the moment and keep the news to themselves, just for that night. Armed with wine and beer, they sat at the table outside until the moon and stars had circumnavigated the sky. They laughed and joked like old times; the money was already working its magic, ironing out all the creases in their relationship. Mark didn't sleep in the spare room that night; the beer only allowed him to make it as far as the couch. Lucy dizzily hauled herself up the stairs, ping-ponging off the walls as she went. Taking her clothes off and throwing them around the bedroom like a drunken stripper, she collapsed into bed, clutching her phone.

Wrestling with sleep, she went into her saved numbers and clicked on "Gold And Treasure". She looked over the numbers through tired squinty eyes before pressing "delete". Her phone was seemingly aware that she was drunk, and not in full control of her own thoughts, as it posed the question: "are you sure you want to delete this number?" Her head rocked backwards and forwards slightly with growing exhaustion. They were just random numbers that didn't mean a damn thing. Lucy clicked save, not entirely ready to believe that, before dropping her phone onto her chest as her body hit the shutdown button.

CHAPTER THREE

Once they had redeemed the winning ticket, the funds were paid into their new joint account within three days. The jackpot had been diluted somewhat, as there had been seven other lucky winners that night. Even so, their share was a healthy £2,857,142.80.

The next few weeks were a whirlwind of celebrations, with shopping trips, new cars and meals out with large groups of friends. Mark loved playing the generous host, while friends and people who barely fell into the bracket of acquaintances happily boarded the gravy train. Lucy took the opportunity to visit her parents, who had retired to Kefalonia two years before. They treated a small group of family and friends who joined them on the Greek island, where they ate, drank, and laughed in the sunshine.

Life was good, with none of the confinements of a normal existence, Mark was a pleasure to be with, like the man she had met three years earlier. It seemed that telling his boss what he could do with his job had given Mark almost as much pleasure as winning the money.

Lucy had also given up work. It was a hard decision to make: she loved her job as a teaching assistant at a special needs school. Leaving the children had been heartbreaking. She had been working there for just over a year, after leaving her previous position as a doctor's receptionist, a thankless job where she had been exposed to disease and illness on a biblical scale.

Her goal had always been to graduate from assistant to teacher; it was the most rewarding job she'd ever had, and she had formed a special bond with all of the children, especially one little boy. But, like Mark had said, they had a life to live and plans to make. This new life that lay before her was exciting, but also daunting.

On the flight back home, Mark suggested that their next purchase should be a house, along with the garden of her dreams. The snowball effect the money was having, had fused them together and pressed the fast forward button: things most people worked towards for years, they were able to do instantly. When they landed in overcast England, the cool breeze was as refreshing as a cold drink, after two weeks under the magnifying glass of the Greek sun.

As Mark suggested, they started their search for a home, setting a budget of £750,000. Mark wanted a modern house with clean lines, while Lucy wanted something with character.

They searched the Internet, then viewed several properties, most of which had more than benefited from the generosity of the wide-angled lens.

Nothing felt like home. Mark was completely emotionally detached from it all. His only concerns seemed to be the size of the garage and whether the garden had a shed.

It was very different for Lucy: the house had to be just right. She loved her little home, even though it was only rented. Everything was set out just how she liked it, although now Mark had moved back in, it wasn't *quite* how she liked it.

After a week of unsuccessful viewings, Lucy was sitting with her feet up on the couch, scrolling through house after house on her laptop, waiting for one to catch her attention. Sure enough, one did. She clicked on the thumbnail picture, and it enlarged to reveal a handsome, double-fronted period house.

Visually, it ticked all the boxes. Lucy's eyes raised optimistically from the photograph up to the price. 'Offers in excess of £980,000.' It was far more than they wanted to spend. Nevertheless, she continued to go through the pictures of each room, only lingering for a second on each one, eager to see the next. It became more desirable with every click, although, strangely, there were no pictures of the garden. *Mark will never go for it, it's too expensive.* Ignoring her own warning, she went to the description, just to satisfy her curiosity about what it was like outside.

'A fine example of an Edwardian home set in a highly regarded location. Offering generous four bedroom accommodation, off-road parking and large garage.' *Yes!* 'The property also benefits from a large, mature, private garden…'

Lucy read on. Every paragraph did its very best to convince her that this was indeed the house for them. She peeped over the laptop at Mark, who was sat in the chair opposite her, reading a high-performance car magazine.

'Mark.' Her voice hung onto his name in a prolonged way that gave warning of a favour about to be asked. 'Yeeeees?' His answer disguised the, *what do you want?*

'What do you think of this?' Lucy asked, being careful with the way she worded her question.

He draped his magazine over the arm of the chair and groaned himself out of his settled position.

'What have you seen?' he asked, kneeling behind the arm of the couch and peering over her shoulder. 'Oh, that's nice.' That wasn't the reaction she had been expecting. 'Er… that's not.' He had obviously seen the price.

'It ticks all the boxes.'

'Yes, including the 'too expensive' one.'

'It has got a garage.' She screwed up her nose, hoping the cutie look would help.

A whisper of a sigh left his slightly curved lips, and Lucy sensed a small victory.

'Can we just have a look at it? And if it's not 100% perfect, I'll forget about it.'

'I think the price makes it not 100% perfect, don't you?'

'Please?'

His eyes roved over the screen of the laptop for a few seconds. 'Okay, but we're only looking.'

She tipped her head back and kissed him on the cheek. 'Thank you.'

Mark got up and returned to his chair. 'I mean it, Lu,' he said, but his face didn't match his words and Lucy grinned to herself from behind the cover of the screen.

'Okay.'

Kingsfellow Real Estate were the selling agents. They would be receiving a call from Miss Eaton first thing in the morning.

Sure enough, as soon as the kitchen clock's hands reached 9 o'clock the next morning Lucy started punching Kingsfellow's number into her phone. A very well-spoken lady informed her that the house was vacant, and that there had been a lot of interest in the property, which made Lucy even more eager to see it.

12.30 was to be their time slot, and Mr Kingsfellow himself would be showing them around. Lucy thanked the lady on the end of the line and hung up. She was excited, but also worried that someone might buy it before the hands of the clock made it to 12.30.

But the morning went on and the appointment was not cancelled. Miraculously, it seemed no one had made an offer on Lucy's dream house.

She drove them through the quiet suburb, passing houses of various styles and sizes, ranging from moderate-sized homes to mansions. The cool calm voice of the satnav advised her to take the next left; Lucy followed her instructions, turning into Southshaw Avenue. It was a wide leafy road bordered by trees of dinosaur proportions.

They drove slowly under the canopy of the green giants, whose thick branches thinned out as they stretched across the road in an attempt to touch their fellow species.

'Bloody hell, Mark, look at these houses.' Driving the short distance to the end of the road, they stared in awe at the impressive buildings that sat behind iron gates and stone walls.

The property they were viewing was by far the smallest of all its contemporaries. Lucy parked the car outside Number 10, which was the last house in the avenue.

'This is it,' said Mark, peering up at the house through the car window.

'Let's go see,' grinned Lucy.

They got out of the car to take a closer look and stood in front of the low-level brick wall that swept around the front of the property. A grey gravel driveway curved away from the road, delivering anyone who travelled along it to the main entrance, and also the sacred garage, which sat between the house and next door. Two tall bay windows sitting on stone sills flanked the old white front door, and were screened by sunlight-bleached curtains. The windows above were a mirror image of the ones below, and the grey slate roof sat like a trilby on top of the grand house.

Lucy loved it the moment she saw it. 'What do you think?' She wanted to hear Mark's opinion before confessing her love.

His eyes climbed the red brick walls, and up to the apex of the roof, but before he could answer, a deep metallic rasp filled the air, A black Porsche 911 Turbo swung around the corner like it was on rails and came to an immediate stop within inches of Lucy's white BMW. Their attention had been taken away from the house by the sleek, gleaming, black machine's dramatic entrance. They both stared open-mouthed, but from the glare of the sun on the tinted windows, all they could see were deformed reflections of themselves.

The staccato burble of the engine ceased, the door opened and a tall dark-haired man athletically sprang up from the white leather driving seat. He carelessly slammed the door shut. It seemed he had dressed to match the sports car: his black shoes matched the glossy paintwork, and slim, sleek fitting black trousers finished off with a dazzlingly white tailored shirt, tieless, and open several buttons down from the neck. He ran his hand through his long black hair, which was swept back and hanging a fraction above the sharp edge of his shirt collar.

The mystery man gave them a fast smile, matching the brilliance of his shirt. He wasn't what Lucy had been expecting; she had imagined a stuffy little fat man with a sweaty top lip and a clipboard. He looked like a slim Chippendale, albeit one who was fully dressed. Lucy half-expected him to start gyrating and tear his shirt off – or was that just wishful thinking?

He confidently strode over with the swagger of a stripper, flicking his unruly fringe back into place. He greeted them with a welcoming smile, holding his hand out to Mark, while keeping his flinty eyes fixed on Lucy.

'You must be Mr and Mrs Eaton.'

'Oh, no. Well, yes, I'm Lucy Eaton, and this is my partner, Mark Smith.' Lucy felt a warm flush to her face; his eyes had lingered on hers for longer than was usual when two strangers meet. Once his hand had briefly greeted Mark's, it gently took Lucy's.

'It's a pleasure to meet you, Miss Eaton.' Her eyes

jumped nervously over to Mark, and Mr Confident followed them, before finally acknowledging her partner with a small nod. 'Mr Smith.'

'Please, Lucy and Mark is fine.'

'Very well. I'm Sebastian Kingsfellow.' His long fingers splayed across his chest as he gave his introduction. 'And I'll have the pleasure of showing you around this gem of a house.' He reached into his pocket and took out a small bunch of keys. 'So, guys, shall we take a look inside?' He threw the keys in to the air and caught them in his clenched fist.

'Yes, please,' Lucy answered for both of them. Mark was unusually quiet.

'Follow me.'

She held Mark's hand and shrugged her shoulders, smiling enthusiastically as their feet crunched in unison along the gravel driveway, following Mr Chippendale. Sebastian rattled the tarnished brass key through the escutcheon and paused; he turned to them with his eyebrows raised, rippling his forehead. 'You're going to love this place.' Lucy squeezed Mark's hand with building anticipation as Sebastian turned the key and opened the door, fanning out a collection of mail across the Minton tiled floor.

'Come in, guys. This being an Edwardian house, it has large square rooms, and as you can see, a rather generous hallway.'

They stepped into the greeting point of the home, and were met with the musty smell of time gone by. The property hadn't been touched for quite some time, and by the look of the wallpaper and stair carpet, Lucy was thinking fifty to sixty years maybe. Their eyes darted left and right, up and down, taking it all in.

'I know it's dated, but it's only cosmetic, and easily fixed with a lick of paint.' Mr Kingsfellow spoke with a very clipped English accent and Lucy doubted he knew one end of a paintbrush from the other.

It *was* dated, but the wide panelled doors, beautiful geometric floor and period features gave it a wealth of character. Lucy was hooked. *I want this house!*

'So, first impressions?' Sebastian asked, watching her closely.

'Mmm, it's nice.' She didn't want to seem too keen.

Sebastian's lips twitched; he looked as if he was about to smile, but clearly thought better of it.

'I'll show you upstairs first.'

They headed up the stairs in a line, with Lucy in the middle. As promised, all the rooms were large and square, and the dated theme continued throughout the first floor. It didn't matter to Lucy, with the opening of each door her feelings for the house only strengthened. It felt right; it felt like home.

She deliberately didn't look out at the garden from the bedroom windows, she wanted to save that surprise until last. They headed back downstairs. Mark had hardly spoken, but Kingsfellow had no such trouble; his easy banter flowed like water from a tap as they trailed behind him from room to room listening to his narration.

They finally arrived at the door of the last room they were to view. Sebastian put his hand on the handle, then paused for dramatic effect, like the showman he was. He looked back at them over his shoulder; glossy black hair arced around his face, and the corner of his mouth was hitched up, giving them a glimpse of a diamond-white canine.

'This is where you guys get lucky. The vendors intended to fully renovate this place, and the first room they did was the most expensive room in any home, the kitchen.'

Finishing his introduction, he swung the door open to a very different room. They stepped onto the light beige travertine tiles, and it was like they had travelled in a time machine and accelerated to the present; it was such a huge contrast to the rest of the house. A pristine white ceiling bounced light around the spacious room, the musty smell had been banished and what could only be described as *newness* filled the air.

Perfectly positioned spotlights lit the black work-surface, which rested on ivory and pale-grey bespoke units. A huge double range cooker sat snugly in a spot of its own built into the chimney breast and surrounded by matching units. A beautiful three-casement window with leaded fanlights above, sat over a Belfast sink and stretched up to the ceiling, only stopping to allow the elegant cornice to glide over it.

'It's amazing,' Lucy gushed. Playing it cool went out the window. The stylish room was a fine example of the potential of the property.

'Wow, this is more like it.' Even Mark seemed impressed.

'It is gorgeous, isn't it?' remarked Kingsfellow with his arms spread while rotating, ever the showman. Throughout the tour, his eyes had barely left Lucy's face, although so far Mark had been too busy looking for reasons not to buy the house to notice. She wandered around the island sitting in the centre of the showroom, and as her hand glided over the cool black work surface, she could feel Sebastian's heavy gaze. He was leaning with his hand against the wall; her eyes routinely flicked over to check if he was still watching, which indeed he was.

'Why did they only get as far as the kitchen?' It was the first question Mark had asked.

Sebastian stood upright and slipped his hands into his pockets. 'I sold them the property, they've been here for six months, but unfortunately they decided to separate. There have been rumours of infidelity... bad news for them; good news for you, my friend.' As he prowled past Mark, he slapped him on the shoulder playfully, like they were two friends on a night out.

'Why's that?' asked Mark.

'Because I know that they are desperate to sell, and with you being cash buyers, you have the position of power.' The expert salesman had now turned his attention to the chink in the armour, knowing full well that Lucy was smitten.

'I'm selling another property at the bottom of the avenue, Number 6, and that's on at £1.8 million.' He swept back the unruly fringe that had made another attempt to be front of show.

'£1.8 million!' Mark had taken the bait and Sebastian's eyes seemed to sparkle with enthusiasm.

This time Lucy was watching him; she wanted him to work his magic, to persuade Mark that this was the house for them. The two men stood face to face. Mark: blond, slim, but displaying a little paunch pushing against his T-shirt. His jeans desperately clinging onto his hips, screaming out for a belt. He was an everyday man, Mr Generic. Sebastian: tall, slim, like a long distance runner, long dark hair black as night, his clothes obviously chosen with great care, anything but generic.

'You can't lose on this place, trust me.'

The words, 'trust me' didn't seem to sit well with him, in Lucy's opinion.

'So, which one of you is the gardener?' Sebastian's index finger flicked between Lucy and Mark.

'That will be Lucy.' Mark joined in with the finger pointing game and poked one in her direction. 'She loves gardening.'

'Good, because that's exactly what this one needs: love, and lots of it.' Sebastian unlocked a set of bi-fold doors that sat in the dining area of the kitchen and slid them open.

They stepped out onto a paved area, which was the only thing stopping the marauding weeds from reaching the house. It was from one extreme to another; the perfect designer kitchen, with not a thing to do in it, to the amalgamation of miscellaneous flora.

'Shit, you weren't joking.' This wouldn't be a selling point for Mark.

The whole scene looked like a war between plants and trees: holly wildly grew into magnolias, which were in turn battling it out for space with a huge horse chestnut tree, while ivy spread like veins around the garden, wrapping itself around everything and anything. The fluffy heads of dandelions poked up above the chaos like little microphones, capturing the action of the ongoing conflict.

Lucy's eyes cut through the weed and bramble, envisaging a very different picture.

There were many well-established mature trees and shrubs that had taken a lifetime to develop into the static works of art they now were. That was the one thing money couldn't buy: time.

'It's beautiful.' She spoke the words to herself.

'What? It's a bloody mess.' Mark said, shaking his head repeatedly.

'No...'her eyes flitted across the garden like a butterfly. 'It's all there, you just can't see it.'

'That's what I like to hear: positivity,' enthused Sebastian.

'Mmm,' groaned Mark. He turned away to look at a brick building that jutted out past the back of the house. 'Is that the garage?' Mark's interest in the garden had withered the moment he saw that there was more to do than just cut the grass.

'It's a great space. Come on, I'll show you.' Kingsfellow placed his hand on Mark's back and ushered him away from the negative selling point. Being a man, he'd have known the importance of the garage. Lucy, being a woman, had no interest in the garage; instead, she rescued an old garden chair from drowning in the deep grass and sat, planning.

A soft breeze tickled the leaves of the trees and made a sound like the ocean lapping on a sandy beach. The seemingly inhospitable garden was a paradise for birdlife, and their note-perfect tunes intermittently serenaded her; it was so tranquil.

The two men's voices echoed from the man cave. It seemed as though some male bonding was going on. She caught the odd word here and there, mixed with manly laughter. They returned from the nerve centre of the home, sniggering like two boys telling dirty jokes. It seemed Kingsfellow was very good at reading people.

'Seriously, take her for a spin around the block, and I guarantee you'll be buying one before the week's over.'

'No, I couldn't.'

'Couldn't what?' Lucy wondered what they were talking about.

'I was just telling Seb that I'm looking for a high performance car at the moment.'

Seb?

'He said I could take his for a drive.'

Sebastian held the keys in his hand, waiting.

'You're not used to powerful cars though, are you?' She could see by the sudden plummet of Mark's eyebrows that she had dented his masculinity.

'Yes I am… in fact, I think I will take you up on that offer, Seb.'

Without hesitation, Mark's new best friend threw the keys over to him.

'Be gentle with her,' he grinned.

'I promise.' Mark grinned back. 'I'll only be five minutes.'

'Be careful,' said Lucy.

'Don't worry, I will,' he called out, hurrying off into the house.

'Good man.' Sebastian's smile remained, but it had somehow changed its meaning. He stepped slowly over to Lucy. 'So, Miss Eaton, do you like what you see?'

She was still sitting, and he was standing almost right next to her with his hands on his hips and his crotch awkwardly level with her face. There was more than a hint of suggestion in his voice. She looked up to his face; the sun decided to make an appearance from behind the white clouds and sat blinding her above his head. Lucy screwed up her eyes and shaded them with her hand.

'Er… yes, I do. It's a lovely house.' Now that Mark had gone, the atmosphere had completely changed. She heard the roar of the Porsche as Mark headed off for his joyride.

'Is there anything *you* would like to test-drive?' Her eyes hastily scrambled away from his and stopped briefly on his seemingly protruding crotch, catching a glimpse of her shocked face in the reflection of his chrome belt buckle.

'What – what do you mean?' She needlessly played with her hair; it felt as though a thousand eyes were on her.

'I mean the built-in appliances.' He held out his hand and she took it, eager to put some distance between her face and his lower body.

'After you.' He gestured towards the house.

Lucy made her way back to the open doors and noticed that her footsteps were alone. Stepping over the threshold, she looked back to see Kingsfellow standing in the glorious sunshine, his feet shoulder-width apart, hands in pockets, eyes narrow and tongue slowly gliding across his bottom lip.

Bloody hell, he's got some nerve!

She hurried back into the kitchen and randomly started opening cupboard doors; Lucy heard the bi-fold doors being closed and then locked.

'I noticed you didn't look out of the bedroom windows.' He addressed the back of her head while she examined the empty spaces.

'Didn't I?' He hadn't missed a thing.

'No, you didn't, Miss Eaton.'

His, "Miss Eaton," had a very provocative ring to it.

'Please, call me Lucy.'

'Let's take a look.' He held the door to the hall open and beckoned her with a tilt of his head.

'Erm, yes, okay.' *Hurry up Mark!* She didn't make eye contact as she passed, but gave a polite smile. Lucy stopped at the bottom of the stairs. 'You lead the way.' She encouraged him with the palm of her hand.

He stood in close proximity to her. 'No, no, ladies first, I insist.' The look on his face was somewhere between confident and smug.

Shit! I knew he'd say that. 'Thank you.' She climbed the stairs, trying not to wiggle her bottom, knowing full well where his eyes would be. Her red pencil trousers felt very tight all of a sudden.

The chatty Mr Kingsfellow was now very muted.

'That is absolutely perfect,' he purred.

Lucy almost hopped onto the landing and spun around. 'What is?' she asked accusingly.

He was standing several steps down, running the tips of his fingers over the handrail.

'The craftsmanship of this staircase, it's very high quality.'

'Mmm.' She nodded and waited for him to pass, and lead the way into the bedroom.

Where the hell is Mark?

She entered the bedroom hesitantly, and stood at the window several feet away from him, looking out at the jungle.

'Do you like what you see?'

She had a feeling he wasn't referring to the garden and was cautious with her answer.

'Mmm,' she simply nodded once again, not wanting to encourage any risqué replies.

No encouragement seemed to be needed. 'You can't wait to get your hands on it, can you?'

Lucy couldn't believe how brazen this man was, and her thoughts which should have been on the house and garden, had been sabotaged by suggestive innuendos.

'You are very... bold, Mr Kingsfellow. Do you treat all your clients this way?' She knew her reply was playing along with his game, but it was impossible to ignore, and strangely, she didn't feel threatened by him at all.

His hand once again swept back the tenacious fringe; the action had become something of his trademark now. 'Only the smoking hot ones, Miss Eaton.'

She turned to meet his gaze; his eyebrows raised languidly, completely unashamed.

'Do you think it's appropriate, Mr Kingsfellow?' She was careful not to sound as though she was telling him off, but didn't want to sound like she was encouraging him either. However, Lucy had to admit, it was flattering to have such an attractive man flirting with her, even if it was borderline sexual harassment.

'Who am I to say what is and isn't appropriate? All I can say in my defence is that I'm a man who knows what he wants.' A shameless smile paraded across his face.

Her interaction with him had eased her nervousness, and she found herself wondering what he would say next, almost excited by it.

She didn't have to wait long. 'Do you think that this garden will give you the fulfilment in life you crave, Miss Eaton? Or will you have to look elsewhere for that? I suspect the latter.'

Her shocked expression elicited his hasty, but unapologetic reply. 'Before you slap my face, let me just say that it's a perfectly valid question.'

That was his job: reading people, gauging their thoughts and spotting the tell-tale signs of body language. Had he seen something between her and Mark? A weakness, maybe? Or was he so in love with himself that he thought that every woman who came into contact with him instantly wanted to drop her knickers?

The sound of mechanical thunder rattled the windows; just like its owner, the Porsche liked to let everyone know when it had arrived.

'Shall we let my boyfriend back in?'

Sebastian chuckled to himself, maybe sensing he was on the right track. 'Yes, I suppose we shall. It would be rude not to, wouldn't it?'

'Yes, it would, Mr Kingsfellow.' Lucy wore a wry smile, now getting to grips with the way the game worked. Sure enough, Mark tapped on the door, wanting to be let in.

'After you.' He tried his luck once more, but the slight curve of his lips gave away the fact that he expected rejection.

And he was right. 'Er, no. I think I'll let you lead the way this time, Mr Kingsfellow.'

'As you wish, Miss Eaton.'

Lucy stayed upstairs for a moment, while Rudolf Valentino re-incarnated went down to open the door. Now she could focus her attention on what she had come to see.

'Are you ready, Lu?' Mark called.

'Yes, I'll be down in a minute.' She was ready to move in. Lucy took what she hoped wouldn't be her last look around, before going down to join Mark outside the front of the house.

He was adoringly stroking the German masterpiece with his eyes. 'Lu, this car is amazing; what a machine.'

Lucy struggled to muster any interest. She wanted to get the conversation back to the house.

'She's a beauty, alright. The best damn ride you'll ever have.' The arrival of Mark hadn't curbed Kingsfellow's suggestive remarks, and he studied Lucy from head to toe while Mark was admiring the backside of the black beauty.

'Mark, can we have a chat?' She tried to ignore the fact that she was being visually undressed by a stranger.

'Yeah, of course.'

'I'll give you guys some privacy.'

Kingsfellow was at least thoughtful enough to allow them some time alone – plus, Lucy was sure he was keen to close the deal.

'Thank you,' said Lucy.

'No problem, take as long as you like.'

She waited until he had entered the house. Mark was reluctant to leave his newfound love.

'What do you think?' she asked, nervous as to what the reply would be.

'It's fantastic.'

Yes!

'Handles like a dream.'

'Not the bloody car, Mark. The house.'

'Oh, yeah. Sorry.' His boyish, animated face turned into a grownup pessimistic, negative one.

'I'm not sure, Lu: the garden's a huge job.'

'Don't worry about the garden. I'll take care of that.' She was prepared for that one. 'What do you think about the house?'

Mark couldn't come up with any valid reason as to why they shouldn't buy the house, none that Lucy didn't have an answer for anyway. She played on the fact that the garage had room for two, possibly three cars, which seemed to soften his furrowed brow.

'So guys, have you written out that cheque yet?' It seemed Sebastian's generous invitation to take as long as they liked had turned out to be an empty one. He had returned within five minutes and was back in full salesman mode.

They discussed money, and as offers were meant to be over £980,000, the expert advised them to come in at £985,000. After some to-ing and fro-ing, Mark was persuaded by Kingsfellow's advice that the property was an excellent investment opportunity, and he finally agreed to make an offer at the suggested price. Hugs and kisses were followed by the shaking of hands. Sebastian said that because he *liked* them, he was going to cancel all other viewings until he had received an answer about their offer. On the condition that they would allow him to call in now and again, to see how the house and particularly the garden were progressing, as he was keen to see how that developed. Mark agreed in an instant, and said he was welcome anytime.

'I'll be in touch as soon as I hear any news, okay guys?' Kingsfellow said, shaking Mark's hand and warmly patting him on the arm. 'Miss Eaton.' He nodded with a grace that wouldn't have been out of place in the Edwardian period, before returning to his personal *fräulein*. Mark surprisingly turned his attention to the house, and for reasons unknown to her, Lucy looked over her shoulder at

Sebastian who was standing behind his car door, like he was waiting for her to look back at him. He wiggled his fingers at her with a wink, and she snapped her head back to face the house.

Damn, he doesn't need any more encouragement. Why had she looked back? Lucy thought that it probably wouldn't be very long before she received a *progress* visit. Kingsfellow left in the same manner by which he had arrived, like an armed robber on the run from the police. All houses have a compromise of one sort or another: for Mark it was the garden, but Lucy had never expected that hers would be an amorous playboy salesman.

CHAPTER FOUR

Thankfully, they didn't have to wait too long: at 4.55 that very day they received a phone call informing them that their offer had been accepted. Lucy was so excited and shed a few tears of relief after being on tenterhooks for most of the day. Even Mark was upbeat: eager to give the garage a purpose again, he had already arranged a tour of all the most prestigious car dealerships. The next few weeks were combined with packing, lazy lunches and shopping for their new home together, which included buying an assortment of gardening equipment. She couldn't wait to get amongst the bramble and weeds to see what lay hidden underneath.

The move went smoothly, mainly because they paid someone else to do it for them.

Lucy wandered around the house with a glass of wine, wearing a cloak of calm contentedness wrapped around her. She totally loved it, even though, with the gangs of cardboard boxes occupying every room, it looked like a warehouse.

Mark's burning desire for a man machine couldn't be restrained any longer, and like most male lottery winners, he went for the trophy purchase: a Ferrari. Despite Lucy's request for something not too ostentatious, he opted for a bright yellow convertible, turning heads wherever they drove, which Mark loved and Lucy loathed.

He was on the drive washing his pride and joy for the third time that week because Mother Nature had inconsiderately scattered the earth with rain, leaving water stains on the bonnet. Despite the fuss he had made over the garage, the car was parked on the drive every night at a particular angle for all the neighbours to covet with envy.

Lucy was standing in the doorway, unseen by Mark, holding a cold beer for him. She watched for a moment; his hand was doing a hundred revolutions per minute, polishing the paintwork until his reflection was clearly visible. They had been getting on well, although their time together seemed less intimate Without the routine of work, they had been entirely preoccupied with what to spend their money on next.

'You'll wash it away.'

Mark raised his head and smiled, mopping his brow with his forearm. She strolled over and handed him the open bottle.

'Thanks, you must have read my mind.' He tipped his head back and let the cool beer flood down his throat. 'I was just thinking about grabbing a beer.'

'That's because I know you so well.'

Mark threw the polishing cloth onto the bonnet. 'Yes, you do, don't you.' He leaned into her, stretching his neck out and pecked her on the lips.

'Shall we have a cosy evening in tomorrow?' asked Lucy. 'We haven't had one for ages.'

'Tomorrow?' Mark took another swig from the bottle. He seemed hesitant. 'Yeah, we'll see.'

She stepped closer to him and softly massaged between his shoulder blades with the palm of her hand.

'I can soon get the living room sorted. I thought we could enjoy a nice night curled up in our new home – maybe watch a movie?'

Mark finished his drink, placing the empty bottle onto the floor; he began to polish the yellow metal. She was about to run through a few more of his options for tomorrow night's entertainment when her attention was caught by a gold Mercedes, which sailed slowly past them and pulled into the drive next door.

'That's the neighbours. Let's go and say hello.' She placed her wine glass down, not wanting to give the wrong impression.

'I wanted to get this finished,' grumbled Mark, both hands spread out on the bonnet.

'Come on, it won't take long.' Lucy went on ahead of him, unclipping her hair, letting the brown locks tumble around her make-up-free face. Lucy called Mark along, who was dawdling with the polishing cloth still in his grasp, like an obstinate five-year-old holding his comfort blanket.

The neighbour's property was double the size of theirs, and screened from the road by a high hedge, which hadn't been pruned in quite some time. She caught a glimpse of a lady wearing cream suit trousers and a white shawl hurrying under the arched entrance.

'Hello, hello.' Lucy waved, and quickened her step, but

heard the door slam.

Mark stood at the border of the drive. 'Never mind, we'll catch them another time.'

'I'll knock on the door, I think we should introduce ourselves, don't you?'

He rolled his eyes at the inconvenience; Lucy waited for him to join her before walking the remaining distance to the front door. She pressed the brass button and clearly heard the bell ring. Casting her eyes around while waiting, she thought the place looked very unkempt.

Leaves from seasons past lay scattered around the perimeter, and an army of weeds had squeezed up between the gaps in the paving. There was no answer. She tried again. Mark huffed and puffed, petulantly checking his watch. Lucy could just about see a contorted image through the pretty stained glass of the front door.

'Who is it?' a stern lady's voice called out, some distance away from the door.

Lucy gave Mark an apprehensive flash of her eyes before answering. 'Sorry to bother you. We're from next door.' There was silence where there should have been a reply.

'We just thought we would say hello and introduce ourselves.'

The obscure figure began to writhe in the green and red glass as it approached. A heavy lock turned, then another; the door opened a mere three inches, with the rattle of the chain restricting it. Half a face appeared.

A suspicious eye darted between them.

'Hello, I'm Lucy, and this is my partner, Mark.' He waved the polishing cloth at her with his introduction, staying several steps behind Lucy. The cold grey eye continued to pass between them. Lucy spoke with growing unease. 'We moved in yesterday, and as you probably know, we've got quite a task clearing the garden. So I'll apologise in advance for any noise we may cause over the next few weeks.' Lucy gave the sweetest, friendliest smile she could muster; it was met with painful muteness.

Mark decided to try his charm. 'We won the lottery, you know.'

Lucy winced with embarrassment at his inappropriate outburst. The lone eye instantly fixed Mark in its sights, and the thinly plucked eyebrow arched its back like a dog about to attack.

'Nearly £3,000,000. That's how we bought that place.' He nodded at their new home.

'I hope we haven't disturbed you,' Lucy butted in. It was unnerving talking to half a face, especially one that didn't talk back.

'I am rather busy, so if you'll excuse me,' The harsh reply had an intolerant tone to it.

'Oh, of course, sor—' The door slammed and the locks were re-engaged. '-ry.' Lucy turned slowly to face Mark; his expression matched her feelings of shock at how rude that was.

'Charming,' he said.

They strolled back up the driveway together. 'Nice to meet you too. Did you have to say that we'd won the lottery?'

'Why, what's wrong with that?'

'Well, it's not the first thing I'd spring into the conversation the moment I met someone.'

Lucy took another look back at the house and thought she saw the bedroom curtain twitch.

Mark returned to his valeting obsession, while Lucy began to sort through the contents of the cardboard boxes with growing annoyance at their neighbour's un-neighbourly greeting.

The next morning Lucy paid another one of her regular visits to the school where she had once worked. Mark paid another one of his regular visits to the golf course.

She was surprised at how much she had missed the children and her colleagues. It had been a lovely place to work and she was toying with the idea of returning part-time as a volunteer. It was everyone's dream to live a life of leisure, but she soon realised that life needed a purpose, a reason to get up in the morning.

Lucy returned home in the early afternoon. Curiously, she checked to see if the lone car was still parked up next door, which it was.She intended on donning her gardening clothes and joining the battle, armed with loppers and various instruments of torture.

She had arranged for a landscape gardening company to come out at two o'clock to give her a quote for clearing the bulk of it, knowing full well it was too big a job for her alone. Two o'clock came and went with no sign of the supposedly "reliable and efficient" company. Lucy rang them several times, only to be told to leave a message after the beep.

Frustrated and annoyed, she surveyed her efforts over the last few hours; she hadn't even scratched the surface. Lucy flopped down in the old garden chair she had rescued and took out her phone. She Googled local gardeners and scrolled down the list, briefly reading each introduction until one caught her eye: 'GD Landscape Gardeners. Old-fashioned, dependable, reliable. Established 1977. Call for a free, no-obligation quote'. Lucy decided to do just that and spoke to a very friendly man who said he would be there in an hour. She instructed him to come around to the side gate, and after thanking him hung up feeling better, knowing the cavalry were on their way.

Just as she was about to put her phone away it pinged with a text from Mark. *I've got a surprise for you this evening x,'* it read

Now she was doubly excited and let her mind wander what he might have in store while she set about raking up what she'd so far managed to cut back.

GD Landscapes certainly lived up to their claim of being reliable: there was a knock at the gate within the hour.

Lucy dropped her rake in the tangled pile of weeds and went around to unbolt the gate.

'Is that GD Landscapes?' she asked just to make sure it wasn't a certain real-estate love god.

'Yes it is, my dear.'

The voice that hopped over the timber barrier was that of an elderly man. She opened the gate and her eyes confirmed what her ears had already told her.

'Hello, I'm George, George Dalton.' A white haired gentleman held out his hand, and his face spread with an authentic smile. Silver rimmed glasses sat perched in his equally silver hair. He was wearing faded jeans with tell-tale damp patches at the knees, and a dark green polo shirt with his company logo embroidered across the left breast pocket. He gently enveloped her fingers; his bark-like skin slightly scratching Lucy's novice hand as they shook.

'Nice to meet you, George, I'm Lucy. Do you want to take a look at the garden?'

'Yes, certainly, my dear.'

'I've been trying to tackle it myself, but it's quite a big job.' She chatted to him as they walked the short distance back to the jungle.

'This is it.' Lucy bit down on her lip and watched him from the corner of her eye, expecting the worst. He dropped his glasses down from their silver bed onto his nose, like a knight lowering his visor, ready for battle. He walked across the small area she had cleared and wadded into the waist height growth. Lucy followed behind him, walking in the channel he was creating.

George came to a halt and ran a soil-stained finger over the transparent whiskers that peppered his jawline.

'What do you think?' Her trepidation was building; she was expecting a sharp intake of air followed by the headshake of doom.

He turned and looked down at her over his glasses. 'I think you've got a beautiful garden here, Lucy. It's all there, it's just hidden.' He gave her the perfect answer, and she felt reassured by his confidence.

'Let's see what else we have here, Mind your step, my darlin'.' He had a very calm, unhurried demeanour – that was something that came with age and experience. Lucy warmed to him straight away. He took her on a tour of her own garden, pointing out every species of tree, shrub and flower, quoting their Latin names.

It was clear to her that he was a man who loved his work. They spent almost an hour rambling around the potential paradise before returning back to the house.

'So, George, can you help me?' They stood side by side, facing the job at hand.

George raised his glasses, resting them in their previous spot. 'This is where I'm supposed to say that I'm very busy, and not sure if I can fit you in.' He leaned his head to the side and looked at her over his glasses, forgetting they were on his forehead. The serious expression didn't sit well on his face, then his snowy-white eyebrows, in unison with the corners of his mouth playfully.

'We're not busy at all. We can come tomorrow if you like?'

Lucy had decided he had got the job after speaking to him for just five minutes. They talked money and he reassured her that he was as honest as the day was long, of which she had no doubt.

He kindly insisted on helping her put all of the gardening equipment away, then told her, in a very fatherly way, to leave the garden for them tomorrow. She walked him back to his pick-up and they said their goodbyes. George drove away, giving her a thumbs-up, and Lucy smiled to herself. He was lovely; she was glad that the other company had been so slack. Heading back through the side gate, she heard her phone ringing on the plastic chair where she had left it. Lucy managed to grab it before it rang off. 'Hello, Mark.'

'I'll be back in five. Make me a coffee, babe?'

'Okay, bye.'

She brushed herself down and kicked off her shoes before going into the kitchen to make the requested beverage.

She was pouring the milk into Mark's coffee when she

heard the key in the door. He came in loaded with bags and dropped them at the bottom of the stairs.

'Hi, did you make that coffee?' he asked, entering the kitchen.

'Yes I did. There you go.'

'Thanks, babe.' He kissed her on the forehead and took the hot drink from her. 'You look nice,' he said jokingly, before taking a sip of his coffee and sitting down at the island. 'Been playing Rambo in the garden have we?' He nodded at her dirty jeans, which still had signs of the mass slaughter she had been involved in.

Lucy drank her water, too hot for coffee – and glanced down at herself.

'I've been having great fun playing in the jungle, thank you. You should try it.'

Mark didn't bother to answer that one.

'I've got some help coming tomorrow.'

'Really?' He rested his elbows on the cool black granite work surface. 'And are they bringing dynamite?'

'You may laugh.' She placed her empty glass into the sink. 'But just you wait and see, mister. Anyway, I'm going for a nice shower. I'll tell you all about it later.'

'Good, because I've got your surprise coming any minute now, and I've got to get it ready.'

Lucy placed her hands on her hips and eyed him suspiciously. 'What is it?'

'Off you go, please,' he said, taking a quick glance at the kitchen clock.

'I'm all excited now, can I have just a little clue?' She pinched her fingers in front of her screwed-up eyes.

'Shower.' He pointed upstairs. Lucy blew a raspberry at him as she headed barefoot into the hallway.

As soon as Mark was out of sight she took a sneak peek into the bags he had left by the stairs. New jeans, shirts and underwear, a pair of shoes and some more beauty products for the Ferrari. She looked back to the kitchen to make sure the coast was clear. It was: she could hear Mark on the phone to one of his friends.

She pulled out the last bag, which was bright orange. On it, in black lettering, was written *"Dress 2 Impress: fancy dress for all occasions"*.Lucy peered into the bag and found a white naval officer's uniform,complete with cap. Her face shot back to the kitchen, now definitely not wanting to be caught. *So, we are having a night in then.*

She closed the bag and crept upstairs to the bathroom, quite shocked. Mark had never gone for role play before; maybe he also realised that their sex life needed a bit of sizzle. Turning on the shower she stepped in; the cloudy water pooled around her feet while she wondered what was arriving for her.

Early evening was upon them and she was keen to see what Mark had in store for her. Showered, she towel-dried her hair, slipped on some sexy lingerie, and applied the basics of make-up: racy red lipstick and mascara. Like the lingerie, it wouldn't be staying on for very long. She put on her pale pink satin nightgown, knotting the floaty material at the waist, and hurried downstairs. All the bags had disappeared from their resting spot; she could hear rustling noises coming from the lounge.

'Mark?'

'Don't come in, not yet,' he called out while the mysterious rustling continued.

Lucy waited patiently by the door, shaking her head with a silly grin at the thought of Mark in uniform – standing to attention, in more ways than one.

'Okay, Lu, close your eyes.'

She followed his instructions and heard the rattle of the old doorknob as Mark opened the door; the sudden displacement of air gently blew her fringe and rippled the gossamer gown.

'Keep them closed.' Holding her hand, he led her into the room.

'Can I open my eyes now?

'Yes, you can.'

Lucy's eyelids drew back slowly, and her broad smile waned. Mark had changed his clothes, but he wasn't wearing the uniform.

'Ta-da!' He clapped his hands and held them out at arm's length, like he was introducing a cabaret act. Instead, he was revealing a huge flatscreen TV, which sat awkwardly in the corner of the room, blocking out half the light from the bay window.

'A TV?' Lucy struggled to conceal her disappointment.

'Yeah, awesome isn't it?' Mark began collecting the discarded bubble wrap and cardboard.

'But we already have a TV.' She did her best not to frown, but the very last thing she expected was this.

'This is no ordinary TV.' Mark reeled off the technical specifications, but his words got mangled amongst Lucy's thoughts.

Where's the uniform? Maybe he plans to put it on later.

'And that's not all, I've got you a little something else.' He exited the room carrying the rubbish.

Aha, Here we go.

'I want you to sit back, relax and enjoy the show,' he called out from the hallway, and popped his head around the doorframe. 'Because I have, for your delectation...'

The smile had now returned to Lucy's face.

'Your all-time favourite movie, *Pretty Woman.*'

It didn't bother to hang around.

'And you can now enjoy it in high definition.' He came back into the room waggling a blu-ray edition of the aforementioned movie, his face a picture of self-satisfaction.

Maybe she was being ungrateful – it was one of her favourite movies. He had obviously made an effort.

She decided that her lingerie would stay on for a while, even though it was made for pleasure, not comfort.

'Sit yourself down.' He stood behind her and placed his hands on her hips, gently pushing her towards the couch. 'Put your feet up.'

Lucy sat down. Mark grabbed a couple more cushions from the chairs and propped her up on a plump downy bed. He put the disc into the player and handed her the controls to the technological wonder as he passed, heading for the kitchen.

On his return, Mark was carrying an open bottle of white wine in one hand and a suitable glass in the other. He knelt down next to her and expertly poured the wine.

'There you go.' He handed her the long-stemmed glass.

'Thank you,' she replied, feeling more than a little guilty for initially being disappointed. It was so sweet of him to think of her like this, and after all, she had asked for a cosy night in.

'There's no need to cook tonight, because I've ordered

a curry from an award-winning restaurant, and it should be here in about fifteen minutes.' Mark got to his feet. 'Is there anything else you would like?'

'Yes, a kiss please.' Lucy tipped her head back, lying in her comfy spot.

Mark craned over and kissed her on the cheek, before she could turn to meet his lips with hers.

'Right then, that's you settled.' He stood up straight and scratched behind his ear.

'I, erm, I won't be too late back.'

'What? You're going out?' Lucy sat upright while he rubbed the back of his neck, keeping his eyes on the TV, which had got tired of waiting and started the movie automatically.

'Yeah.'

'Where to?'

'I'm just catching up with a few of the boys I haven't seen for a while. Didn't I tell you about it in the week?' He turned his face towards her, but his gaze was firmly fixed on Julia Roberts in thigh length boots.

'No, you didn't. I thought we were going to have a night in together? Aren't you going to watch this with me?'

'You know it's not my thing, babe.' His eyes darted across to her then back to the screen. 'Just relax, you've worked hard in the garden today.' She knew Mark well enough to know that he probably hadn't even taken a look to see what she had done in the garden.

'I'll see you later.' He quickly made his exit while Lucy was in the calm period between shock and anger. The door slammed, and the Ferrari roared out its farewell. A larger-than-life Richard Gere did his best to distract her, but unwanted thoughts still occupied her attention.

Was this the beginning of Mark returning to his old ways? Maybe *he was* just meeting up with a few old friends. He definitely hadn't mentioned it to her, as he suggested. Lucy's stomach turned at the thought of where he may really be going.

There was a knock at the door. It was the award winning Indian meal – for one.

It didn't get the chance to impress that evening, and spent the night in the containers it was delivered in. A succession of scenarios were chasing each other around her mind; she plucked out the ones that were easiest to digest. *He'll be home in a few hours… won't he?*

A few hours came and went. Mr Gere and Miss Roberts had long left the living room to live happily ever after in fantasyland. Even Mark's phone had shut down for the night, refusing to take any calls. Lucy, tired of waiting, finally went to bed, having got her wish of an evening in, although it hadn't been cosy and she hadn't expected to be spending it alone.

CHAPTER FIVE

The slam of a car door stirred Lucy from her sleep. She lay there, listening to the mumbling voices, while her mind and body re-booted. The disappointing recollection of last night was first in the queue.

She rolled her head over on the plump pillow to face Mark's side of the bed, knowing full well that he wouldn't be there.

A clattering noise had joined in with the mumbles outside; Lucy patted the bed down, letting her hand do her eyes' work, looking for her phone. No calls, or messages. The time inconspicuously hid in the top corner of the screen. 'Shit!' Finding its hiding place, and seeing that it was 8.05, she kicked the duvet off and launched herself out of bed.

Lucy staggered over to the window, her legs still playing catch-up, and parted the curtains just enough for her left eye to confirm what she already knew. It was George, on time and unloading his equipment from the back of his dark green pick-up.

He was directing a teenage boy, who floundered around in his baggy jeans like he too, had just woken. Staying up late waiting for Mark had caused her to oversleep. Dropping to her knees she very slowly opened the curtains, then scurried across the carpet on all fours until she was clear of the window.

She flung open one of the suitcases containing the clothes that were yet to be put away. Every box and bag was labelled, except the suitcases. Lucy hastily rummaged through the neatly folded garments, throwing them over her shoulder as she desperately tried to find something suitable to put on. She didn't want George thinking that she was too idle to get up on time for them.

Suitcase number one was only offering winter sweaters, socks, thongs and push-up bras. 'Shit, shit, shit.' She wanted to beat them to the side gate. She pounced on case number two. It was full of Mark's clothes; his grey sweatpants sat on top offering their services.

'Oh sod it, they'll do.' Lucy hopped around the bedroom slipping her legs into Mark's pants, which were way too long. Pulling them up under her boobs she threw on one of her sweaters that were now strewn all over the bedroom, and tied her hair in a ponytail with a thong, as it seemed all her hair grips where hiding. Holding onto the sweatpants Lucy ran down the stairs; on her way into the kitchen she passed a pair of flip-flops loitering around, so she put them to good use.

Armed with the key, she heaved the bi-fold doors to one side and quickly made her way to the gate. George's voice approached as Lucy rattled the key in the lock; she opened the gate and found George with his arm stretched out, reaching for the handle.

'That was good timing, good morning, Lucy. How are you?'

'Morning,' she sang, pleased with herself for completing her mission. 'I'm fine, thank you.'

'This is Adam, my apprentice.' George turned to the side to reveal a young lad hiding under a mop of ginger hair that threatened to suffocate his face.

'Nice to meet you, Adam.'

His lips rose with the motion of his head in acknowledgment of their introduction.

'Adam, can you start bringing the gear around please, mate.'

Adam nodded silently from under his ginger veil; he trundled off with his jeans hanging low, leaving his purple underwear on view. Lucy thought he bore a striking resemblance to Scooby Doo's pal, Shaggy.

'And pull your trousers up, man.' George shook his head at Lucy, bringing out her first smile of the day.

'The youth of today,' he sighed. 'It seems it's the fashion to show your undergarments these days.'

He removed his glasses and took out a handkerchief from his back pocket.

'He's a good lad though,' he said, cleaning the lenses. 'So, my sweet,' he slipped his glasses back into place, 'we're going to continue with where you left off and trim it all back. Then we'll have a better idea of what we want to do, okay?'

'Yes, that's fine. I can't wait to see it all cleared. It's exciting. Can I get you a drink before you start?' Mark's pants slowly started slipping down. Lucy abruptly folded her arms, trapping the waistband.

'We'd love a cup of tea, please – two sugars in each. Thank you.'

'Two teas coming up.'

Lucy made her way back to the house. As soon as she was out of sight, she hauled the waistband back up under her boobs. She prepared the cups while the kettle rumbled and she wondered where the hell Mark was. He better have a damn good excuse when he got back.

She made their drinks and placed them on a plastic tray with a selection of biscuits. Carefully, Lucy carried them outside, hoping her braless breasts would hold the unruly pants in place. Just as she was stepping out into the garden she heard her phone ringing in the bedroom.

That will be Mark, no doubt.

Lucy quickened her step to a canter, hoping to get to the call. Her eyes fixed on the trembling cups and her hips wiggling in a fruitless attempt to slow the decline of the slippery sweatpants. George and Adam were out the front, and if she didn't get their drinks to them soon she would be handing them over bare-arsed. Her eyes still locked on the clinking cups, she flew around the corner of the house, heading for the gate with increasing urgency.

BANG! She came to an immediate stop and the tray clashed into a solid wall of green, sending the cups falling to their doom, exploding hot tea onto the paving.

Lucy dropped to her haunches to pick up the fractured ceramic and came face to face with a well-worn pair of tea-splattered, sandy-coloured work boots. Her eyes climbed up the laces and onto the thick black socks scrunched down above the ankle; bronze, diamond-shaped calf muscles sprouted from them.

It wasn't George, and it definitely wasn't Shaggy. With growing curiosity, she continued the ascent and reached the hem of a grey pair of shorts, which finished just above the knee and having an embarrassing wet patch right over the crotch area.

'Are you okay?'

A large hand dropped down level with her face accompanying the question; the thick brown fingers opened in offer of help. Lucy's hands had forgotten all about their task. She dried them on her thighs, brushed her fringe from her eyes and looked up to the face from which the deep throaty question had come. The sun observed her from over the shoulder of the stranger and was too powerful for her eyes to bear. She accepted the kind offer and placed her fingers in the coarse grip of the hand offered. She was helped to her feet and was greeted by the embroidered emblem of *GD Landscape Gardeners*.

Lucy looked up into the clear blue eyes of the man-wall she had just crashed into. The stranger looked down at her from under the frayed peak of a faded black baseball cap; his warm eyes had a competent familiarity about them. Facial hair covered his square jaw and had crossed the line from stubble to beard. The perfectly formed lips moved once again, but her brain was putting all its capability into the power of sightfocusing entirely on what she could see – and what a sight he was.

'Miss, are you all right?' His voice poured into her ears.

'What? Oh, sorry, yes, I'm fine.' She snapped her gaze away from his captivating face to take a look at the damage.

'I'm so sorry; I've soaked you,' she said through her

splayed fingers, feeling the fever in her cheeks building as the stranger quite obviously, and without the slightest hint of shame, took a tour of her body. His manly perfection had seduced any offence she should have felt as the roving eyes were joined by a wry smile.

'Are you wet?'

'What?' She was shocked, but still not offended. 'What do you mean?'

His tongue bulged in his cheek, as he appeared to be wrestling with a smile. 'Your clothes... are they wet?'

You now could have fried an egg on her face; spontaneous combustion was surely imminent. Could she have made herself look any more stupid?

'No, my clothes aren't wet, funnily enough.'

She meant to give a girly giggle, but her mind was suffering from the effects of testosterone overdose, and it came out as a grunt. To top it all off, her somewhat erratic breathing had dislodged the sweat pants from under her breasts, and they had decided that they would rather keep her ankles company. Before they dropped like a sky-diver from a plane, Lucy's hands sprang into action and clamped each side of her hips, catching the abandoning material. She breathed a silent sigh of relief, trying not to stare at his chest, which was clearly not happy at being constrained and was pushing hard against its green barrier. The fresh, minty laundered smell was at odds with the appearance of his well-worn clothes.

'You're a little early, don't you think?' This time he unashamedly let the look of amusement have free rein over his face.

'Too early?' His contagious smile caused her to reciprocate like a dorky teenager. He gave a slight nod; his eyes bounced off her chest and back up to her confused face. Lucy, still smiling, bowed her head to take a look at herself; unintentionally, a whimper of utter embarrassment escaped her.

She stood in the neon flip-flops from Greece, wearing Mark's clown-like pants, which were hitched up over her tummy. But the pièce de résistance was the red sweater, complete with a picture of Rudolph the Red Nose Reindeer, grinning madly like he had full-blown rabies, pulling Santa Claus on his sleigh. Santa was giving a big thumbs-up, and the words *'I Love Christmas'* were emblazoned underneath.

It was something she'd bought for the school's Christmas party last year. Lucy screwed her eyes tight shut, wishing a sinkhole would appear and swallow her up. As the ground beneath her feet was safe and sound she raised her head, besieged with mortification, and forced her lips to form some semblance of a smile.

'Everybody loves Christmas!' It was the first thing that had come to mind, and the very second the words had trotted off her tongue she wanted to haul them back in. *There you go, just in case I didn't look fucking stupid enough already, that ought to do it!*

A deep chuckle thundered from his throat.

George joined them and slapped the bearded brain-scrambler on the back. 'You've met the third Musketeer then.'

'What have you done?' George asked Musketeer Number Three, seeing the broken cups.

'When anything breaks, why do you automatically think it's me?' Aramis asked, turning to George, who threw a wink at Lucy.

She took advantage of this diversion to admire his handsome profile; tawny coloured hair curled and kinked out from under the band of his baseball cap, his strong jawline was shadowed by his beard, which crept down his thick neck.

'Because, it usually is. Where are my manners? Lucy, this is Joseph, my son.'

She unintentionally compared the two men's faces, searching for some resemblance, but could find little in the way of similarity, except for his eyes: there was an honesty in them that evoked an instant feeling of trust.

'Lucy.' Joseph tilted his head and touched the peak of his cap like cowboys do in the movies.

'Nice to meet you, Joseph.' She batted her eyelashes, trying to regain some femininity.

'Don't you worry about the mess; Joseph will clean it up. Adam,' called George, 'bring the dust pan and brush, will you, lad?'

'No, don't worry about it; I'll do it. I'll make you another drink first.'

'Thanks, Lucy.' George wandered back out to his pick-up.

She did a 180 in her luminous footwear, and shuffled along back to the shelter of the kitchen with her hands still firmly on her hips.

'Black coffee for me, thanks. No sugar.' His gruff voice tapped her on the shoulder, and she could feel the weight of his stare.

'Okay.' She slung her reply back at him, not stopping until she was out of sight. Making it into the kitchen she planted her elbows onto the hard surface of the island and dropped her head into her hands. *Everybody loves Christmas?*

Oooh Gooooood!

She shook her head, trying to dislodge the thought. *I mean, what are the odds? I go out to open the gate, dressed like a pissed-up child's entertainer, and bump into Gerard Butler, who's come to cut the fucking grass!* She pulled the knotted thong out from her hair, and the sound of knuckles onglass sent her shooting bolt upright, which threw her hair into as many geometric angles aswere possible. Mr Butler's stunt double stood at the bi-fold doors, holding the tray full ofbroken cups.

'Where do you want this?' His face bore the ghost of his earlier amusement.

'Oh, er… I'll take it.' She strutted down to him, a hand held firmly at her hip, keeping hold of the unruly pants. Lucy's free hand eagerly shot up to take the tray and flicked her black and white spotted thong onto it.

They stood there for a moment, both of them holding onto the round plastic tray, their eyes fixed on the knickers. Her eyeballs were attempting to vacate their sockets as they rose to meet his composed stare.

'Going commando today?' he drawled.

'No, they were in my…' She pointed to her head before balling them up with both hands and stuffing them into her pocket. In a fluster she took the tray from him; Mark's pants spotted their chance, and like a lead weight, dropped to the ground. The world stopped turning on its axis at that very moment. They both stood motionless, Lucy's still, bulging eyes holding his line of sight. She could feel the knitted band of her jumper across her hips, but wasn't sure if it was low enough to cover her own lady garden.

Joseph's dulcet tones were first to ripple the perfectly

still airwaves. 'I find it very freeing myself.' *Say something you twit!* All her vocabulary was too mortified to show its face. A tremulous hand smoothed over her perpendicular hair, with no effect at all.

Joseph cleared his throat. His eyes creased faintly at the corners, indicating the smile that no doubt lay below the surface. 'I'll be in the grass, if you need me.' He indicated in such direction with a thumb over his shoulder.

'Okay... I'll make your drinks now,' uttered Lucy while her hand confirmed that the red waistband was indeed covering her modesty – just.

He turned and headed out, his gaze never dropping below hers. Lucy waited for his footsteps to fade, before folding at the waist to retrieve the absconding clothing. With great haste, she retreated to the safety of her bedroom.

Flopping down onto the bed she sank her fingers into her unruly locks, replaying the farce that had just played out downstairs.

Why didn't George tell her he was bringing his son? Lucy wasn't the sort of girl who had a roving eye, although yes, she did appreciate a good-looking man – the same as any other self-respecting woman did. He had taken her completely by surprise, in more ways than one. She was sure if she'd have looked up the word 'masculine' in the dictionary there would have been a picture of Joseph Dalton. There was something about him, and the fact that she couldn't quite define what it was both intrigued and alarmed her at the same time. Despite the fact that she was now in the privacy of her room, her hands had yet to regain their composure.

She had promised them drinks long ago, but first she

needed to redeem her dignity with make-up and perfume. The fancydress costume was cast onto the bathroom floor with a vow to burn them for inflicting such a mental scar, and the shower was charged with the task of taking her hair down. It was Suzie's day off work; Lucy was meant to be meeting her for brunch, but now she really didn't want to go.

After showering, she wrapped herself in towels and picked up her phone to see who the missed call was from. It was Suzie. Still no calls from Mark. There was no way she was going to put up with this shit anymore. This is exactly the sort of thing he'd done in the past. To teach him a lesson she was going to spend the day with the botanical love-hunk that had come to her gardening aid.

Yes it was childish, but he had pissed her off, and not only that, Lucy wanted to watch the garden evolve with every step. Well, that's the excuse she gave herself.

CHAPTER SIX

Lucy selected Suzie's number. She felt guilty for cancelling at such short notice, but after pacing the bedroom talking herself into meeting her, then out of it again, she finally plucked up the courage to cancel.

She pressed 'call' and held the phone against her damp hair.

'Hi Lu.'

Suzie's voice lacked its usual enthusiasm.

'Hi Suzie, is everything alright?'

'I'm a bad friend. I can't make brunch today, I'm sorry.'

'That's okay, don't worry about it, there'll be another time.' Lucy was relieved; she hated lying to her best friend.

'They're short-staffed at work so I've got to go in. Bummer, eh?'

'To be honest, Suzie, that helps me out.' Lucy ambled back into the bathroom, put the call on loudspeaker and placed the phone on the window sill. 'I've got the gardeners in and I want to keep an eye on him – I mean them!' *Shit.*

74

She squeezed toothpaste onto her toothbrush; and examined her eyebrows for stray hairs in the mirror, which rested on the sink waiting to be hung.

'Don't tell me: pot-bellied middle-aged men, wandering around with a cup of tea glued to one hand, scratching their arses.'

'Erm, yeah, you know the sort.' Lucy's hand masked her eyes, and she shook her head in shame.

'I'll let you go and crack the whip then. Are we still on for the barbecue this Saturday?'

'Yeah, course. That's why they're here, I'm trying to clear some of the mess so we don't lose any guests.'

Do you want me to bring anything?'

'No, just your lovely self.'

'Okay, chick, see you Saturday.'

'Oh, Suzie, one last thing. Was that brother of yours with Mark last night?' Pete was a nice guy, very quiet. He and Mark had become unlikely friends not long after Lucy's relationship with Mark had started.

'I don't know to be honest. He's still living with me while he's in between women; he didn't come home last night. Has Mark gone AWOL again?'

'No, no, I knew he'd be out all night; I just wondered if Pete was with him, that's all.' Lucy didn't want Suzie to think she was being used as a doormat all over again. 'Okay, Suz, have fun at work, see you on Saturday at four.'

'Can't wait. Bye, babe.'

'Bye, Suz.'

She descended the stairs in her retro red Nike sneakers; her hair was tied back in a high ponytail, and her glossy fringe shaded her freshly plucked eyebrows, just above her long lashes.

Lucy's self-confidence needed some underpinning after the morning's fiasco; smoke-grey three-quarter leggings helped with that, adhering to her shapely legs, while the red fitted polo shirt modestly covered her round bottom. It wasn't her usual gardening attire, but she had to restore her reputation as a perfectly sane woman. Once again she carried out their drinks, now quite some time after they were first promised. George was running through the starting procedure for the industrial machine with Shaggy, whose posture was so bad he looked like he'd had his spine removed.

'Two teas with sugar,' Lucy called out, getting their attention.

'You're a darlin'.' Thank you, Lucy.' George lifted the cups from the tray and handed one to his silent apprentice.

'Very sporty,' he gestured to her clothing with his cup. 'Off to the gym?' he asked, taking a sip of his tea.

'No, I just threw these on.' Lucy looked down at herself as though she wasn't sure what she had thrown on.

'Is that for Joseph?' asked George, pointing to the lone cup balancing on the tray.

'Yes, it is.'

'I'll take it to him if you like.' George raised his hand, in expectation of delivering Joseph's coffee.

'No, it's okay; I don't mind.' She drew the tray away protectively. She wanted to deliver it so he could witness her usual appearance. Usual, apart from the lash-thickening mascara, rose-coloured lip gloss and a light dusting of foundation. Other than that, she was *au naturel*.

'He's somewhere in the middle of the garden, if you can find him.'

'Okay, thanks, George.' Lucy turned, heading for the waist height wilderness.

'Watch your step, darlin'.' It's very uneven.'

'I will.' She took the cup from the tray before treading the bumpy ground, following the droning buzz of the petrol engine. She staggered her way through, doing her best not to spill his coffee. There he was. He had his back to her and was pivoting from left to right while the petrol-powered machine extended the flattened area. Unlike Adam, he stood tall and straight. Lucy swept her fringe to one side and straightened her T-shirt. Why the hell did she feel so nervous? She was only taking him his coffee. She expelled a lungful of air through her round pouty lips. 'Excuse me!' Her voice was cancelled out by the resounding noise of the tool. 'Excuse me!' Treading carefully, she headed into his peripheral vision, waving her hand in the air. Joseph's concentration flashed across to her; he cut the engine, removed the supporting harness from over his shoulder and placed the trimmer on the decapitated cuttings.

'I've finally got that coffee you asked for.' She stepped into the flattened zone with the cup back on the tray. Joseph slapped the palms of his hands together as he approached her, the tinge of amusement still present under the peak of his cap.

'Hello, my name's Joseph.' His hand extended with the spread of his grin.

Has he got sunstroke? She wasn't quite sure what to say. 'I'm… Lucy…' Eventually she accepted his hand's invitation, his soft touch contradicted the coarse skin of his fingers. 'Thanks,' he said, taking the white coffee cup.

'You better be careful out here. There's a crazy lady running around in a red Christmas sweater, throwing hot drinks over anyone who comes into contact with her.' He tactfully used the cup to conceal the obvious smirk that was adorning his face. Lucy didn't have any such props to use, so her sunshine smile was completely exposed.

'Really? A Christmas sweater, you say? How awful.'

'Yes, it was very bright – hurt my eyes, in fact.'

Lucy giggled, pressing her palm against the side of her face. 'I'm sorry, I didn't mean to scare you.'

His gloriously handsome face looked down on her from its lofty height with a broad smile. Not a smug, cocky smile, but an authentic, reassuring one.

'Hey, I'm a fine one to talk,' his arms splayed out. 'Look at me.'

Yes, Just look at you.

'My tuxedo is at the dry cleaners. Gym today?'

'Oh no, these are my old gardening clothes.' A total lie: they'd only been worn one other time, and that was in the changing room.

'You've got quite a garden here.' Joseph surveyed the area he had yet to cut through while Lucy guiltily let her eyes feast. No man could look this good without there being a flaw of some kind.

The baseball cap. He's probably bald, with a great big egg-shaped head.

'Do you live here on your own?' Joseph raised his hat and mopped his brow with a muscular forearm. A thick head of hair swirled in different directions like a tempestuous ocean, drowning her theory. Visually, there were no flaws.

'No, I live with my partner, Mark.'

Yes, Mark her partner, yet here she was dressing to impress Mr Butler's *doppelgänger*. It wasn't like she was flirting; she was merely admiring nature's fine work. If God had created man in his own image, then God was a hottie, and Eve was one lucky bitch.

Joseph looked into a non-existent distance and nodded ever so slightly. 'He's not the gardening type, I'm guessing?' He surmised correctly, although Mark's absence was a bit of a giveaway.

'Not really, I'm the one with the love of gardening.'

'Well there's a lot to love here.' He finished his coffee and placed it back onto the tray. He picked up the trimmer and paused, eyebrows raised, his direct stare cutting through the air with hypnotic power.

'Nice to finally meet the real Lucy Eaton.' His eyebrows dropped and the lips raised.

He arced the strap over his head, and with a snap of his arm the modern-day scythe screamed back into life. Rooted to the spot, she watched his backside as he strode into the overgrowth to continue with his rhythmical twists.

'Nice to meet you too… Joseph Dalton.' Even his name had a certain something about it. She took it for a test drive, several times, while making her way back to the house.

She thought about what he had said about 'the real you'. The comment was highly appreciated: she was pleased to have given him a more accurate image of herself. Lucy noticed that the sound of Joseph's tool had remained steady. She rubbernecked to see a mirror image of Joseph doing exactly the same thing, his mouth hitched up at the corner in a knowing way. Instantly returning her face in the direction of travel, she wondered if she should have returned the smile. Now having self-consciousness riding on her shoulder, Lucy grabbed her ponytail and ran it through her fist, feeling the need to do something, anything. The noise from the machinery remained unchanged, as it idled breathlessly.

He's still bloody watching me.

A large conifer tree, heavily laden with pine needles, was to be her shelter. Now she had an audience, the performance began. Holding her head high, she returned the tray to its original position, level with her shoulder, she sashayed her stuff over the uneven landscape.

Yes, Mr Dalton, not so scary now, eh?

'Argh!' One of her trotting feet stepped into a pothole and her ankle turned into Play-Doh, causing her to disappear into the sea of green, throwing the tray into the air like a frisbee. *Bollocks!* Lucy lay there, hoping and praying that he hadn't witnessed the graceless tumble. *He must think I'm aright idiot.* She wasn't far from the house, and considered doing a military crawl back to base. Lying on her back, staring into the big blue sky with both her palms squashing cheeks, she tried to force yet another embarrassing image from her mind. At that precise moment, Joseph's face appeared in her window of blue.

'Need a hand?'

At the speed of light, her hands hid themselves behind her head, like she was sunbathing.

'What?' *Why the fuck do I keep saying 'What'? He must think I'm stone deaf.* 'Oh, no… I was just watching the clouds go by.' The summer cherries would have been sick with envy at the colour of her cheeks.

He stood, hands on hips, and tipped his head back to take a look at the wonderful cloud formations, to find not even a puff of mist. He crouched down next to her; the depth of the sky was no match for his eyes.

'Did you hurt yourself?'

Lucy's hand rested on her fringe-covered forehead. 'You must think I'm a total idiot.'

His beard made way for another genuine, Mr Dalton smile. 'Of course not.'

Lucy propped herself up on her elbows, which exaggerated the effectiveness of her push-up bra. It didn't go unnoticed.

She pushed herself up and sat on her bottom with her knees raised. Lucy sucked in the air as she felt a biting sting at her ankle. 'Ow, ow, ow! I think I've sprained it.'

'I'll help you into the house.'

'Thank you.'

She raised her hand to be pulled to her feet, but he ignored it, sliding one arm under her legs and the other around her back. As if gravity had been switched off, he raised her in his arms with what seemed like no effort at all. Strangely, she didn't feel awkward, maybe because his eyes weren't upon her, although hers were upon him. She kept her head low and her eyes high, covertly appreciating his rugged perfection.

Joseph held her securely next to his chest, his body was hard, not like Mark's. It seemed wrong to make the comparison but she couldn't help it. There was an understated capability about him, like driving a fast car slowly, or ambling along on a horse; the raw power was there, lying dormant, waiting to be called upon.

They passed George and Adam, who were busy

beavering away with their backs to them. Joseph kicked the toecaps of his boots against the step, knocking off some of the cuttings. He carried her into the kitchen, and with no sign of fatigue, gently placed her onto one of the stools that stood around the granite island.

'Do you have any ice?'

Her glossy lips peeled apart to answer, but the slamming of the front door interrupted her. It was Mark. A slight pang of disappointment took her by surprise. Lucy's head turned from the hall back to Joseph, who remained loyally fixed to the spot, waiting to be told to stand down.

'That's Mark, I'll be fine now... Thank you, Joseph.'

'Any time, Lucy.'

She held her breath, bravely holding his stare until Mark entered, still wearing his Ralph Lauren sunnies.

'Morning.'

The greeting didn't sit well with his tone, and Lucy instantly knew that he was in one of his un-negotiable moods. He carelessly threw the car keys onto the island and peered at Lucy over his sunglasses.

'You going to the gym?'

'No, I am not going to the gym. I've just twisted my ankle in the garden. This is Joseph, he helped me back into the house. He's from GD Landscapes.'

Joseph took a step forward and offered his hand. 'Nice to meet you, Mark.'

Mark turned his attention to the fridge and his back to Joseph. 'Yeah, you too, mate.'

He opened the fridge, which was a couple of degrees warmer than his greeting, and cracked open a can of Coke.

Lucy cringed with embarrassment and looked to Joseph

apologetically, but his eyes were fixed on Mark's back. His tongue traced the line of his bottom lip while his open hand slowly returned to his side, closing into a fist before relaxing again. He clearly wasn't happy at being snubbed.

'I'll leave you to it.' Joseph nodded at Lucy and took one last look at Mark before heading back to the garden.

She held back her agitation until Joseph had gone, then pivoted on her chair.

Mark closed the fridge door and drained the can of its contents. He turned around, removing his specs and dropped them into the breast pocket of his grey shirt.

'He could have cleaned his mess up.' Mark put the empty can down next to the toaster. His hand slid along the work surface as he walked around to the window above the sink. He turned his back to Lucy once again, favouring the view through the window. She looked back to the path Joseph had taken. There were a few remnants from the garden scattered over the tiles.

'I could say the same about you.' She held on tightly to her self-restraint, feeling a full-blown argument was brewing.

He nonchalantly turned his head a mere ten degrees. 'That empty can doesn't go next to the toaster, it goes in the bin.'

She was pissed off at him anyway, but he was acting like a total arsehole. 'What the hell's got into you today? Before you answer that, you can tell me where you were last night?' Her self-restraint had always been a slippery bugger.

A sharp stab of air left his lips, like he was blowing out a candle. 'I knew I'd have this.' He held his position.

'Have what, exactly?'

'The third degree.'

Lucy's already thin patience was now threadbare.

'You think because you bought me *Pretty Woman* on DVD and a takeaway curry that you have the right to go gallivanting off all night, without so much as a phone call…?' In the right situation silence could be extremely antagonistic.

'Can you at least face me when I'm talking to you?'

Mark's hands hid in his pockets and like a sullen child he shuffled around to face her.

'I met the lads at the King's Arms. It was Roger's birthday and we all got a bit carried away and had too much to drink, so I crashed out on Roger's couch.'

She had prepared her reproach, but before she got chance to vent it Mark hastily butted in.

'Before you ask, my phone was dead.' He took the evidence from his pocket and repeatedly pressed the power button to prove his point.

'You're the only one with a phone then?'

Confrontation was a great painkiller; she had completely forgotten about her ankle.

'Of course not, but you know what I'm like with numbers.' That was certainly true. His reliance on technology tended to disengage his brain.

'Don't they have taxis where Roger lives? Who is this *Roger*, anyway?'

'You know, I used to work with him.' Mark hunched his shoulders and held out upturned palms, as though everyone knew who Roger was.

'I thought you hated everyone at work?' Lucy folded her arms. Watching Mark closely she contemplated his story, feeling her agitation subside. She wasn't in the mood for a fight, especially while they had people there – even though the noise from outside masked their raised voices.

'Roger was alright. I always got on with him.' Mark's tone had softened slightly. He went back to the empty can and deposited it into a larger, stainless steel one. It seemed he was climbing down from his high horse.

'Look, I'm sorry, okay? I should have come home last night, but I had too much to drink and I had a terrible night's sleep on Roger's couch, and I've woken up grouchy.' Mark made his way to the stool next to her and perched his backside on it, keeping one foot on the floor.

Lucy looked into his eyes; he did look tired. 'Just give me some thought, Mark, and more importantly, some respect.' He broke eye contact to check his nails, nodding submissively.

'What have you got planned for today?' Mark subtly steered away from the subject.

'I was supposed to be meeting Suzie, but she couldn't make it, so I'm spending the day here. Just to make sure the guys know what to do.'

'Well in that case I'm going to have a quick shower, and go for a round of golf.' He laced his fingers behind his head and stretched. 'Try and shake off this crabby mood – is that okay?'

'Yeah, that's fine. So long as you come home tonight.' She couldn't resist one last stinging remark.

He took it on the chin and climbed off the stool, kissing her on her cold shoulder.

'Are you going to say hello to the guys?' She rotated herself around to face him.

'There's another two out there somewhere.'

Mark clung onto the chunky architrave of the hall

frame and looked out of the kitchen window.

'In a minute, when I've had a shower.' He gave the timber a friendly tap with his hand and headed up the stairs, rather energetically for a tired man. He *probably* was telling the truth about last night; he always did have to be the ringleader. It was the *probably* part she didn't like.

CHAPTER SEVEN

Lucy ate her breakfast while a bag of frozen peas administered first aid to her ankle. Thankfully the injury wasn't as bad as she had first thought. She loaded the last spoonful of cereal into her mouth when there was a knock at the front door. Dispensing with the frozen peas, she quickly put her empty bowl into the dishwasher and hobbled across the Minton floor. Opening the door she was greeted by a man in the winter years of his life. He was impeccably dressed in taupe chinos and a navy, double-breasted blazer with bright gold buttons and an even brighter smile.

'Good morning, young lady. I do hope I'm not interrupting you?' He waited for conformation, displaying a '70s game show host smile.

'No, can I help you?'

'Allow me to introduce myself.' He straightened the already straight, perfectly formed Windsor knot of his sage-green tie, which sat between a pale blue collar. 'My name is Charles St Clair.'

A sprightly hand shot out towards her, matching the enthusiasm of his theatrical introduction. Lucy's brow pinched, she was about to announce that whatever it was he was selling, she wasn't interested.

'I live next door with my wife, Tabitha.'

'Oh! Nice to meet you, Charles.'

She let go of the door, which she'd been holding protectively close and shook Mr St Clair's clammy hand.

'I'm Lucy. Lucy Eaton.'

'A pleasure to meet you, Lucy. The reason I've called round—'

'Come in, Charles, please.' She interrupted him to offer the invitation.

'Why, thank you.' He stepped up into the hallway while Lucy held the door open for him.

She led the way into the best room in the house, as all the other ones looked like they had just moved in, which of course, they had.

'Can I get you a drink?'

'No, thank you. Now, where was I...?' His hand rose up, lightly patting over his wavy hair to check that the Brylcreem was doing its job. 'Oh yes, the reason I've called round is because my wife is worrying herself silly.' He paused and dropped his fingers into the pocket of his blazer.

'Why's that?'

'Well, some time ago we were broken into whilst we were in bed.'

'God, how awful,' she interjected, placing her hand over her mouth in horror at the very thought.

'Indeed.' Charles nodded gravely. 'Luckily, we slept through the whole thing, but consequently, as a result of that night she is very wary of anyone that comes to the house unannounced.' His free hand expressively danced around to the tune of his voice. 'So when you called to introduce yourselves, not knowing who you were, she panicked somewhat.'

That would explain her strange behaviour.

'That's why she didn't answer the door, you see.' He brushed his index finger over a very neat, ash-grey moustache that was clipped to millimetre perfection and was colour-coordinated with his slicked back hair.

'Tell her not to worry about it. It's fine, really.'

'Oh, but she is. I've been away in France – we have a home there which is currently being renovated.'

He looked like the sort of person who would have a home in France. Lucy privately made assumptions about Mr St Clair, based purely on his appearance.

'Do you want me to go and see her now? I don't want her worrying.'

Lucy's offer was genuine: she really wanted to have a good relationship with her new neighbours. Her last ones always seemed to pretend not to have seen her when clearly they had.

'That's why I'm here; we would love you both to join us this evening for a drink or two.' He spoke with a very upper-class accent, but not in a snooty way.

'That's very kind of you. Yes, we would love to.'

'Wonderful, how does eight o'clock sound?'

'Absolutely fine.'

'Good, that's settled then.'

The two neighbours continued talking, making general conversation about their houses and gardens. Charles told her that they had neglected their own property in recent years, since they had spent most of their time overseas. He did most of the talking. Lucy was happy to listen to him. He was obviously an educated man but he had a very easy demeanour about him, and coupled with his watery pale-green eyes shadowed by black eyebrows that weren't quite as well manicured as his moustache, she found him very endearing. When they finished their chat, he bade her good day, and in a refined fashion he clipped across the tiles in his tan brogues, leaving Lucy smiling to herself. There were still a few gentlemen around, after all.

Mark's aftershave announced his arrival. He appeared in the kitchen, raking his fingers through his dishevelled towel-dried hair. Lucy half-filled three tall glasses with ice, and took a bottle of lemonade from the fridge.

'Okay, I'm off, babe. See you later.'

She unscrewed the cap from the bottle and turned to say goodbye. 'You look very smart for golf, don't you?'

Mark's head dropped to take a look at his attire. This was another outfit she couldn't recall ever seeing.

'Not really, it's a very select club you know.'

She wouldn't know, as she had never been interested in knocking a little white-pitted ball around acres of land.

'Before you disappear, we're going around to next door for drinks at eight.' The ice cracked as the lemonade hit, and a flurry of bubbles rushed to the rim of the glass.

'Not the one-eyed witch?' His face displayed utter distaste at the idea.

'Her husband Charles came round while you were in the shower. He's lovely.'

She rummaged around in the kitchen drawer, then pulled out the car charger for his phone and dangled it at arm's length. 'I'll explain it all to you later, *don't* be late.'

'Do we have to?' Mark whined, as he took the white cable and coiled it around his fingers.

'Yes, I've said we would go now. His wife's name is Tabitha.' She screwed the cap back on the glass bottle and placed it back in the fridge.

'Charley and Tabby, I bet they're a barrel of laughs.' He slipped the cable into his skinny grey trousers.

'See you later.' He kissed her on the back of the head and made his way to the front door.

'Eight o'clock!'

'I know, I know, eight o'clock.'

'Mark..... .' The door latched. 'You're not going to say hello to the guys then?'

She clenched the trinity of chilled glasses with both hands. Stepping outside she noticed a great divide in the jungle; Joseph had cleared a pathway for her. George was meandering along the aisle, some distance ahead, chatting on his phone. Lucy followed up behind him while the ice cubes played a delicate tune on the cool glass.

She cautiously placed one foot in front of the other; she didn't want another twisted ankle, although it might have been worth it just to get trucked around the garden in Joseph's capable arms. Her concentration lifted from the sloshing beverage to see George, who had stopped dead in his tracks. He slowly lowered his left hand, which was holding the phone, while raising his right hand to massage the back of his neck. She could tell from his body language that something was wrong.

Lucy slowed her pace, then stopped when Joseph came into view. He was on his knees in the middle of what looked like a blast zone. He had cleared a large perimeter, cutting down everything in his path, except for a lone poppy.

He knelt in the desolation, staring at the pale red tissue-like petals fluttering in the whisper of a breeze. A lonely splash of colour amongst the slain greenery, its long wiry stem reached the delicate flower up to him as if it were asking for mercy.

George, motionless, watched his son, and Lucy watched them both, unnoticed. Joseph's hand skimmed over his beard and rested on his thigh. Was he hurt? Why was George hesitating? Lucy was confused by the whole scene, but knew she was witness to something. George put his phone away, shaking his head gently, he continued towards Joseph.

'How you getting on there, son?' His question was delivered at a higher volume than was necessary, giving warning of his approach. Lucy had stepped off the track and was hiding behind an overgrown amalgamation of bushes.

Joseph started at the sound of his father's voice; the flower that he had shown so much compassion for was ripped from its place on earth, and crushed in his fist.

'Good, good, I'm good.' He looked startled and rose to his feet quickly.

Lucy's hands began to cramp holding the now freezing cold glasses. She quietly edged deeper into her hiding place. She knew it was wrong of her to be eavesdropping, but intrigue had overruled good manners.

'I've sent Adam to get the sandwiches. You've done well, son.' George surveyed the progress.

'This is a big job. We could do with another pair of hands, you know, Dad. You need to start taking it a bit easier.'

'We'll manage, son, we'll manage.' They both looked out at nothing. There was an awkwardness between them, like they were avoiding something. 'I was thinking… there's a service of remembrance tonight.'

'Dad,' Joseph half-sighed, half-groaned, 'we've already had this conversation: you know the church thing isn't me.' He removed his cap and clamped his thumb and fingers on his temples.

'I know, I know, but they've got the choir tonight. They're practising for their competition. They've made the finals.'

Joseph stood with his head held up to the sky, his face knotted with concentration.

'It'll only be an hour… you can light a candle for your mother.'

The knots were undone at the mention of the woman that gave him life. He looked over at the old man, whose face she couldn't see.

'What do you say?' asked George.

There was great affection in Joseph's eyes as a reluctant smile developed.

'You always did know how to persuade me.'

'Come on, just an hour with your old dad, eh?'

'Okay,' Joseph nodded as he slipped his cap back on. The adulation between them was evident, and although their conversation hadn't been anything out of the ordinary, Lucy was touched by the gentleness of their exchange.

The sound of the side gate closing alerted her to the approach of someone. It had to be Adam.

Shit!

She had been flushed out, and had to make a move before Adam caught her snooping in the bushes.

'Drinks, anyone?' she called out with the enthusiasm of an am-dram extra, before stepping out from behind the bush like she had been beamed down from the Starship Enterprise.

'Let me help you with those.' George hurried over. Taking the glasses from her, he handed one to Joseph. 'You should've come along the track that Joseph cut out. You'll twist your ankle if you're not careful.'

She guiltily peered up through her lashes at Mr Dalton, Jr. who was waiting to receive her stare.

The very thought of having his eyes upon her evoked a crippling self-consciousness – why was that? Her arms flopped about having no purpose now George had gallantly taken the glasses, so she knotted them across her chest. She only had to be within fifty feet of this man to feel his presence. It hung in the air like a thick fog, interfering with the natural rhythm of her breathing. Lucy sporadically stole glances at him to see if he was still watching her… he was. She wasn't sure if Mark going to play golf was a good thing or not, as a stream of inappropriate questions involuntarily pinged into her mind's inbox.

'Adam's here – about time too,' said George.

Lucy looked over her shoulder to see the young apprentice, who was holding three white parcels aloft.

'We're going to have a quick sandwich, Lucy, okay?'

'Of course, you don't have to ask.'

George's phone rang in his breast pocket. 'Excuse me.' He pulled out the phone and squinted at the screen from behind his glasses. 'Hello, John… sorry about that…' He strolled around aimlessly with his glass of lemonade, in the way people do when they talk on the phone.

'Do you want to share my sandwich?' Joseph sipped on the cool liquid, which was the exact opposite of his appearance. Hot didn't do him justice; he made all the Diet Coke men look like the Hunchback of Notre Dame. She didn't know how to respond to his question: was he joking or not?

'That's very kind of you, but I've already had breakfast.'

She couldn't look him in the face for more than a few seconds. It was like staring at the sun; you could glance at it quickly and admire its wonder and beauty, but to look for too long was dangerous.

'Shall we?' He motioned towards the pathway that he had specially prepared for her.

Being his father's son, he waited for the lady to go first. Lucy squeaked out a pathetic 'thank you,' and they left George deep in conversation, making his own crop circle. As they headed back to the house, Lucy turned her head from left to right, casually taking in her surroundings.

But really she was trying to see how close he was. It seemed he had left enough distance between them to get a full view of her. She stretched the hem of her T-shirt down over her bottom, knowing full well that his eyes were feasting on it. Her bottom was the one part of her that she was proud of; she wasn't particularly big breasted – but, like Suzie always said, 'any more than a handful is a waste.' The round full cheeks seemed to know that they were being admired, as they jumped around like two puppies vying for attention, easing her T-shirt up over her curvy hips. His silence was very telling and also very unnerving. 'Sorry about Mark, earlier.' Why the hell did she mention, Mark? Was it her brain's way of reminding her she was taken?

'Don't worry about it, it's fine. How's the ankle?' His voice was like audible chocolate: thick, velvety, addictive. 'You look fine – the ankle, I mean.'

It was a good job he couldn't see her face, which looked far from fine; it was twisting into various hideous expressions while she desperately tried to think of something witty – or at least coherent – to say. But Joseph Dalton, who she couldn't even see, had thrown a glitch into her system. *Actually, it feels terribly weak – can you carry me?* 'It's fine, thank you.' *Coward!*

Much to her relief they arrived back at the house. Adam had set out three camping chairs in a row, facing the garden. He sat in the end chair with his face buried in his sandwich, his fingers stained with runny egg yolk. Lucy turned to her trailing partner, keeping her line of vision below the horizon of his eyes.

'Shall I take that for you?' She reached out for the dry glass.

'Thanks.'

Lucy grabbed the glass by the rim, making sure she didn't touch his fingers.

'Are you sure you don't want some?'

Was the question entirely innocent? There seemed to be more than a hint of playfulness in his voice.

'Sorry?' She bravely raised her face to his and searched through her portfolio of expressions, looking for the cool, calm and collected one. All that was available was blushing adolescent.

'My sandwich...'

A sparkle of mischief shimmered in his eyes. He was

toying with her. It seemed the effect he had on her hadn't gone unnoticed.

'I'd love some, but I already have a sandwich.' Her heart crash-banged like a big bass drum as she courageously tried to match his innuendo with a clever euphemism. Every single drop of moisture had evaporated from her mouth, and as hard as she tried, her appearance didn't match the boldness of her words. Joseph's eyebrows hitched up under the shade of his baseball cap; for a brief moment she took the risk and stared at the sun. It was bright, it was beautiful and it was dangerous.

Adam, who was an oblivious witness to their little *tete-a-tete*, butted in. 'Your sandwich is gonna be cold, Joe.' His words were churned up with a mouthful of food.

Joseph looked to the young man, and Lucy cowardly hot-footed it back into the house, her chest rising and falling with a breathlessness that was inexplicable.

She poured herself a glass of water with jittering hands to combat her sudden drought. *Jesus, what the hell is wrong with me?* The strange loss of control was not welcome; she needed a mundane task to restore some balance. Lucy took herself upstairs and began to put away the clothes that were still packed. She busied herself with hanging, folding and sorting, the gardener never far from her thoughts. Now she had felt the heat of the sun, the cold reality of things didn't seem quite so appealing.

CHAPTER EIGHT

Joseph stood under the canopy of the old church gate and stared at the ecclesiastical archway and its foreboding doors. The house of God was one place he didn't think his presence was appropriate, but he had promised his dad. He couldn't let him down and indeed he wouldn't.

He lifted the thick cast-iron latch; the old hook and band hinges groaned their disapproval at having to be of service once again. Joseph made his way along the uneven pathway past the weathered stones that crookedly sprouted from the earth, each one a marker for a life now spent. He briefly paused at the heavy-set doors before entering.

Even a blind man would have known he was in a church from the distinctive, musky smell of incense. It had been burned there for hundreds of years, impregnating the very fabric of the building.

The cold stone church housed a warm welcome; a mixture of people formed the population of the place, but it was the older generation that held the majority.

George proudly introduced him to almost everyone;

pleasantries and smiles were traded. He recognised many of the faces from his mother's funeral, although there had been no smiles that day.

'Father Brian, you remember my son, Joseph?'

'Of course I do.' Father Brian was another member of the white-haired club, although for his advanced years he looked remarkably youthful; maybe that was the result of a sinless life.

'Good to see you again, Joseph.'

'You too.' He had a strong grip for such a slight man, and apart from the bright white square that sat in the centre of his neck, he was dressed like a hitman. They chatted for a while, George silently observing them.

Bushy white eyebrows that arced around his autumn-brown eyes gave him a sympathetic appearance. He seemed to be searching Joseph's face with inquisitive concentration.

'I'm glad you could join us this evening. Now if you'll excuse me, I'd better get the show started.'

Joseph was never one to be lost for words, but he simply smiled politely. He should have felt at ease there, at peace, but it was quite the opposite. His heart rate was steady, except it thumped harder in his chest. The last time he had been here was for his mother's funeral. She had been a regular at St Francis's and when she died his father had taken her place, although he had never been a religious man. Maybe it helped him feel closer to her, as it had been the last place they were together as man and wife before her body was returned back to the earth.

Everyone took their seats; father and son sat on the end of the middle pew, next to the left aisle. Joseph cast his eyes around the vast space, which seemed twice as large as its external appearance would have led you to believe.

God's shepherd ascended the mini-staircase of the intricately carved pulpit to welcome his faithful flock. Before delivering his sermon, Father Brian gave out thank you's, happy birthdays and a reminder about the jumble sale taking place the following Saturday to raise funds for essential repair work to the steeple. The service was performed with professional enthusiasm and wit; he was both articulate and engaging.

Joseph randomly surveyed the congregation who were looking to the man in black to give them answers, promises of a better life, a better world – one where the horrors of our world would cease to exist and only good and righteousness would prevail. He had a captive audience, preaching to the converted; who wouldn't want to believe in such a paradise?

Joseph knew a very different world from the one promised: one where good and righteousness were the underdog; a world where horrors that most men couldn't imagine played out, unchallenged, below the blindfolded gaze of heaven.

He silenced his thoughts, and heard a sample of the Good Book being quoted. What could it hurt if it gave them a sense of security, even if it was a false one? The service shuffled along as these things did. Joseph started to feel a little more at ease, his mind preoccupied with people-watching. Father Brian announced with great pride and excitement that the choir would be giving a special performance ahead of their upcoming competition. This caused quite a stir, and a wave of nondescript mumbles rippled around the bobbing heads, before ebbing back in respectful silence as the mighty organ, which looked like a medieval fortress, made its presence known.

Warm, fluting harmonic tones drifted invisibly through the air, building in volume, filling the enormous space with sound, reverberating through the oak pews. The choir joined the flow of euphony, their clear sharp voices capturing the emotion that the composer had carefully crafted. They sang of great love and honour, of the finality of death and the glory of God Almighty, who would welcome us with open arms to live an everlasting life at his side.

The pitch of their voices raised in celestial perfection as the sound swirled around Joseph. It became more than just music: it was like a winter wind biting at him; it was memories, regrets and pain. His feeling of comfort had abandoned him.

The relentless angelic harmony washed over every square inch of the ancient building, reaching into his soul, confronting his demons, challenging the great shame he carried in his heart. Joseph tightened his mouth; his nostrils flared frantically drawing in air trying to calm the unwelcome feelings.

His eyes raised as if they had a will of their own, and he found himself looking upon the image he had deliberately been avoiding. Suspended from the horizontal collar beam of the great timber roof was a life-size effigy of Jesus Christ nailed to the cross. A crown of thorns punctured his skin and the blood of a man ran from the Son of God. The ubiquitous stare of the bright blue compassionate eyes found him.

He wasn't a man of faith, life had driven it from him, but as he looked up into the face of Christ and listened to the angelic voices, tears began to spill, rushing to the concealment of his beard. Emotional control had been taken from him, but he fought hard to regain it; every muscle in his body was locked in a battle of wills.

He felt the hand of his father gently tap him twice on the knee and tenderly rest there. The simple action telling him, *it's okay, son. Don't be ashamed; go ahead and weep.* Heavenly intonation showed no mercy, conjuring up images he knew would never leave him, and the simple touch of his father's hand was all it took.

His body unlocked, submitting to the moment; tears of repentance solemnly filed down his skin. Tears for his much loved mother, tears for the pain he had caused, for that one moment in time that had changed his life irrevocably.

Having broken him, the ethereal, angelic voices slowly drew back, vacating the space they had so powerfully possessed. Upon their silence, the crack of palms filled the stillness with a much deserved round of applause. Joseph exhaled with relief; the outpouring had left him with an unexpected feeling of serenity.

His hand discreetly towelled his face while Father Brian finished his sermon, displaying great magnetism for such a small man, and welcomed everyone to join him for tea and biscuits. A choir of creaks followed his announcement, as everyone raised from the old benches.

'Why don't you go and light a candle for your mother?'

Joseph nodded in answer to his father's suggestion, suspecting his vocal cords weren't up to the task.

Using the pew in front, he pulled himself to his feet and walked into the intimate space of the south transept. Several rows of candles sat tiered above one another on a black metal frame, providing a subtle light to a marble sculpture of the Virgin Mary. Her upturned open palms were held out from under flowing robes, inviting him to add to the lights of remembrance. He delved into his jeans pocket, pulled out some loose change and dropped it into the donation box.

The metallic clash was unsympathetically amplified in the respectful silence.

Holding his chosen candle, he transferred the flame from its neighbour and placed it on the top tier. It shone bright and steadily for a dearly loved mother and wife; an involuntary smile snuck onto his lips at the memory of her beautiful, kind face. God, he missed her.

Joseph hesitantly reached out for another candle, then looked over his shoulder, feeling the presence of someone watching. George nodded his approval, and one more candle fought back the darkness. It slowly burned away unlike like the pain that had burned inside of him, every single day, never fading, never dying.

'Come on, son, let's get a cup of tea, eh?' His father threw out a lifeline to pull him from the darkness that was never far away.

Joseph clutched his tea and biscuit self-consciously while his dad had his ear chewed off by a large lady with an equally large head of curly hair. The chink of cups and saucers rang out like church bells amongst the chitter chatter. Joseph kept his back to man's savior; his body was in the present but his mind lingered in the past.

'Joseph,' the warm tone of the Irish brogue gave away its owner. He turned to look down at the youthful face of the old priest.

'How did you enjoy the choir?'

'It was… stirring.'

'Yes, they're fantastic aren't they? I'm sure they'll do well in the competition.'

'I'm sure they will.' Joseph sipped the hot sweet tea, wishing it were something cold and alcoholic.

'And how are you keeping, Joseph?' Father Brian's eyes pinched the slightest fraction; Joseph sensed his father's involvement in what seemed like an innocent question.

'I take each day as it comes, good or bad.' He could have given a generic answer, but the rousing atmosphere had left the door of honesty ajar.

'You'd be more than welcome at our Sunday service, Joseph.' The man in black's voice was calming and soothing, but most of all it carried compassion effortlessly; he was very well suited to his chosen career.

Being a man that spoke his mind, Joseph saw no benefit in skirting around the issue. 'I'm not a believer, I'm afraid, but thank you.'

'May I ask why you came tonight?'

'Dad asked me to,' His eyes pointed to the man in question, who was inconspicuously watching them from behind a cluster of tight curls.

'You mean to say you've never looked up to the sky and uttered the words, "please, God?"'

'Yes, I have, but every time I asked for help, it seems he was out to lunch.'

Joseph's satirical comment inflicted an asymmetrical smile on its receiver.

'Life doesn't always travel the path we intended it to, and sometimes tragedies are suffered along the way.'

God's sales rep paused, allowing Joseph to anticipate his next line.

'But time's a great healer?'

A broad smile creased the boyish face, giving away his true age. 'Yes, that's the old cliché, isn't it? Before I received the calling to serve God, my wife and I lived in Galway, west Ireland. One day we were driving to go and visit my wife's mother, when out of nowhere a car careered into the side of ours.' The creases faded along with the smile. 'Our six-month-old daughter was in the back seat.' He seemed to age five years in five seconds. 'She was seriously hurt. We spent a week living in the intensive care unit, and my lord, I prayed, I promised and I asked...' The slight tremble of his chin indicated the difficulty of his story.

'She died eight days after the accident...' His voice , like the short life of his child.

Joseph's eyes fell to the floor, searching for something to say.

'I'm sorry.' The inadequate remark was all he had to offer; he was feeling increasingly uncomfortable with this conversation.

'Not a single day...' Father Brian's voice fractured once more. 'Not a single day goes by when I don't think of her...' What I'm trying to say is that there are some things you never get over, but you build your life around the reality of it. Joseph, I know your pain, and I know that you are a good man. I'm not trying to tell you that God has forgiven you, I'm telling you that *you* have to forgive yourself.'

Despite his black attire, there was a luminosity about this little man, an unvarnished truth. The eyes of two very different generations locked, and in those few seconds of silence more was articulated than had been over the last few minutes.

A wealth of knowledge from a long life lived was contained behind the windows to the soul. Joseph knew he was looking straight into his heart; it felt almost cathartic.

'Brian, you must try my pecan sponge.' The lady with a mass of curls waded in with a wedge of cake that left very little of the plate still visible.

'Why, Janet, you know I'm watching my figure. But I'll do my best to get through it.'

Janet handed over the plate with a large dollop of self-pride, reiterating that she had made it specially. She kindly asked Joseph if he would like to try some; he respectfully declined and decided that it was as good a time as any to make his exit.

'It was nice talking to you, Father Brian.' The two men pressed palms. 'Thank you.'

'Any time, Joseph, I'm here any time. Shall I save a seat for you on Sunday?'

'No, thank you, you won't be seeing my face here again, I'm afraid.' He tried to deliver the reply in the nicest way possible. Father Brian accepted it with good grace, and possibly a twitch of doubt to the lips.

'Take care now, Joseph.'

'You too.'

Excusing and apologising through the gang of people, he placed his half-empty cup and uneaten biscuit onto the refreshment table.

His father made his way over to him. 'Everything alright, son?' It was a loaded question.

'Yeah, fine. I'm going to make a move now.'

'Oh.' George fiddled with his fingers and drew a deep breath to speak.

His son reached an arm over his shoulder and kissed

him on the forehead, like he occasionally did, usually on his father's birthday.

'See you in the morning, Dad.'

George patted his son on the back and Joseph headed for the exit.

'Don't be late in the morning,' he called out. It wasn't what he had intended to say, but the moment had gone.

Joseph stepped back into the 21st century. He had a friend at home which shared his initials, and always helped to ease his troubles. It was a full, unopened litre of help just waiting to wash it all away for another night.

CHAPTER NINE

It was 7.45 p.m., and there was still no sign of Mark. Lucy had deliberately not called him: he knew full well before he left the house, that they'd been invited next door. He wasn't a child that needed reminding constantly, he was a grown man.

She was already pissed off, having found his golf shoes while putting away their clothes. She decided to reserve judgment until he came home. *You can play golf in normal footwear after all, can't you?*

The front door slammed. Lucy paused for a moment holding her hair up with one hand and a hairpin in the other. 'Don't panic, I'm back,' Mark hollered up the stairs.

She inserted the final pin and glanced at her Rolex. It was now 7.50 p.m. She would never have spent that much on a watch; Mark had bought a matching diamond encrusted his-and-hers set when he was having one of his 'we've got money to burn,' days. Having witnessed Charles's dapper appearance earlier that day, she felt a little bling needed to be on show.

Mark clumped up the stairs, sounding as though he had lead boots on; he came into the bathroom with his hands held up in surrender. Lucy shook her head at him in the mirror. It was too late for an argument, and she really wanted to make a good impression on the new neighbours.

'You've been gone for ages; how long does a round of golf take?'

Her hair looked perfectly fine, but she still had to fiddle with it.

'It's not a two minute game, you know.' He started to unbutton his shirt.

'What are you doing?' She turned from the reflection to face the real man.

'I'm having a shower – why?'

'Why? Did you get hit on the head with a golf ball? We're meant to be next door at eight o'clock.'

She hated to be late and always prided herself on being on time.

'Alright, calm down. It's only next door. I'll be two minutes.' He dropped his trousers and kicked them off into the corner. Lucy turned back to the looking glass and stooped down to triple-check her hair.

'Can you please hang this mirror, Mark?'

'Never mind the mirror,' his voice echoed from behind the psychedelic shower curtain as the water spat and stuttered into action. 'We've got to get a new bathroom suite fitted. I hate this crappy shower.'

Lucy pondered whether or not to mention the golf shoes.

'You know you left your golf shoes here?'

She looked at the '60s shower curtain; it really was horrid.

'What?' he gurgled. 'I know. I bought a new pair from the club; mine were a bit tight anyway.'

Lucy wished she had posed the question while his face was in view. The slight hesitation in his voice wasn't comforting; she decided not to push it. They hadn't got time for it, and Mark would only need the slightest excuse not to go. True to his word, he was showered within the self-imposed time limit.

A pair of charcoal trousers and a blue pinstriped shirt lay on the bed waiting to be occupied.

'Put these on quickly.'

He made no objections to her choice and obeyed orders.

'Do I look okay?' Lucy asked.

She wanted to look smart, but not too smart, and casual, but not too casual. The white tailored trousers and cobalt hem blouse seemed to fit her convoluted fashion brief.

'Yeah, you look fine, babe.'

His words hit her ear canal before his pupil landed on her appearance.

Shoes on and a spray of cologne, and Mark was ready. Keys in hand, Lucy jangled down the stairs, grabbed the bottle of wine she'd left by the door and marched double-time to Number 9.

Mark trailed behind her, tapping away on his phone. According to the bling it was 8.05 p.m.

Damn! 'Come on, Mark.'

'Okay, keep your knickers on.'

I will be tonight, don't you worry.

She stood at the mouth of the driveway and waited for him; he sauntered along with the enthusiasm of a funeral procession.

'Put your phone away now, and switch it onto silent.'

'Okay, Mother. What's got into you tonight?'

'Nothing,' she snapped. 'I just want to make a good impression.'

Mark leaving things until the very last minute hadn't helped her stress levels. Plus she was anxious about meeting the other half of Tabitha's face, especially after their first encounter. More annoyingly, the folding and putting away of an infinite amount of clothing hadn't diluted the unnerving effect of the gardener. She didn't like it. It was unwelcome, not to mention inconvenient, and although Mr Dalton wouldn't be there this evening, she had somehow dressed with him in mind. Lucy stubbornly refused to admit this to herself, but it was true.

Life's timing could be truly terrible sometimes. She linked arms with the man fate had chosen for her, who lately seemed more enamoured with electronic gadgets or small white pitted balls. They walked the short distance together; Lucy fingered the brass button which activated an almost comical ding-dong sound inside.

'Mark.' He was still enveloped in an intimate moment with technology.

She watched him briefly, not as his partner, rather as a customer in a cafe who watches strangers, making assumptions about their personality based on a fleeting moment in time.

The old Mark seemed to be creeping his way back into her life. After today, she needed him to be the man she fell in love with. Their defences needed to be strong, because she feared an attack was imminent.

He broke his attention from the illuminated screen for a moment, and witnessed her café-customer stare.

'What?'

'Nothing.' Lucy didn't want to have to tell him how she wanted, no, needed him to be. It was the one thing that should have been natural, instinctive.

'You look nice.' The sterile words were blurted out, void of any real sentiment, like when you say hello to a stranger in an elevator.

Her lips curled under one another in acknowledgment while the twin locks were being released. This time the door opened fully, unhindered by any chains.

'Lucy! Welcome.'

Charles was, as she expected, dressed to the high standards of a time gone by, complete with a mustard-coloured, paisley-patterned cravat.

'Sorry we're late. It's my fault, I was having hair trouble.' She took a hit for the team.

'Not at all.' A ringless right hand perched on her shoulder; he leaned in and kissed the air, the sharp edges of his engineered moustache grazed the soft skin of her cheek.

'This is my partner, Mark.'

Thankfully Charles didn't air-kiss Mark, but greeted him in the more traditional way.

'A pleasure to meet you, young man.'

'You too.'

The front door was closed and both locks returned to duty. They waited for directions in the dull, three-quarter-panelled hallway. The timber floor matched the deep tone of the walls, as did the heavy-set staircase; it was not conductive to a light and airy atmosphere. No furniture or clutter of any kind could be seen in the naked room.

'I wasn't sure which you would prefer, so I took a chance and brought red.'

'Why that's very kind of you, Lucy, thank you.' Taking the bottle from her, he cradled it in his hand while inspecting the label. 'My wife loves red wine; you chose well, my dear.'

The fact that her novice choice had met with his well-seasoned palate was a small relief.

Where is his wife?

'If you'd like to enter through the door behind you, my dear, you should find Tabitha.'

Lucy's stomach turned with the rotation of the doorknob. Charles was such a lovely man, so surely Mrs St Clair would be too. The dark door swung silently on its hinges, revealing more and more of the unfamiliar room. A large antique cabinet stood with its back to the wall and was adorned with an eclectic mix of ornaments. Original parquet flooring did nothing to help lift the shadowy gloom. Two well-worn, French provincial style lounge suites faced each other in front of the smoke-stained open fireplace.

Lucy crossed the threshold into the aged, but still opulent room, which bore the same scent as their home once had. Unless they were playing a game of hide and seek, it seemed there was no one there.

Stepping from behind the blind side of the door, Lucy took in the uninterrupted view. Mark shuffled in behind her.

'Tabitha, our guests have arrived,' George announced to the seemingly empty room. The pivoting figure of a woman snared Lucy's eye. She was standing at the bay window, perfectly camouflaged next to the thick plum curtains.

Tabitha approached with an open hand on the end of a straight arm. Lucy met her halfway, but the extended limb refused to buckle, keeping the two women as far apart as possible.

'Nice to finally meet you, Tabitha. I'm Lucy.' The other half of her face was a perfect match with its neighbour.

'The same to you too.'

Her pigmentation-free hair was tightly scraped back, which served as a DIY face-lift, pulling out some of the wrinkles from years already spent. Lucy was amazed the words had managed to squeeze through such a tight mouth. Lipstick must have lasted her years, as there was very little lip to apply any to. With the introduction of Mark came another stern, business-like handshake, along with a smile her face clearly wasn't happy giving. Charles heartily informed his wife of their neighbour's kind gift, and a 'thank you' managed to work its way to freedom, which was the extent of her interest in the matter.

Charles was director of their get-together again; he invited them to take a seat and played the role of barman. Lucy requested a vodka and tonic; it wasn't her usual tipple but she needed something as close to an anaesthetic as was possible, because it seemed the evening was going to be painful. Mark hadn't read them at all well, and asked for a beer.

'Wine or spirits, old boy,' was the stunned reply from Charles.

They both sat with their knees raised way higher than their bottoms, thanks to the antique state of the springs. Tabitha sat opposite them, her hand draped over the rolled arm of the chair like a sleeping cat.

For a few moments, the only sound in the room came from Charles tinkling the crystal and from an ornate, dirty gold clock which sat on the fireplace and kept time on proceedings, interjecting with the regularity of a dripping tap. Having issued his guests with drinks, Charles gave a tall glass of gin and tonic to his wife and sank next to her.

'So, what is it you do for a living, Mark?' Charles started the evening's banter.

'I'm a man of leisure these days.'

'Really? May I ask why that is?'

Oh god, here comes the lottery story again.

No detail was spared in Mark's telling of their good fortune. Both Mr and Mrs St Clair seemed genuinely interested in the tale.

Having heard the story every time they came into contact with anyone who hadn't, Lucy dismissed it as white noise, and secretly browsed through the well-stocked bookcase that sat in the alcove of the fire place. Shakespeare's complete works graced the shelves along with other esteemed writers from generations long gone. The only things in the bookcase that weren't literary works of art were financial journals and thick, heavy banking encyclopaedias, which must have been more a test of self-will to read rather than a test of intelligence.

Returning her attention back to the conversation, Lucy found the storm cloud grey eyes of Mrs St Clair shadowing her. She offered a submissive smile; one half of the older lady's mouth bent up at the corner, like a rusty old bar.

Charles was the same affable character she had met earlier that day. He explained how a heart scare had forced him to retire from a long and very successful career in the banking industry; complimenting them on their shrewd investment in the neighbouring property, he also warned them that the amount they had won was not a never-ending pot of cash. The latter piece of advice was very welcome to Lucy: boating magazines had been mysteriously appearing around the house, it seemed Mark was itching to make another big purchase.

'Are you retired now, Tabitha?'

Deciding not to be so judgemental, Lucy had a stab at engaging her fellow female in conversation.

'Yes, I am retired now, I worked in accountancy.' Tabitha's voice was clear, sharp and flat. Like the blade of a sword, it cut straight to the point.

'That's how we met actually: we both had a love of figures, and Tabitha had a figure I loved.' A chuckle unsuitably burst from the amateur comedian on a wheeze of air, into the sombre room. His dearly beloved shifted in her seat and emitted a throat-clearing cough, clearly not amused by his attempt at a risqué joke.

Holy fuck, this is awkward. I'll never hear the end of this from Mark. Another half an hour and we're out of here.

She finished her drink and requested the use of their bathroom – not because she needed it, but because it would help to kill another five minutes of this disastrous meeting.

'The bathroom?' Charles looked at his wife briefly. 'Yes of course, I'll show you the way.'

Lucy managed to haul herself out of the pothole and handed her glass to Mark, who flashed her a wide-eyed look of panic at the prospect of being left alone with Mrs Chatterbox.

'Follow me, young lady.' Charles led her from the

oppressive atmosphere and up the wide old staircase, which apart from a well-worn runner in the centre, was as bare as the rest of the hall. He made a point of showing her the exact door, which Lucy thought was strange, but put it down to his old fashioned manners. She thanked him and entered the small room, wondering if he would wait for her.

The groan of the stairs answered her question. The bathroom needed attention, and was in keeping with the rest of the house. She stood looking at her watch, willing the time to pass quickly. She was now feeling the effects of the vodka, having downed it like a teenager in Ibiza. *What the hell gets an accountant going? Maybe I should throw some maths questions at her, or ask her opinion on the tax system.* To make sure her bathroom visit seemed genuine, Lucy flushed the toilet and opened the door half-expecting to find their host waiting to escort her back downstairs.

Charles's voice – and only Charles's voice could still be heard from downstairs, trying to entertain and amuse. On closing the bathroom door she noticed that the one facing her was slightly open. Maybe his wife felt that her and Mark weren't good enough to be living in Southshaw Avenue, because they were lottery winners. *Let's take a look, Mrs, to see why you're so high and mighty.* Her imagined reasons for Tabitha's distant presence were a good enough excuse for Lucy to sneak a peek at one of the ice queen's bedrooms. She crept over on tiptoes, somehow thinking it would be quieter, and stretched her neck around the enticing door.

The room wasn't what she had been expecting. There was no antique furniture – in fact, there was no furniture at all. A shadeless bulb hung from the ceiling, decorated with dust-laden cobwebs. A threadbare curtain, which matched the age of the property, clung to its track, while its twin lay curled up on the bare floorboards like a dead animal.

It was such a gloomy room that even the wallpaper was trying to escape, peeling away from the borders of the ceiling. Maybe it was a spare room. It was a big house for just two people; they didn't appear to have any children – at least there were no photos to suggest otherwise. Having aroused her curiosity further, she wondered what lay behind the other doors; they weren't so accommodating and sat tightly in their frames. It had been a few minutes since the toilet had announced she was returning, so she did just that.

Lucy fell back into the crater, and Mark handed over her glass, refilled, whilst explaining to Charles all about his efforts to lower his golf handicap.

Bloody golf. Can this get any worse?

Gulping down half a glass of vodka, she threw out a question in an attempt to veer away from the most boring sport in the world, second to cricket. 'Do you have any shared interests?'

By including both of them she had covered all the bases; Charles was sure to answer for them. And so he did.

'We love the arts, don't we, dear?'

The pursed lips refused exit to any vocabulary, and so a raised eyebrow accompanied a shallow nod of the head.

'I especially love the theatre.'

The heavy lids lifted above Charles' animated eyes. 'George Bernard Shaw, Tennessee Williams… but I have to say one of my favourites is Arthur Miller.'

His wife didn't seem to share his keen interest in Mr Miller or any of his fellow playwrights; in fact the conversation had roused the most reaction they had seen all night. She turned to look directly at the side of his face. Charles leaned forward, elbows on his knees, like a man settling in for a long conversation, leaving Medusa scowling at the back of his head.

'*Death of a Salesman* is a truly remarkable play, but I feel that *The Crucible* has to be near the top of anyone's list as one of the best plays ever written.'

It was quite clear that this really was his passion; every facial muscle worked harmoniously with his gesticulating hands, illustrating his opinion in a very sincere way.

'I don't think you can beat Bruce.' Everyone's attention turned to Mark.

'Bruce?' The heavy lids fell back into place contributing to Charles' perplexed expression.

'Yeah, Bruce Willis. *Die Hard* is a classic – I don't think you can top it.' The screaming silence was an extremely unwelcome guest.

Fuck me, Mark, Bruce Willis!

'Quite,' muttered Charles.

Playing with her earlobe, Lucy turned her head away from Mark, pretending he was her imaginary friend. 'Do you go to the theatre often?'

'Not as often—'

'I think we could all do with a top-up, Charles.' Having interrupted him, Tabitha pressed her cut-crystal glass against his arm. He stayed in his forward position and twisted to look at her. 'Yes... Of course, I forgot myself for a moment.' Her words clearly had another meaning; subserviently, he attended to her request.

The whole evening had been awash with unease, and this was yet another unsettling scene. Feeling the stress of a lack of sparkling conversation, Lucy had been sipping away, with the purpose of simply having something to do. Charles was rather heavy-handed with the alcohol. Another drink and she'd be pissed. Nonetheless, when asked, she accepted yet another one, as did Mark.

'And what is it that you do with your days, Lucy?' The pitch of Tabitha's voice probably had dogs everywhere howling in agony.

'I was a teaching assistant at a special needs school. I still work there part-time as a volunteer.'

Lucy addressed looked Satan's sister straight in the eyes; her cream and brown high-neck blouse and long black skirt were as closed-off as her personality.

She made no response to the returned answer; her cat's arse of a mouth seemed to constrict even more under the shade of her long hard nose.

'How interesting. It must be a very rewarding job.' Mr St Clair filled in the gaps as ever.

'It is. We're currently fund raising to build a sensory room and garden, and ultimately we want to install a specially equipped pool.'

Drinks were handed around and Charles returned to his place at the right hand of his master. Lucy explained all about the fundraising fete that the school would be holding and offered an invitation to them both, knowing full well that only one of them might attend. Yet again, Charles answered for them both; they seemed to have the same relationship that a ventriloquist has with their dummy. The dummy did all the talking, but the ventriloquist was the one who chose the words.

'I'm afraid we've got other engagements that weekend, but we'll certainly make a donation.' Thanking him, Lucy used the excuse of having to prepare for the aforementioned fete as a way to escape any further torture; the topics of conversation were quickly diminishing.

Lucy took away any sadistic pleasure Tabitha may have gotten from snubbing them once more, by telling her to stay where she was and lying through her teeth about how nice it had been to meet her. Ever the gentleman, Charles escorted them out. One more air kiss and a warm handshake, then freedom was theirs. The neighbours had certainly proved the old cliché of opposites attracting to be true; he was a lovely old gentleman, and she was a horrible old bitch.

The alcohol had now taken effect; she clung to Mark's arm, steadying herself. There must have been half a bottle of vodka in those three drinks. They maintained silence until they were well and truly out of range.

'Can you believe that?' Lucy was pissed off at having wasted an evening.

'I know, who doesn't have a TV in their lounge in this day and age?'

'What? Not that, I mean the talking corpse that was propped up next to Charles.'

'Yeah, she was a bit odd, wasn't she?' Mark turned the key and they stepped into the new familiarity of their home.

'Odd? That's putting it mildly. Fucking weird would be a more suitable term.' Lucy was angry at how much effort had gone into not making them feel welcome at all.

Having suffered the trauma of being in a room with no TV, Mark went to restore balance in front of their own futuristic picture box.

Lucy decided to have an early night. She climbed into

bed and just before she clicked off the light, the arm of the red Christmas sweater she had stuffed into a plastic bag of unwanted clothes, reminded her of another painful but memorable moment from that day.

Everything was painted black with the extinguishing of the incandescent light. Darkness was a blank canvas for a wandering mind, and so the memory of Joseph Dalton escorted her into the prelude to another day.

CHAPTER TEN

The blank page of a new day opened and Lucy rose early. It was school today; the little white lie she had told to the neighbours the night before about having to prepare for the summer fete had been a half-truth. She headed downstairs, leaving Mark sprawled out on the bed looking like he had fallen from a great height, snoring like a hippo. She scribbled out a post-it note and stuck it next to the kettle, informing Sleeping Beauty not to forget to make the guys plenty of drinks. With no map in life to follow, Mark had slipped into student-like habits, watching TV until the early hours and then sleeping right through the a.m. part of the day.

With the gate unlocked and all three cups were lined up, just needing boiling water. Lucy checked the time on her cheap plastic watch. The Rolex had been returned to its extravagant box, being far too ostentatious for most of life's occasions. It was almost eight o'clock; they'd be there any minute. She decided to skip breakfast as her stomach hula-hooped while her hands betrayed her otherwise calm appearance. She blamed it on the vodka from last night, knowing full well it wasn't that.

Rehearsing her script of what she may say, Lucy busied herself, tidying things that were already fine as they were. The kettle was moved a few millimetres, the toaster had its crumb-less surface wiped. Her handbag didn't manage to escape either, and was unceremoniously hauled from the stool and dumped by the hall door. If she didn't leave by eight o'clock she'd be late.

George's white hair bobbed across the kitchen window. The kettle began its first task of the day, and Lucy went out to wish them good morning. Adam traipsed behind George, carrying some of their tools for the day's work ahead.

'Lucy, how are you this fine morning?' chirped George, full of beans.

'Good, thank you. And how are you?'

'Fighting fit, my dear.'

She stole a glance over George's shoulder, looking at the corner of the house, around which she expected his son to appear. 'I'm going to be out for most of the day, but Mark will be here if you need anything.'

'I'm sure we'll be okay, my darlin'.'

'I'll make you a drink before I go.'

'You spoil us too much. Don't worry about it if you've got to go – we'll be fine.'

'No, I don't have to leave just yet.' She should have left five minutes ago. Lucy shuffled back to the kitchen and paused with her foot on the threshold, then took another look at the corner before entering the house. *Where's Joseph?* Having poured the water into their cups, Lucy hurried into the lounge and peeked over the giant TV through the window to see if his truck was there. It wasn't.

Another time check told her that she was now officially late.

She hurried back to the kitchen, finished their drinks and delivered them to George, who thanked her and gave her an update on their intended plans for the day, while Adam filled a rather mean-looking lawn mower with petrol.

She nodded occasionally, trying to give the appearance of listening, but all she wanted to do was ask one question. 'George,' she cut in, placing her hand on his forearm. 'I trust you implicitly, you don't have to justify yourself to me.'

The skin on his cheeks tightened as they rose above that familiar smile of his. 'Am I rambling on? It's one of the traits of old age you know.'

'No, of course not.' She felt guilty for interrupting him. 'I know you won't do me wrong.' It was a genuine answer; she felt at home in his company.

'Okay, my darlin'.' The sandpaper skin of his free hand affectionately rubbed her reassuring one.

'I've made Joseph a coffee. Is he in today?'

George quietly sighed. 'He should be by now.' He removed his glasses and pinched the bridge of his nose; the usually jovial eyes recast to one of concern. 'I'm sorry, Lucy, he's usually very punctual; it's just he's…' His brow displayed signs of a heavy burden.

'He's what, George?' Her interest in the man in question needed no encouragement.

The worried parent's eyebrows huddled together; his gaze floated from left to right as though he was in silent discussion with himself. 'He's—'

'Morning.' Who would have thought those seven letters could have such an impact when caressed by the right voice?

'He's finally here.'

George's relief was plain to see; his chest dropped like he'd been holding his breath. 'What time do you call this?' It was meant to be a criticism, but the soft tone couldn't carry it off.

'Give me a break; I'm only ten minutes late. I'll work over.'

Lucy bent down and picked up his coffee. Her legs had lost 80% of their capability on his arrival; uncontrollable nerves ran riot. She walked the short distance to him, carrying his hot drink in both hands. Adrenaline coursed through her veins, his presence having the same effect as a bungee jump. She stood on the edge of a large drop, facing him.

His bootlaces were undone, and his T-shirt was untucked, the collar half-up. Everything about his appearance told her that he hadn't long jumped out of bed. It didn't matter. He could have been wearing a pink tutu and a tank top; on this man anything would have looked good. George left them alone and took Adam up the garden to show him his task for the day.

'Black coffee, no sugar.' Lucy held out the red cup.

'Thanks, you remembered,' he croaked, taking the cup and lifting it to take a sip.

'How could I forget?'

That certainly hadn't been on her pre-rehearsed list of things to say; the inappropriate remark stopped the coffee an inch from his parted lips. Lucy's heart rate redlined, and a fresh batch of blood was delivered straight to her face;

flustered and embarrassed, she stumbled over her words. 'I'm sorry, that was—'

'Very nice of you,' he cut in, slowly lowering the untouched cup.

His black cap was pulled down low, shading his face, but she could see that his eyes were red and swollen. The inappropriate remark had fired out of her mouth as an attempt to override the feeling of powerlessness that seemed to overwhelm her when he was around.

A suggestive wise crack was the expected reply, but his words were quite the opposite. There was a definite vulnerability to him that morning and it drew her in. Lucy searched his face and he searched hers.

It was a look that burned into her soul and stopped her dead. He was like a different man; sadness clung to his handsome face. But for a handful of words they were complete strangers, yet Lucy was drawn to him in an inexplicable way; more familiarity would have led her to ask what was wrong. Strangers or not, there was no denying the unspoken connection between them. The encrypted acknowledgement was there, if only for a very brief period.

'Come on, lad, we've got work to do.' George returned, disconnecting them, oblivious to his intrusion.

Lucy jolted into action. 'Yes, I'm late for work.' She spun around and marched into the house, wishing them all a good day as she fought against every fibre of her being that was telling her to look back at him one last time.

Scooping her bag from the floor, she stood at the front door, her hand resting on her thumping breast. The faint sound of Mark snoring drew her attention to the top of the stairs. *Dear God, what am I doing?* Guilty regret shamed her; she had deliberately waited to see him – why? Not having the answer to that question, Lucy decided to focus her thoughts on the day ahead and a special little boy who she had missed so much.

Driving away to add her car into the multi coloured traffic jam, she wished that for those few charged moments she could have read his mind.

CHAPTER ELEVEN

Lucy thoroughly enjoyed her day at Tall Trees Special School. So many people had jobs that didn't make a scrap of difference to anyone, apart from the guy who was counting the cash, but Lucy wasn't one of them: love, laughter and compassion were the tools she used with these little people, who were the closest you could possibly get to angels, minus the wings.

Their virgin minds were so innocent and uncontaminated by the world, full of wonder, always happy to see you and blissfully unaware of the struggle that one day awaited them, when they left this sanctuary of people who knew and understood their delicate, vulnerable natures. Many tears had been shed late at night, thinking of what struggles lay ahead for these kids. Fortunately, most of them came from secure, loving families – although that wasn't the case for her friend Sam. His little life had made her heart ache the most; it was because of him that she'd decided to do more days at the school. She needed to satisfy her own overpowering need to know that he was okay and happy. The flipside was that she had to go through the agony of witnessing sorrow on the face of a six-year old boy when it was time to go to his so-called home – a place where drugs and alcohol took precedence over cuddles and bedtime stories. He was seldom far from her thoughts.

Lucy arrived home to find Adam just as he was when she had left that morning, carrying machinery, this time back to George's truck.

She parked her BMW on the drive. The absence of the Italian banana-mobile was a slight giveaway that Mark was out. Having used her rear view mirror for vanity reasons, she was confident that her face was all in order and exited the car.

'Hi, Adam. All done?'

'Hello. Yeah, for today.'

The briefest eye contact was made; being a man – well, a boy – of few words, Lucy was impressed: he'd almost made a full sentence.

Rather than going through the house, she went around to the rear garden. She was feeling quite pleased with herself, and having okayed it with Mrs Shoesmith, the head teacher, she had a proposal for the two Mr Daltons.

'Quick, look sharp: the boss is here,' said George out of the corner of his mouth upon seeing her.

'I expect a written report on today's progress, Mr Dalton.' She played along with the joke.

'Right away, ma'am – do you want it written in blood as always?'

Lucy's giggles drew the curtain on their little act. At the side of the house a huge pile of garden debris blocked her view of any progress they may have made. George explained that Joseph and Adam had cleared the whole area, and that the next day he would bring the mulcher to chew it all up and take the debris away in time for their barbecue.

She couldn't wait to take a look at the ongoing transformation. George went to see what Adam was up to, mumbling something about him playing on his phone again. She walked alongside the red brick of the house, eager to see what the tangled mass was hiding.

The sight that lay before her was like a flash of lightning, making her stop, wide-eyed and open-mouthed. She absorbed the affecting sight, the beautiful work of Mother Nature: her eyes were gifted the vision of Joseph, shirtless, emptying a wheelbarrow, adding to the already substantial mountain. It had been a humid, overcast day, but the sun made an appearance right at that very moment, putting the star of the show into the spotlight.

'Phwoar.' The toneless noise escaped her body involuntarily, like she had swallowed a golf ball.

Fuck! Did I just say that out loud?

He lifted the wheelbarrow and shook the contents free; the strong arms that had carried her so easily were on full display.

He was a perfect anatomical guide; each muscle clearly defined: full round shoulders carved into swollen biceps, the contours of which were piped with thick veins leading to lightly haired forearms, which Thor himself would have been proud of. His T-shirt hung down the back of his legs, tucked into his shorts. He looked to be a very capable man in every aspect that a man needed to be.

'Hello, Lucy. Good day?'

His sinfully thick, chocolate-gateau-with-extra-cream voice alerted her to the fact her eyes were still touring the continent of his naked torso.

'Good! Yes… thank you, very good.' *Come on, Lucy. Get your shit together!*

He dropped the wheelbarrow and walked the few steps over to her. Lucy rested her hand over her brow, shielding her eyes, not from the sun, but from the half-naked bronze demigod that towered above her.

'How do you think it's looking?'

'Fucking gorgeous' was her brain's impulsive offering; as he was referring to the garden, she chose a more suitable reply.

'I can't believe how much you've cleared; it's looking really good.'

He was standing close; the earthy, smoky, resinous smell of hard work pricked her nose. It was quietly addictive, like hot tar, or the gorgeous smell of the barista's magical machine. Lucy silently drew in the cocktail of pheromones, filling her lungs to capacity.

'There's still some more to come out, but we're getting there.'

He seemed in a very different mood from how he had been that morning. His line of sight followed Lucy's, looking out over the day's efforts. She took the chance to give his chest an appraisal; it fitted in perfectly with the rest of him.

Hard, full and defined, even the quantity of his hair was perfect. Like chiffon, it covered his chest but didn't conceal anything, tapering down over the bumpy road of his abs and disappearing into the black waistband of his underwear, which poked out above his shorts.

A simple tattoo sat where his heart was. There was no design or particular font to it, just a name: *Aashna*. A basic, functional reminder; ridiculously, Lucy felt a pang of resentment that someone had affected him so much that their name had been bled into his skin forever.

The exotic inscription conjured up images of a Tahitian beauty; hair black as coal, cascading like a waterfall down her back. Large, deep, dark eyes bordered with the longest lashes and a body that any man would kill for. Who was she? Lover? Wife? His fingers were ringless – not that that meant anything: he could have taken his wedding ring off while at work.

Joseph noticed that they weren't sharing the same view. He looked back at Lucy and caught her pondering the strangely intriguing name. She looked up and caught a flicker of annoyance that twitched in his eyes.

Immediately, he pulled his T-shirt out and manoeuvred his body back into it. She sensed he was uncomfortable. Should she apologise for invading his privacy, even though it was on plain view? The face he had been wearing that morning had made a return.

'Right, I'd better get packed up.'

'Mmm, yes' was all she could think of to say, and he returned to the wheelbarrow.

What she really wanted to do was make him a coffee and sit down and talk with him until the tag team that were the sun and the moon had each had their turn to shine.

How could the details of a stranger's life suddenly hold such interest? The uncomfortable silence forced to her act; Lucy rummaged in her bag, needlessly pretending to look for the house keys. Joseph rumbled the barrow out to his pick-up, a high-pitched squeak screamed out from the wheel with each revolution and seemed to highlight their lack of conversation.

His unexpected change of mood had left her wondering whether or not her idea was a good one.

She finally plucked the small bunch of keys out, after stirring them around her bag needlessly. Allowing some distance between them, Lucy followed his path to the roadside.

'Is that everything?' asked George.

Joseph carelessly tossed the unfortunate barrow into the back of his pick-up. 'Yep, that's the lot.'

Adam was already seated and belted. 'Okay, Lucy, we're going to leave you in peace now.' George opened the door to his truck.

'George, can I have a quick word before you go?'

'Yes, my dear, of course you can.'

'For the last few weeks we've been having guest speakers come into school and talk about their job and the role they play in society.' George gave her his full attention, listening intently, while Joseph restlessly prowled around in the background.

'We've had the usual ones: police, ambulance, fire brigade. I thought you might consider doing a little spot for us?' She poised the question nervously, Joseph's lack of interest not helping. 'You don't have to if you don't want to.' She quickly threw him the get-out option, not sure if it was agreeable to him.

It was: George didn't hesitate for a moment. 'Why, we'd be honoured, Lucy. Thank you.'

'We?' His son's lack of attention had obviously been a pretence.

'When do you want us?' George ignored Joseph's

interjection.

'Er…' Lucy looked from Mr Dalton, Jr to Mr Dalton, Snr, unsure whether or not to continue. 'Any day's fine,' she eventually said.

George had either missed, or had simply decided to ignore the glare that Joseph was throwing his way. He leant with both his hands on the back of his father's truck, arms locked; he dropped his head, allowing the baseball cap to act as a visor, but it was quite clear he was unhappy about his father volunteering him.

'Monday at two o'clock?'The pitch of her voice was unsure of the question.

'Two o'clock it is.' George tapped the roof of his vehicle with a nod, like an auctioneer completing a sale.

Lucy smiled appreciatively, masking the unease she felt from his son's mannerisms.

'Great. Well, I'll let you go, and I'll fill you in on the details tomorrow.' She didn't want to prolong the tension any more than was necessary.

'Okey-dokey, we'll see you bright and early in the morning.' He turned to Joseph. 'Are you coming around tonight?'

'I'll call in after my run.'

'Not too late though,' remarked George as he climbed into the driver's seat. 'Enjoy your evening, Lucy,' he called out of the open window before driving away.

Joseph walked around his truck to the driver's side, removed his cap, and ruffled his hair.

'Lucy…' He paused for the shortest time but long enough to indicate that he wanted to say something. Her breath had been confiscated; she transferred her weight from one foot to another nervously, anticipating what it was he might say.

Doubt cast over his face, and a nod was all that was offered. He opened the door of his truck with an air of defeat. Lucy's breath returned, suddenly gasping for the right thing to say in a confusing situation, desperate to keep him there for just a moment longer to soak up the inexplicable, hypnotic, addictive aura that surrounded him.

He threw his cap onto the dashboard.

'See you in the –' Lucy began, but the door slammed with resounding finality.Too late; the moment had gone. '… Morning, Joseph.' Her guilty tongue caressed his name, holding onto it for as long as possible. She watched him drive away, ignoring the alien sadness turning inside of her; Joseph's unpretentious work vehicle turned the corner passing its antithesis.

Mark tore along the otherwise quiet avenue and reversed onto the driveway, parking in the exact same spot as he always did. The powerful engine was revved twice before it was put to sleep, roaring out its dominance, as was now the custom. He climbed out of the enveloping seat and waved to Lucy, all sunglasses and teeth.

She was still stood at the roadside struck with another loss for words, but this time for a very different reason. There was nothing to say; he had little or no interest in her work at the school and no interest in the garden at all.

'You coming in, babe?' he called out, his key already in the door.

'Yeah, I've got to get some stuff out of the car, I'll just be a minute.'

'Okay.' He entered, leaving the door open.

There was nothing in the car; she wanted some time to

get back onto the right frequency. Lucy took in the view of the rather grand house, the Ferrari suitably complimenting the property with its garish elegance.

They had no money worries. It all seemed perfect. So why was she still looking at the corner that Joseph's truck had turned? Was she an ungrateful person? Greedy? Selfish? *Jesus, how much more can anyone want?*

Lucy's feet carried her into paradise, but her mind still lingered on the corner that had taken him out of view.

CHAPTER TWELVE

When George and his son arrived the next morning, Lucy kept her distance. Mark was sent out with their usual morning drink; he was spending the day at home as they had to get ready for their barbecue on Saturday.

Lucy was glad of his presence: not only because various bits of garden furniture needed to be assembled, but him just being there would force her to focus on things other than Joseph Dalton, who inconsiderately, looked his usual dangerous self.

The humidity was equal to that of the day before, but his shirt remained on, which, while she was thankful, it did strike her as being an insult akin to putting a blanket over a Van Gogh.

Busying herself getting the house ship-shape, Lucy waited for a chance to catch George on his own. She filled him in on the protocol for their visit to Tall Trees and took a few details for the routine security checks. She so wanted to invite them to their get-together, especially after all the hard work they had put in, but just being in Joseph's company was hard work in itself. George looked tired; he was getting on in years to be doing such a physical job, even though the two younger men did the bulk of the work.

Rather than risk offending him by asking him to take a rest, Lucy astutely asked him if he wouldn't mind trying out the oversized garden table and chairs that had been delivered that morning.

'I'd be delighted for my bottom to give you its opinion,' he joked as he pulled out the chair at the head of the oblong table.

The sigh of a man that welcomed the respite slipped from his lips as the bench took his weight.

'Oh, very nice, very nice indeed.' His hands slid to and fro over the undulating curve of the teak armrests, stirring the air with the faint leathery smell of freshly cut timber.

'Beautiful, Lucy, beautiful.' His head nodded as his eyes skirted around the table, counting the chairs. 'Twelve, I don't think I know that many people,' he chortled. Removing his glasses, he placed them on the table. Her intention to keep out of the way had slipped somewhat, and Lucy sat in the chair next to him, which had a view over the garden. She felt genuine affection for George.

'It is a bit big,' said Lucy. 'Mark likes to impress.'

A short spurt of air shot out of George's nose accompanied by the expression of a man who'd had plenty of experience with male egos.

'How long have you been doing this for?' Lucy asked.

'Gardening?'

'Yes.'

'Since God was a boy, my dear.'

Lucy smiled at him. He always had a witty answer. His

son was at the very back of the garden with Adam and wandered in and out of sight behind the green curtain of a weeping willow.

'Have you and Joseph always worked together?'

'Mmm… he's been with me a while.' The slight pause was uncharacteristic of him.

'Would retirement not suit you?'

It occurred to her that the question could have been offensive to him. 'I'm sorry, George, I didn't mean that you're too old or anything.'

'I know you didn't, sweetheart. In my mind I'm a young man, unfortunately the mirror tells me otherwise. I fully intended to retire but….' His hands held each other while the curve of his lips faltered. 'My wife died two years ago.' Heavy lids cloaked his eyes as he looked at the dull gold band he turned with his thumb and index finger.

'Oh, George, I'm so sorry.' She tenderly laid her hand over his. It was a hushed apology for being the cause of his painful recall. 'I'm sure she was beautiful.'

'She was,' he boasted proudly, raising his head high. 'She was too good for me… her name was Rose.' He stopped short. His lips folded in on themselves and once again the ring that was given with a solemn vow, drew his attention.

Lucy unintentionally found herself examining the lines that life had carved into his face. It was a reminder that time would not falter in its never-ending quest.

'We bought a motorhome to travel around Europe for six months, but the big man upstairs had other ideas. I never even got to drive it out of our street.' George turned to face the open space he had helped to clear. 'It's not the same on your own… I do miss her.' He was such a lovely man. It was heartbreaking to see the shadow of his loss hanging over him; she held on tight to her own composure, feeling the threat of tears.

George picked up his glasses and placed them on the end of his nose. He tapped the table lightly with his fingers. It was clear to see from his glassy, unfocused stare that the movie of his life was playing in his mind.

'I stay at work because I love it, and… because I don't want to be lonely.' He looked straight into Lucy's eyes with a hint of embarrassment. That was a profoundly honest thing to admit – especially for a man his age.

'The lads keep me young, and I get to spend every day with my son, keep an eye on him.' The last part was missing the humorous tone she would have expected it to have.

'Trouble, is he?' Her playful smile proposed a lighter mood.

He turned once again to look at his flesh and blood; the loose skin under his eyes tightened as they pinched. The pride he felt was obvious. 'Nooo… I couldn't ask for better.' A tinge of sadness clung to the positive reply.

Lucy felt awful. He was fine before he sat down with her; It was all the excuse she needed.

'George.'

'Yes, sweetheart?'

'I'd be honoured if you could come to the barbecue tomorrow.'

He finger slid his glasses up the bridge of his nose into the correct position. 'You're not feeling sorry for an old man, are you?' It was said light-heartedly disguising the truth of the question.

Lucy answered sincerely: 'absolutely not. It's family and

friends only, and you fall into that bracket now, George.'

Colour returned to his face as a broad smile stretched out.

'Well, in that case, I happily accept your kind invitation – thank you. Now, I had better go and check up on those two rascals.' He got to his feet, pushing against the table to help him.

'The invitation extends to Joseph and Adam also.'

'That's very kind of you, Lucy, although I don't think you'll see Adam. He likes to spend his weekends skateboarding.' He simultaneously rolled his eyes and shook his head. 'Kids…'

Carefully placing the chair back into position, he made his way towards the rascals.

'What about Joseph?' Unsure whether or not to ask the question, when she finally did, it shot out rather abruptly. Part of her desperately wanted him to come, but she also wanted to relax and enjoy the day, and she was anything *but* relaxed when in his presence.

George turned around. 'I'm not sure about Joseph; I'll ask him.' His shoulders had only made it to 90 degrees before he was halted again.

'Tell him he's welcome to bring his wife or partner.' The intended nonchalance was shot to pieces by the questioning raise in the tone of her voice, and not helped by her child-like fiddling with her hair.

'Joseph's a single man, Lucy.'

Her heart seemed to skip a beat, and a cocktail of euphoria and relief filled her tummy.

'For this week anyway.' The sting of his parting reply brought Lucy to her senses like a slap to the face. Having erased all her vocabulary with his last remark, Lucy allowed him to leave. Joseph certainly wouldn't have any trouble attracting female attention, and from what his father had said, it seemed he had no problems enjoying that fact.

Flashes of gorgeous leggy blondes draping themselves all over him taunted and teased her bruised heart. Jealousy was a strange creature and indeed *had* always been a stranger to Lucy, but since Mr Dalton had arrived they were beginning to get better acquainted. If he was single, who was the Tahitian beauty, Aashna?

She watched George approach his son and place his hand on his shoulder, stopping him working. They must have been discussing her offer; Joseph glanced in her direction. Lucy's eyes worked to their best ability, trying to pick up on any kind of movement that may have given an indication of his decision. There was a nod of the head. *Yes!* Then a shake. *No!* Shrugging of shoulders coupled with insignificant hand gestures gave no evidence of an affirmative answer. Either way, she had to know: it would drive her crazy otherwise. The chair grated against the coarse paving as she stood. She took a deep breath and hoped her legs would hold out until she reached them.

'Ready, babe?' Mark's unexpected interjection startled her. He stood in the doorway with her car keys dangling from his fingers.

'What?'

'Meat?'

'Oh, yeah.' She'd forgotten that he wanted to pick up their order from the butchers in her car. Apparently it was against the law to carry sausages in a Ferrari.

The two men had finished their conversation and returned to their duties, leaving her none the wiser.

'I've checked the forecast, and so long as the

weatherman has got his facts right, it should be a fine day, weather-wise.'

'Mmm, good.' Her lacklustre reply seemed to sail right over Mark's head. He made his way through the house, whistling tunelessly.

The clock raced towards home time for the hired help. Mark and Lucy hadn't far to go and would be back before then. The question had to be asked, otherwise it would dominate her thoughts all evening, and she had at least a dozen other things that required her attention. Two short toots from the car horn delivered a blunt message as to Mark's eagerness to get his hands on the enormous order of flesh he had requested. Making sure she had a means of paying and her mobile, she closed the front door and climbed into the driver's seat.

Mark stabbed at the buttons on the radio like he was typing his PIN number into a cash machine, listening to only a split second of whatever was playing before denouncing it as "shit, shit, and more shit."

'Don't you have any decent music at all?' It sounded like more of an accusation than a question.

'Like what?'

'Something with a beat, a bit of life to it – dance music.' He opened the glove-box and started to shuffle through the small CD collection which she kept there, tutting in disgust absence of low-quality, electronically produced rubbish that could be created on any laptop. High-energy rave music was the last thing he needed: he seemed agitated by something.

'Hey, this is my car, thank you.' She took the stack of CDs from him, annoyed by his sudden mood change, and put them back in the glove box, slamming it shut. 'If you want to drive around in a mobile disco then you can do that in the Italian banana-mobile.'

'Don't fucking call it that, it's a fucking Ferrari!' Ripples and lines gathered like storm clouds on his usually smooth forehead. He was so fractious; she knew they were right on the edge of an argument over nothing at all. 'That is a state-of-the-art automotive machine sitting right there.' He jabbed violently at the window of his door, leaving a smeared fingerprint.

Something was bothering him; he was always irritable when stressed. Was it Joseph? Had he noticed a change in her behaviour when he was around? Maybe it was the make-up? Usually she didn't wear that much, but her mascara and lippy had certainly taken a bashing lately.

'Jesus, Mark, okay. It was only a joke.' Lucy broke eye contact to put her seat belt on and started the car. Mark chose to observe the view through his smudged window; he rocked his heel up and down on the ball of his foot, shaking his leg restlessly. There was definitely something wrong. Lucy reversed out of the drive, knowing full well that only meaningless conversation would dissipate the mood.

'So, you did post the invitation to the St Clairs didn't you?' She knew he had, several days ago.

'Yeah, they've had their invite.' He had mastered the art of delivering a deadpan reply perfectly.

She ignored the peevish tone of his answer. 'I like Charles, but I'm not sure about his wife; to be honest, I'm hoping she doesn't come. What do you think?'

The passing scenery held no interest, and his attention returned to the space they sat in.

'I've invited someone today.' Although her question

had been ignored she was glad to hear rationality had returned to his voice.

'Who's that then?'

'Seb.'

Mark's mood may have been settling, but the mention of that name had the opposite effect on hers.

'Seb? As in Kingsfellow?'

'Yeah.'

Oh for fuck sake, no. 'Really… and, is he coming?'

'He's playing tennis in the morning until twelve, so he said he'd pop by around two-ish.'

'It'll be nice to see him again.'

Fucking wonderful! Why the hell has he asked Kingsfellow?

'I can't wait to show him the car.' There was the answer. Mark had to get one up on his automotive rival. The only thing the two men had in common was they both drove supercars in a country that was littered with speed cameras.

Was now a good time to mention that she had invited someone else also? Not quite having the courage to announce it, she mulled it over all the way to the butchers, not sure what he would say when he knew Dalton Senior and Junior had been invited.

They eventually arrived home with enough raw meat to feed the entire lion population of the Kruger National Park. There was a vacant spot where Joseph's truck once sat. George was fastening the cover on his pick-up and waved to them as they parked up. Lucy unclipped her belt before turning the engine off and hastily exited the car, hoping to get to George and ask the burning question without Mark hearing. Unfortunately, George had ambled down the drive to them, removing any such chance.

'We're all done, folks; everything's cleared away. Joseph's taken the last trailerload. The next step is to start cultivating the ground and getting rid of all the weed roots.'

Mark opened the boot, rudely ignoring the considerate explanation George was giving.

'It's not perfect, but at least your guests can wander around without the risk of getting lost in the overgrowth.'

'Thank you so much for all of your hard work. I can't believe the difference; it looks twice as big now.' She had hoped that Mark would start to transport the meat into the house, but opening the boot was as far as he got before the overwhelming desire to check on his state-of-the-art banana-mobile drew him back to the machine. There was no chance of asking the question now Mark was in earshot, especially as she hadn't even told him they were invited.

'Do you want me to give you a hand with those bags before I go?' That was typical of his generous nature, which only served to highlight how appalling Mark's behaviour was.

'No, George, you've done more than enough, thank you. Go and enjoy your Friday evening.' His face shrugged off the weariness that the day had hung on him, to gift her with a gracious smile.

'You too, my darlin'. Bye, Mark.'

Mark was crouched down in front of his car, rubbing off a splattered insect with his thumb. Haughtily, he silently raised his hand in the air; the dead insects taking preference.

George's smile sailed out to an empty port with a half wave of his hand that ended as a gentle tap on his thigh.

The old man rocked from one foot to the other as he trudged back to his pick-up. Lucy's heart pained at the thought of him returning to an empty home, the honesty of their earlier conversation still on her mind. She waved to him cheerily until he had driven away.

As soon as he was gone, Mark's interest in the minuscule spots ceased.

'Right, shall we get this lot in then?' He sprang to his feet.

Lucy was fuming at the display of pretentiousness he had shown to a man who was anything but.

You can be a real prick sometimes, Mark.

She observed him through very different eyes with a lowered level of respect while he grabbed bag after bag and hauled them out of the boot. Now wasn't the time for an argument – they still had far too much to do for tomorrow – but the boiling indignation gave rise to the confidence to confess her inviting them.

In fact, it would be a pleasure to slap him in the face with it.

'Because the guys have worked so hard this week, I decided to invite them also.' Her antagonism was very well hidden.

Mark stood laden with heavy bags, his shoulders sloped unnaturally low. 'The gardeners?' The tart effect his words had was clear to see, and clouds gathered once again; it looked like Joseph *was* the problem after all.

'Yes, the gardeners.'

'Why exactly?'

Petulance in a grown man was so unattractive, Lucy thought.

'Because, if you'd bothered to take your attention away

from your golf clubs or that bloody car for a minute, you would have seen that they've cleared the equivalent of half a rainforest back there.'

It wasn't a great example of how to avoid an argument, but it was the right thing to say.

'They've been paid for it, haven't they?'

'Yes they've been paid for it, but –'

He couldn't wait for his turn. 'I don't think we should be associating ourselves with that class of people.'

Mark's sulky stare rested on her shoulder, either because he knew it was an absurd thing to say or it was an excuse for the real reason he didn't want them there.

'Have you lost your senses?' The fight to keep the conversation civil was becoming increasingly difficult. 'George is one of the most decent men I've ever met, and if you had been bothered to speak to him for a few minutes, you'd see that too.'

The words flew out fast and fluidly as all honest ones did. Mark had now become petulance personified; his tongue poked around in his cheek while his eyes waltzed around her feet in a hand-in-the-face, "whatever" kind of way. Nonetheless, she wasn't going to let the crass comment pass so easily.

'And what do you mean 'that class of people'? Have you forgotten already that not so very long ago, you were in that category? And almost everyone who is coming tomorrow will be too.'

Lucy stood tall in the knowledge that the truth embellished her point.

Mark was stiff with defiance although the downcast expression on his face conceded defeat. Setting a wrong right was incredibly empowering, and she was going to make sure he would think twice before he decided to put himself on a pedestal.

'Anyway, we're all equal; no one's better than anyone else because they live in a bigger house or drive a faster car.'

'Oh, here we go with the special needs teacher spiel.' 'Fuck you 'was her first, less than eloquent impulse. He was on shaky ground when it came to this subject, and he knew it.

She held her tongue and Mark retreated into the house, his fingers blue from the cutting weight of the plastic bags. She allowed him to have the last word, simply for the sake of a successful get-together tomorrow. What she wouldn't allow, and certainly couldn't live with, was a man who held himself in such high opinion to the detriment of others.

CHAPTER THIRTEEN

On the odd rare occasion, the weathermen's predictions were accurate. Fortunately for Lucy and Mark this was one of those occasions. A scattering of candy-floss clouds drifted like leaves on a pond across the powder-blue canvas of the sky.

Suzie had arrived early to help with the final preparations; despite Lucy's protests that she would be fine, she was glad of her help, and company. The hosts had barely spoken to each other the night before; Lucy had decided to let him marinate in his own juices – like the steak.

Having a cheerful third person in the house made it difficult for his sulking to continue without making himself look like an arsehole. So he became the "we've got people over" Mark, which was virtually an admission of guilt. He kept out of the way by attending to the manly tasks, such as setting up the brand-new, Winnebago-sized stainless steel barbecue. It was of course the largest and most expensive one in the store.

The two old friends mercilessly skewered various pieces of fruit and cheese onto cocktail sticks. Mark wasn't the only one guilty of over-indulgence: the kitchen looked like an international food market. The homely smell of fresh crusty baguettes was in stark contrast to the exotic, tangy zest of the mouthwatering mini fruit cocktails.

A flamboyant coffee-infused chocolate gateau pompously rested under a glass cover next to an army of assorted canapés, which sat on white plates in perfectly straight lines, waiting for deployment.

Cute little cupcakes were assembled on three-tiered stands, like bubbly teenage girls in pleated skirts, with pink and yellow quiffed icing. A seductive, deep-red cherry cheesecake lay sprawled out on an elevated bone-china stand, looking arrogant in the knowledge that no man or woman could resist its sublime delights. It was like a who's who of party food, and there wasn't an inch of work surface that didn't have some culinary delight occupying it.

With everything under control and time to spare, the two ladies headed upstairs to ready themselves.

Despite the busy morning and Suzie's company, the butterflies in her stomach still remained; her mind had taken on a will of its own, wandering into thoughts that weren't suitable for an attached woman.

'The house is fab,' Suzie said through her T-shirt as she pulled it over her head. 'I love it.'

'Thank you, we love it too.'

They had seen each other virtually naked many times, both being around the same size, very often they would share a cubicle when trying on clothes. Today though, Lucy felt strangely self-conscious.

Suzie peeled off her black leggings, unaware of her

friend's hesitation. Lucy had never compared herself with Suzie, but she found her hand gliding over her tummy while she covertly eyed her friend's tight flat one. She had a great figure; tiny ankles and knees served to enhance her shapely calves and athletic thighs. There were no straight lines in her make-up; she was a continuous flow of feminine curves.

'Mark's quiet today, isn't he?' Suzie trotted around the bedroom and hung her dress on the knob of the tall chest of drawers, her lacy white bra and thong complementing the golden hue of her flawless skin.

'Is he?' Lucy dismissed the remark and turned her back, delving into the wardrobe to retrieve her dress for the day.

'You two getting on okay?' It wasn't an out-of-the-ordinary question for Suzie to ask, but somehow Lucy found the truth uncomfortable, even though they had shared many bottles of wine discussing Mark, and men in general, without limits.

'Yeah, of course, everything's fine.' She removed the clear plastic bag covering the maxi dress and laid it on the bed.

'I always knew you two were meant for each other. It just doesn't seem right: Lucy with no Mark. It's like gin without tonic – bloody awful.'

Arms raised and hands behind her neck, Suzie attached a silver necklace, which immediately disappeared into her upheaved cleavage.

'I'm glad you said gin and tonic, and not fish and chips.' Lucy attempted to be her usual self, but didn't quite feel like playing today.

'You've got a bit more class about you. Is that what you're wearing?' Suzie nodded to the dress lying on the bed.

'Yes – what do you think?' Lucy nibbled on the nail of her little finger, forgetting that only last night she had painstakingly coated them with Chanel Rouge Rubis. 'Is it a bit... frumpy?'

She'd loved it in the store, but after seeing Suzie's sexy little number, it had lost its sparkle.

'No, don't be daft. It's elegant, very you.'

Lucy had been really looking forward to this day. She didn't want to feel uneasy and jittery, but increasingly, that was how she was feeling.

'It'll be great to catch up with everyone.'

Suzie relieved the coat hanger of its duties. Even the zipper sounded sexy as it lazily buzzed its way down. She bent down and stepped into the dress gathered on the floor, while Lucy slid hanger after hanger in her wardrobe with a steady pace, knowing full well that there was nothing suitable. Still, she went through the exercise of frustrating herself.

'Zip me up, Lu.'

The wardrobe door was closed with frustration; Suzie held her locks to the side of her face. The zip purred suggestively on the way up as the material knitted together, embracing the petite frame it would intimately be spending the day with.

Suzie spun around. Her blonde hair fanned out in sync with her dress and fell perfectly around her pretty face. 'How do I look?' Only a confident woman would wear such a dress. Suzie knew full well how she looked. 'Will I do?'

For the very first time in all their friendship, Lucy had the bitter taste of jealousy. The champagne-pink Jacquard skater dress was simply stunning. A deep V neckline unashamedly exploited her best feature, outlining the two mounds of plump flesh snuggled together, creating a deep, dark crevasse that would draw any man's eyes.

It wasn't just any man's eyes she was concerned about. Suzie's already small waist looked positively tiny with the fabric flared over her feminine form, ceasing some distance from the knee. Her already shapely legs were enhanced by the elevating, high-heeled nude sandals; the diamanté ankle strap was both elegant and sexual at the same time.

'It's only a barbecue, you know.' The words came out with a titter. Instantly she felt awful by the sight of her friend's affected smile. 'You look absolutely beautiful, Suzie,' she quickly counteracted her first statement before it was too late.

'Do you think I look overdressed?' Suzie looked down at herself, smoothing her French-manicured fingers over the pleated skirt.

Lucy didn't allow a single second to pass before she answered. 'No, Suzie. No, you don't.' With guilt tutting in her ear, she reached out and held both of her friend's hands tightly.

'You look beautiful, you really do.' A heavy dose of sincerity was added to her voice while chastising herself for being such a bitch.

'Aww, thank you. Now come on, girly, get your glad rags on. You'll have people arriving soon. Do you mind if I steal some of your hairspray?'

'Of course not, help yourself. It's in the bathroom.'

Her friend strutted out of the bedroom, the hem of her dress waving with the sway of her hips. Lucy looked down at her attire lying on the bed like a lifeless corpse, flat, uninhabited.

Suzie was right: the guests would be arriving any minute; there was no time for a fashion meltdown.

'Shall I go down and tell Mark he can come up now, Lu?' Suzie called out between hisses of spray.

'Do you mind?'

'No, I'm all done – apart from adding another coat of lipstick. I'll go and tell him.'

Right, come on, for God's sake!

She stripped off her clothes and laid the bohemian dress on the bed. It was lovely, with its fuchsia and green lines swirling into one another up to the fuchsia belt that sat below the breastline… but it wasn't sexy. Slipping it on over her head, the black bodice's plunging neckline crisscrossed over her breasts, which were not as ample as her friend's.

She looked… *nice*. That was the word she felt most suited her appearance. Lucy took the clip from the back of her hair, doubled over and ruffled her fingers through her long locks. Springing back up, the dark chocolate swirls of hair bounced, kinking and curling down her back and onto her chest. She slipped on her strappy sandals and crossed the landing to the bathroom.

Mark was at the top of the stairs. 'You look nice.' His choice of words made Lucy smile to herself. Not the compliment she would have liked. Gorgeous, hot or beautiful would have helped to bolster her flagging self-confidence.

'Thanks,' she replied. That was obviously his peace offering; he would now act like a cross word had never been exchanged between them.

'I'm gonna put my shorts on I think; it's gonna be hot today,' he called out from the bedroom, confirming what she already knew. Familiarity giving the illusion of psychic abilities.

Lucy stooped down to take a look at her *nice* appearance in the mirror, which still hadn't been hung on the wall. She was usually a confident dresser, but today she knew that no matter what she wore it wouldn't be right.

A spray or two of Coco Mademoiselle added to the polluted mist in the bathroom. She traced over her full lips with the matching partner to her nails. Without dwelling on her reflection any more, she headed down to meet Suzie in the kitchen, who had popped open one of the bottles of Moet and was undertaking the task of filling the champagne glasses for each guest upon their arrival.

She placed her handmade sign on the drive, requesting all callers to enter via the side gate, as everyone would be in the garden.

Five minutes after the official beginning of the party, and with no one there, she began to panic at the vast amount of food there was, thinking no one was going to come.

But come they did. And in great numbers.

Mark had obviously been playing Mr Popular at the Golf Club, as there were more than just a few faces that Lucy didn't recognise. It didn't matter; things were going great. Shrieks of laughter jumped above the conversation of friends. They all agreed that they should do this more often. But of course, never did.

The house and garden was a sea of people. The men had dressed casually in the non-fussy way that men do, while the ladies were quite the opposite. Suzie's outfit certainly wasn't over-the-top. After climbing the stairs a dozen times to show people around the house, doing the equivalent of a half-marathon, Lucy invited all to wander freely as they wished.

Mark was on fine form and played the part of himself with award-winning skill. He donned a joke apron, with a picture of a woman's body clad in stockings and suspenders, while taking charge of the industrial-sized BBQ, which looked like a prop from *Star Wars*. Suzie's brother, Pete, played sous chef. He was quite the opposite of Mark in many ways, although he spent most of his time at Mark's side helping to deliver endless fat steaks and swollen sausages. Lucy mingled amongst her guests, making sure everyone was watered and fed, stopping to chat for a while, but always making sure she was positioned with a view of the corner of the house. Despite the abundance of food, very little had passed her lips. Expectation had stolen her appetite. She glanced for the umpteenth time at the spot that revealed all and any guests and saw Charles appear. He looked ever the gentleman with an affable smile under his precision-cut moustache, and wearing an ivory straw fedora hat. A cashmere sweater was draped over his shoulders, loosely knotted. He confidently made his way amongst the strangers, nodding and smiling while his eyes searched for the host.

Lucy was relieved, but not surprised, to see that he was wifeless.

'Charles!' She waved her hand, catching his attention.

He waved back in acknowledgement. 'Lucy, so nice to see you again.' He reached for her hand and kissed each side of her face, as was his way.

'And you, Charles. Thank you for coming. No Tabitha?'

'No, I'm afraid not. She sends her apologies.' He held up a black patent wine bag, and Lucy caught sight of the Bollinger emblem on top of the red box.

'Oh Charles, you didn't have to do that. It's very kind of you, thank you.'

'Not at all. My wife... she's not very comfortable in the company of strangers.'

'Charles, you don't have to explain.'

'No,' he interrupted. 'I want to. She has recently been diagnosed with bi-polar disorder, and it's blighted our lives.'

'Oh no, I'm sorry to hear that.'

'She was always such a bubbly, outgoing, confident woman,' he began, standing close to Lucy and speaking quietly. 'But ever since the break-in she has started to have panic attacks. She wouldn't go out on her own at night and she stopped seeing her friends. It's been a slow decline ever since. These days Tabitha is a very different woman from the one she once was.'

'Charles, I don't know what to say. Is there anything we can do?'

'Yes, just carry on being your usual, normal self. I'm determined to get my wife back and live as normal a life as possible. So if you see her out, please go and say hello or even have a little chat with her.'

'Yes, of course, I will.'

'I'm sure you noticed her unease when you and your good man came to visit the other evening.'

Lucy wasn't sure how to answer that one. 'Hmmm, she

did seem – quiet.'

'It was all my fault. I thought she might have loosened up once you had been introduced, but she was racked with nerves all evening and retired to bed in tears the minute you departed.'

Lucy felt terrible for being quick to jump to conclusions about Tabitha. Dealing with special needs children, she had become aware that sometimes, there's an underlying reason for what seemed like odd behaviour. She could see that evening had been playing on his mind.

'I'm always here if you ever need a cup of tea and a chat – or maybe something stronger.'

His melancholy face brightened. 'Thank you, Lucy. That means a great deal to me. Now, that's enough doom and gloom for such a wonderful day.' He looked around with a cheery expression. 'I have to say, this seems to be a great success.'

Charles shared similar qualities to George, although the two men were opposites in many ways. They were from a generation where manners, respect, and decorum mattered more than the latest mobile phone. Lucy took the liberty of linking arms with him.

'Come with me, Mr St Clair. Let's get you something to eat and drink, shall we?'

He placed his cool hand upon hers, which was draped over his forearm.

'Well, that sounds most agreeable, young lady. Thank you.'

Leading him to the banquet-sized teak table, she thought about the strange ways that relationships change over time. Men were always seen as hunters, gatherers, protectors, but when they reached a certain age, the roles seemed to reverse, and the female instinct was to nurture and protect. Maybe it had something to do with the loss of virility, which most men conceded to graciously.

Sitting him at the table, she made good on her promise and placed a hearty plate full of food in front of him, along with a generous glass of white wine. He thanked her profusely and instantly struck up a conversation with the stranger to his left. Lucy took a moment to take it all in. Everything was going well: the food was being eaten and the drink drunk, and the sun was smiling upon them all.

Suzie was balancing a plate of nibbles on her fingertips, deep in conversation with Mark, whose barbecue was adorned with empty green beer bottles.

Suzie's brother, Pete came out of the house, taking a bite of chocolate gateaux. She squeezed through the chattering mob to go and have a word with him.

'You having a good time, Pete?'

'Mmmm,' he dabbed the flakes of chocolate from the corners of his mouth and licked his teeth clean before speaking. 'Yes, thank you. The food's awesome.' His eyes flicked guiltily to his plate, which also had a generous slice of the seductive cherry cheesecake. 'Sorry, I couldn't decide which one to choose between.'

'Please, eat as much as you like – that's what it's there for. So how are you? Still staying with Suzie?'

'I'm fine, thanks, I'm hoping to get a place of my own soon.' He nodded the whole time he spoke and found it hard to maintain eye contact, preferring the contents of his plate. Pete was a kind, gentle man, very quiet and inoffensive, slightly overweight and clumsy-looking, with an innocent face that matched his nature. For as long as Lucy had known him, he had arranged his dirty, shoulder-length blond hair in the same shaggy style, which was really no style at all.

'Are you seeing anyone at the moment?' His head ceased nodding.

'Not at the moment, no.'

He looked up from the plate, but avoided Lucy's face. Despite his age, the mention of girls seemed to bring out the blushing teenager in him.

'It's hard to find a good woman these days,' she said.

'It is, it is…' The incessant nodding returned. It was very difficult to strike up a conversation with a monosyllabic man. Lucy wondered what the hell he and Mark talked about. Mark probably did all the talking, and Pete did all the nodding. Maybe the old cliché was true: it was the quiet ones you had to watch out for.

Lucy was searching for another topic of conversation to attempt, when her heart fluttered at the sight of George stepping around the corner of the house.Out of his work wear he looked very different indeed; clothes do maketh the man after all. She was pleased to see him, but was also desperate to see his son. Her eyes stayed firm at the point from which he had appeared. She held her breath waiting for him.

Pete offered no help in filling the silence that had taken hold. Needing air, Lucy exhaled, feeling a mix of hope and disappointment.

'Excuse me, Pete, there's someone I need to say hello to.'

'Sure.' He was as frugal as ever with his words, and Lucy left him to attend to the 1200 calories on his plate.

George had wasted no time since arriving and had already infected a smile or two as he greeted strangers with his disarming charm.

'Got room for an old one?' He spotted Lucy hurrying towards him. She wrapped her arms around his shoulders and affectionately gifted him a kiss on the cheek.

'What have I done to deserve that?' He returned the hug, softly patting her back.

'That's for gracing us with your wonderful company,' she beamed at him.

He raised his glasses off the bridge of his nose a fraction, seemingly moved by her genuine affection.

'And these are for you.' George held up a generous bouquet of white lilies and powder-pink roses.

'Oh, George,' she took a moment to admire their unparalleled beauty. 'They are stunning, thank you so much.' That earned him another kiss.

'Lilies were always my wife's favourite…' the reminder had caught him off-guard. Lucy placed her hand on his arm and George cleared his throat with a cough. 'And I don't know a woman that doesn't love roses.'

'That is true. I almost didn't recognise you for a moment.'

'Yes, these are my posh glasses,' he said, referring to his new black-rimmed spectacles.

'Very handsome.'

'Thank you, kind lady.' Now, finally, she could ask the question that refused to be ignored, and then maybe she could get on with enjoying the day.

'Will Joseph be joining us?' she asked, hoping her smile looked carefree, but fearing that it might show her desperation.

'I'm not sure. He goes out Thursday and Friday nights, so it depends…'

'On whether he's picked up a girl?' Her hand shot up to her mouth. 'Sorry, George, I didn't mean to say that out loud. Why would I say that?' She mumbled through her fingers.

He gently removed her hand with a chortle. 'I was going to say 'if he's had a late night'. But yes, I think your answer would be more accurate.'

Her lips fought to hide the bitter disappointment.

'Saying I look different – look at you.' He stepped back to view her in her entirety. 'You look gorgeous.' That was her first 'gorgeous' of the day, and it had been spoken with sincerity by an honest man.

'Thank you, George. Now come with me. There's someone I would like to introduce you to; I think you'll have a few things in common.'

'Okay, lead the way, my darlin'.' Lucy felt comfortable enough to take his hand and led him to the table, where Charles was deep in conversation with everyone around him. She introduced George as her friend, as well as the sculptor and creator of the transformed grounds. He made his way around everyone, shaking hands and exchanging names as he went.

Lucy sat him next to Charles, having a feeling the two men would have much to talk about. She headed into the kitchen, placed the flowers in a vase and sat them proudly in the centre of the kitchen window before returning to the garden.

Like a waitress in a busy restaurant, she checked that everyone was okay for food and drink before taking the liberty of choosing a plateful of food for George. From the applause and roars of laughter she could hear, she guessed that her instincts had been right: the two men had clearly already formed a double act.

Accepting that Joseph wouldn't be making an appearance, and somewhat relieved by this fact, Lucy popped the cork of Charles's bottle of Bollinger, and poured herself a tall glass of the golden fizz, which slipped down a little too easily. She topped up her glass, then made her way back into the garden to mingle.

'There you are.' The clear-cut diction inferred only one owner. She screwed her eyes tight shut for a moment, hoping it wasn't him and wishing it was another.

Lucy looked over her shoulder. Sebastian Kingsfellow stood with his hands in his pockets, dressed head to toe in linen, somehow managing to be completely creaseless as if he had levitated there.

'Mr Kingsfellow, nice to see you.' She stood still, causing him to advance. He took her hand and raised it to his lips. 'It's *very* nice to see you too, Lucy.'

'Call me Sebastian, I insist.' He held his lips on her fingers for longer than was comfortable, or necessary, forcing her to pull away.

'"Mr Kingsfellow" is far too formal. We are friends after all, aren't we?'

Black Ray-Bans sat across the top of his head, acting as a makeshift headband for his unruly fringe. She nervously sipped her drink with more frequency than was usual.

'What do you think of the garden?' The question was used as an excuse to look anywhere but at him. Sebastian's gaze was too direct, intense, obtrusive.

'Fantastic. You look fucking hot.' His eyes hadn't been anywhere other than on her. He wasn't there to see the garden.

'I don't think that was an appropriate thing to say –

especially   not   between   friends.'

'It was more appropriate than my initial thought, which was to say I want to stick my head under that dress and bury my face in your pussy until you scream for mercy.' There was no hesitation or embarrassment in what he said. He spoke with the superiority of a man who was used to getting whatever he wanted in life.

Lucy's mouth dried with nervous unease; she moistened it with more Bollinger. From the rising temperature of her face, she knew that he could see the effect he was having, albeit misguided.

'No answer, Lucy? I'll take that as a "yes, please" then shall I?'

For fuck's sake, speak!

'Do you always talk like that to attached women?' She forced herself to hold his sleazy stare.

'Mark's a nice guy. I like him, but tell me it's not boring when he fucks you. I bet you have sex on the same days every week and in the same position.'

He gave her the opportunity to reply. She revealingly let it pass.

'Sex has become a chore, hasn't it? Something that has to be done, like going to the supermarket or cleaning the toilet.'

He took a step closer, his cologne within range. 'Has he ever made you beg for an orgasm, Lucy?'

Not being a natural liar, she struggled with the direct interrogation, remaining silent at all the wrong moments.

'Well, has he?'

Sex *had* become routine, but wasn't that the same for every long-term couple?

'I'm   perfectly   happy   with   all   aspects   of   my

relationship.' He leaned in closer still; watching her lips with greed in his eyes. 'I don't believe you.'

'Believe what?' Mark had approached without either of them being aware.

Lucy jumped. Her drink sloshed over the rim of the glass; Sebastian didn't flinch in the slightest and held out his hand. Mark was too preoccupied with his new friend to notice Lucy's startled face.

'I was just saying that I can't believe how much work you've done here. The place looks amazing.' He was in full charm mode, and the teeth were out in force.

'Thanks. It has been hard work, but we're getting there.'

Lucy's mouth fell open at the shameless bullshit that so easily rode out of Mark's mouth.

Is arsehole contagious?

'Did you see my girl when you came in?' Mark smirked.

'It's not the gorgeous Italian piece is it?'

The two men only had eyes for each other, and little did either know, it was all bravado, on both sides.

'That's my girl.'

'You lucky bastard, you.' Sebastian punched Mark on the shoulder, a sickening gesture of male bullshit. She detested it when men spoke of cars like they were women; how would they like it if women referred to their shoes in the same way?

Although, many women did gain more pleasure from their shoe addiction than they did from their men.

Now they had reached the physical contact level of friendship, Mark placed his hand on his buddy's shoulder. 'I'm going to extend the same courtesy to you that you extended me.'

'Oh really, and what is that?' asked Sebastian.

'I'm gonna let you take my girl for a ride.'

Lucy was halfway through swallowing yet another mouthful of alcohol, and snorted at his unintentionally inappropriate comment; spilling her drink all over her hands, she hunched over, coughing and spluttering.

'Steady, steady.' Mark patted her on the back, which was of no help whatsoever.

'Are you alright, babe?'

'Yes, I'm fine.' She dabbed her chin with the back of her hand. 'I just sneezed.'

'So what do you say?' That was the extent of Mark's concern.

'Well, looking at the sexy little minx. I'm sure I could ride around with her all night long.'

Lucy found it staggering that Mark hadn't picked up on the innuendo.

'I bet you could. Give me ten minutes: I've just promised to show my friend Tony the car.'

'Take as long as you like, Mark. I'm not going anywhere.'

Great.

'Can you keep an eye on the barbecue, babe? I've put the last of the steak on.'

'Yeah that's fine.' It was the perfect excuse she needed to escape.

'I'll keep you company, shall I?' oiled Kingsfellow, once Mark was away from them.

'Don't be too long, Mark,' she called out as he headed back through the house, removing the joke apron and leaving her in the same predicament as before.

'I bet you'd like to take a look at my meat, wouldn't you?'

'That's enough. Don't talk to me like that. You're wasting your breath: I'm perfectly happy with Mark.' Lucy didn't give him a chance to interject and strode off, incredulous at the fact that Sebastian Kingdick actually thought that was the way women liked to be talked to.

She threw a scowl his way. He hadn't moved an inch and seemed to take great pleasure in the rousing effect he had inflicted. Emptying her glass, Lucy manned the stainless steel meat beast, knowing full well it would take much more than that to discourage a man like Kingsfellow.

She stole a look to confirm what she already knew, he was sauntering along in his brown leather sandals. He removed his glasses and hung them on his white linen shirt revealing a little more of his hairless tanned chest.

Lucy reached for the barbecue spatula, which, with its serrated edge, resembled a medieval instrument of torture. A rap on the knuckles should calm him down. She glanced around with ever-increasing unease as he approached, flicking and tossing his hair like he was starring in a shampoo commercial.

'I'm sorry. It's an affliction I have. I simply can't help but speak my mind when I see a woman I want.' He stood close once again, boxing her in between him and the garage wall.

'You need to work harder with that.' She pointed the utensil at his chest in warning.

'Easy tiger.' He held both hands up in surrender. 'Wouldn't that make a great spanking tool?'

'Do you think of nothing else? Have you only come

here to harass me?'

'In answer to your first question: no, I don't think of anything else when you're in my vicinity.' He spoke low, doing his best to coat his words with lust, instead they just dripped with smarm.

She knew once Mark started with his car he would lose all awareness of time and bore the fuck out of that poor bastard Tony by rattling on and on about shit no one cared about.

She was increasingly agitated, because the observational shark had spotted the holes in her and Mark's relationship. Never in her life had she been faced with such supreme arrogance.

'I never did tell you the story of the previous owners, did I?'

She should have told him she wasn't interested and to fuck off before she chopped his dick off and served it to him in a bun with ketchup. The trouble was that now that he had mentioned it, she was curious.

'No, you didn't.'

'Mr and Mrs Templeton viewed this house four times before they finally purchased it. Mrs Templeton loved what she saw, but Mr Templeton was reluctant. His concern was not only the garden, but also the aged state of the house. But his wife just *had* to have it.' His eyelids were heavy, laden with perverseness. 'And have it she did. On their fourth visit, Mr Templeton wandered the grounds in careful contemplation of his possible investment and commitment. Mrs Templeton and I watched him from that very bedroom window that you and I stood at, while I fucked the hell out of her from behind.' His top lip buckled like a snarling dog.

He displayed no shame while telling the story, which Lucy had no doubt was true. Sebastian watched her reaction closely like he was looking for any sign that it had excited her too. 'And that is how you have come to be the current custodians of this house.'

Lucy wondered if, in some crazy warped way, he thought that Lucy was living there because of his actions.

'Do you honestly think that scenario will play out again?'

Pitted dimples appeared in his cheeks, and his mouth stretched to its maximum capacity, displaying a cocksure grin. 'I know it will, Lucy.'

She looked at him dead in the face. His half-cocked eyebrow and smirking lips were a representation of decadence and immorality at its most brazen.

The intense heat from the grill couldn't stop the cold morose feeling that crawled over her skin. He fully believed what he had said, and that thought alarmed her.

'Dream on,' she quipped with a snort.

'Like I said, Mark's a nice guy, but you need a man to take charge.'

Maybe it was a kind of sixth sense, but something told Lucy to look to her left. Acting on impulse, she was generously rewarded. Her line of vision shot straight like an arrow, skimming Sebastian's shoulder and completely avoiding all other bodies until it landed on its target, Joseph Dalton.

'And, believe me, I *am* a take-charge man.' His words fell to the ground like spent shells from a rifle – dead, used.

'Good.' She slapped the spatula against his chest and he took hold of it. 'You can take charge of the barbecue.

Mind you don't burn your sausage.'

She didn't waste the power of sight and speech on Mr Fabulous any longer, and made her way to the one person she was sure wouldn't show.

He hadn't seen her, but he was scanning the crowd. Lucy realised that once she was in his presence she would probably crumble and turn into a gibbering mess. Pausing halfway through her journey she indulged in a little voyeurism. She covertly hid behind the generous frame of Mike, one of Mark's golfing mates, who was the human equivalent of a hippo. Joseph came in and out of view as he navigated slowly around the groups of friends.

Her beats per minute increased; the rhythm of her heart was almost audible.

A tight white T-shirt hung over faded, navy shorts. The baseball cap had been given the day off, and black Converse boots finished off his casual look perfectly. He certainly wasn't as crisp as Sebastian, but his carefree appearance was real – and the effect this man was having was certainly all too real. Lucy chastised herself: she couldn't believe that when she first met Sebastian, she had found him attractive. In the presence of a genuine man he seemed plastic, with his creaseless clothes, whiter-than-white teeth, baby-smooth jawline and black glossy hair.

Joseph was uncluttered and unfussy. His rugged face had lines, but in all the right places. His hair wasn't styled within an inch of its life and that only added to his raw appeal.

Suzie and a group of the girls had already spotted him. She couldn't procrastinate any longer.

She had so wanted him to come, despite telling herself otherwise, and here he was. Taking several shots of oxygen, she tousled her hair and stepped from behind her hiding place.

I'm an attractive, confident woman. This is my domain. I am in complete control and will hold my own.

He stood in one spot, slowly turning, trying to find a familiar face amongst the strangers. He found one. Lucy's. His eyes narrowed as she approached. He made no secret of the fact that he was studying her appearance from top to bottom. With but a whisper of a smile on his handsome face, her confidence dripped away like the fat from cooking sausages. To top it all off, her composure had just handed in its resignation.

'Hello, I'm surprised to see you here.'

'Lucy.' He gave her his cowboy nod. 'Good surprise or bad?'

The urge to drop her eyes to the floor and fiddle with her fingers was almost overwhelming.

She held her nerve and looked up into his face. 'Good... very good.' The first 'good' could have been taken as a general comment. But the second one was unmistakably flirtatious. Her nerve cracked. 'I'm sorry, I meant –'

'I know what you meant,' he interrupted, slicing across her babble. Lucy fought to control her breathing. Her chest heaved with a mixture of feelings: nervousness, excitement and guilt. She watched the eyes of the man in front of her trek from her jawline up to her forehead and down over her nose. Stopping for a rest on her full, open red lips before making their way over the form of her dress.

He shook his head, so slightly it was almost imperceptible.

'You look . . . beautiful.' His stare impaled her, giving full validation to what he had said. Lucy almost choked on her own breath. Of all the compliments she had received that day – nice, pretty, gorgeous, lovely – the one she most wanted to hear was spoken with the upmost sincerity, that beckoned tears from a man she hardly knew. Her eyelashes fluttered in an attempt to fan away the threatening spillage.

'I noticed yesterday that you were inundated with wine, so I brought beer.' He held up a yellow and blue box with six Corona bottles poking out of the top. 'And,' he reached into his pocket and pulled out a lime, 'just in case you didn't have one.' He threw it into the air, then caught it, wearing the most infectious smile she had witnessed for a long time.

'What sort of household do you think this is, that we don't have limes?'

'Well, you are a lady who likes the finer things in life.' His open hand fanned over her appearance. 'I figured that you'd probably prefer to lie in a bath full of goat's milk, with limes on your eyes rather than sticking them into bottles of beer.'

Lucy giggled. 'You're slightly off-track: it's meant to be cucumbers on your eyes.' She paused. 'You'd be surprised what I like.'

'Would I?'

Now, unintentionally, she had slipped back into flirting.

'Would you care to join me?' He opened the box and held up two bottles in his one hand. 'Or are you a champagne and wine kind of girl?'

'I'd love to join you.'

Even if he had held up two bottles of horse piss, she

would have shared them with him. Thankfully it was beer, and she did like beer.

'Follow me. I'll slice the lime and you can say hello to your dad.'

As they both made their way to the house, Lucy noticed that Pete was now manning the barbecue. Sebastian was nowhere to be seen. She didn't care now Joseph was here and she had his full attention.

The laughter coming from around the table was a joy to hear. The whole day had gone so well and things were only getting better.

'George, look who I found loitering around.' Lucy thumbed over her shoulder, and his son stepped out from behind her.

'Everyone, this is my boy, Joseph,' George announced, with great pride. Joseph held up the two beers in acknowledgement of everyone while Lucy went into the kitchen to slice the fruit.

She managed to find a clear space for the timber chopping board amongst the empty glasses and crumb-filled plates. She was eager to get back to Joseph, and erratically searched the drawers, looking for a sharp knife, but they were all playing hide-and-seek.

'Why can I never find anything when I want it?' She looked around at the disarray. The kitchen bore the evidence of a great party. It looked like they hadn't washed up for a year.

'Dishwasher.' She opened the door to the machine that, to her, was man's greatest invention, second to the wheel. Finding their hiding place, she took a clean knife out and slammed the door with growing unease. She had always been nervous in his presence, but was even more so now, knowing that he was out there waiting for her.

The fruit was dissected and she hurried out, holding the two slivers in the palm of her hand. Lucy returned to the scene to find all as it was when she left, apart from that there was no Joseph. After a few moments she caught a glimpse of him and her heart sank. He was standing talking to Suzie. Her friend's composure spoke volumes. Her head was slightly tilted to one side, wearing a permanent smile. One leg was bent against the other in a very feminine way. Suzie was holding what should have been Lucy's beer with both hands, and every time Joseph made her laugh, it was all the excuse Suzie needed to touch his arm. She was working her beauty to the very best of her ability. Why wouldn't she? They were both single people; there was nothing wrong with it, except that Lucy didn't like it… she didn't like it at all.

CHAPTER FOURTEEN

Lucy Eaton, partner of Mark Smith. Mr & Mrs Gin and Tonic. Millionaires living the fairy tale. She had never envied anyone in her life; jealousy simply hadn't existed in her world – until now, that was. She couldn't bear not knowing what was being said between them for a moment longer.

Just before she came into view, she forced a smile onto her face.

'Here she is: our wonderful hostess and my lovely friend,' said Suzie.

'Everything okay?' That was the closest she could get to *'what are you talking about'* without actually saying it.

'I was just saying how I'm always stuck at a loose end on Saturdays, as you've all got men in your lives, and I'm the only single girl,' Suzie tutted with fake annoyance.

Well played, Suzie, not very subtle though.

'There you go,' Joseph said, offering an open bottle to Lucy.

'Thanks.' She gripped the cool glass and opened the

hand that was holding the slices of lime.

'I've only cut two.' There was no way she was leaving them alone.

'That's okay – Suzie can have mine.' He took the fruit and stuck it in the neck of Suzie's bottle. 'There you go.' He flashed a grin at her.

'Aww, thank you.' Suzie held up her bottle in thanks and he gave her the cowboy nod. Lucy felt wounded; it was as if he had cheated on her. She thought the cowboy nod was for her only.

'I didn't think you liked beer, Suzie?'

'Yeah.' She tasted the beverage in question as if to validate her answer. Lucy knew her friend well enough to know that she would swallow anything to impress a man she liked. And it was clear to see that she liked Mr Dalton very much.

'So what's a typical Saturday evening's entertainment for you, Joey?'

Joey? What the...? It's Joseph. Lucy caught herself frowning at Suzie.

'It depends really. There's a bar on Bridges Street in town that has some good live bands.'

It seemed that her brother's habit of nodding incessantly was hereditary, either that or Suzie had a spring for a neck.

'Oh I've heard about that. Is it called Tommy's?'

'Yeah, that's the one.'

'I've always wanted to go there.' Suzie was brazenly dropping hints at every opportunity.

Lucy's head turned left to right like a spectator at a tennis match, listening to the verbal volleys, feeling herself becoming more and more invisible as they *'got to know each another.'* What she should have been doing was asking him if he wanted anything to eat, and maybe going and cut another slice of lime for him. That was the hostess's role, wasn't it?

Looking after her guests. All day she had thought of nothing else, secretly hoping that he would come, and now here he was. The elation of seeing his face had evoked such a high that Lucy was now plummeting from it. She thought he had come to see her, but the reality was simply that he had turned up at some barbecue he had been invited to. That's all.

She felt foolish for feeling disappointed, and ashamed for inwardly berating her best friend.

'Thursdays or Fridays tend to be the best nights, I've found,' said Joseph.

'Maybe I'll see you there one night?' Suzie suggested.

'Maybe.' He tipped his bottle up, emptying it. 'Excuse me, ladies, I'm going to grab another beer. Do either of you want anything?'

'I'm fine, thank you, Joey,' Suzie gushed.

'Lucy?' He looked down at her and she looked up at him.

Can I have your undivided attention, just for five minutes?

'No, thank you.'

He walked between the two friends, heading for the table where he had left his drinks.

They both turned to watch him, their shoulders touching. 'Fucking hell, Lucy.'

'What?'

'You know what... You kept him quiet didn't you?'

'I didn't think he'd come to be honest.' Lucy swerved the question.

'How's my lipstick? Is it okay?'

'It's fine.'

'Do I have any salad between my teeth?' Suzie curled her top lip under itself and presented her perfectly straight gnashers for inspection.

'All clean. You look fantastic, relax.'

'This beer's bloody horrible, and I hate lime. It's like sucking on bleach – ugh!' That had always been Suzie's problem. She'd go along with things she didn't really like or agree with, and then wonder why her relationships never worked out.

They both watched him stop to talk to his father and Charles.

'He's not looking, is he?'

Suzie hid her drink behind her back and emptied the bottle. The beer splashed onto the cropped, coarse weed grass and was consumed by the thirsty, parched ground.

'Is he single?'

'Er... I... think he has got someone special.' Lucy scratched the tip of her nose to check it wasn't growing.

'Well, I'll have to make him think twice about that then.' Suzie flicked and fluffed her hair, which had no effect on her appearance but seemingly made her feel more attractive. As both their attention was fixed on Joseph a hundred feet away, they hadn't noticed that Sebastian had approached them.

'Lucy, how naughty of you not to tell me that you have such a gorgeous friend.'

Hearing those words, Suzie grew a couple of inches in height. Her back arched, breasts heaved out and the feminine knee was bent once again.

He introduced himself with great importance and

pomposity, then kissed Suzie's hand, lingering for so long that Lucy thought he was trying to suck the sapphire ring from her finger.

'Where have they been hiding you, then?'

'I've been here ages, you haven't been looking hard enough.' Suzie giggled, enjoying being a single woman.

'Well, I can tell you I am looking now, and it's hard…'

'Oh my life!' Suzie shrieked with laughter, her hand over her mouth, imitating an innocence that had forsaken her long ago.

Lucy spotted a chance to exit and let Suzie watch the show on her own. It was too late: Joseph was just a few feet away, and was viewing his fellow male with a questioning look. *This should be fun.*

Sebastian was halfway through a raucous howl, brought on by his own rapier wit, when he did a double take at the bearded, broad shouldered stranger. The sparkle in his eyes was dimmed by Joseph's presence. Lucy was glad of his return, but uneasy at what would happen when the two polar opposites meet.

'Hello, who do we have here then?' asked Sebastian, still displaying overdose levels of self-assurance.

Lucy introduced the two men, who shook hands vigorously and exchanged pleasantries. Joseph's company seemed to be having the same effect on Sebastian, who also began to play with his hair.

'So how do you know my girl Lucy?' This was him staking a claim.

'We did the garden, my dad and I.'

'You're the gardener?' Sebastian sniggered disparagingly. Lucy's whole body tensed with unease. She glanced at Joseph, but he seemed to be remaining composed and good-natured.

'What's so funny about that?' Joseph asked.

'Nothing,' Sebastian smirked. 'It's just my dry sense of humour.'

Lucy knew that, in Sebastian's eyes, Joseph's vocation put him way below his own eminent profession of estate agent. The childish laugh he had given only revealed his threatened masculinity, and said way more about his self-confidence than he realised.

'Sebastian was the estate agent we purchased the house from,' Lucy explained, foreseeing the pomposity of the man in question's flowery version.

'Kingsfellow Real Estate.' He spoke rather too loudly, as all insecure, arrogant men did. 'You must have seen the boards. I have over 800 properties on my books in London and across the surrounding area.' He wasn't going to settle for Lucy's factual explanation. The more he boasted and bragged, the less impressive he seemed. 'You can't go anywhere without seeing my name. I'm a big deal when it comes to real estate.' Lucy could only imagine what must have been going through Joseph's mind. Probably much the same as was going through hers: dickhead, arsehole, prick—all the expletives that suited such a man.

'So, Suzie, what do you do with yourself all day, apart from looking fabulous?' She giggled girlishly, completely loving the cheesy one-liners.

'I'm a customer care manager for a large fashion retailer.' Several bats of her lashes accompanied her answer.

'Well you could certainly take care of me, you little fox.' Suzie held onto his arm, doubled up with laughter;

Sebastian joined in, he had no qualms about laughing at his own jokes.

Taking advantage of their distraction, Joseph stole a glance at Lucy. The corner of his mouth had hitched up and his eyes narrowed slightly, affected by the preposterous behaviour of Mr Fantastic. It was only for a second or two but it was comforting, genuine, and somehow placed her at ease. He wasn't threatened in the slightest. Sebastian's attempts to make himself look more important and successful only helped to elevate Joseph to another level.

'I've yet to take your man's pride and joy out for a spin. I didn't have the heart to tell him that my Porsche is the much faster car.'

But of course it is.

'German engineering, it simply can't be beaten.'

'You drive a Porsche?' Suzie had found another excuse for physical contact.

'It's a Porsche 911 Turbo S Coupé. Brand new. Drives like a dream. Naught to sixty in 3.1 seconds.'

'I love Porsches. They are sooo sexy, aren't they?'

Lucy was both embarrassed and pleased by her friend's blatant flirting. Pleased, because she knew Joseph lived on this planet and was probably feeling embarrassed by their displays of desperation.

'Very sexy, that's why it suits me. What do you drive, Jim?'

Joseph smiled, accepting the deliberate mistake affably.

'His name's Joseph,' Lucy was quick to correct him.

'I drive a Toyota pick-up. Several years old, drives like a tank and does nought to sixty… eventually.' It was Lucy's turn for the giggles. 'I had to pass on a Porsche, I couldn't get a lawnmower in the back.' Joseph sipped his beer and winked at Lucy. She took it as a signal, rightly or wrongly, that she was on his team.

The quip raised a smile from Suzie, who bit on her lip to stop it developing into anything more.

Strangely, Sebastian didn't seem to see the funny side of it.

'The only thing that my car carries are my Louis Vuitton bags.' Both hands slicked back his long hair and landed on his hips in defiance.

'Seb!' They all looked around to see Mark standing by the house, jangling his car keys.

'Duty calls, I'm afraid. Excuse me, ladies. Nice to meet you, John.'

He didn't hang around to be corrected this time. With a flick of his head and a swish of his plumage, the proud, if not delusional, peacock, pranced off in all his creaseless linen glory.

'You too, Sid,' Joseph called out, playing along with the fun and games.

Sebastian's head turned a quarter upon hearing the retort, but he stayed his course pretending that he was out of earshot.

'They say the greatest love is to love yourself. I don't think your friend has got any worries if that's true,' Joseph laughed to himself. Lucy could see that he was in a contented, comfortable mood. He radiated warmth and affected a part of her that she hadn't thought existed.

When Mark had called his driving buddy he hadn't batted an eyelid at Joseph, so what had his problem been last night, Lucy asked herself.

Lucy *so* wished that Suzie wasn't there. She desperately

wanted to take advantage of his receptive mood. He was like a thick book with a very intriguing cover, and Lucy wanted to see what was on each and every page.

'I like a confident man. Confidence is very alluring to women.' Suzie audaciously ran the tip of her middle finger around the head of the beer bottle while gazing submissively through the fan of her false lashes.

'Are you a confident man when it comes to women, Joey?'

Lucy's mouth fell open, aghast at Suzie's tenacious resolve to let this man know that she was his to do with whatever he so wished.

'You look like a very capable man.' She held the bottle to her lips, then seemingly remembered how much she disliked its contents.

Joseph was about to answer when Mark's shrill voice butted in.

Lucy's stomach churned at the call, although she hadn't done anything wrong; she knew that the question *what the hell are you doing talking to him?* was sure to be catapulted her way.

She looked across to Mark, acknowledging him. 'Can you move your car, babe? It's blocking me in.'

Surprised and relieved, at the simple and painless request, she was also irritated at having to leave Joseph alone with Suzie. She could imagine what she might be suggesting in her absence.

'Sorry, won't be a moment.' Lucy shrugged, giving a tight-lipped smile, knowing full well that Suzie would go in for the kill, and being a beautiful sexy woman, Joseph surely wouldn't need much persuading. Then Lucy would have to endure the torturous stories of how wonderful he was. This little scenario played out in her mind in great detail, like a time-lapse video, zooming through every intimacy of their imaginary meeting.

Her legs passed each other with increasing speed and agitation at her facilitating such eventualities by inviting the opportunity.

'Can't you move it, Mark?'

He was leaning out of the kitchen, clinging to the doorframe by his fingertips; his eyes had a misty glaze that indicated high levels of alcohol in the blood.

'How much have you had to drink?' asked Lucy.

'I've had enough, and then a bit more.' As with all drunks, his eyebrows seemed to regard his inebriation as being their chance to shine. 'Don't worry, my flower, I'm not driving; I'm the navigator. Seb is the pilot.'

Dear God. Boys and their toys.

'Right, let me get my keys.'

Mark headed out to his car, which was being revved impatiently. Lucy followed, enquiring on her way whether people had had enough to eat. She rummaged through the receipts, make-up, hairbrush and emergency tampons that cluttered her bag.

Retrieving her keys, she manoeuvred her car over a few feet to allow Starsky and Hutch to hit the streets. The high-performance machine inappropriately thundered away.

Prick.

She was anxious to get back to Joseph, but on her way through the house she was stopped by a small herd of mature ladies who simply had to know the origin of every *vol-au-vent* and cake.

They were at that age where the pleasures of taste

superseded the pleasures of the flesh – their Body Mass Indexes being testimony to the fact. Lucy played the dutiful host all the while eager to get away. She waited for an extended silence, which would enable her to request to be excused.

The conversation jumped from cakes and pastries to carpets and curtains. Lucy smiled through gritted teeth, her face at odds with her thoughts. Although the four ladies were utterly charming and they had only been chatting for a matter of minutes, urgency had no concept of time. She tried to gauge what was an acceptable amount of revolutions of the kitchen clock hands before making her excuses.

Finally escaping, she made her way back into the garden, and was relieved to see that Suzie was no longer with Joseph. He was now sat at the table in conversation with his dad. She was curious to know what had been said between them while she was away.

Lucy retraced her steps back to Suzie, who was now accompanied by Claire and Sonya, who they had been good friends with for many years.

Claire was a larger-than-life woman in every sense of the word, and appeared to have an amalgamation of two bodies: she was broad-chested with arms that any wrestler would have been proud of, which were at odds with her svelte legs.

Never short of something to say, she had a happy round face and a kind heart.

'Here she is, the lady of the house,' said Claire.

'Hi girls, everything all right?' Lucy asked. They all answered at once, all agreeing that the day had been a great success.

'There you go, chick.' Suzie held out a bulbous glass of wine full to the brim. 'Bloody hell, Suzie, are you trying to get me drunk?'

'It's a party isn't it? Besides, it will help you get rid of the taste of that awful beer.'

Lucy skimmed her lips over the rim of the glass and sucked up some of the liquid to avoid it spilling down her dress.

'Have you had enough to eat, Sonya?' Sonya was the yin to Claire's yang. She was a fragile woman with a delicate build and Lucy hoped she hadn't caused offence with her innocent question by insinuating that she wasn't eating properly, although her skeletal appearance did suggest that this might be the case.

'Yes, thank you, I'm stuffed.' Sonya patted the hollow where her tummy should have been.

'I notice you didn't ask me the same question, you cheeky cow!' Claire piped up, her rosy cheeks full of good humour.

'I knew you didn't have to be asked twice, lady, that's why!'

'That's the truth: the food was beautiful.'

'Oh, thanks, Claire.'

'Hey, talking of beautiful – you kept that quiet, didn't you?' Suzie repeated her earlier question with more volume than was necessary; the alcohol tinkering with her senses.

'What?' Lucy knew very well what.

'What do you mean *what*?' Suzie's chin retracted into her neck. 'Joey, the gardener, that's bloody *what*!'

The wine glass went straight up to Lucy's face for cover.

'Joseph, you mean?' She hated Suzie calling him Joey,

as if they had a special connection.

'Yeah.' Suzie conveyed her indifference with a shrug of her shoulders.

'He's a nice guy.'

'Lucy Eaton, unless you're registered blind, you can't tell me he's not fucking gorgeous.'

'Is this the guy in the white T-shirt with the beard?' Claire asked.

'Yeah, Joey the gardener,' Suzie confirmed.

'He's your fucking gardener! Oh yes, now he is a honey.' Claire pouted out her thin lips as best she could, and her eyelids met each other deviously. 'You go girl.'

Lucy didn't know how to react; she felt uneasy about the subject matter, but not acknowledging his attractiveness probably be more telling.

'He is very handsome,' Sonya chipped in. Lucy was glad that at least one of her friends had some reserve.

'And, guess what I've got?' Suzie's manicured claws reached into her plunging neckline and jiggled one of her generous breasts. 'I got his number.' She produced Joseph's business card from her bra. Lucy felt her cheeks blanch. She had wanted Joseph to attend so she could chat with him, maybe get to know him a little better. Her plans had proved unsuccessful for her, and fortuitous for Suzie.

'You did?' Lucy hoped some sort of agreeable expression had formed on her face.

'You don't mind, do you?' Obviously not by Suzie's question.

'No, no, of course not.' Her facial muscles took the strain and heaved the corners of her mouth in opposite directions to where they had fallen.

'Good, because that's one gardener who needs to give

my bush some serious attention.'

'Suzie!' Lucy's reprimand was drowned out by the girls' salacious cackling.

'I know, I'm terrible, but I've gone *so* long without sex. The vibrator just isn't pushing my buttons any more, if you'll pardon the pun. I think I'm turning cannibal: I need flesh, I need meat.'

'Calm down, woman,' chirped Claire. 'I'll get you a cold flannel and a sausage from the barbecue.'

'Make sure it's a big one then, and don't leave me alone, I'm not sure what I might do with it.'

Another round of smutty giggles were served.

Lucy did her best but could not find the energy to partake. The conversation continued along the same theme, and even though they were all good friends she felt like a stranger listening in on a private conversation. She nodded and smiled on cue, but all the while a concoction of irrational thoughts about Joseph and Suzie's potential meeting served to isolate and taunt her further.

Giving the excuse that she needed a toilet break, she took herself off to the privacy of the first floor and wandered through the rooms like a lost soul. Was she acting like a spoilt brat because she couldn't have Joseph's attention?

It didn't matter how much she vilified herself. She simply could not dispel the foreign mixture of feelings. Rushes of excitement were shadowed by guilt, which courted remorse, leading her to thoughts she had so far evaded.

"Live life with no regrets." That was what her grandmother had once told her, it was an ideological fantasy. How many people lived a life full of regret? Squandering the years away, justifying the loss with promises of *'one day.'*

The arrival of Joseph Dalton had introduced her to the possibility of such a future, and it filled her with a fear that should have been ill suited in the world of premium post codes and Porsches.

The unapologetic dissonance of Mark's car returning, interrupted her thoughts.

It was time to paint on a smile and flounce around like she didn't have a care in the world. Which was true. So why didn't it feel that way? Driver and navigator entered the house. Lucy waited a few minutes for Sebastian to find a victim before joining the fracas unnoticed.

Since Joseph's attention was still on his father, Suzie latched on to Sebastian, leaving Yin and Yang exactly where Lucy had left them. She spent the next couple of hours doing the rounds flitting from guest to guest. Almost everyone made a comment about how she was living the millionaire lifestyle. Their envious, but complimentary words only left her feeling more and more unappreciative of Lady Luck's blessing.

A sure sign of an unsuccessful party is an early mass exodus of people, making excuses such as, *'the dog is on his own, so we'll have to get back.'* They must have got something right, because no such excuses were uttered and no one made any advances towards departing – apart from George, that is. Despite Mark's ignorance the day before, George displayed the evidence of his good character and sought out Mark with an offer of his hand along with his gratitude.

Lucy watched them from her distant spot peering over

Bob's shoulder, who, along with the odd interjection from his wife Jane, was telling the fascinatingly boring story of their recent trip to Portugal, in excruciating detail. Lucy dropped in the odd, 'yeah,' with a nod, disguising the fact that she had long since tuned out the monotonous din of his endless story.

Searching, George spotted her and made his way over. He was alone, so that must have meant that Joseph was staying. Lucy exchanged 'yeah,' for 'sounds lovely, Bob,' and made the fact that George was leaving an excuse for her to get away.

'Going already, George?'

'I'm afraid so: I play dominoes on Saturday evening with a few friends from church. I've had a lovely time though, thank you for inviting us. Everyone's been very welcoming.'

'It's you I should be thanking: this day would have never happened if you and the guys hadn't worked your magic.'

He dismissed the much-warranted praise with a flap of his hand. 'Enough of that, young lady; it's been our pleasure. We'll get there, eh?'

'Yes, we will.' Lucy gave him a cuddle and kissed him fondly on the cheek.

'That rogue son of mine is hitching a lift with me. Thirty-two years old and I am still chauffeuring him around.'

'Joseph is leaving too?'

Her instinct was to look for Suzie, who, if she stood any closer to Seb would have been wearing his clothes.

'He's meeting a friend in town – or so he tells me.'

'I didn't get to speak to you both very much today.' It

was a desperate attempt to scrounge the smallest morsel of time with the one and only guest she really wanted to talk to.

'That's okay, my darlin', you've got a lot of people to get around. Besides, you've got us all next week, so you'll be sick of the sight of us.' He playfully elbowed her arm. 'Enjoy the rest of your evening, Lucy, we'll see you at the school on Monday at two.'

She stood planted to the spot and watched him slowly make his way towards the house. 'Thank you for the flowers, George.'

'You're very welcome,' he called out. Joseph rose from the table, waved to his companions and met his father. They chatted briefly, and the younger man looked in her direction, before Dalton Sr. took his exit.

Joseph kept his distance, his face fixed on her, seeming to hesitate. Just the very act of his eyes taking in her image set off a strange reaction inside of her. *Was he staying after all? Get over there, you idiot.* But before her foot had left the ground, he raised his hand, dashing any hopes of him staying. It stayed aloft momentarily, no smile was offered. The hand fell like a checkered racing flag, signalling his passage out. Lucy watched his every step, paralysed with the desire to stop him, until his image was stolen from her.

It wasn't the only thing that had been stolen. The party had lost its party mood. The misery of his leaving was equal to the euphoria of his arrival.

What the hell was she thinking? That they were going to spend all afternoon chatting uninterrupted? With a house and garden full of people; she knew that was impossible. Expectation isn't bound by logic, so disappointment was always destined to be the victor.

The summer evening brought an elongated dusk that fought back the outset of nightfall admirably, before falling to the dominant darkness. Saturday neared the end of its slot on the calendar, and the merry people absconded with empty offers of help to tidy the post-party chaos. Suzie had left some time ago on the arm of a very smug Mr Kingsfellow, who, from the look of his twisted smile, seemed to think that he had inflicted a torturous envy that she would wrestle with the whole night through, but in reality she couldn't have cared less.

When placed alongside Joseph, Sebastian seemed as insignificant as a speck of dust, despite his designer clothes, salon-condition hair and racing machine. Those things were no match for the raw, unpolluted magnetism that radiated from Joseph. He illuminated her soul with the brightest light, the like of which she had no previous memory of...

And it was that which Lucy would wrestle with the whole night through.

CHAPTER FIFTEEN

Lucy awoke to greet Sunday morning with tangled hair and tangled thoughts. Her body was alone in the warm haven of their bed. Mark had probably fallen asleep in front of his treasured TV watching some 1950s war movie that only late-night security guards and insomnia sufferers were awake for. She rolled on to her side and pulled the duvet up over her head. It was yet another bright day – no consideration shown for the delicate condition of late-night wine drinkers. She had intended to spend another half an hour curled up, but her bladder had other ideas.

Hauling herself out of bed, Lucy threw on her dressing gown and, on tiptoes, wobbled from side to side into the damp air of the bathroom. The mirror was thankfully frosted with a slowly dissipating coat of condensation. It seemed Mark was already up and showered.

Having answered the call of nature, she took to the stairs with all the finesse of Frankenstein's monster. The door to the kitchen was open and the tinkling of a spoon on ceramic rang out. As she approached the kitchen, a panoramic view of the battle zone opened up. Mark was sitting at the island surrounded by the evidence of their party; his breakfast bowl occupied the only spot that wasn't covered by drink-stained glasses, or plates of half-eaten sandwiches and sausage rolls.

'Oh my god.' The palm of her hand dribbled down her cheek. 'Did we have an earthquake in the night?'

'Morning. It's not as bad as it looks.' Only a man would have said that. Mark's slightly darker shade of damp blond hair was stuck to his forehead. He was dressed complete with shoes.

'You're going out?' she asked, scraping a congealed layer of mascara from her eyes.

'Mmm...' He crunched through his muesli before answering. 'I'm taking Pete home and then I might go and practise my swing.' Both *Pete'* and *'golf'* stuck out in his statement.

'Pete?'

'Morning,' she heard a voice reply.

Lucy stepped through the doorway avoiding a discarded chicken wing, and sure enough, there was Pete, sat at the dining table at the other end of the kitchen, caressing a large mug of tea.

'Oh, hello. I didn't know you were here.'

'He won't be for much longer,' Mark hopped off his stool. 'Ready mate?'

'You're going now? What about all this mess?' The delivery of her question was much more controlled because of Pete's company.

'Don't worry about it, babe, we'll do it when I get back.' He pecked her on the cheek and made his way down the hall, Pete lumbered along behind him.

'Thanks, Lucy for all the...' He made circles with his fingers, encompassing the leftovers.

'You're welcome, Pete. Tell that sister of yours to call me when she gets a chance.'

'Will do.'

The door closed, leaving Lucy alone with the remains of a house full of people. It was Suzie who was meant to be staying the night, and then helping her with the aftermath. Still, Lucy was grateful for small mercies. Suzie could have left with Joseph last night, which would have made the job of facing the mess all the more arduous. If the level of disorder represented the success of their day, then it had been one fucking hell of a party. She didn't know where to start.

Mark knew full well that she couldn't just leave it until later. She needed him to redeem himself in some small way, to pull her back from the brink and stem the flow of unwelcome thoughts that was threatening to drown their relationship. He was living the life of a single man, expecting Lucy to tag along. Lately she had felt more like his mother than his lover.

Almost certain that Mark's swing practice would develop into a full eighteen holes, she began the sobering task of returning order to what used to be a functioning kitchen.

Lucy's psychic abilities were fairly accurate, after all. Mark returned at 9:30, and on seeing the kitchen back to its usual state, made a light remark about *'the fairies'* having visited, before plonking his backside in front of the TV. Lucy was all fired up, but for the sake of getting a good night's sleep she decided to save it until the morning.

'I'm going to bed, Mark.' She stood in the doorway, looking at the back of his head.

'You're early, aren't you?' He was stretched out on the couch with the magic wand in his hand, switching from channel to channel, viewing a mere second of each programme.

'I've got work tomorrow.' The whole living room flashed like a strobe light.

'What, on a Monday?'

'Yes, I told you I was going to do more days. I might even go back full time.'

'That's just fucking stupid.' The comment was mumbled as if it was meant for his ears only.

She couldn't let that pass.

'And why is it *fucking stupid*,' Mark?' She entered the room and stood at his side.

'Because who works when they don't have to? Only a fool works for free.' His arrogant snort only added to the antagonism of him not taking his eyes off the changing channels.

'What the hell is wrong with you just lately?'

He offered no answer.

Ironically, he had managed to find a 1950s war movie. The sound of machine gun fire and explosions inflamed her all the more. Lucy hit the *'off'* button, putting an end to the fictional battle, but beginning a very real one.

'Come on, you've been acting strange ever since we moved into this house.'

'Is this because you tidied the kitchen?' He tossed the remote on to his lap and finally made eye contact.

'You know damn well it's not about that, although it would have been nice to have had a little help.'

'Just go to bed.' His eyes returned to the blank screen.

'Not until you tell me what's wrong. Is it the sudden change in lifestyle?'

He folded his arms tightly across his chest.

'Is it because you feel like you haven't got a role in life anymore?'

'Don't psychoanalyse me! You can save that shit for those fucking retards you teach,' he spat the words out with such vehemence.

'Don't you ever – *ever* – refer to those innocent babies in that way again.' Lucy replied, leaning over him punctuating every word with a jab of her finger. 'How fucking dare you! I do it because I care... because I want to make a difference to their little lives and these poor kids need all the help they can get.' She was close to tears, but despite the rage managed to remain in control.

He showed no remorse for his thoughtless comment.

'There but for the grace of god go I. You'd do well to remember that, Mark.'

'Fuck me, here we go! Gone all religious now, have we?'

'You know full well what I mean.'

'Finished?' The sardonic response did him no favours. Retrieving the controls, he turned the TV back on.

'At this moment in time Mark, I am very close to being finished with you.'

'Goodnight, then.' The non-stop channel hopping resumed.

'If you love that thing so much you can fucking sleep down here with it tonight.' She walked out calmly then slammed the door.

Why was he being like this? Each one of these

incidents took another bite out of her love for him and right now it was looking pretty ravaged. She lay in bed that night with a light head and a heavy heart. A pool of despair spilled from her eyes, following a path across her face and down past her ears.

Lucy's journey in life no longer seemed defined as it once was, and after that night she didn't think it ever would be again.

CHAPTER SIXTEEN

Lucy woke early, filled with a sense of purpose for the day ahead. George and his son would be arriving at the school at two o'clock; she was looking forward to seeing how they would interact with the children. There was no doubt that George would keep them all entertained; it was his son she was unsure of.

Dressed in an ensemble of navy-blue slim-fitting trousers that accentuated her bottom, paired with a tailored, crisp white blouse and white patent flats, she was careful to make sure that her look was not too out of the ordinary. After a light application of maintenance make-up, the splendour of her sumptuous head of hair, which was always tied back for school, was allowed to hang freely, bouncing and kinking with her every movement, like a vivacious child ignorant of its sublime beauty.

Lucy headed straight out the door; she didn't want a repeat of last night.

After parking in her usual bay, Lucy entered into the old building, feeling a strange sense of tranquility. The parting of last night's tears had left a feeling of calm that the release of strong emotions often did. She was looking forward to seeing the little boy that had melted and broke her heart in equal measure.

The usual fun and frolics involved with imparting knowledge to ones so young and innocent kept all three ladies on their toes. Mrs Timpson was a very compassionate teacher, and despite thirty-five years in the profession, approached each day as fresh and filled with enthusiasm as if it was her first. She was something of a role model to Lucy, who had nothing but admiration for this quietly competent woman.

Chloe was also a teaching assistant. She was a radiant young girl who was eager to please and very often did.

For most of their day, they fielded the same repeat questions.

'Is Mr Dalton the gardener here yet?'

Little did they know that Lucy shared their eagerness, having inspected the white clock on the wall with impatient frequency. Eventually time delivers all things, and at five minutes to two the phone rang and Mrs Timpson left to greet the visitors and escort them back to the room.

Chloe sat with her legs folded on the multi-coloured woven rug with the waiting children, who were all jittering with excitement. Lucy too, had the jitters, she sat on one of the miniature desks behind the group, facing the door. Her palms were clammy at the thought of seeing him outside their usual environment. It seemed very strange that he was coming to her workplace.

The door opened and the two men followed Mrs Timpson into the room, each holding a hessian bag.

Joseph's eyes found her instantly, and it was like receiving a physical blow to the chest. He had no idea of the effect he had on her.

The garbled hum of excitement began to rise in volume, and hellos were sporadically

flung out at the visitors.

'Settle down children, settle down now please,' the soft, but commanding voice of Mrs

Timpson executed its meaning effectively.

Father and son were both wearing denim and their trademark dark green polo shirts. Joseph respectfully removed his baseball cap and George winked at Lucy from behind his posh black-rimmed glasses and placed the bag he was holding down at his feet.

Lucy and Joseph exchanged a silent greeting. He seemed very subdued; he didn't share the ease of his father.

Joseph had been in some tricky situations in his time to say the least, but he was more nervous than he had ever been as he listened to Mrs Timpson's introduction. He glanced across at his father who was standing with his hands clasped in front of him. His face bore as much excitement as the children's. He would make a fantastic grandfather. He had certainly been a great father – and indeed still was. But he was more than that: he was his best friend. At that moment, it dawned on Joseph that he needed his dad now, just as much as these vulnerable kids needed theirs. He knew his darkest secrets and had shared his pain, much to the detriment of his own contentment.

Keeping his line of vision high above the wondrous stares of the children, Joseph thumbed the peak of his cap with the apprehension of a man ill at ease with his position.

'So let's give a warm welcome to Mr Dalton, Sr. and Mr Dalton, Jr.'

The tiny patter of their infantile palms set George springing into action. He won the crowd over instantly with the promise of gifts. He had thoughtfully brought each child a colourful pair of gardening gloves, which they were instructed to wear for use later on. Joseph played the dutiful assistant and handed out their gifts and even helped some of the little ones put them on.

George was truly magnificent, and after a child-friendly description of what their work entailed, he went on to describe the science and wonders of horticulture, and how all life, animal and human, relied on it so heavily.

He even tackled the complex subject of photosynthesis with impressive simplicity and eloquence.

A sure sign of his success was Mrs Timpson's silence, as she had often been compelled to intervene with previous guests when the flow of words had dried up. George showed masterful skill in involving his son as well. Joseph seemed to benefit from his father's infectious confidence and began to answer the minihecklers' questions, no matter how obscure they were.

Lucy paid special attention to her little friend Sam as he knelt, quietly taking it all in.

Professionally, it was wrong to have a favourite, but the heart doesn't understand rules and regulations. She shared an affinity with this little boy. Maybe it was his situation, but whatever the case, he certainly occupied her thoughts more than was professionally acceptable.

'OK then, hands up, who wants to grow their own

flower?' Rapturous calls of 'me, me, me,' answered George's question, along with fourteen sets of hands swaying in the air like little flowers themselves. George asked Mrs Timpson for permission to take one of the tables outside, which was gladly granted. Chloe sprang to her feet and opened the double doors that led to a small tarmac courtyard.

Joseph grabbed the bag of compost he had left in the corridor, and Lucy, along with Mrs Timpson, carried one of the small, child-scale tables out into the sunshine. A row of little brown plastic pots were lined up, and aprons were donned on the wise instruction of the veteran teacher.

The children ran around in the fresh air, full of excitement, except for one little girl who had Down's syndrome. She clung to Joseph's leg with a smile as big and bright as the summer sun. He held his hands out awkwardly, unsure of what to do.

'That's our cuddle monster,' Lucy smiled. He appeared utterly taken aback by the honest show of affection. 'She doesn't bite,' Lucy said, seeing an excuse to talk to him. She knotted the last apron and stepped over to them.

He looked so vulnerable. Somehow the balance of control had reversed: he was obviously out of his comfort zone.

'Talk to her,' Lucy encouraged.

'Hello... what's your name?'

'Amy,' came the shy reply. He looked back at Lucy for further guidance, with an almost childlike stare. She encouraged him with a nod, her smile affected by the touching awkwardness of the scene.

'Amy... that's a beautiful name. Can I see your face?' She raised her head slowly, fixing her big hazel eyes upon him.

'Wow, aren't you gorgeous.' That was it – the barrier had been broken by her look of pure innocence, an innocence that wasn't aware of any disability that she one day would be all too aware of.

'I love flowers, and I love you too.' Her face was hidden from view once again, her arms unyielding in their tight grip.

'And how old are you, Amy?'

'Six,' her face popped up to answer, then hid away again.

'Six years old. You're a big girl now, eh? Do you want to show me how to plant a sunflower seed, because I'm not sure if I know how to do it?' he said, softening his gruff voice to a gentle rumble.

'I know how to do it!' she exclaimed. Releasing his leg from its captivity, she took his hand and pulled him down to his knees. Joseph was guided by Amy, who imitated what she perceived as adult behaviour with glorious animation.

George was surrounded by eager hands and was sprinkled with soil. Chloe had been instructed to make tea and coffee for the visitors, and Mrs Timpson had also disappeared somewhere. Having imparted her knowledge, Amy decided that George would benefit from her tutoring and directed Joseph to carry on as she had instructed, before skipping away.

Lucy had been observing Sam with curiosity. He was standing near George but hadn't taken his eyes off Joseph. Spotting the vacancy Sam shuffled his way over to Joseph. Lucy took a step back, interested to see how they would interact with each other.

Sam tugged on the back of Joseph's T-shirt to gain his attention. He looked over his shoulder and saw the little golden-haired boy gazing up at him, his rich, deep-brown eyes striking against the paleness of his skin. The polo shirt he wore was several sizes too big for his slight frame and just about scraped in to the category of white.

'Hello, little man, what's your name?'

They made eye contact, and the child immediately looked away.

'Samuel Crispin. I'm six and a half and I like trains and lawnmowers and hats.' There was very little pause between his words. Tellingly, he was eyeing up Joseph's cap that he had placed in the centre of the table. Joseph turned around to face him and sat on the floor to take the weight off his knees.

'Everyone calls me Sam – you can call me Sam.'

'Nice to meet you, Sam. My name is Joseph, but you can call me Joe if you like.'

The boy's clothes bore the signs of previous owners. His grey trousers, a lighter shade at the knees, were several inches shy of his scuffed black shoes, which were wrinkled with the evidence of many miles travelled.

'Mr Joe, do you have a lawnmower?'

'Yes, we have three.'

'Can I see one?' He began to rock from side to side, rubbing the palms of his hands together.

'I don't have one here today, I'm sorry, Sam.'

The little boy's hands fell to his sides with disappointment and he ran the worn seam of his trousers between his thumb and finger.

'I've got a picture of one. Do you want to see it?'

His hands shot back up and he flapped them both like

he had burnt his fingers.

'Yes please.' He began to shake them even more vigorously. Seeing Joseph's perplexed

expression, Lucy stepped in to explain. 'He flaps his hands when he's excited.'

'Oh, I see.'

Joseph delved into his pocket, took out his wallet and pulled out a business card that was gnarled at the corners. He handed the card over which showed a picture of a man pushing a lawnmower.

'There you go, how's that?'

Sam took it and held it with both hands, his eyes examining every square millimetre.

'Mr Joe, can I keep this?' His attention was still fixed on the card.

'Yeah, of course you can.'

'Thank you so much, Mr Joe, you're the bestest man ever.'

Joseph looked over at Lucy, and they exchanged slightly cheerless smiles.

Sam reeled off both phone numbers on the card, one of which was Joseph's, the other his father's. Lucy had already checked both against Lady Lavinia's numbers, no match.

'Do you have a best friend, Mr Joe?'

'Yes I do. He's right there,' Joseph pointed to his father.

Sam finally took his eyes off the card and followed the pointing finger.

'My dad. Is your dad your best friend?'

The delicate child, small, even for his age, tellingly didn't answer. It sharpened Joseph's observation of him.

The boy was in the years of life that should have been blissfully ignorant of the woes of the world, but the dark circles under his eyes and his sallow complexion suggested otherwise. He cut a very lonely figure for one so young.

Then, without a single word, Sam wandered back into the classroom, Joseph watched him go, open-mouthed.

'Did I say something wrong?' he asked Lucy.

She too, looked forlorn. 'No, I'll explain later.' Her eyes diverted from Joseph, and he watched her face flush as her hand cupped her mouth. Like a river ready to burst its banks, her eyes threatened to spill.

He turned his head to the right to see what it was that was having such an effect on her. Sam was tottering back to them carrying a tatty old brown teddy. Its big shiny black eyes matched the sadness of the boy's. The aged toffee-coloured toy was missing an ear and its nose had been crudely stitched back together.

'This is Charlie, he's my bestest friend in the whole world. Miss Lucy gave him to me.'

The lady in question turned away, dabbing her eyes.

'Do you want to hold him? You can if you want to.'

'I'd love to.'

Sam knelt down next to Joseph and held out the sorry-looking bear. 'You'll have to give him back though.' He gripped his friend tightly.

Joseph smiled tenderly at the boy. 'I promise.' The little fingers opened.

'Let's have a look at him, then...' Joseph gave the toy a general examination. 'What are all these black dots?' He took a closer look. 'Are they—'

'They're burns,' Sam said, matter-of-factly.

'Burns?'

'Cigarette burns,' Lucy explained, arms folded lips pursed.

'Sometimes Charlie is naughty, and Daddy gets angry at him.'

'Does he now? And does he get angry with you?'

Another unanswered question. Sam held out his meagre hand; the tips of each minute nail were black with dirt.

Joseph ruffled the fur of the toy, as you would a friendly dog, then handed him back. 'He

looks very old. Have you had him long?'

'I got him at Christmas.' Sam took the bear into his embrace, uneasy at Joseph's interest

in him.

'Christmas? He's had a hard life hasn't he? And did you have lots of other presents?'

Sam's face turned to the sky while he pondered the question. 'Well... I got Charlie, and... I got... some chocolate biscuits too...'

That was clearly the end of the Christmas gift list. It was becoming more and more arduous for Joseph to keep smiling while listening to the poor little boy. It was time to get onto another subject.

'Do you like stories, Sam?'

'I love stories. Charlie reads me a story every bedtime.' Having gained some confidence in Joseph, Sam was now making eye contact, albeit intermittently.

'I love stories too.'

'Will you tell me a bedtime story, Mr Joe?'

'What, now?'

'Noooo, silly, it's not bedtime now. I mean when it's real bedtime.' He made full contact visually, and emotionally.

Sadness was draped like a heavy blanket over the shoulders of this boy. Empathy spilled from

Joseph's heart, he raised his hand and ruffled the mop of blond hair. Sam's enquiring eyes held their nerve waiting for an answer. Joseph had never been comfortable with lying, especially to a child that lived a life of utter disappointment. But there was some comfort in the deception of brightening his days for a while. 'I'd love to, Sam,' he nodded, spreading his mouth as wide as he could to validate the hollow promise. 'Okay children, it's tidy-away time before we all go home,' they heard Mrs Timpson say.

She had made an appearance along with Mrs Shoesmith, the headteacher; a stern but fair woman of small stature. Her frizzy russet hair was backcombed into a huge bun, a style that had been all well and good in her heyday, but now only made her look dated.

'Bye, Mr Joe,' Sam said, standing up and going to join his contemporaries.

'Hey, Sam,' Joseph said. Sam stood in the doorway, waiting, while Joseph used the table to push himself to his feet. Joseph picked up his cap and went over to Sam.

'Why don't you have this? I think it will look better on you.'

The little boy's neck was craned right back, looking up at Joseph towering over him. His whole face lifted with the effect of the kind gesture.

'Really?'

Joseph placed the cap on his head, and the peak slipped down over his face. Sam tipped it back with his free hand.

'It fits me!' A semblance of colour had seeped into his

delighted face.

'Mind how you go, Sam. And take good care of Charlie.'

'I will. Thanks for my presents, Mr Joe.' Off he went, teddy bear in one hand and the peak of his new, old cap in the other.

Lucy busied herself clearing things away while Mrs Shoesmith was around. All the time watching man and boy, teeth clenched trying to keep it together. What was he trying to do to her? She had wanted him to be hopeless with the children. She had wanted him to be stand-offish and cold, but he wasn't. He was warm, kind, and utterly charming, and Lucy hated him for it, for making her admiration grow.

Joseph returned to Lucy, who was lining up all the brown plastic plant pots against the wall. She looked up from her crouched position, pretending she hadn't noticed his approach.

'Oh, hi. Thank you for making a fuss of Sam.'

'It was a pleasure.'

A helping hand lowered; Lucy took it and got to her feet, savouring the feel of her skin on his. She released his fingers with some reluctance.

'So what is the story with Sam, anyway?'

The face that haunted her nights was now present in her day. He wasn't making small talk; it was a genuine question. *Why couldn't Mark be more like this?*

'Where do I begin? Sam has autism, which is a lifelong developmental condition that affects how he communicates and relates to others, and the world in general.'

She filled her lungs with oxygen and let it seep from

her lips that were about to tell the history of Samuel Crispin.

'But that's not all he has to contend with. He was born to a mother and father who care more about feeding their drug and alcohol addiction than feeding their child. He's been in and out of care since he was a baby. His mother has spent just about half her life in prison for prostitution and drug-pushing. He lives with his father, locked in a dingy first-floor flat, and every night he sleeps in a dirty bed.'

The speed at which she spoke had increased with her frustration, which was born from the disabling feeling of powerlessness.

'Why isn't he in care now?'

'Because his shit of a father has wised up over the years – he knows how to play the system. The only reason he wants Sam is for the welfare benefits.'

'What about social services? Don't they check up on him?'

The subject matter had rendered her usual nervousness around Joseph impotent, as all thoughts focused on Sam.

'He has regular checks, but he knows how to keep things just about acceptable and taking

a child from a parent is always the very last resort.

'The fact that he has no interaction with anyone outside of school is not a crime. Or that his clothes are old and dirty, and he lives in a world without love or compassion, or any understanding of his disability…' Her voice stumbled for a moment.

Joseph folded his arms, his face stern.

'Without the right guidance and care that boy will be lost to the world, and he'll spend his whole life scared and confused… I'm sorry.' The tips of her fingers smoothed the ripples on her brow.

'What for? For caring? You're a good woman, Lucy Eaton. Don't ever be sorry for caring; it's what sets you apart.'

She had tried to have this conversation with Mark so many times. Why couldn't he have said that, just once? Let her know that there was a quality about her that he admired other than her ability to keep the house tidy and make sure the bills were paid on time. Instead, it had to come from the one man that it shouldn't have. The sedate tones of his voice eased the pain of one ailment, but accelerated the sickness of another. Lucy's love for Mark was on the edge of extinction, not helped, of course, by his self-destructive temperament.

'It's just that I see so much potential in him: he's such a loving little boy, although he doesn't like to be cuddled or hugged. But that's one barrier I hope to break down in time.'

'I'm sure you will, Lucy. I'm sure you will.'

'Black coffee, no sugar.' Chloe said, returning with the visitors' drinks

'Thank you, Chloe.' She was witness to the heart-melting Dalton smile, which, judging by Chloe's face, lived up to its reputation. Even though Joseph was twice her age, his good looks hadn't gone unappreciated.

Joseph was beckoned over by Mrs Timpson, and Lucy began the task of getting the children ready for home, along with Chloe.

'Mr Dalton, I was just telling Mrs Shoesmith how entertaining both you and your father have been this afternoon,' Mrs Timpson introduced him to the matriarch. She had a big presence for such a short woman, barely five foot, even in heels.

'We've been booked to do another gig, Joseph,' said George, with some delight.

'We would love you to come back in a few weeks to give another talk to the children of

Class 6.' Mrs Shoesmith had a very direct way of speaking. 'We have plans to develop a garden and vegetable patch for the children to tend. I'm sure you will help to fire their enthusiasm. And we would very much appreciate your expertise.'

'We're happy to help in any way we can,' said George, finishing his tea.

'Good! And will we be seeing you at our fundraising fete this Saturday?'

'I hadn't mentioned it to them actually,' confessed Mrs Timpson with a pinch of unease.

The headmistress then went on to explain, in some detail, the need to raise funds to pay for the planned sensory room and swimming pool, because of the government's woeful levels of funding for schools in general.

'I have a prior engagement, but Joseph will be sure to show his support.' His father took it upon himself to volunteer his son's support.

'Wonderful. Well, I'm sure you two gentlemen would like to go home now, so let me thank you for your time today, and I look forward to seeing you both again very soon.' On completion of her business like statement, she removed herself with great pace.

Mrs Timpson added to the appreciation and thanked

them profusely before helping her

colleagues to round up the troops. The two men collected their belongings and called out their farewell to all the kids, which was returned with a joyful, inharmonious chorus.

'Lucy, will we see you tomorrow?' asked George. Joseph was stood in the corridor holding the door open.

'Yes you will.' She kissed him on the cheek. 'Thank you so much for today, you were both brilliant.'

She rubbed George's arm affectionately, then noticed that Joseph was peering into the classroom with a half-cocked smile. She looked over her shoulder to see the cause of his amusement. Sam was standing in front of the crescent-moon-shaped mirror, admiring his new hat with the great pleasure. of a child that is utterly unspoilt in every sense of the word. The simple sight brought joy to her heart; she turned her view back to the bearer of the gift. 'Thank you.'

He remained silent. The cowboy nod gave notice of his understanding.

'Bye, Lucy.' George's voice was low and considerate. He had spotted the humbling sight too.

'Bye, guys.'

The door closed and they made their way along the corridors, which were decorated with artwork from the school's population, and then out to the car park, now full of cars, school buses and parents waiting to collect their children.

'That went well didn't it, eh, Joseph?'

'Better than I expected.'

Their travelling speed slowed to a crawl as they reached the point where they had to part.

George was parked by the green, corroding cast-iron gates, Joseph in the row

closest to the building.

'Son… I'm very proud of you today, it's a step in the right direction.'

The clouds drifted along in their unhurried way, exposing the afternoon sun. George squinted; under the harsh light that unforgivingly showed all of his 72 years spent on this earth.

'Yeah,' Joseph nodded, lost for words, but all too aware of what a burden he had been.

'Right then, I'll see you in the morning.' George's voice adopted a whimsical rhythm realising that he had picked the wrong place for a heartfelt conversation.

'See you in the morning, Dad.'

His father turned and steadily made his way back to his pick-up, hands in pockets, head

held low, ruminating perhaps about the afternoon's events. Joseph took a moment to watch the man that had spent most of his life safeguarding him, and yet still was not shrinking from his responsibilities.

'Hey, Dad.'

Most of the male occupants of the car park looked to see who was calling them, along with George. The distance between them didn't dilute the charged silence as Father and son stared at each other with a reticent understanding that only comes from a close bond.

'Any time, kiddo.' George spared him the words, and giving a wink, continued on his path.

Kiddo. He hadn't called him that since he was a little boy. He was lucky to have a man who transcended the title father.

Floods of children rushed towards their parents with happy faces, some carrying paintings, others proudly clutching cardboard sculptures.

Joseph pulled back the cover on his pick-up. He put the bags of spare pots and gloves in the back, clipped the cover back into place, and climbed into the cab. His hand reached for his absent cap out of habit, forgetting he had given it away. While the children dispersed, he spent five minutes tidying the dashboard which was littered with paperwork and receipts. Putting his seatbelt on, he started the engine and checked his mirrors.

In the passenger wing mirror was a tall thin man in grey sweatpants and an old green checked shirt. The noise of the engine masked what he was saying, but it was clear that he was annoyed about something. His image moved out of frame, and was replaced with another; it was Sam. He was still wearing the hat, carrying his bag with a broken demeanour.

Joseph cut the engine and dropped the windows.

'Come on, you little shit, I've got things to do! Fucking hurry up!'

A switch flicked in Joseph, he had been in a nice, calm, positive mood up until that point. He unclipped the seatbelt, climbed out and closed the door quietly. Sam was still some way behind the man. He knew this must be his father from what Lucy had told him.

Joseph was hidden behind the large 4 x 4 but had a clear view through the back windows. The boy's father had stopped in front of the dented bonnet of an old red Honda. He had a hard, thin, drawn face. The corners of his mouth reached for the floor, a symptom of a tortured mind that had developed from existing in a chemical world.

'I should make you fucking walk home for being so slow!'

Joseph's fingers joined forces to form two hard balls of flesh and bone. He instinctively assessed the target. The thin body was curved over, craving the sustenance of more than just alcohol, his mind wasn't the only thing that was weak.

'Come on you little cunt,' the malnourished face spewed out the words with unbelievable hate.

Joseph's jaw clamped shut. It was taking all his willpower to hold back, not because he wanted to ignore what was happening, but because he wasn't sure if he would know when to stop.

The boy finally caught up. His face was still lowered towards the floor, arms close by his sides.

'What's that you've got on your fucking head?' The weasel quickly scanned the car park to see if anyone was around before snatching the hat from his head, sending Sam stumbling forwards. 'Who gave you this? That fucking do-gooding bitch Miss Eaton?'

Hold back… hold back, Joseph told himself, burning with rage.

He opened the door and threw the hat into the old car, Sam didn't dare raise his eyes from the ground. Joseph bit down on his knuckle. *Just get in your truck and drive away, or this won't end well.*

Sam's father crouched down in front of the quivering wreck of a child. 'You better start showing me some fucking respect, you little cunt. Do you want a cuddle…?'

He thrust his open hand towards Sam's face, stopping just an inch before striking him, causing the boy to wince like a frightened animal. 'Or a hug?' The open hand turned into a fist.

Jesus Christ, that's what he thinks hugs and cuddles are? That was the tipping point; to walk away would be to turn his back on any humanity he possessed.

Joseph came out of his cover and strode toward the mark who had his back to him, shoving Sam into the back seat. He would give him a fighting chance before hospitalising him. The deadly weapons raised, ready for attack.

'Mr Dalton!' The shrill voice stopped him in his tracks

He turned around to see Mrs Shoesmith, arms folded, head held high.

'I'd like a word with you, please.'

Joseph looked back to his intended destination.

'Now!' she demanded.

The car door slammed. Sam's father seemed surprised to see a stranger in such close proximity to him. He bravely – and foolishly gave Joseph a grimacing look, unaware of how close he had been to serious harm. The beat-up old car spluttered into life and stuttered away.

Joseph caught a glimpse of Sam through the cloud of blue smoke, sobbing in the back seat. The car faltered beyond the borders of the school and out of sight.

Mrs Shoesmith was no doubt determined to show him who was boss and stood firm, making Joseph go to her. He approached the miniature lady with mixed emotions, relieved that he had been removed from the situation, but frustrated that it hadn't been resolved.

'Mr Dalton, I don't think it is your place to interfere in

matters that have no concern to you.'

'Did you see or hear any of what that boy was just subjected to?'

'I did.' The concrete mask remained in place.

'And you expect me to let that pass?'

'I expect you to let us deal with school problems, Mr Dalton.'

'And are you dealing with it?' A slight protrusion in her jaw insinuated her lack of experience with being the one having questions fired at.

'The authorities are fully aware of Samuel's situation.'

'So what are they doing about it?'

'Mr Dalton, who do you think you are to question me about a child who has had no connection to you whatsoever?' She attempted to shout him down like one of her pupils.

'I'm a man who will not turn a blind eye to child abuse.'

Each continued staring at the other, neither prepared to give way.

'And what did you plan to do, mmm…? Have a little *chat* with him?'

Joseph remained silent but steadfast.

'No, I thought not. I don't expect a blunt instrument like you to understand this, but violence solves nothing, Mr Dalton.'

'Blunt instrument? That's a very presumptuous thing for the head of a special needs school to say.'

A twitch of her shrivelled lips showed she conceded the point.

'And how often do you think Sam gets slapped and punched around for being a hindrance to his junkie father.' She shifted uncomfortably on her spot. 'You can bet that what you just saw was only the tip of the iceberg. Violence should always be the last resort, but the ugly truth is that for some, it's the only thing that works. If I witness that again, I will not fail to act.'

Seeing no point in continuing a conversation which could be unending, Joseph walked back to his truck.

'And the soles of your boots will never touch the ground within these gates, Mr Dalton, you can be sure of that.'

He opened the cab door and paused. 'Maybe not, but at least I'll be able to sleep at night… can you?' He climbed in, slammed the door and drove away.

Mrs Shoesmith defiantly stood her ground and remained in his rear view mirror until he had turned the corner.

If only his parting comment had been true. The thing was, he didn't sleep at night; he

hadn't for a long time – not without the aid of Jack Daniels. That night was no different to any other, except now there were two more people keeping him awake. One was a good woman that deserved a happy, complication-free life; the other a mere child that lived his life under the threat of violence, confused and afraid.

CHAPTER SEVENTEEN

Mark acted as if everything was tickety-boo and not a cross word had passed between them. The only evidence of mild guilt was the spaghetti bolognese and glass of wine that was waiting for her when she arrived home. Lucy played along with the pretence; she was too exhausted for anything else. It had been an emotional day for many reasons; reasons that should have been left behind the moment her key slid into the lock, but the shadow of her thoughts could not be escaped. Bland conversation accompanied the cuisine equivalent. Mark chatted away about his plans to transform the bathroom, while Lucy used the act of eating to reminisce about her time with Lady Lavinia, nodding occasionally to give the impression of listening.

One sentence in particular was at the forefront of her mind: *'I see that you don't like facing up to the hard work that a relationship entails.'* There was definitely some truth to that statement. Mark certainly was hard work. Maybe she was losing sight of reality, captivated by a handsome stranger, who by his father's own admission, was with a different woman from one week to the next, no doubt breaking hearts as he went. She needed to get her head out of the clouds and focus on what was real.

Their relationship wasn't perfect, whose was? Bottling things up was a sure-fire way to

destruction. They needed time to get to know one another again. A holiday, that's what they needed – just the two of them. Once the garden was finished. They could fly somewhere, anywhere, for secluded, lazy days and romantic nights.

Lucy was looking for reasons for feelings she didn't understand, as all people did when the legs of life started to wobble. There's a need to make sense of things, to have control, even if it's only an imitation of it. That day would be the death of her silly schoolgirl crush. In a couple of weeks the garden would be complete and they would return to being strangers to one another's lives once more.

It seemed Mother Nature agreed that there should be some distance between them. It rained night and day for the next three days, halting all work. George called every day to update her on the predicted weather forecast and also to have a friendly chat. Lucy resisted the urge to enquire about Joseph, determined to stick to her self-imposed prohibition. She spent most of her time at school, helping to prepare for Saturday's fete.

On Thursday evening, George made his usual phone call. Finally there was to be a break in the weather and it would be all systems go for Friday. Lucy's stomach fluttered at the thought of seeing Joseph the next day, having been weaned off his image for a few days.

Mark was out having drinks with *'the boys'* so the house

was quiet. But silence holds no peace for a doubtful mind. Lucy put on some music and, feeling the need for distraction, decided to call Suzie. She hadn't heard from her since the party, which was unusual. She flopped down on the couch having found a station playing elevator music, and searched through her contacts until she came to '*Floozy Suzie*'. They both had nicknames for each other: '*Loose Lucy*' was hers, and no more flattering. Lucy let the phone ring for longer than she usually would have. She wanted to speak to her friend, and despite her new resolution to avoid all things Joseph-related, she had been plagued with thoughts about whether Suzie had called him.

'Hey chick,' Suzie eventually answered, with her usual zest.

'Hey Suzie. Not interrupting you, am I?'

'No, I was in the shower. I've got a hot date tonight.'

Lucy's whole body braced itself for the verbal impact. Her free hand kneaded the decorative pillow that lay upon her lap as she silently prayed for it not to be Joseph.

'Anyone I know?' The panic was well hidden.

'Might be…' The childish retort had Lucy up on her feet, still clutching the cushion.

'It's not Joseph, is it?' She gave the most unconvincing chuckle and sank her nails into the soft pillow.

'Joey? He doesn't answer his bloody phone.'

Lucy felt a sudden sense of relief, quite the opposite of what she had been expecting.

'I've left him messages so I'm expecting a call back any day now.'

Any relief was short lived. Suzie wasn't ready to give up chasing him, but then what girl would be?

'How did it go with Sebastian?' She wanted to get

Suzie's thoughts as far away as possible from Joseph.

'Well, let's just say… his car isn't the only thing that's fast, and his talk *is* the only thing that's big.' That revelation was hardly surprising.

'I am sorry, Suzie. Has he had the bullet then?'

'Everyone deserves a second chance. When he calls, I'll agree to see him again. It would be rude not to, wouldn't it?'

'Absolutely.' Having given Sebastian what he wanted, Lucy doubted that call would ever transpire.

'How's your week been?'

'Good thanks, we're busy at school getting ready for the fete.'

'Oh shit, I forgot all about that. I'm so sorry, Lu: I can't make it.'

'Can you not?'

'No, sorry, chick, I can't.' No further explanation was offered, which was strange, as they had never kept secrets from each other. 'You don't need me there anyway. I'm sure it will be a great day.'

'Yeah, I am looking forward to it. So, are you going to tell me who the mystery man is?'

'Let me see how tonight goes.' Suzie was never usually this guarded. 'I'm going to have to go, Lu. I haven't done my hair yet, and I'm meant to be leaving in half an hour.'

'Okay, I'll let you go – have fun. I'll talk to you later. Bye, Suzie.'

'Bye, Lu.'

She hung up, then stared at the screen, wondering who it was Suzie was seeing. Clearly someone that Lucy knew. Suzie was certainly keeping all her options open, that's for sure. Of course, that was her prerogative. The thing that bothered Lucy most, was that Joseph was one of those options.

Friday arrived, bringing with it relief from the rain. Lucy was feeling in an efficient mood and made a list of all the things she wanted to get done that day. Mark was still in bed recovering from another late night. She had heard him return, but pretended to be asleep for fear of possible drunken amorous advances.

George and his men arrived at their usual time. Lucy delivered their customary hot drinks and had a little chat with George before removing herself from harms way to make toffee apples for the following day's event.

It took her a couple of hours, but Lucy finally completed her torture of the innocent fruit. They had been staked through the heart and then mercilessly dunked in red-hot chocolate, before suffering the humiliation of being covered in pink and yellow sprinkles.

Her victims sat cooling on the greaseproof paper, while Lucy industriously set about filling the prize bags, ready for the lucky dip. A faint tap at the front door made her stop what she was doing, one hand full of sweets and the other holding a blue polka-dot bag. She listened, not sure if her ears weren't playing tricks on her. There was another series of knocks, louder this time. She dropped the sweets into the bag and went to see who the caller was. She opened the door and found Charles standing there, looking as dapper and well-groomed as ever.

'Good morning, Lucy!'

'Morning, Charles.'

'I didn't want to knock too loudly; I wasn't sure if you were out of bed yet as the curtains are still drawn.'

'I've been up for hours. Mark had a late night so he's

catching up on his sleep, come in.' She beckoned him in with a smile. 'Tea, coffee?'

'Tea please, Lucy, but only if it's not too much trouble.'

He shuffled his tasselled suede loafers on the bristled mat before he crossed the threshold.

'It's no trouble at all. How's Tabitha?'

'She's… her usual self shall we say.'

Lucy's chin dimpled in sympathy. 'Come through to the kitchen, you'll have to excuse the mess, I'm making goodies for the school fete.'

'How wonderful.'

Lucy swished her open hand proudly over her creations like a magician's assistant.

'What do you think?'

'I must say they look delicious.'

'You can have one if you like.'

Lucy topped up the kettle, smiling to herself at the thought of Charles munching on a toffee apple while dressed for dinner at the Ritz.

'It's a tad early for me, but thank you anyway.' He ventured over to the window. 'I see Mr Dalton and Co. have returned.'

The skin around his eyes creased and folded as he focused, signifying a man that had let vanity get in the way of necessity.

'Yes, I'm so glad. Sugar?'

'One please.'

'It all looks a bit bare now they've taken all the rubbish out. We need to start putting things back in.'

'Well you certainly have the right man for the job; George is a man of great integrity.' He made his way back to the toffee apples, perhaps tempted by her offer.

'Isn't he just? I think he's wonderful. To be honest, I'll be sad to see them go.'

George and Charles were two very different characters; but Lucy was equally fond of both.

He was obviously very wealthy and successful, but there was no arrogance about him.

'There you go.'

She placed his drink on the island, and had made the assumption that he only ever drank tea from a cup *and* saucer.

Lucy took the weight off her feet and sat on one of the stools.

'Take a seat, Charles.' She tapped the granite work surface of the island.

'Why, thank you.' He viewed the modern seating with some trepidation, before climbing onto a stool with all the awkwardness she would have expected of a traditional man of his age.

'So, a big day at the school tomorrow?'

'Yes, the kids are going to love it.'

'I'm sorry we can't make it. We've got so much planned: I'm taking Tabitha to our house in Verdant, Vendée.' His pronunciation was perfect.

'The renovations are almost complete. She hasn't visited for some time now, so the transformation will be a nice surprise for her.'

'It sounds idyllic.'

'Mmm.'

Taking a sip of his tea, he placed the cup back onto its saucer. 'I have to admit, it's a beautiful place. Used to be an old farmhouse, set in rolling hills with ten acres of land. It is secluded, but that's what appealed to us. I'm hoping the break will do her good. So, tell me, how much do you need to raise for the… swimming pool and garden?'

'And a sensory room, yes.'

'Sensory room,' he said, poking his finger in the air. 'I knew I'd forgotten something.'

'That's the scary part. The total build cost is estimated to be between £850,000 and £1.1 million.'

Her eyebrows raised as she mentioned the numerical milestone.

'Right,' he said. The figures clearly didn't have the same effect on Charles as they did on Lucy.

'And what funds do you have at this current time?'

'£243,000, so we still have a long way to go. We're applying for extra funding, and if that's successful, it will push us closer to our target.'

'But it won't get you there?'

'No. Maybe halfway, but at least that would mean we could start work on the sensory room.'

'I see.' He stroked the short spikes of his carefully trimmed moustache with youthful-looking fingers, the sign of a man that had avoided hard labour for most of his life. 'May I volunteer a suggestion?'

'Please do, we would be grateful for any advice.'

The suggestion remained hidden as he deliberated what he was about to say. His expression had switched to one of great seriousness that all men of standing seemed to bear, as though the fate of the world hinged on their every decision.

A faint groan preceded his words. 'Dear me, I shouldn't really, Tabitha would be livid if she knew.'

Lucy wasn't sure if he was talking to her; it appeared he was externalising his thoughts.

'I'm sorry, I'm rambling, aren't I? Let me explain: four years ago now, I suffered a massive heart attack, brought on by stress and long hours at work.'

'Oh my god.' It had never occurred to her that he had retired because of ill health, he looked so fit.

'I made a lot of money for a small, but close-knit group of people, who I considered to be friends as well clients. However, upon my illness, they took their spoils and discarded our friendship.'

The disappointment was clearly still fresh. For any proud man, humiliation always left its mark.

'Charles, don't worry. It's very kind of you to offer, but I don't want to cause you any hassle, and I especially wouldn't want to put a strain on your health. You relax and enjoy your retirement. We'll find another way.'

He pondered Lucy's words with a knitted brow, his fingers tapping the white porcelain cup.

'No,' he said, sounding defiant and raising a few inches in his seat. 'I want to help. And what better cause could I apply myself to?'

Had he been offended? Did he think she thought him not up to the task? Whatever it was, his masculinity was firing on all cylinders.

'Are you sure, Charles?'

'I am. Now, what I'm about to suggest is no doubt unorthodox, but it will get you what you want, and quickly.' The sense of importance he had felt in his younger days had been summoned up, and he was clearly intent on reliving them.

'I'm all ears.' Lucy clasped her hands together and leant forward, eager to hear his expert advice.

'I'll prepare a detailed investment plan, with multiple

options and the predicted return listed for each one. I am happy to provide any credentials and proof of my highly successful, unblemished track record in investment banking. Once I have everything in order, we can make an appointment to present our proposal to the board of governors to invest the sum of £240,000, which, I can tell you now, will save you *years* in fundraising events. Plus, it will allow the children to enjoy the new additions sooner rather than later.'

He took a sip of his tea, his eyes bright with excitement of re-entering the arena that he once excelled in.

'Charles –'

'I know it's not going to be easy,' he interrupted, anticipating the hurdles she was about to lay before them.

'It certainly won't be easy; what it will be is impossible. They can't even paint the parking bays on the car park without having weeks of endless meetings. The politics are unbelievable.'

'I'd only need twenty minutes with them – surely that's not too much to ask?'

Lucy shook her head with a smile, touched by his eagerness to help.

'Charles, don't waste your time, I know they won't go for it.'

'Are you quite sure?

'I'm afraid so.' She couldn't help but feel disappointed. What he was proposing was far too revolutionary. In a world of bureaucracy, the wheels of progress turned very slowly.

'That's a damn shame. Narrow-mindedness cripples so many.' He attempted to cross his legs, but the stool began to pivot and he thought better of it, placing his hands on the surface of the island in an attempt to stop the rotation.

'It would be great to get things moving along – so many of the kids would benefit from having a pool.'

Sam had never even seen a swimming pool – or the ocean, for that matter. It was going to take years for them to raise the money, and considering the amount of time it would take to complete the project, Lucy knew that Sam might not even be there to see it.

'I have an idea,' declared Lucy.

'Is it my turn to be all ears?' joked Charles, flicking an elongated lobe.

'What if I was to invest my money? And donate any profits that I make to the school?'

The youthful finger returned to its grooming duties. 'That would be incredibly generous of you, Lucy. Maybe you should think about that one for a while and have a talk to Mark about it.'

'What is there to think about? My money or the school's – it doesn't make any difference. Mark and I have separate accounts. That was the easiest way to stop the disagreements about what we spend the money on – this way he doesn't have to know.'

Charles cautiously scratched the top of his head with his little finger, making sure not to displace a single hair. He gazed around the room as he pondered her suggestion.

'Are you entirely sure about this?'

She began to fill with excitement at the distant prospect of advancing the school's plans.

'You're confident it will have a successful outcome?'

'Absolutely,' he answered without hesitation. Lucy couldn't stop the joy from showing on her face.

'Well then, Mr St Clair, if your offer still stands, I will

gladly accept it.'

She extended her hand to seal the deal. Charles hesitated, his eyes fixing on Lucy's for a moment. Did he hear the voice of his wife dictating to him? Apparently not. His stare softened, and his moustache spread as he smiled.

'It will be my honour to assist you, Miss Eaton.' His hand made the journey to hers and the deal was set.

Lucy hunched her shoulders and gave an impromptu round of applause.

'Oh, I'm so excited! So what happens next?'

'First of all, young lady, I'm going to give you a few days to fully consider what you are proposing to undertake. And then, if you wish to proceed, I will discuss the finer points of my investment plan with you in full.' He had switched from neighbour to banker in the blink of an eye.

Lucy knew she was in good hands. There was an air of professional capability that didn't allow doubt to draw a breath.

'And as a sign of my utmost confidence in this venture being nothing but a success, I will personally guarantee your investment, however large it may be,' he continued.

She wasn't entirely sure of what he meant by that. 'You'll personally guarantee?'

'What I am saying is, in the highly unlikely event of the investment making a loss, I will

personally underwrite all and any losses, guaranteeing that there is absolutely no risk to you whatsoever.'

She was stunned. 'Wow! Charles, I don't know what to say… I'm speechless.'

Close to tears at his benevolence, she slid off her stool and went over to give him a hug.

Her fingertips met each other across the back of this small-framed gentleman. Words could not express the enormous gratitude she felt, and neither could she: her throat was constricted by the affecting generosity.

'You are very welcome, my dear Lucy.'

She hung on, gently rocking him from side to side on his stool, until her emotions unlocked the gate to her voice. She pulled away, her hands resting on the padded shoulders of his blazer 'thank you, Charles.'

'No, thank you, Lucy. You are allowing me to relive a life I thought was long gone.' His hands reached up and took hold of Lucy's. 'Now, the only thing that I ask of you is that this remains our secret, because if Tabitha were to find out, it would cause her untold stress.'

'My lips are sealed.'

'Good.' He released her hands and reached into his inside pocket. 'I know in the grand scheme of things that this is just a drop in the ocean, but every penny helps.' He pulled out an oblong piece of paper and handed it to Lucy.

'Charles! Really?' It was a cheque for £5,000 made out to Tall Trees Special Needs School. 'That's too much!'

He frowned away her comment and took a sip of his tepid tea. 'Nonsense, we're happy to help a worthy cause. Besides, we have more money than we could ever need, and no children of our own to leave it to. We support a small group of charities that we feel are very worthy.' The cup clinked against the saucer on its docking. Charles tentatively climbed down from his perch and buttoned his tailor-made, brown dogtooth jacket. 'And yours is one of them.'

Lucy was still holding the cheque in both hands. 'I don't know what to say…'

'You have said enough, my dear. You have a good heart, and that must be applauded and encouraged. Now I don't want to hear any more about it, okay?' His head dropped, a lone eyebrow raised in faux-sternness.

'Yes, sir!'

'I will leave you to your duties as I have a suitcase to pack. We fly out tonight.' He leaned in for the air kiss and Lucy stretched out her neck, making her cheek available.

'We may stay the week; it depends on how my good lady wife is.'

He made his way back to the entrance door that was now to be his exit.

'Give my regards to Mark – and George.' Unlatching the door, he stepped out onto the mat.

'Is that the most expensive cup of tea you've ever had?' Lucy joked.

'I'm sure it will yield the best return of *any* investment I have ever made, my dear Lucy.'

He almost had her close to tears again. He didn't wait for, or indeed want, any more praise.

'*Au revoir,*' sprightly, he took his leave with a hand held in the air. 'Good luck for tomorrow!'

'Thank you, Charles. Have a safe trip.'

She waited until he was hidden from her view before closing the door. Lucy sat on the stairs with her head in her hands, bowled over by how lucky she had been to have met such wonderful kind men as Charles and George. Joseph attempted to add himself to that elite line-up, but was refused entry.

Now full of determination and psyched up about the rosy future for Tall Trees, she felt in control enough to allow Joseph to enter her thoughts.

Her handbag was in what had now become its designated place, on the fourth step up. Seeing it there reminded her of the obligation she had promised to fulfil. Dipping her hand inside she retrieved the folded piece of paper that was to be delivered to Joseph. She didn't open it: the contents of the plain white piece of paper had proved to be too affecting on her first viewing.

Friday morning held little interest for Mark; he waited for the afternoon before he opened his eyes to the world. Unlike Charles, he cared not for what time of day toffee apples should be consumed, so his breakfast consisted of a combination of chocolate and fruit, washed down with a Coke.

He spent the remainder of the afternoon slobbering around the house with his hands in his baggy white shorts, like a tourist without a map; periodically taking a rest on the couch to watch the adverts for various amazing new exercise machines that could transform your body in just three minutes a day. Once fully recovered he would make yet another pilgrimage to the sacred fridge to gaze upon its contents, thinking somehow that there would be an item of food he wished to devour that he hadn't spotted on his four other trips that afternoon.

He huffed and puffed around the house like the Big Bad Wolf. Lucy knew he was waiting for her blessing to go out. The only reason he was there was because he felt he had to be, as he very rarely was. She let him simmer in his stupor, busy enough to not be annoyed by his moping. With tasks to complete, the fingers on the clock seemed to march double time and the end of the working day soon arrived for the team.

Lucy kept her distance from the gardeners all day, as

she had intended to, but was yet to deliver the folded piece of paper. Having finished making her third Victoria sponge, Lucy dusted the icing sugar from her hands and picked up her delivery. Taking a deep breath she left the warm sugar-infused air of the kitchen to take in the earthy atmosphere of the open air.

George gave his usual daily update, telling her that the last three days of rain had been a blessing in disguise as it had softened the earth, making it easier to turn over. He wished her luck for tomorrow and needlessly explained his reasons for not being able to attend, apologising several times over before instructing Adam to get the envelope, which he dutifully did. George handed it to Lucy, leaving his muddy fingerprints on the pure white paper.

He told her the value of his donation, which was no match for Charles's but was equally as generous in terms of social status and income. Lucy thanked him in the same way she had her neighbourly benefactor. Kissing him on the cheek, he declared that she had "made his weekend" and left with a promise to return on Monday.

Joseph waved to his father and wheeled down the garden, a piece of machinery that looked like a medieval instrument of torture. Lucy waited for him, feeling guilty for breaking her own promise to herself.

He was wearing a new old brown baseball cap with white stitching and a mesh back. Her mouth became drier with every closing step his sullied boots took. The simple question and message she had to ask, held the intimidation of a speech to a crowd of hundreds.

'Lucy,' he said, stopping in front of her, still holding on to the handles of the machine.

'Love the new hat.'

He smiled, and suddenly her heart reminded her why she needed to keep her distance.

'Yeah, some kid swindled me out of my old one. I'm a sucker for a cute face.'

'Yes, your father told me you were.' His eyes pinched at her remark.

'Will we see you at some point tomorrow?' she added quickly, trying to cover her previous comment.

His eyes dropped to the cold, mud-caked steel of the machine in his grasp.

'I don't think I can make it tomorrow.'

'But you said you would.' Her disappointed reply drew his attention away from the machine.

'No, my dad said I would.'

'Oh…'

Joseph offered no further explanation.

'I'm sure you'll all have a good day. Enjoy your weekend, Lucy.' With that, man and machine moved on. She closed her eyes, mentally kicking herself for having virtually insisted that he attend. Lucy held up the paper she was meant to deliver. It seemed so contrived to give it to him now, but she had promised.

'Joseph.'

He stopped and turned his head a fraction.

'I was asked to give you this.' She walked over to him and held out the folded piece of paper.

Placing his load down, he wiped his hands on his chest before taking what was offered.

'What is it?' he asked, viewing it with some suspicion.

'Open it.'

He did, and Lucy watched him closely. His mouth parted slightly as if to take a silent gasp. She couldn't see his eyes because his head was held down, but the flickering of his lashes indicated that he was studying the picture Sam had drawn for him.

He saw a big stick man holding the hand of a little stick boy, both of them wearing hats and big smiles. They were standing among jagged green lines of the long grass, while an egg-shaped, bright yellow sun hung in the corner, shining down on them. The tip of his tongue ran over his top lip before it sealed together with its partner.

Lucy's tears had stained the paper from when she first read the simple message which was; 'to Mr Joe my bezt frinb iN the hole worlb.'

'He would love to see you tomorrow; he hasn't stopped talking about you all week.'

Joseph's fingers massaged the edges of the rectangle.

'I would, too...' Was that the right thing to say, she immediately asked herself. Maybe not, but it was the truth – how could the truth ever be wrong?

The magnetic picture continued to hold his attention, but finally, he folded it back together and slipped it into the side pocket of his shorts.

'What time does it start?' His voice was hushed.

'10.30.'

She needed to know his eyes had seen the need in hers before he left.

No wishes would be granted today. Joseph turned away, taking hold of the handles of his equipment, making sure his thoughts weren't on show.

'I'll see what I can do.' He moved on, out of sight, around the side of the house.

'Bye...'

The farewell fell short of its target. After being in his

company for but a moment her intentions had crumbled. It was wrong of her to have put him on the spot like that; he hadn't seemed very happy about it. With the evidence of how weak her self-restraint was, Lucy had to admit that it would be for the best if he didn't attend.

'Is it alright if I have a slice of this cake, babe?'

She turned to answer Mark's pointless question. The cake was already sliced and plated. The distinctive sound of Joseph's truck driving away stole her attention for a moment.

'Lu?'

'What?' Her head snapped up from its sagging position. 'Oh, yes. That's fine.'

'Cheers.'

Half of the generous slice was gone before he stepped foot back into the house.

Lucy had slipped back into that void between irrational and logical. Not everyone can have their cake and eat it.

CHAPTER EIGHTEEN

Lucy's suggestion of providing a school bus to pick up children was a success. Their parents welcomed – and in many cases needed – the respite.

She had volunteered her services as an escort, having already been to the school earlier that morning to drop off her wares.

The bus picked her up from her home and they travelled a 40 minute route, collecting excited children along the way. Sam was on that list; and in truth, he was the reason for her suggesting the pick-up/drop-off service. She knew full well that his father wouldn't have brought him and that he would welcome the chance to be rid of him for the day.

Sam was the last on the list. The quality of the view outside the window declined steadily as they drove deeper into the suburb where he lived. There was rubbish everywhere, lying where it had been dropped or where the wind had taken it. They passed row after row of houses, each one an exact replica of its conjoined twin, some of them barricaded with heavy metal shutters. None of them bore any welcoming or homely features whatsoever. Brick walls were tattooed with crude remarks and the street names of those who relished the infamy of making the place so squalid.

David, the driver, who had been singing along to pop music with the children, fell silent. He and Lucy exchanged troubled glances; they could find no redeeming qualities in the place. No greenery of any kind could be seen: concrete and brick covered every square inch. Broken glass and bits of wood lay strewn around randomly, as if a tornado had passed through. Her heart sank to see the jungle-like environment that Sam had to endure.

'7B, isn't it?' asked David.

'That's it there: the one with the old red car.' Lucy had never been there before, but recognised the beat-up vehicle.

They pulled up outside a row of three-storey flats. The iron railings that bordered a small space to the front of each block had been removed and the battered red Honda filled most of the space.

It was surrounded by junk: an old car battery, spare wheels and a soiled mattress that wasn't fit for a dog to lie on, never mind a human being

David tooted the horn, and the bus doors concertinaed open.

As Lucy stood on the steps, her eyes ascended to the second floor window. One of the panes of glass was broken and all daylight had been shut out by dark curtains,they began to ruffle, she was just about able to make out Sam's face through the grimy glass. Suddenly he was gone, and moments later he burst through   the communal door with a wide smile, running like the devil himself was chasing him, holding on to his precious hat.

Lucy stepped off the bus to clear his entry and welcome him.

'Good Morning, mister' she mustered as much enthusiasm as the oppressive environment would allow.

'Is Mr Joe coming today, Miss Lucy?' The peak of the cap fell down as he raised his face towards her.

She crouched in front of him. 'Where have you gone?' she asked, tipping the hat back.

'Oh! There you are!' Even when he smiled there was a shadow of sadness on his little face.

'Is he?' He was so excited. 'Because you said that he was, so that means he has to, doesn't it?'

Placing her hands on his slight shoulders, Lucy looked into those deep-brown, wondrous eyes of his, surprisingly, he held her gaze, keen for the answer, no doubt.

'Sam, we are going to have lots of fun today, I promise. But Mr Joe is very busy.' The brightness dimmed noticeably. 'So I don't think he can make it.'

To see so much disappointment on the face of a six-year-old, who never asked for anything from life, was hard to bear.

'But we're going to have the best day ever, okay?' she said.

Eye contact ceased. The top of the baseball cap was now where his face was. Her heart ached for him. If only he had known how much she wanted Joseph there too.

'I've got you a present.' The mention of a gift had no effect. 'When we get to school I'll give it to you. Now come on, mister, on you get.'

Lucy and Sam climbed on board. He was wearing the

same school uniform he had worn all week, which stank of cigarette smoke.

'Morning, young man,' David greeted him cheerily.

Sam kept his head down and raised his hand in acknowledgement.

Before taking her seat at the front of the bus, Lucy watched him fall listlessly into his seat and gaze out at the bleak view of his callously titled *home*.

'Let's get out of here, eh,' David said, closing the doors.

'Yeah, and quickly.'

The wheels on the bus went round and round as they drove through the ruins of the rundown area until the view was replaced by one they were more accustomed to. The music played and David was brilliant, encouraging all the children to sing along, getting them all into the spirit of things. All apart from one.

When they pulled into the car park the children all shot to their feet, seeing that there was a fire engine parked there with kids clambering all over it. The local fire brigade had kindly come down for the day, along with the police, whose squad car horn was being fully tested by each enthusiastic young driver.

The bus came to a halt and there was a mini-stampede for the exit doors, which were flung open, letting the euphoria of youth run free.

'Have a good day, kids!' David bellowed above the excited chatter.

As well as being last on, Sam was last off. He sauntered his way along to Lucy who held out her hand for him.

'Thank you for taking me here,' he said to David, before reaching up for Lucy's hand.

'It's been my pleasure, young man,' David smiled at the

boy with a heavy dose of sympathy.

Helping him off the bus, Lucy grabbed the paper bag that held his gift.

'Okay, Sam, shall we go and see the fire engine first, then I'll give you your present?'

He nodded, letting go of her hand and adjusting his headwear. Lucy began to walk along, her companion at her side. Every single one of his peers wore clothing other than their school uniform.

It was very busy, busier than she had imagined, helped perhaps by the fact that the late July day was behaving just as it was meant to.

Parents and grandparents, family and friends, all had come in droves. The screams and laughter of a new generation boisterously sang out with unrestrained delight. Lucy was kept busy returning smiles and waving to all the familiar faces that came into view.

'Do you want to sit in the driver's...?' He wasn't where he was meant to be, at her side. 'Sam?' She looked around from left to right. 'Sam!' Lucy caught a flash of him between the roving bodies, heading away from her.

Where is he going? She looked ahead, following his suggested path. Without warning, her body released a heart-wrenching sigh; her breath was stolen and her eyes smarted, threatening to ruin her mascara.

The little boy was running towards his best friend in the whole world.

Joseph was leaning against the back of his truck with his arms folded. He raised a hand to Lucy, who stood on the spot, witnessing the scene from afar, knowing that if that little boy hugged him, she would lose control completely.

Sam slowed his pace as he neared Joseph, who beamed at the boy, and they high-fived.

Joseph must have made a complimentary comment about his cap as Sam started fiddling with it proudly. Lucy remained standing where she was, the distance only adding to the power of such a simple moment. They both started to walk back towards her, Sam's delighted face hopping between Joseph's and Lucy's, silently telling her that he was there.

She pulled the bobble from her hair and ruffled it free of itself, trying to look as casual about it as possible. Joseph didn't stop talking to Sam, who hung on his every word while they walked.

God, he looked good: a thick brown belt hugged the waistband of his faded jeans, coupled with a tight, navy-blue wide-necked collarless T-shirt, its three buttons undone, teasing her with a view of his muscular chest. How could someone dress in such a casual way and have such a deliberate effect?

Would he stay long? It didn't matter: he was here, Sam was happy… and so was she.

'Miss Lucy,' Joseph nodded in that way that she liked to think was special to her.

'Mr Joe,' she retorted, doing her best to imitate his gesture. 'I didn't think we'd see you today.'

'I couldn't let my best buddy down now, could I?' He patted Sam gently on the shoulder with a wink. The two adults' faces engaged. Sam's smile was still on his lips, and Joseph looked calm, at ease with himself. It was very disarming, and left her with a strange feeling of being able to confess anything to him.

'He's very, very, pleased to see you.'

'Is he?' They weren't talking about Sam now.

'Yes, he is.' This man melted self-control like a blowtorch on an ice cube. 'Are you, pleased to see *him*?'

She feared his answer, yet hungered for it.

'Always.' The smile had gone; he shot straight from the hip, his words piercing like a bullet, the sweet pain hurting yet pleasing in unison, stealing any and all riposte.

'Miss Lucy, can we show Mr Joe the fire engine, please?' Sam asked, saving her from drowning in words she could not say.

'Shall we?' said Joseph.

Sam flapped his hands excitedly, hopping on the spot.

'Come on, then,' said Lucy.

He ran on, stopping periodically to make sure they were following.

'Thank you, it really means the world to him.' He seemed uncomfortable with the well-deserved gratitude.

'Please don't thank me. It's the least I can do.'

He walked ahead of Lucy, catching up with Sam. 'Do you want some help, little man?' Without waiting for an answer, he lifted Sam up and placed him in the driver's seat. Sam bounced around, pretending to drive.

'Come on, Mr Joe. Quick! Look at this, it's amazing!' Joseph asked the supervising fireman for permission to join Sam, then climbed on alongside him.

He was so happy; he looked like a different child. His eyes were bright and he had a glow in his cheeks. He looked carefree, just as he should have been.

'Do you want to join them, Mum?' asked the fireman from under his bushy ginger moustache, which completely curtained his mouth.

'Oh, no. I'm not... I'm fine, thanks.'

She decided to go along with the fantasy that Sam was hers, hers to love and care for. After all, he was, if only for that day.

'Come on, don't be a spoilsport. Tell her, Sam,' Joseph said, laughing, infecting her with the giggles.

'Quick, Miss Lucy, we're going to be late!' Sam was still bouncing up and down, completely in the moment. She had never seen him like this.

'I think you're going to have to join them, the chief has spoken,' the fireman said. His ginger moustache spread but there was still no sign of any mouth.

Lucy shook her head, still chuckling away to herself.

'Okay, let me in.'

Reaching up, she took hold of the yellow grab rails and pulled herself up. Joseph held her arm, helping her in, and she sat down next to him.

'We're all on board, chief. Where are we going?' said Joseph.

'To the park!' The little hands slid over the bottom half of the steering wheel, pretending to drive them.

Joseph played along. 'Is there a fire in the park?' he asked, in a melodramatic tone.

'No, I would like to play on the swings and then feed the ducks. I've never done that before.'

Joseph and Lucy looked at each other, their playful smiles extinguished by just how simple the child's dream was.

'And then what would we do?'

Joseph's voice now lacked enthusiasm. He wasn't playing anymore; His question was secretly delving into the stark emptiness of the boy's life.

'We would have a lovely picnic together, draw some

pictures and then you would read me a bedtime story, like you said you would, remember, Mr Joe?'

'I remember, Sam.'

Lucy saw that Sam's words were weighing heavily on Joseph. His face fell, and he passed a hand over his beard, clearly affected by the boy's state of indigence. She felt it too, but she was determined that the day would be a happy one.

'Shall we let some of the other children have a go, Sam?' A small queue of impatient children had formed.

'Okay,' he sang out. The moustachioed fireman offered his hand to Lucy, helping her out of the vehicle, before very kindly lifting Sam down.

Joseph jumped down, looking more fireman-like than the real McCoy. He thanked the officer with a brotherly slap to the shoulder.

'What's next then, face painting?' Joseph asked, bent over, his hands braced on his knees.

'Can I be Spider-Man?' The little hands flapped in excitement.

'You can be anything you want to be.'

It was a joy to see him interact with Joseph. All the teachers at the school were female, so Sam had no male role model in his life – none who were worthy of the title, anyway.

'Calm down boys! First of all, Sam, you come with me to get your present, and Mr Joe will wait here for us. Okay?'

But instead of being excited about the promise of a gift, he became uneasy and fidgety.

'You will be here when we come back, won't you, Mr Joe?' The man in question crouched down in front of the boy. He was very perceptive of Sam's character.

'I will not move from this spot until you come back, no matter what.'

His feelings of concern chased away Sam happily skipped off with Lucy.

'Won't be a moment.' She thanked him with her eyes, and they headed towards the school.

Joseph remained crouched down, taking in the sight. They were both fine examples of all that was good and pure in the world… unlike him.

Haunting memories surfaced to keep him company, reminding him of the revulsion that a kind, beautiful woman like Lucy would surely feel if she knew his sin. As he rose to his feet so did the self-contempt, it usually struck in the evening, when he was alone, resting. But there could be no such thing as rest when memories as fresh as the moment fate had created them, returned to torment. That's when he would wash it all away. But since he didn't having any Jack Daniels readily available, he was going to have to go cold turkey.

What the hell was he doing there anyway? Trying to appease his guilty conscience? Did he really think that a day of lollipops and sunshine was going to erase the past? The sad reality was that even if he walked the earth for a thousand years, he would never forget what he had done.

It was rarely far from his thoughts, whether conscious or subconscious. He was contaminated with the venom of self-loathing.

Taking in the happy scenes around him, he suddenly felt like an inappropriate prop. He felt a strong urge to leave right then, to hide away with a bottle. But he had promised to stay, and despite all the other things he may have been, he was a man of his word.

Trying to focus on the present, he fixed his eyes on the door they had gone through. It opened and out came Sam, wearing red shorts, white Nike trainers and a white Nike T-shirt. He marched back most of the way with his head down, proudly examining his new outfit.

Lucy never took her eyes off Sam, watching his every step with surrogate pride.

'Doesn't he look smart?' Sam stood to attention, his head held high.

'Very smart,' Joseph nodded, giving him a thumbs-up. 'In fact, I think you are the smartest boy here.'

'Really?' Sam ran his hands over his clean, fresh clothes, obviously not used to such basic luxury.

'Really.' Joseph held out his palm, Sam slapped it, dancing on his toes from one foot to the other.

'Do you want to go on the bouncy castle?' asked Lucy.

'Oh yes, please.'

'Lead the way then Sam. Everyone's on the sports field.'

His eyes bright with enthusiasm, he adjusted his cap. It didn't go with his outfit at all but there was no way he was going to take it off. They crossed the car park, entering the school through the old glazed metal doors, walked a short distance along the corridor and back out into the open air.

The grassy sports field was a hive of activity. Lines of green and white marquees formed a semicircle. It was like a family-friendly version of the Saturday market that Lucy loved so much. There were tables filled with homemade cakes, books of all genres, cuddly toys that were looking for new homes, bottles of alcohol stood side by side with their softer brothers, while the adults tried their luck at the tombola, hoping to win the harder alternatives.

Sam flapped his hands excitedly. It must have been a wondrous sight to him compared to the colourless wasteland that was his everyday reality. The joyous sound of unity rang out; conversations danced with laughter and there seemed to be a smile on every face. Balloons and bunting hung on every table and tent, while the invisible tempting smell of hot dogs and onions whispered its way through the temperate summer air.

As soon as Sam saw the bright yellow bouncy castle sat in the centre of the day's activities, he bolted towards it.

'Make sure you take your shoes off, Sam,' Lucy called.

The new shoes went flying in opposite directions as Sam disappeared behind the multicoloured wall of air.

'He's a good kid,' said Joseph, handing payment to the lady supervising.

'Yeah, he is.' Lucy watched Sam playing, looking happy and carefree. She questioned whether or not today would really be good for him. They were giving him a taste of what childhood should be like, only to be snatched away from him at 4 o'clock. Sorry, kid, fun's over; get back on the bus to hell.

'You okay?' asked Joseph.

'Mmm.'

Her eyes stayed on Sam.

'You're worried about him, aren't you?' She nodded, concentrating on controlling her feelings.

He didn't know what to say. Having witnessed Sam's father's treatment of him, he knew she had good reason to be worried.

'Want to tell me about it?'

'Oh,' sighed Lucy, 'you don't want to listen to me going on.'

'I could listen to you all day.' That caught her attention. 'It's not healthy to keep things bottled up inside.'

Lucy looked up into his face and saw that it wasn't an empty offer. Mark had never shown the slightest interest in any aspect of her involvement with the school.

'He's such a lovely kid – gentle, kind. His autism means that for him, the world will at times be a scary, confusing place. But he has so much potential: with the right nurturing he could live a full, independent life...' Lucy nodded to herself. 'I know he can.'

Sam was busy momentarily defying gravity. Spotting he had an audience, he acknowledged them with a wave.

Lucy conscripted a smile and wiggled her fingers back at him. His predicament was the thorn that festered in her mind.

'He's got learning difficulties, as have all the kids in our school, and we have the privileged position to be able to influence these children's lives. There's a spark in Sam, but it's being stifled by the life he has outside this building. What hopes and aspirations can he have when all the odds are against him? I'm waiting for that bastard to put a foot wrong, and then maybe Sam can be free of him.'

'You're talking about his dad.'

Lucy felt her good mood slipping. 'I'm sorry, it's not your problem. I shouldn't be boring you with it.' She turned to see that Joseph was now the one watching Sam solemnly.

'I think he's a lucky boy to have someone special like you watching over him.'

How could he have such command of her emotions? She took cover behind the sunglasses that were hooked on her plum-coloured, boat-necked blouse.

'Are you… staying for the day? Or…' With her confidence bolstered by the tinted lenses she could look upon his face without fear of giving herself away.

'I was just going to show my face for another hour.'

'Oh, that's… fine.'

'But…' he began, then paused.

'But?'

He drew breath to answer but held onto the words, then reached out to her face with both his hands.

'Don't hide your eyes; they're far too beautiful.'

She carefully removed her shaded defences, freeing a stray curl that brushed her cheek. Wide-eyed and scared of the impact that his words might have, Lucy took in the soul-searching depths of his contemplation, ravenous for the next line of words that would either delight or destroy her spirits.

'Do you want me . . . to stay? Or is it best if I go?' It seemed more than just an innocent question – at least it did to Lucy. She swallowed hard, trying to summon some moisture to lubricate her reply.

'I want you…' Microscopic attention was applied to assessing the effect of her answer. 'To stay, Mr Dalton.' Her voice was barely breaking from the slumber of a whisper. It *was* more than an innocent answer.

His mouth closed and the pulse of his clenched jaw throbbed beneath his beard.

'Then I shall stay, Ms Eaton.' He hooked her sunglasses back on her blouse and with a touch as gentle as the summer breeze, he set the rogue curl back into place.

'Now, let's give him a day he'll remember. No more worries today. God willing, he's got a bright future ahead of him.'

'I hope so. Do you believe in God, Joseph?'

He turned his face away to Sam, the jaw pulsing once again, 'I believe in people like you, Lucy.'

'Mr Dalton.' The chilled greeting had an official dominance to it, which was ill-suited to the day. Mrs Shoesmith strode over to them; she looked out of place amongst the casualness of the day, dressed in her usual stuffy business attire, so that no one would forget that she was the one in charge.

'Mrs Shoesmith.' Joseph returned her greeting with all the warmth of a strained professional relationship.

'Lucy, nice to see you.'

'Hi, Priscilla. Isn't it busy?'

'I suspected it would be.' Her answer was a sure sign that she did not like to let go of the reins.

Sam's enthusiasm for bouncing was all gone, he was now sitting on the blue mat, attempting to put on his laced-up shoes.

'Excuse me.' Lucy went to his aid.

The head teacher's keen eyes waited until Lucy was far enough away before turning them on Joseph. 'What brings you here today, Mr Dalton?' Her face straight, making no attempt to be cordial.

'I'm showing my support.'

'For whom?'

'For those that need it most,' retorted Joseph.

'The boy's father, is he here today?'

Joseph rested his hands on his hips, his head bowed towards the diminutive dictator.

'You're worried I'm going to cause trouble?'

'Is he?' she asked, sharp-tongued and insistent.

'You know better than I do that he'll be in some crack den, spending the money that's meant to feed his child.'

She clasped her hands behind her back. The lines around her top lip tightened and her neck elongated, as if she was trying to gain more height. She knew the power of her superiority was impotent outside of her command.

'I'm going to be watching you very closely, Mr Dalton.'

Lucy was heading back with Sam.

'And who's going to be watching him?' Joseph nodded towards the boy, 'Huh?'

The matriarch's bosom inflated and her chin twitched at the show of blatant insolence. Lucy and Sam's return uncocked the scathing reply that must have been loaded in the chamber.

'Hello, Mrs Shoesmith.' Sam obediently knew his place.

'Hello, Samuel.' He was one of the few people who was smaller in stature than she was.

'Well, I have to make sure I get to see everyone, so I'll leave you to enjoy the day.'

Both Lucy and Sam wished her a good day, but having taken only two steps into her departure Mrs Shoesmith stopped and turned on her spool heels. 'We shall continue with our conversation another time, Mr Dalton.'

'I look forward to it.'

Having fired this warning shot, she continued on her royal tour.

'What were you talking about?' asked Lucy.

'Philanthropy.'

Lucy frowned, confused by his answer.

Joseph cracked the air with a clap of his hands.

'Right, are you ready to go and win some toys?'

Sam tipped his head back to look up at Joseph, open-mouthed with surprise. 'Toys? For me?'

Joseph crouched down to answer the humble little voice.

'As many as we can carry.' His huge fist playfully skimmed Sam's chin. 'I'm going to need your help though, okay?'

Sam's head bobbed up and down in definite agreement, his fingers knotted in front of his chest.

'I'm very good at helping, I am, Mr Joe.'

'What are we waiting for then? Let's go!' Joseph strode away, swinging his arms in make-believe running. Sam followed, also swinging his arms, having to run to keep up.

Lucy stole a minute of the day to watch them, more confused than ever. Was he really this nice? Or was she being lined up as one of his weekend conquests? Lucy told herself she was over-thinking things, and that she needed to relax. As Mrs Shoesmith had said: enjoy the day, because come tomorrow it will be lost forever.

Before rejoining Joseph and Sam, Lucy took out her phone to send Mark a message, telling him that she would be tied up all day, selling jam on one of the stalls.

Mark had promised to come down at some point, and although Lucy hadn't believed for a moment that he would, she now wanted to make sure that he definitely wouldn't. *It's only a little white lie. There's nothing at the fete of any interest to him anyway. He'll be relieved to get out of it.* The excuses lined up as she typed out the message. Excuses are usually a precursor for regrets; still, adults are free to make their own decisions and mistakes.

The moment her finger touched the 'send' icon, Lucy knew she had taken another step closer to the edge.

CHAPTER NINETEEN

'How's that?' asked Joseph.

'Higher,' instructed Sam.

'There?'

'Yes.'

'Say the word, little man.'

'Fire!' Joseph's hand cut through the air, throwing the ball with pinpoint accuracy. With a loud thwack the ball connected with its target, knocking the coconut to the ground.

'Yes!'

Joseph flung his arms in the air, celebrating his victory. Lucy applauded, while Sam jumped up and down, shaking his hands in total joy.

'Take your pick, Sam, which one would you like?'

Sam deliberated, holding his finger to his lips and looking at the menagerie of cuddly animals, large and small.

'Can I have the little doggy?' Sam posed his question to the elderly stallholder, holding his hands up, awaiting the prize.

A black and white, floppy-eared puppy was handed down to him along with congratulations and instructions to take good care of him.

Sam thanked the kindly old man. His manners were impeccable, and quite unexpected, considering his parentage. He lovingly stroked the soft toy, holding it close to his delighted face.

'Isn't he adorable,' said Lucy, tickling a floppy ear. 'What are you going to call him?'

'Lucky.' He kissed his mute friend's soft fur.

'That's lovely, Sam.' Lucy mouthed a *'thank you'* to the man responsible.

Joseph's cheeks rose attempting a smile, but the sight of an underprivileged child clutching onto a soft toy that was unwanted by someone else was cruelly ironic.

He slapped his palms together once more to dispel the thought. 'It's your turn to show me your skills now, Sam. How are you at catching ducks?'

'I'm actually really good, I think.'

'Come and show me, then. There's a Hook-a-Duck over there.'

They spent the day working their way around each and every stall. Lucy revelled in Sam's unrestrained joy and was struck by Joseph's innate kindness. He had taken charge of the day, making Sam laugh with his silly stories, and unwittingly revealing another side of himself, which was dangerously intriguing to her.

She wanted to turn the pages of his mind, to know who he was and what he wanted. Lucy didn't feel any guilt for spending the day with a man whom she hardly knew, probably because of the very public setting. But she was sure that if they had been alone, her mind would have led her to a place saturated with reprehensible thoughts.

He had, however, been a perfect gentleman– although she had still caught him checking her out more than a few times.

The day neared its end and the thick crowds of people began to thin. Sam was sitting with a small group of children, engrossed in the tumultuous life of Mr Punch and his abusive wife Judy. As promised, his face had been used as a canvas for a Spider-Man mask. Lucy and Joseph took a back seat on the cool green grass to sample a moment of grown-up time.

'Don't you feel sorry for Mr Punch?' Joseph lay on his side, propped up on his elbow. 'Domestic abuse in a relationship is a terrible thing, don't you think?' An eyebrow raised playfully as he feigned concern.

'Well, some people like to be smacked, don't they?' Lucy smiled into her plastic cup of Pimm's, her eyebrows equally aerobatic.

A baritone chuckle rumbled from his chest. 'Do they now? I wouldn't know, having spent most of my life living in a Tibetan monastery.' A smile wriggled across his lips.

'Really? I didn't know that about you. How interesting.'

'Yes,' giving a melodramatic sigh, accompanied with a shake of his head. 'I'm uneducated in the ways of the world… I need a good teacher.'

Averting her stare, Lucy plucked blades of grass, feeling a flush of nervous excitement flowing through her body. Just knowing he was looking at her made Lucy fidget; she ruffled her hair, fiddled with her earlobes, scratched itches that weren't there.

It had been a great day. But she couldn't deny it was

nice to have him all to herself.

'What is it you do again?' he asked teasingly.

'I happen to be a teacher.'

'No!'

'Yes!' Their childish game was fun, and after all, they weren't doing anything wrong: they were just joking, not flirting with each other.

'Are you any good though?'

'I'm the best.' Her confident answer misrepresented of what was really going on in her head. Nevertheless, her gaze was the dominant one. Joseph broke eye contact to watch Mr Punch being chased by a crocodile with a mouth full of sausages. Now he was the one scratching and fumbling with his face.

'Do you need private tuition, Mr Dalton?' Lucy asked, emboldened by his seeming distraction and nervousness, and wrongly feeling she had the upper hand.

He pushed himself up and sat facing her. His strong forearms were linked around his raised knees.

'It has to be intensive, I like to delve deep into matters, Ms Eaton.' They had definitely strayed from joking now. The suggestive remark coupled with the unflinching attention he was paying her reasserted the fact that he was in fact the one at ease. Was it so wrong to enjoy the company of a man who wasn't her partner?

Right or wrong, she would have been more than happy just to stand in his shadow. His affecting presence was like the far reaches of our galaxy, unexplained.

'Don't you have an answer for me, Miss Eaton?'

'Some things are better left unsaid.' Running out of witty answers, she could see that things were heading to a place that was off limits.

The glint in his eye faded. 'I'm sorry, I've over stepped the mark.'

'No, Joseph.' *You haven't.*

'Lucy!' A tall lady in a long flowing floral dress approached them, fanning the air with a sheet of paper.

'Hi, Jan – everything okay?'

'Yes, fine…' Jan stopped in mid-flow, noticing Joseph. Her long fingers spread out on her chest.

'Oh, hello there.'

'Hi,' replied Joseph, palm raised.

Lucy introduced Jan to the reason her train of thought had been derailed. She bent her stalk-like legs and curtsied to touch palms with him.

'Have you had a nice day, Joseph? Oh, sorry, listen to me being over familiar, Mr Dalton.'

She swooned, fannying around with her short, kinky blonde hair.

'Joseph is just fine, and yes, we have had a great day, thank you.'

Jan was 41 and on husband number four – and by the looks of things she was sizing up number five.

'Jan,' Lucy called, somewhat annoyed at having been simultaneously interrupted and ignored.

'Yes?' Jan said, managing to unhook her eyes from Joseph just long enough to answer Lucy.

'You were saying?'

'Oh yes… silly me, I'm daydreaming,' she chortled, in a high-pitched tone that must have set dogs howling for miles around.

I think you mean fantasising, don't you, Jan?

'Just to let you know, I have the list of children riding David's bus and we will be setting off in five minutes.'

'Oh, so... you're going on the bus?'

'Yes, my hubby's got the car, men and their football.' She threw her eyes over in a huge arc. 'David has to pass virtually by my house. You don't mind switching, do you?'

'Er...'

'Super! I'll round up the troops, Samuel, come along now please!'

'I'll bring Sam over,' Lucy insisted, leaving Jan with a slightly pained expression on her gaunt face.

'If you wish,' she said loftily, turning and prancing away, like a thirteen-year-old having a hissy fit.

Lucy felt miffed at being bulldozed like that. She had assumed that she would have taken Sam back on the bus. Joseph had by now risen to his feet and was brushing away the grass cuttings from his T-shirt.

For Lucy, the contentment of the day had been turned on its head. This was the part she hadn't been looking forward to: sending him off on the bus, back to the cage that was his life.

Mr Punch and his friends took their bows to the tiny patter of hands, and the curtain fell on all of the day's performances. Sam was still smiling at the antics of the wooden puppets when Lucy told him it was time to go home. Home: a word that was usually synonymous with love, safety and warmth, but which for this six-year-old had a very different meaning.

The bright smile that had lit up his face faded, his eyes dulled; the heavy chains that awaited the boy just a short drive away were already upon him.

Joseph carried the two large bags of toys. He had stayed true to his promise and with the

determination of an athlete at the Olympics, had paid

his money and competed in every single game and challenge to win Sam a prize.

They headed back towards the spot where the day had started, a blink of an eye ago. Many of Sam's fellow pupils were still full of the excitement of the day, and were running around, vocalising their infinite energy.

There were no more hops and skips for Sam. He walked to his carriage at the pace of a funeral procession, nodding in solemn agreement at Lucy's commentary on how wonderful the day had been. No matter how hard she tried, it seemed nothing could evoke a smile.

'Come along Samuel.' Jan said. She was waiting by the open doors of the bus, holding the list of names.

'I'll put these on, shall I?' Joseph stepped onto the bus, holding the two bags, drawing Jan away from her post to follow him.

Lucy crouched down on her haunches, then knelt down on the warm tarmac. 'It's time to go now. Mr David will help you with your bags when you get back.' She refused to use the word 'home' as it was a very gross exaggeration of the truth. 'I am very proud of you, Sam. You've been such a good boy.' His eyes hadn't budged from staring at a spot on her shoulder; the despondency that riddled the infancy of his life was a torment that had been gathering strength in Lucy. The school days were few and far between when she hadn't shed a tear for his what seemed, helpless plight.

'Sam,' her voice was a mere whisper – any more and it would break. 'Look at me sweetheart, please.' The lids of his eyes slowly peeled back and his cavernous brown eyes fulfilled her request, if only for a few seconds, allowing her to see more than a child could ever put into words.

'Before you know it, it will be Monday.'

It was a poor consolation, but all she could offer. He gave a slight, slow nod.

Joseph's shadow cast out, announcing his presence. He kept a respectful distance between them before being invited to say goodbye. Lucy had been amazed at how at ease he had been with them, but now that ease seemed to abandon him.

His hand massaged the back of his neck as he stepped over to the boy. 'Make sure you take good care of all those new friends of yours, now, you hear?' His voice was cheery, which seemed inappropriate, but necessary.

Lucy rose to her feet and stepped to one side.

Joseph looked vexed: hellos and goodbyes were always the most awkward parts of a meeting.

'I want to say thank you, for giving me a day that I didn't expect.'

There was an overly sweet tone that adults tend to use when speaking to children; Joseph hadn't adopted that, but Lucy doubted Sam would understand the somewhat cryptic nature of his message, although it was spoken in such a genuine manner that she was also sure it would translate in some way.

It seemed that even Jan had picked up on the poignancy of the moment, judging by her uncharacteristic silence.

Lucy and Joseph shared a blank look, not quite sure what to say or do. Sam reached out and took hold of Joseph's leg, who raised his hands in surrender. They exchanged very different looks this time.

'Thank you, Mr Joe, for being my friend.'

The simple sight of the little boy's head tilted back,

looking up at Joseph who was looking down at him, stole her breath and touched her soul. It was an memorable snapshot in time.

Joseph's face was etched with a look akin to anguish. His lips folded inwards, his brow lowered and his eyes were almost closed. Slowly his startled hands fell, down and down they went until they were resting on Sam's insignificant shoulders.

A thousand words written by Shakespeare himself could not have conveyed the look that lived in this child's beautiful eyes at that very moment it was more than Lucy could bear.

She sharply sucked in air, which was immediately trapped by a body fighting its natural urges. Her nails dug into the flesh of her thighs in a futile attempt to stop the tears from falling, but fall they did, the tiny drops spreading in diameter as they were absorbed by her blouse.

The gentle compression of a hand on her shoulder drew her attention. Jan handed her a small wad of neatly folded tissues, Lucy took them without a word, having no confidence in her voice.

Sam released his friend and with a greater composure than that of his elders, did what had to be done, and boarded the bus.

The doors closed, cutting the umbilical cord of their day together. Sam went and sat by a window, but chose not to look at them. Despite that, Lucy still waved with one hand, stemming the flow with the other. Turning its back on them, the bus couriered him away from the love, support, and protection of the school and back to the blunt reality of 7B Eden Row.

CHAPTER TWENTY

Slightly embarrassed by her lack of self-control, Lucy went up a gear into hyperactive and immediately volunteered to stay behind for an hour to pack everything away. Joseph was kind enough to offer to assist them, despite being given the option to leave. Thanks to an army of hands the field reverted back to its usual empty, functional self in no time. Having no ride home, Lucy called Mark to ask him to pick her up. His automated voice told her several times that he was busy right now, but he would be sure to call back ASAP.

'He's not answering. I'll ask one of the girls if they can drop me back.'

'No you won't. Come on, I'll take you home.' He didn't bother to wait for an answer, and began to make his way back to his pick-up. Lucy paused in artificial consideration. It didn't seem quite right to accept instantly.

Seeing that she wasn't following, Joseph stopped.

'You'll be perfectly safe, scout's honour.' He held three fingers grouped together, against his temple, saluting.

Conceding to a smile, Lucy closed the distance between them. 'Are you sure it's not out of your way?'

'Not at all.'

'Well in that case, thank you.'

Side by side, they proceeded back to the car park.

'Will I be safe?' He elbowed her arm playfully. 'I mean, I don't know you very well.' The humour was a welcome distraction from the ache of saying goodbye to Sam.

'My mother always told me never to pick up strangers, and here I am, going against her best advice,' he said.

'I'm not a stranger, am I?'

'Well, I'm not sure: I don't really know you that well. A man has to be careful these days.'

'You'll have to get to know me then, won't you?' Because they were walking and not facing each other, it made it easier for her to be bold.

'I'd very much like that.' Their arrival at Joseph's pick-up interrupted the flow of conversation, which was veering into sinful, but nevertheless exciting, territory.

'Now I have to warn you: once you've been in this baby that Ferrari will never be the same again.' The door was opened for her.

'Thank you, Mr Dalton.'

She climbed up onto the big fleshy seat, placing a fitness magazine that sat there onto the dashboard. Closing the door, he made his way around to the driver's side. The cab gently rocked as the seat cushioned his weight. The door slammed, sealing the confined space.

'We've got all the mod cons,' he cajoled, sprinkling his fingers over the dashboard.

'So I see, I'm very impressed.'

'It's even got brakes.'

'No!'

'Yep, so we'll be able to stop if we want to.' He slipped the key into the ignition.

'The question is, do you know when to stop, Mr Joe?' *Jesus! Where did that one come from?*

A hiss of air escaped from his cheeks, which were ballooned above the hairline of his beard; his eyes never left the dials.

'I always used to…' On his command the engine sparked into action. He twisted from the waist to face her, his arm resting on the steering wheel. 'This could be a bumpy ride, Lucy. You're going to need protection.' Palpitations and flutters caused by the smouldering suggestion of his words wreaked havoc with the natural balance of her body.

'What!' As much as Lucy liked to think she could match his risqué wit, after suffering a direct hit such as this, her counterstrokes all but surrendered.

'Protection, Miss Lucy. It's the sensible thing to do.' His hand sailed through the thick, heavy air across to her face. Like a tortoise trying to hide in its shell, Lucy's neck retracted, she gasped with the sudden shock of what was happening. The skin of his wrist brushed her locks; she quickly scanned to see if anyone was watching, the coast was clear.

The hairs of his forearm bowed under the hurricane of her laboured breathing, and Lucy closed her eyes, preparing herself for his next move.

'There you go.'

She peeked through her lashes. He pulled the seatbelt out, and held it for her.

Stupidity replaced apprehension with the speed of light.

'Thanks...'

She took the clip from him and closed her eyes again, wincing with embarrassment tinged with a slight hint of disappointment. The click of Joseph's seatbelt interrupted her self-conscious musing.

'Safety first, Miss Eaton. Safety first.'

He gave yet another cheeky wink, which he roguishly seemed to take great pleasure in, fully aware of his predominance. First gear was selected, the driver's window retracted into the door, allowing cooler air in to chase away the magnified temperature of the afternoon. It was a welcome relief to her crimson cheeks, scorched by the heat of the moment. They drove from the school premises at walking pace, following the flow of the last remaining patrons, who were carrying large cuddly toys, a balloon or two ascending above them.

Once clear of the pedestrians they gathered speed and reached a comfortable pace. It was nice to be driven home without sudden violent acceleration and abrupt breaking, which was Mark's style of driving.

'You're not going to believe this, but I actually do prefer your truck to the Ferrari.'

'I bet you say that to all the boys.' A hint of scepticism laced his voice. It did seem a rather silly thing to say, it was true though.

'No really, the seats are too low and hard, and it's a hard ride.'

Joseph afforded himself a quick glance at his passenger, the curl of his lips screamed mischief.

'So you prefer a soft ride, rather than a hard one?' If it was inappropriate to smile at such a question, it seemed her face was unaware of the fact.

An answer came to Lucy, equal in its unsuitability. The tip of her tongue buttoned itself to her top lip, while she considered her next tactic in this verbal game of chess.

Lucy made her move. 'Well that all depends on what I'm riding, doesn't it... Mr Joe?'

Queen takes bishop.

The cable-like lines in his forearm rippled, as his hand choked the leather steering wheel. His redundant arm was resting on the open window, disturbing the aerodynamics and causing a flutter of air to tousle his thick head of hair.

'Most hard rides turn soft in time, I think you'll find.'

'Some sooner than others.' Her tummy tumbled with the thrill and excitement of their exchange. She had him all to herself, if only for a while.

Because he was bound to the responsibility of driving, Lucy felt emboldened by her visual advantage. His smouldering eyes exerted a power over her brain's ability to function normally, but at that moment they were focused on the road, so she was fully *compos mentis*.

'Do you have any plans for this evening, Mr Dalton?'

'Nothing that can't be cancelled. Why? Where are you taking me?'

It was a suggestive joke uttered by a singleton. Lucy certainly wasn't single, but the urge to answer as such was hard to resist.

'I may go into town, there's a good band playing at Tommy's tonight.'

'On your own or...'

'It will be rammed with people, so I won't be on my own.' He cleverly avoided the question.

'I may even bump into your friend Suzie.'

Of all the things he could have said, that was the very last thing she wanted to hear. It was wrong of her to feel that way about her best friend, but feel that way she did. Was he teasing her, or was it an innocent comment?

'She's been trying to get in touch with you. Have you returned any of her calls?'

'I've been meaning to.'

'Suzie's a great girl, but she's had a bad run of men lately,' the compliment was served along with a warning.

'There's a lot of us about, I'm afraid.'

This was her chance to dig a little deeper. 'Do you include yourself in that bracket?'

Although his face was in profile, it was clear his humorous mood had waned.

'Let's just say, I'm going to be on Santa's naughty list for a while.'

The frosty, cloaked reply only stoked her curiosity.

'Want to tell me about it?'

A red light halted their journey. He turned to Lucy, his eyes wide and as deep as wishing wells, focused on the present but only seeing the past. Instinct told her to reach out to him, to take his hand and beg him to share his thoughts, but morals and so-called right and wrong prohibited any such action. Her window of opportunity was gone with the illumination of the green light.

He faced the windscreen once more and smoothly moved them on their way. 'I wouldn't want to ruin your day,' his voice suddenly sounded weary, but there was a slight intonation that he wanted to say more.

'What if I wanted to know?'

Joseph seemed to contemplate the offer for an agonisingly long time. 'What if… I didn't want you to know?'

'Then I would respect that, but if ever you changed your mind, I'd be ready to listen.'

Whatever it was that he was wrestling with, its gravity was obvious. The next minute or two was filled with nothing but the purr of the engine. Lucy ruminated what it might be that he was so guarded about. She was oblivious to the passing scenery, her field of vision contained entirely within the cab. Entering the boundaries of Lucy's neighbourhood, the unease of arriving home raised its head. What would Mark say about Joseph bringing her home?

She didn't care: this was one thing that was worth an argument. Turning the corner into her road the fitness magazine drifted across the dashboard. Lucy shot her hand out to grab it at the same time that Joseph did, trapping both under his heavy warm paw.

He parked up and killed the engine, keeping his hand in place.

'You got there before me.' He set her free from the welcome captivity, drawing his fingers slowly across her skin, reluctance to let go disguised by the delicateness of his withdrawal. With the release came the realisation of where they were. Her white BMW had the drive all to itself; Joseph had also noted Mark's absence.

'Thank you for today. It was kind of you to spend your Saturday with Sam. You've made his day… and mine.' Why did the truth feel so dishonest?

'It was my pleasure, Lucy.' The low softness of his voice was reassuringly comfortable. Now that she was at the point of separation, her words played truant once again. It was talk or get out time.

'Er, I don't suppose… do you, do you want to come in for a coffee?'

Bloody hell Lucy, couldn't you come up with something a bit more original than that!

She sat with her knees tight together, hands smoothing her thighs, feeling the wrenching regret increase with every painful second that he didn't answer.

He was perfectly still, apart from his eyes, which studiously avoided hers.

'Lucy, I've got some –'

'Of course, of course,' she cut him off, embarrassed by her own suggestion. 'You've got other things to do – I've got a ton of stuff to do myself.'

He let her give him his excuse, and she wittered on with the speed of an auctioneer, exposing the unease that was strangling her.

'I won't keep you any longer.' She unclipped the seat belt, opened the door and stepped down onto the pavement. 'I'll see you Monday?'

'I'm afraid so.'

His attempt at a smile was not reassuring. She had embarrassed herself and ruined an otherwise perfect day, she told herself.

'Bye, Joseph.'

'Bye, Lucy.'

She shoved the door to, the lock clicking like snapping fingers dismissing her away.

Walking the drive she knew that of all the day's events the look of reluctance on his face was the one that would play over and over again in her mind. Pulling the house keys from her denim shorts, a bass drum-like sound caught her attention, along with her breath.

'Black coffee, no sugar.'

Joseph's voice tapped her on the shoulder and sent her heart galloping. She puffed out a lungful of air, trying to ease her tension before turning to see the magnificent glory of him approaching, armed with a killer smile, his hand sweeping through his thick swirls of hair.

'I haven't forgotten, you know.' Her confident repose was a complete contrast to the shaking hand that took several attempts to slot the key into the lock.

'Come through to the kitchen.' She did just that, leaving Joseph to close the door.

Mark had left the kitchen as he usually did, scattered with dirty plates and cups, even though the dishwasher was empty.

'Sorry about the mess.' She began to round up the dinnerware.

'One coffee coming up in just a minute, unless you'd like something else?'

'I would like something else,' he admitted.

'We've got orange juice, apple juice, Coke, lemonade. I'd offer you a beer but you're driving.' She opened the dishwasher door, pulled out the rack and began to load the plates in neat rows.

Busy worrying about the mess, she hadn't heard his approach.

'I don't want any of those, I want you.'

His voice was resolute and froze Lucy on the spot, hunched over, with the dregs from the coffee cup she was holding dripping onto the lined up plates. He bent down, swapping the cup for his hand, and they rose together, his fingers firmly clamped on hers.

'I think you want me too.'

Her face was level with his chest. Lucy tried to regulate her breathing, which had become spasmodic at the thought of crossing the line. She had always wondered if he found her attractive, this was definite confirmation that he did. His curled index finger hooked under her chin and softly raised her face to his, with her heart pounding in her rib cage like a trapped animal pleading for freedom.

'Tell me if I'm wrong, and I'll walk out of here right now.'

It was poor consolation, but he looked uneasy too. A tornado of thoughts and emotions tore around inside her. The answer to his question charged at the closed gate of her lips like a raging bull that had been driven crazy by its confinement; morality was the only thing holding her back.

Her hesitation softened his grip and broke his gaze, the look of rejection flashed across his downcast face. Joseph nodded, answering his own question before turning away and heading for the door, each footstep on the hall tiles a countdown to his departure.

To admit that she wanted him, to say those words was to admit that her life was a lie, but to let him go would surely be to deceive herself. Before his hand had touched the latch she let her thoughts taste the freedom they had so craved. 'Stay… please.'

Joseph stood with his back to her, head held low facing his optional exit. Had her hesitation influenced him too? Not wanting her bravery to go to waste, Lucy made her way towards him, anxiety rising with each step.

She had never done a parachute jump before, but imagined this was exactly how it felt right before stepping from the plane, and hoping that chance would favour you.

He turned around upon her final step.

'Are you sure you want this? I can only give you now, nothing more.'

It was time to roll the dice, to take the gamble. She would rather have one moment with him than live a lifetime of *what if?*'

A half step more put them toe-to-toe.

'I'll take whatever you can give me,' she uttered tremulously, tipping her head back in submission to his offer. Her long hair swung like a curtain down her back; although she was fully clothed, she had never felt more exposed in her life.

Joseph's chest rose and fell deeply, his jaw clenched, nostrils flared, the sound of air rushing in to oxygenate his aroused body was intensified by the silence of the house. Mark could've returned at any moment, it didn't matter; she was in a trance, waiting for his lips to make themselves known to her. Joseph lowered his head, but stopped short, his mouth slightly open, refusing to budge any more, making her meet him halfway. Lucy placed both her hands on the full round plates of muscle hiding under his T-shirt. The heat from his body seared through the taut cotton.

With the grace of a prima ballerina she rose onto the very tips of her toes, so close to the prize. Racked with nerves but driven by desire, she stretched her neck, feeling his breath on her face. Her eyes closed and the softness of their lips met, slowly, gently skimming over each other, taking Lucy to a place she hadn't been to in a long time, turning fantasy into reality as they tasted each other for the first time. His tongue politely introduced itself to the border of her lips before becoming acquainted with the inside of her welcoming mouth.

The support of his strong arm wrapped around her

waist relieved the weight from her toes, while a hand slipped under the silky mane of hair and held her head, applying light pressure the insistence of his mouth, sending a surge of animalistic hormones flooding through her brain and body. Nerves had been slapped down by biology, that sleeping feeling that, once roused, simply has to be attended to.

Lucy hung from his T-shirt, popping the only button that was fastened, desperate to know the feel of his skin.

'Upstairs.'

Dropping back down to her feet, she tugged at the material that she jealously wanted to trade places with. Having no fear or shame, Lucy took hold of his thick fingers and led him up the stairs. They did not speak. Words were of no use; only actions could douse the fire that had burned inside her from the very second he had entered her world.

The door to her and Mark's bedroom stood firm within its frame, while the rather more liberal door to the spare room welcomingly stood clear of its post.

It was a bright sunny room with a brand-new double bed; a white cover free duvet was peacefully sprawled out over it. The late afternoon sun hung low in the sky, and cast a projection of light through the windows turning the wall opposite into a makeshift cinema screen. Their silhouettes, the stars of the show, met and synthesised into one. Disfigured shadows of raw passion played out to the cardboard boxes full of books and picture frames that would spend their entire lives hidden and packed away, like most people's hopes, dreams and desires.

This wasn't the case for Lucy: the torment, want, and secrets were being exorcised, purged, and it felt good, it felt right, even though it was so wrong.

Those lips that she had ached to feel were now feasting on her neck with a growing ferocity. She felt his teeth grazing against her skin, working up to her earlobe, causing a burst of prickles to explode like a great firework across her, sapping the strength from her legs.

Lucy pulled his T-shirt free of the waistband. 'Off,' she commanded, surfing an involuntary groan of pleasure that was released as he tugged an earlobe with his teeth. The tip of his nose dipped into her ear, delivering fluctuating bursts of air, affirming his longing was equal to hers.

Joseph broke contact, crossed his arms and lifted the T-shirt up and over his head, turning it inside out as he did so; his back fanned out from his rib cage and tapered down to the kind of waist usually only seen on raunchy calendars. The capable arms dropped to his sides and Lucy took a moment to appreciate the vision that stood before her. *Oh. My. God!* Lucy quickly brushed over the female name that was branded onto his chest – right now, he was hers.

'Anything else you'd like removed?'

Her eyes tore themselves away from the ripped torso, which had whetted more than her appetite, and fell rebukingly on the tarnished gold buckle of his thick brown leather belt.

'Yes, all of it.'

Even Lucy was surprised at how demanding she sounded.

'Whatever the lady wants.' His brown boots and socks were removed first of all, then the pin of his belt was released from the tension of its hold, causing the taut leather to fall limp around his waist. He didn't take his eyes off Lucy, and she couldn't take her eyes off the rolling mounds of muscles that twitched and jumped with each task they were given.

Her bottom lip bore the brunt of her hunger, her teeth sinking into the rose red plumpness, as his hands moved from button to button, about to reveal the fare that her body was to feast on.

The denim crumpled at his feet, anchored by the heavy belt. Tight black shorts obscured the view, but the thick curve of his manhood was clearly visible. Lucy swallowed hard, finding the surreal situation hard to take in.

His thumbs breached the waistband, and Joseph teasingly slid it down over his hips. A dark brown bristle of pubic hair introduced the main act, and as the black band continued to fall, a long, fat tubular member was presented, which twitched upon being freed from its cramped confinement.

He stepped out of his superfluous clothes, his penis bumping against his leg, not yet fully erect but swelling with desire. He was the first man other than Mark that she had seen naked in a long time.

The contrast was a stark one, and so was the emotive power of it. Sex *had* become routine in every way possible. It usually happened after Mark had been drinking, and always at the weekend. Foreplay through to intercourse was always a virtual re-run of the previous week's – or even month's – so-called love-making. Lucy had begun to think she was going off sex.

That was not the case. It seemed her internal organs had liquefied and were seeping into her knickers as she studied every inch of the banquet that stood before her.

He closed the gap between them. 'Your turn, Miss

Eaton.'

She had been quite happy fully clothed, but now the nerves of self-doubt pricked their ears up. What if she didn't meet his expectations? She was hardly Jessica Rabbit, after all.

'Patience, Mr Dalton.' The confident, seductive purr was nothing more than deflection.

Lucy wiggled her hips around the bed and drew the curtains, expecting some concealment but getting very little, as the pale material was no barrier against the ball of fire in the sky.

'I've been patient every single day that I have been in your company.'

The floorboards groaned under his weight as he approached Lucy who was still clinging to the curtain, delaying her turn to strip.

'I have suffered the beauty of your face, endured the smell of your perfume and ached from the sight of your body.' Gently he caught her wrist and removed her hand from the curtain. 'There is no more patience left to give.'

The playful banter was over; they had gone way beyond that. He certainly wasn't joking when he said his patience had all been consumed. Joseph ripped her blouse wide open; buttons flew in all directions with the swift motion. She gasped at the surprise exposure, finding relief in the sheer look of total carnality that was on Joseph's face.

'No more games.'

His voice was like the quiet rumble of thunder, a warning of the impending storm.

Dropping to his knees he wasted no time unbuttoning her shorts, the V-opening displayed her plain white knickers. Joseph's fingers hooked into her back pockets and dragged the denim over the curve of her bottom. Lucy watched from above, feeling as though she was having an out-of-body experience while the exquisite scratch of the coarse hands that tended her garden were now expertly tending to her personal needs, sliding up under her cotton knickers. He grabbed her hips and her thong sliced tight between her cheeks, pulling the material taught across the hot triangular mound. Lowering further still, he buried his face in the heat, nuzzling with his nose, finding the groove.

'Fuck,' Lucy puffed out.

The subtle pressure tantalised the hypersensitive nerve endings of her hidden treasure, closing the shutters on her vision as the divine sense of intimacy spread through her body with fibre-optic speed. Her hands delved into his hair, roaming around unsupervised while her breath shuddered and stuttered its way out. Her head tipped back in abandon as the warmth from his breath soaked the already sodden material, which was now folded inside of her.

His nose rubbed and pushed repeatedly against the magic button, not quite getting to the depths that could be catastrophic, and yet teasing even more so because of the fact. Slipping around to the plump round cheeks of her bottom, the explorative fingers squeezed and fondled like a customer checking the ripeness of an orange. She was ready, waiting to be peeled and eaten. Entering the deep crevice, he separated the ample dunes of meat, stretching the flesh wide, pulling the inflamed lips of her sex open with it.

Lucy dovetailed her fingers behind his neck, arching backwards, forcing his face deeper into her primed pussy with all her upper body weight; driven half-crazy by the lewd need to rip her knickers off and wrap her legs around his face and let him devour her until the demons were slain. Needing air he pulled back, taking a look at his victim. His face glistened with the sheen of his body's attempts to cool the machine in the subdued light of a room that until that afternoon had seen no use. Now it was a den of iniquity, stained by an act of immorality.

When Joseph rose, Lucy couldn't help but focus on the weapon that would commit the crime. It was now bloated by an adrenalin-fuelled heart, which had sent all its reserves to assist in the attack. The fat, bulbous snake head was now fully exposed, having outgrown its skin, hanging just below 90 degrees to his body, heavy with its bulk.

Their mouths sealed again. The faint essence of her body fragranced his lips and their soft tongues entwined like two dolphins exploring the uncharted depths of a hidden passion.

Skin to skin, Lucy's eyes drew shade on the here and now, letting the darkness heighten all other senses: the brush of his beard against her chin, softer than she had expected; the tickle of his chest hair; and the hard contours of a body at the peak of physical perfection, were all first time experiences, an introduction to a body that she was about to become better acquainted with.

Lucy wanted him recklessly, more than she had ever wanted anyone; the desire to satisfy and be satisfied was beyond all reasoning. Frisking down to his erection, her open palm felt the heat as it travelled the long road to its end. Another thunderous rumble reverberated through his chest as her fingers encircled his thick heavy cock, failing to meet each other.

This was going to hurt, but never had she welcomed

pain so readily. With his arm around her waist, Joseph pirouetted Lucy, and sat her on the edge of the bed, breaking their kiss and her grip on his steel-hard dick, now pointed accusingly at her, engorged with a map of thick veins.

Moistening her tingling lips in readiness, Lucy wasn't sure that her mouth would stretch that far without dislocating her jaw. Joseph's eyes bore into hers, glazed with the determination of a man more than capable of completing the task at hand.

She sat square-shouldered, her concealed breasts held high, nipples tight and hard.

'Lie down.' She obeyed his command, disappointed that her mouth wouldn't get to sample the taste of his flesh.

Parting her legs, he slipped his index finger under the embroidered edge of her knickers and drew them to the side, cutting the thong across her rounded cheeks. Lucy raised her arms, fully stretched out, legs spread; the gardener groaning and shaking his head at the sight of her shaven pussy. Sex had always been an activity that took place in darkness, but seeing the lust and need ingrained on his face, empowered Lucy with the confidence to be viewed in such a manner.

'Do you like what you see, Mr Dalton?'

He nodded, with an arched eyebrow that told her he was about to show her exactly how much.

'What are you waiting for then?'

She was approaching desperation, her hands knotting themselves; she feared they may delve down to ease the building tension. The edge of the bed buckled as his knees sank into the duvet; he prowled over her until they were face to face.

'Don't take your eyes off me, this is one thing I don't want to miss.'

Supporting his body weight on one arm, Joseph reached down to position himself. The head of his penis butted against the tumescent lips of her pussy. The fleshy gateway parted as he pleasured himself, causing her to draw breath sharply.

'How's that, good?'

'Mmm,' she closed her eyes momentarily and her hands made a grab for his toned backside, landing on his hips, not quite able to reach.

'Open your eyes, Miss Eaton.' His long deep strokes continued, causing the ballooned head to travel the length of her soaked opening, just nudging at her clitoris, each swipe an appetiser to orgasm.

Lucy's nails sank into his flesh, grappling for leverage, the aroma of her arousal filling the air between them.

'More... give me more,' she begged, her whole body rigid.

'Certainly.'

Weighed down with his chest on hers and her raised arms shackled by a resolute grip, his hips dropped, slicing his monstrous cock into her tight opening. Lucy's back arched with the pain, knowing that pleasure was on the other side while his tongue gagged her mouth, stifling a scream, yet still he forced the fat length deeper and deeper, finally stopping to allow her to get accustomed to it.

'Is that better, Miss Eaton?' he whispered into her gasping mouth, the tip of his nose circling hers.

'Do you want more? I hate to disappoint.'

'More?'

She was stunned by the question. He didn't wait for the answer.

His hot pulsating cock mined to undiscovered depths until their pelvises met, filling Lucy to the brim, sending her into an almost hallucinogenic state.

Her mind scrambled to take in the fullness her body was experiencing, when the perfect fit of his mouth sealed them as one and they shared life-giving air of each other's bodies, submerged in the waters of passion. He withdrew slowly, almost turning her inside out, the wall of her vagina stretched beyond itself, then he plunged back in, oozing out her body's lubrication, sending thick beads of it trickling down into her bottom. He found a steady rhythm, pummelling her into the mattress, the pulse of his meaty erection reaching her belly, relentless in its determined strokes. Back and forth, back and forth. Their bodies bathed in perspiration, Lucy whimpered with each stab driving her closer and closer to the limit of her ecstasy.

This wasn't lovemaking, which happened in a dark room with candlelight, champagne and soft music. No, this was pure unashamed fucking – that unplanned liaison, where only one thing mattered. Her body had finally managed to adjust to the oversized invader that disappeared inside her with each stroke. Joseph's lips pressed down on each other, his eyes shut tight, puffs of air cooling her overheated face.

'Open your eyes, Dalton, I don't want you to miss this either.'

His lashes parted, just enough for her to see that he was nearing his limit too. She clenched her pussy tight, gripping the huge lump of meat exploring her insides. His heavy balls slapping against her arse combined with the tight pull of her thong, crudely yanked aside, slipped her into a decadent place where time and space had no meaning. There were no rights and wrongs, only sensations and emotions.

Lucy's body was heavily self-medicated with the sensual need to achieve her own sexual gratification – that natural desire more powerful than cocaine, a high transcending all other highs in life. With a man like Joseph Dalton, the chances of addiction were highly probable.

It was too late to turn back now: he was inside her body and mind, under her skin, Intravenously seeping into every inch of her being.

His strokes slowed, his breathing shallow. Lucy freed her arms and held his face with both her hands.

'Oh yeah, that's it,' she husked, 'I want it.'

She did: she wanted him to use her and empty his engorged balls deep inside of her, to have the knowledge and comfort that her body had broken him as he would surely break her.

With one final thrust, he paused balls deep, cock spasming as warm semen spurted into her with intermittent bursts. Lucy looked deep into his dilated pupils with privileged fascination, witnessing a brief glimpse of another realm. The blood-shot whites of his eyes returned to their natural state, as the hiss of air rushed through his teeth, relieving the pressure.

Feeling satisfied by the delivery of pure protein, she kissed him, but knowing that she was responsible for his climax made her hornier than ever.

'Keep going, Dalton, I'm not there yet,' The message was whispered into his ear.

He was still buried deep inside of her, his body was

blanketing Lucy, whose face was hidden in the duvet. Joseph lifted himself from the bed, eyes pinched with the sedative aftershock, his mouth wearing the smile of a man who always delivered. He raised her left thigh and with some haste, perhaps with the knowledge that his erection would soon subside, he took hold of her arse, his fingers delving deep, his other hand tightening on the back of her neck. Then he began to dip in and out of the pool of his own release, stretching her bottom wide open, filling her, blissfully sucking and licking her pouting lips.

Lucy clenched and unclenched feeling her climax building, trapped in his forceful grip while he fondled her bottom and fucked her pussy with a single-minded goal.

She could take no more, the vehement swell of need was too strong to hold back. The impalement continued, whipping his cum into a thick cream, his great sword drawing back from the sheath of her body, only to slice once again, gloriously through her inflamed entrance, so tight it was borderline painful.

She could feel every individual knot of veins against the walls of her sex, propelling her to a paradise that was beyond worlds. Everything had its limit and Lucy was on the crest of hers.

His hips rocked, the delving tongue preceding those lips she had dreamt of – so soft, so sensuous, too much to bear. Lucy's hands balled clumps of his hair. Her body was wracked with violent spasms, tearing through every fibre and nerve, whisking her to the divine crescendo of her climax, fracturing around the real life fantasy that weighed over her.

Their eyes locked, sharing a moment of complete purity. A babble of incoherent words and groans bumped into one another, the expenditure of a hard orgasm had lavishly splurged all of her energy. Joseph withdrew and collapsed at her side, gently rocking the bed, leaving her quivering, contracting vagina well and truly fucked.

'You made me work for that, didn't you?' he panted.

'Ooh but it was so good.'

The fatigued reply slipped out quietly, like smoke. Lucy was listlessly floating on a warm undercurrent of satisfaction, her racing breath slowing to a deep, steady rhythm, like the pendulum of a great clock, her exhalations matched her inhalations. Her eyelids were half-closed, like blinds in the midday sun.

'Sorry... I just need a minute,' her whisper as faint as a hummingbird's wings on the air still hot from their passion. The shadow from his hand passed over her face before the melting pressure of his fingers combed through her hair, massaging her scalp.

'Ahh...' Lucy closed her eyes and submitted to her body's suggestion . . . only for a minute.

Joseph slowly rolled to the edge of the bed, being careful not to wake Lucy, who was still lying there, her knickers skewed. He folded the spare half of the duvet over her legs before dressing himself.

He was on autopilot, like when the alarm rings at 5 a.m. and despite your body's every objection you get up to face another day. He laced up his boots, doing his best to ignore her sprawled out beside him. This had been a mistake, complicating things needlessly for both of them. If he had wanted a quick fuck, he should have gone to a bar somewhere. Pulling his T-shirt over his head, he ruffled his hair and made for the stairs. After four determined steps, he stopped in the doorway, fighting the urge to take one more look at her. Slipping his hand into the back pocket of his jeans, Joseph grabbed hold of his keys in encouragement.

It's time to leave, Joe. Despite himself, Joseph turned back to look at Lucy. A shaft of light cut through the gap in the curtains catching the tiny particles in the air that were usually invisible. They floated magically over her like a constellation of stars.

She lay in the blanket of her own glossy hair with the crisp white duvet snaked around her flawless almond skin. The term 'beautiful' was bandied around frivolously these days, but this girl was the very epitome of the word: she was beautiful in every single way.

In truth, he wanted to stay, to rest his sex-weary bones next to hers, but more than that, he wanted her to be happy. Happiness was the one thing that had avoided him. He deserved to suffer the consequence of his past. Sexual gratification was only allowed because of its fleeting existence.

Lucy deserved better, and that, he was not.

CHAPTER TWENTY-ONE

Lucy's eyes fluttered open and she gazed at the shaded bulb peering down at her, suspended from the white ceiling. She lay still for a moment while her scattered thoughts collected themselves and formed an orderly line.

First to present themselves on the stage of consciousness was Joseph Dalton, along with the throbbing beat from her pounded womanhood. She righted her knickers, the elastic hem having bedded itself into her skin, and pondered how long her *minute* had really been.

The room was now darker than it had been when she had closed her eyes. As she sobered up from her reverie, the memory of her adulterous afternoon brought with it a very different mix of feelings altogether. She shot bolt upright, remorse crawling all over her where lust once was.

What the hell have I done.

The buttons from her blouse lay dotted around on the carpet, alongside her discarded clothes, which now lay alone. Jumping to her feet, Lucy balled up the soiled duvet, then hid it behind a couple of boxes and the ironing board. She had never been unfaithful while in any relationship; hypocritically, for her, it was the worst breach of trust there was.

Opening the curtains Lucy pressed her feverish brow against the cool glass, eyes closed, dismayed at herself for being so weak. How was she going to face Mark now? Even worse, how was she going to face Joseph on Monday? Her mind was infested with all manner of thoughts and feelings, and each one left her feeling sicker than the last. The extreme high she had felt during her rendezvous with her fantasy man was gone, leaving behind the anguish of regret.

Crossing the room she snatched her clothes from the floor and made her way to the bathroom, dropping them into the laundry basket along with her underwear. She was about to turn on the shower when the sound of voices seized her attention. *Is that Mark?* Alarm bells rang. *Who's he talking to?* Her fist clenched against her lips as she had an alarming thought. *Is he talking to Joseph? Surely not.*

Unhooking the dressing gown from the back of the bathroom door, she slipped it on and knotted the belt. She trod gingerly to the head of the stairs, pausing, she held her breath, giving her hearing capacity the best advantage possible. Which, from the thudding of her remorseful heart was very little. There were definitely voices, but they were too muffled to be comprehended.

She wanted to hide all night, but knew full well that she couldn't. She crept down the stairs, trepidation ascending with her descent. The voices were coming from the lounge. Lucy stopped several steps from the bottom, leaning over the handrail, her head turned towards the door. A feeling of relief washed over her, allowing a much-needed flow of oxygen to be sucked in and out of her heaving bosom. It was the TV that she could hear. The temporary abatement expired before it had even drawn breath, with the birth of another anxious question. *How long has Mark been back? Had he seen Joseph leaving the house?*

The door to the lounge was only open half an inch. Completing the stairs, she attempted to compose herself, trying to delay the inevitable. Deflating her chest through puckered lips, she scraped her sex-styled hair back and nervously reached out for the handle. Her feelings of apprehension were balanced by the hope that she would find an acquittal waiting for her. Her tongue circled the barren cavity of her mouth, giving herself a countdown from three, Lucy pushed the door open, feeling as nervous as an actor on the opening night of a play. She stepped onto the stage to begin her performance.

'Oh, hello. I didn't know you were back.' Her voice was too high and very animated; she didn't sound like her usual self – because she wasn't her usual self.

'I haven't been in long.' Something was definitely wrong. He sat on the couch in tight formation, his knees touching, one hand cupping his elbow while he gnawed on the thumbnail of his other, his chin tucked into his neck. The artificial conversation from the TV was the only sound filling the dead air space.

Lucy caught sight of the illuminated time on the Blu-ray player. She'd been asleep for over an hour. The problem was that she had no idea how long Joseph had stayed; he could have only left ten minutes earlier for all she knew.

'Have you had a good day?' Despite her best efforts,

she still sounded like a checkout girl in a supermarket.

'Yeah, fine.' He stared blankly at the screen, not watching what was playing out before him.

Lucy stepped deeper into the room, secretly observing. His eyes were red and puffy from the sting of tears. *Oh my god, he knows!*

She hid her trembling hands in the pockets of her gown, trying to rein in her panic, and a cold trickle ran down the inside of her thigh – a timely reminder of her sin, of the gross betrayal she had so easily allowed to happen.

She sat on the chair opposite so that his expressions could be analysed and gauged before placing her bet. It was a cold and calculating thing to do, so unlike her nature, but that is what infatuation and infidelity do to an otherwise kind heart, they warp and twist the rational.

Perched on the edge of her chair, her hands still hidden, she swabbed the inside of her thighs.

'What have you been up to today?'

'Not much,' he answered morosely, his glance darting over to her for only a second. Lucy spotted the question in his eyes as he took note of her bathrobe.

'I had a terrible migraine when I came home, so I went to bed for an hour.' Unchallenged, she watched his face intensely, looking for the slightest twitch or flicker. 'I was just going for a bath when I heard the TV.'

Not a thing. The tension in her body eased somewhat, although she wasn't out of danger yet. Lucy ran through a checklist of things that may have been causing his solemn mood. Was he tired? Hungry? Had someone scratched the car? There was obviously only one way to find out.

'Mark, what's wrong?' Her nerves spiked when he

didn't answer straight away, every second felt like an age.

'Nothing.' It was the stock answer that all men gave when something *was* wrong.

She had two options: either leave him in his stupor, which would make her ill from worry, or pursue the reason he wasn't himself.

'Has something happened?' A shake of his head was the only reply.

She got up and sat next to him. If she was going to get any sleep at all that night, it was essential that she knew what was bothering him, albeit for selfish reasons.

'Come on, Mark, what is it?' It did cross her mind that she might have been encouraging a lion from his cage.

The television received all of his vacant attention, whilst the tip of his finger and thumb moved left to right across his closed lips, as if zipping and unzipping them. The hypocrisy of her hand reassuringly resting on his thigh left a bad taste on her fraudulent tongue.

'Have I done something to upset you?' She kept her voice very submissive, almost apologetic.

'It's not you.' A short passage of time slipped by before he continued, in a strained voice. 'It's me.'

'Why? What have you done?' The focus of her thoughts switched from her own guilt to what was about to be confessed.

'Huh.' His eyes finally moved, randomly scattering across the empty wall opposite.

'Mark?'

'I… am struggling…'

'With what?'

'Everything.' His hands slipped down from his brow, squashing his nose as it passed.

'I've been acting like a total arsehole most of the time, I'm never here when you need me. I'm too busy… fucking around on the golf course, or…' His lungs released some of the pressure. But rather than being concerned for Mark, Lucy was flooded with a rush of relief. He didn't have a clue about her and Joseph; the liberation was invigorating.

'Maybe you are right: maybe I do need a purpose in life. I just… need to get a grip on things, take control of myself.' Now that she was off the hook, Lucy paid more attention to what was being said. He was genuinely upset with himself; she had never seen him like this before. Mark shuffled towards Lucy, his knee touching hers. 'I know one thing,' he took her hand from his thigh, and holding it in both of his, 'I'm going to be a better man for you from now on.'

He looked at her in a way that he hadn't for such a long time. The watery blue of his eyes sparkled beneath the glaze of emotion ready to spill. 'I promise I will. I need you so much. I don't know what I'd do without you.' His grip tightened as he made the pledge.

Lucy knew she had to say something encouraging, reassuring. Mark wiped his eyes, leaving a glossy streak on each temple. She freed her hand, leaned into him and put her arms around his neck.

'Come here,' Lucy said.

Mark leant his head on her shoulder. It could have been her act of betrayal, but Lucy felt detached from his emotion whilst she consoled him.

'I love you,' he mumbled into the pile of her gown.

'And I love you too.' What should have been a very natural thing to say, seemed fictitious.

'How would you feel about becoming my wife?'

That was the last thing she expected him to say, or wanted. Twelve months ago she would have been kicking her heels to be asked such a question, but now… now, she wasn't sure. Fortunately, he remained cuddled into her shoulder so he didn't witness her uncertainty.

'You don't have to ask me such a question, silly.'

'No, I mean it, Lucy.'

'How about we talk about this when you're feeling more like yourself.' She issued a Judas kiss to his cheek. 'Shall we have that movie night you promised me?'

'Yeah, that sounds nice.'

The awkward moment had been sidestepped, but Lucy suspected that there was more to his confession. But under the circumstances, she had no right to question and was glad that her shoulders were now weight-free, her conscience however, was another matter altogether.

Mark ordered a takeaway while Lucy showered. They ate under the flickering light of the TV as a movie played, filling the room with scripted words so Lucy didn't have to. She laid in Mark's attentive arms with her head on his chest. Thoughts of the day floated around her head like bubbles in a champagne glass. She went over every word, every touch, the feel of his skin on hers, more than just a memory. Lucy vowed to herself, over and over, that she would never do anything like that again; the fear of them being caught, still influencing her somewhat. She listened to the contented beat of Mark's heart, now not entirely sure where hers belonged.

.

CHAPTER TWENTY-TWO

Mark began his new resolution with great vigour, bringing Lucy tea and toast in bed, tidying his mess as he went, all well before midday. Most of that Sunday afternoon was spent wandering the corridors of one of the many museums Lucy was constantly trying to get him to visit with her.

If he was bored and uninterested then he was hiding it well, then again, so was Lucy. The effect of sex with another man other than her long-term partner wasn't something that could be brushed away easily.

Mark was perfect company: attentive, funny, and engaging. Even so, Lucy's smiles and conversation didn't flow quite as naturally as it should have. Her attention was taken with the thought of the next day's meeting with Joseph. The shadow of the thought followed her all day long – even the sanctuary of sleep was powerless to her troubles.

Lucy woke just as the sun was stretching its arms, ready

to start another shift. She lay in wait listening for the sound of vehicle number two, anticipating he wouldn't break with habit and arrive after his father. Taking advantage of Mark's considerate spell, she falsely confessed to wanting a lie-in, and asked if Mark wouldn't mind making the guys their usual morning drink. Like a faithful dog sent to fetch a ball, he leapt out of bed, eager to please.

George arrived early as usual. Precisely eight minutes later, the identical noise of his son's truck arriving made her stomach churn. It was her turn to leap out of bed. Lucy's fingers skirted the edge of the curtains. This wasn't a very good start to her promise of abstinence. The bedroom floor was paced for ten minutes before showering and slipping on her old comfy jeans. She left her hair down, knowing it suited her better.

Lucy entered the kitchen, Mark had his back to her and was hunched over the worktop texting on his phone, which he promptly slipped into his back pocket as soon as he noticed her.

'Morning. That wasn't much of a lie-in.'

'No, I know. I couldn't get back off to sleep.'

'Well, now that you're up, how do you fancy a continental breakfast?'

'What?' Her attention was taken up by the view from the window.

'You know, croissants, jam, coffee . . .'

'Yeah, if you like.' She sat in one of the stools and pivoted her back to the glazed side of the room. 'We haven't got any croissants.'

'No, but the bakery on Connaught Road does.' He opened the kitchen drawer and took out her keys. 'You don't mind if I take your car, do you?'

'No, that's fine.'

'I won't be long.' He kissed her on the head and left her alone with temptation. This wasn't going to be as easy as she had supposed. Even before the car had pulled away, the suggestion that this may be her only chance to talk to Joseph paraded itself inappropriately.

What am I supposed to do, hide myself away? There's nothing wrong with saying hello is there?

Most wrongs are committed on the whim of justification, and it was certainly true that a simple 'hello' held no threat to anyone, but the person it would be delivered to did.

There was a knock at the window. Lucy's nails embedded into her thighs and her stomach knotted. He must have heard Mark drive away; clearly he also wanted to seize the opportunity to speak with her.

She fixed a demure smile on her face and swung herself around. On the other side of the glass was George. She felt her smile wane, so bolstered it with a show of teeth. He motioned towards the door. Lucy's bare feet made contact with the cool tiles, she walked to the bi-fold door where George was waiting with a ready smile. Disengaging the lock, she leaned her body weight against the floor-to-ceiling door, sliding it open.

'Good morning, sunshine. How's Monday treating you?' George had mastered the art of being cheery first thing in the morning without being annoying.

'Hello, George. I'm very well, thank you. How about you?'

'Couldn't be better, I feel like an eighteen-year-old. An eighteen-year-old with chronic arthritis and failing eyesight, but never mind.' He was the cause of Lucy's first giggle of the day.

'How did the school fete go?'

'It went very well, thank you. The kids loved it.'

'I'm sorry I couldn't make it, but I had arranged to go and see an old mate of mine. We hadn't seen each other for years so I didn't like to cancel.'

'George, you don't have to explain, that's fine.' Lucy reached out and rubbed his shoulder.

'Joseph tells me he was there too.' She recalled the vision of him leaning on his truck, waiting for her and Sam. If there was a single day of her life she could relive, it would have been that one.

'Yes, he very kindly showed his support,' her answers were measured.

'And was he good?'

'He was better than I could have ever imagined.'

That answer wasn't measured at all. It felt good to be able to say that in the way it was meant; with the cage door open, honesty could fly free without restriction. Fortunately, it soared straight over George's head. It was his turn to chuckle, mistaking sincerity for sarcasm.

'Good, I'm glad he behaved himself; that makes a change. The reason I wanted to speak to you is, you have a horse chestnut tree right at the back of the garden.' He removed his glasses, taking on a more serious tone, and put the tip of one of the arms into the corner of his mouth, like a pipe. 'It's got a very bad case of what's called bleeding canker. It's a virulent disease and I'm afraid the tree won't survive, it has too much bark damage.'

'Dear me, what do you suggest?' She loved her garden, but after all the recent drama in her personal life, she found it difficult to muster any interest.

'It needs to be taken out really. If you don't do it now you'll only be doing it in another three to four months.'

Having issued the prognosis, his glasses were sat back on the end of his nose. He reassured her that in all his years as a gardener he had never cut down a tree without good reason. And despite Lucy's protest that she wholeheartedly trusted his advice, George insisted that she make the trip to the back of the garden to see for herself before he would remove so much as a leaf.

'You go on. Joseph will show you what I mean. I'll get the chainsaw from the truck.'

Here was the perfect excuse to say *hello* to Joseph. She pondered the predicament for a matter of seconds, before deciding that she simply had to know if he had been as affected as she had. Shoving her feet into her old gardening shoes that had been left outside the door, Lucy hurried along knowing that George would only be a few minutes. Halfway along her journey she passed Adam who was head down, arse up. She wished him good morning, but by the time he'd extracted himself from the bush he was in, Lucy had already put some distance between them. The feminine perfume of a voluminous white lilac scented her approach. As she neared its heavy branches, laden with the purest white clusters of bloom, it generously granted her passing with a view to the object of her brisk crossing. Her steps slowed and her heartrate quickened. He had his back to her, head tilted up, looking at the giant he was about to euthanise. With no time to waste she lubricated her lips to ease the passing of the name that had hounded her every thought, whether it was sun or moon in the sky. Lucy's lungs filled with the air that would carry her voice when the electronic drone of his phone kidnapped the moment.

He popped the press stud on his short's side pocket, took out the phone and inspected the screen before answering. She didn't know whether to make herself known or not. 'Hello, Kimberley, are you keeping tabs on me, you naughty girl?'

Lucy rocked backwards, the effect of what he had said hitting her like a crossbow in the chest.

'You know I was going to call you . . .'

She looked back over her shoulder for George. Filled with a detrimental curiosity, she wanted to hear the rest of his conversation.

'Yes, I will be coming to see you... not this weekend, next... you know full well when it is. I bet you've been counting down the days, haven't you, you little minx?'

She listened to his playful tone, the one he had used with her, with unreasonable jealousy, the burn of it rising from her stomach into her chest.

'I'll be staying all weekend – I bet I'm going to need all weekend to recover.'

She felt dizzy and nauseous. How could she have been so foolish? Lucy thought they had a connection. It was more than just a thought, it was a deep feeling that had felt as real as the wind on her face. But it seemed it was just a sentimental illusion; no doubt she was just one in a long line of girls to have been fooled by the mirage.

'Ok, I've got to go... I'm looking forward to seeing you too. Take care, gorgeous, bye.'

Gorgeous? Minx? Naughty Girl. This Kimberley must be really something.

In this entire fucked up situation Lucy was the

adulteress, yet she was the one feeling the ache and torment of betrayal. With the call ended, she now wanted her presence to be known.

'Morning' The off-hand greeting caught him by surprise. Spinning around, his boots created a small dust cloud.

'I didn't hear you coming.' *You fucking did on Saturday.* 'Morning. Dad sent you up to look at the tree, has he?'

Sod the bloody tree, I wanted to see you.

'Yes, he has.' Surely he couldn't ignore what had happened between them?

'If you stand here you can see…' Her own screaming thoughts drowned out whatever the hell he was telling her about the doomed tree.

Joseph's eyes were busy climbing into the foliage. She was waiting for them to fall upon her face, to give her some kind of acknowledgement that she wasn't just another Saturday night fuck.

'…so sooner or later it would have to be felled,' he finished, and Lucy finally got what she had been waiting for.

Silently, she was imploring him to say something, anything meaningful. His brow knitted, confused by her silence.

'Lucy, are you all right?' The question wasn't asked in the context she had wanted it to be.

'I was about to ask you the same thing.'

He shrugged his shoulders. 'I'm fine, why?'

Another arrow was fired, but this one hit the bullseye. It was only her own emotions she was seeing in his eyes, nothing more.

'Why?' she said sharply, abandoning suggestive

subtlety.

'Can you see what I mean, Lucy?' George interrupted, chainsaw in hand.

That was it, the window of opportunity had closed. Had it ever been open? She hadn't had the slightest effect upon him. None whatsoever.

'Er… yes, just… do, do what you have to do, George.'

'Okay, I'm sorry, Lucy.' He passed the instrument of death to his son.

'Yeah… so am I.' Her return journey to the house was a much slower one. The perfume from the lilac tree lost its sweetness on her second passing. She saw Mark stood in the doorway waving a bag of croissants in the air like he was bringing a plane into land.

The chainsaw buzzed as Lucy taxied, crash-landing internally upon reaching the house. She dabbed the moisture from her eyes while Mark's back was turned, blaming the redness of her eyes on hay fever that she had never suffered from. Handing her the morning newspaper, Mark insisted that she sit down and relax while he prepared breakfast. The bold black headlines of scandal and celebrity gossip held no interest for her whatsoever, but she was glad of the concealment it afforded her.

Mark chirped on about shopping for bathroom suites while the buttery fumes of fresh, crusty croissants and the heavy aroma of coffee created what should have been a perfect Monday morning scene. Except, Lucy was there in body alone. Now that the anaesthetising effect of nearly being caught had worn off, she was left feeling raw and confused, even though the situation was entirely black and white: Joseph Dalton was a player and she had been played.

CHAPTER TWENTY-THREE

Tuesday delivered some relief, placing a degree of distance between Lucy and her problem. It was a busy day at school, which should also have provided her with some distraction, except for the fact that Joseph had made a big impact on another life. Sam was constantly asking about him and when would he be visiting the school. It was easy to deceive herself, but a six-year-old boy? One who she cared about deeply; that really took its toll.

Had he any idea about what he had done, what effect he'd had? If he did, then he was a very cold and callous man.

Lucy took the long route home in order to make sure that she wouldn't have to suffer the pain of seeing his face or the distress of hearing his voice. Croissants and spaghetti bolognese were the limits of Mark's skills in the kitchen, but he had given some thought to their dining dilemma and ordered pizza. Lucy wondered how long it would be before he got cabin fever. It was the longest he had spent in the house with her since they had moved in.

Wednesday was just as pitiless as its predecessor. Every day without fail, Sam came to school with the hat that his best friend in the whole wide world had given him. Even her colleagues added to the provocation, by asking how he was and, sending their flush-cheeked regards, which Lucy kept to herself. There was no escape. You can't outrun your own mind.

She drove home slowly to ensure that her arrival at home would be long after his departure. But she still felt a sense of disappointment upon turning the corner and seeing the empty space outside her house. Mark had given up the 'new man' act and slipped back into his old habits. When she got in, he told her that he was going out to catch up with some of his old friends. At least this time he had bothered to wait until she arrived home before going out: a note scribbled on the back of an envelope was his usual method of telling her. He promised not to be late and that tomorrow they would go out for dinner together. Lucy reassured him that it was fine. The truth was, she was relieved to have the place to herself, and not have to go through the library of bathroom brochures he had collected. The last thing on her mind was what shape toilet they needed. Mark left the house long before the smell of his cologne did. Lucy ran a hot bath and drained the cool wine glass, then soaked in a pool of reflection. The hushed crackle of the bubbles disappearing like her silly fantasies was the only sound occupying the room. The tranquil water allowed her body the feeling of weightlessness. If only it could award the same benefit to her mind.

The cooling water forced her to swap the bathtub for bed, but an unsettled mind wasn't conducive to a good night's sleep. Mark came home and slipped under the covers, only an hour later than he said he would be. Lucy pretended she was asleep. That had become the norm lately – pretending.

Thursday was greeted with a determined attitude, despite the sandman leaving her last on his list.

It was her final working day of the week, and it held all of the obstacles every other day had, but bullishly she pushed on through. She had even driven straight home, refusing to let circumstances dictate her life any longer. She arrived to find Joseph's truck had gone, and George in the street, chatting to Charles.

'Hello, Lucy.'

'Hi, George. Hi, Charles.' She closed the car door and made her way over to them.

'I'm glad I caught you; the plants are being delivered tomorrow. I've left the planting plan with Mark. Let me know if there is anything you want to change, or you're not sure of.'

'I'm sure it's all perfect, George.' She had missed seeing him too.

'Will you be here tomorrow?' he asked.

'Yes, I will, I'm afraid.'

'Oh, better not be late in the morning then,' George said, winking at Charles, who was impeccably dressed as usual.

'I can't imagine a man like you ever being late, George,' Charles said, accompanying the compliment with a royal flop of his hand.

'I wish I could say the same about that boy of mine. He's out tonight, so he'll probably be late in the morning, depending on where he ends up sleeping.' George wasn't aware that he had dashed all her day's efforts with that reminder of his son's promiscuity. It was a myth that time was a great healer. If anything, it made things worse. It was like going without water, and Lucy was very, very thirsty.

'Oh to be a young man again, eh, George?' said Charles.

'I wish he'd settle down and find a nice girl like Lucy.' George shook his head with a sigh. 'He does worry me. I'm going off on a tangent, aren't I? Sorry about that. Lucy, I look forward to seeing your lovely face in the morning, and, Charles, it was nice talking to you, sir.'

Charles offered his spotless hand to George's rather dirty one. 'The pleasure was all mine, and remember, as soon as Lucy's garden is finished, you must take a look at our frightful mess.'

'I certainly will. Enjoy your evening, my friends.' George climbed into his truck and drove away in the same calm, steady way that he always conducted himself.

'I know you must be tired from your day at work, Lucy, but could I take up ten minutes of your time to discuss the school investment?'

She needed something to focus on, and this could be just the thing. She had begun to wonder whether he had reneged on his promise, since she hadn't heard from him recently.

'Of course, Charles.'

'Wonderful. Come into the house. Tabitha is at the doctor's so we will have some privacy.' Ever the gentleman, Charles held out his elbow and Lucy linked arms with him.

They sat in the same sumptuous but tired room she

and Mark had when they first visited. Without being asked, she was handed an iced gin-and-tonic in a tall glass. Feeling it rude to decline she accepted with a smile. Charles sat opposite her a notepad in one hand and what looked like a shot of whiskey in the other. He ran through every single detail of what the school hoped to achieve in a very methodical and precise way, complete with figures, dates and timescales. She felt very lucky to have the help of a professional, astute man of business.

After that, Charles moved on to her personal finances and account details, Charles repeatedly reminding her that she could pull out at any time if she was in any way uncomfortable with the investment, which he had delved into with a robust, passionate zeal. Here was a man revisiting his youth, a time when he felt important and necessary. This was his chance to shine, to prove to himself that he still had what it takes, and that age was no barrier to his knowledge or ability. By now she had reached the bottom of her glass, and Charles was still talking in terms that were unknown to her. He promised once again to produce a detailed document for her perusal. Having finished his monologue, he apologised for turning the ten minutes into an hour and offered her another drink, which she politely declined. Lucy clawed at the near-threadbare arm of the chair and managed to hoist her bottom out of the sunken seat. The effect of not having eaten properly for four days and consuming a large glass of alcohol, sent her head spinning as she reached the dizzy heights of her two-inch heels. Charles kindly held on to her elbow and led her to the front door as you would an elderly relative or a young child. She thanked him for his generous involvement, overshot the air kiss and bumped clumsily into his cheek. She was at that strange point of having a completely sober mind, and an ever so slightly drunken body.

Lucy completed the short journey to her front door successfully, having adjusted to her chemically altered state.

'I'm upstairs, babe,' Mark called out on the closing of the door.

Shoes kicked off, her handbag took its usual spot on the fourth step and she expended what little energy she had on climbing the stairs to find Mark ironing a shirt in just his shorts and socks.

'Hi.' She flopped down on the bed like wet cardboard, drowsy from the large G&T.

'How's your day been?' Mark asked through a cloud of steam.

'Yeah, not bad,' she answered, lying down next to his freshly pressed, navy jeans. 'Are you going out tonight?' Her tone was as carefree as she could make it. It wasn't a criticism. 'Yeah, we both are. We're going for dinner, remember?' She didn't. 'Oh, yes.'

Her arms rose above her head languidly; the bed felt so soft and welcoming. When she had wanted sleep last night it couldn't be found, now it was courting her with its slumberous spell. She seemed to sink a little deeper into the bed with every long, slow exhale.

'Mark... can we cancel tonight? I don't really feel like it,' she mumbled, her lashes knitting together.

The iron was placed upright with more force than was necessary. It snorted a steaming cloud of disapproval that curled up into the air. Mark transferred all his weight onto one leg, hand on hip, tongue poking around in his cheek. It was a look that needed no accompanying words.

'I'll go and have a shower,' she said. Anything for a peaceful evening; at least she wouldn't have to cook.

The taxi arrived, beeping impatiently. Lucy offered to drive, but Mark's insistent ways had lay dormant for long enough.

'Got everything? Have you got the house keys?' He opened the door and signalled to the driver that they were on their way.

'Keys are in my pocket, and my phone is in my bag.'

'Right, let's go.' Mark clapped his hands, rubbing them together.

'Is my hair okay?' Lucy flicked her fringe from one side to the other, neither side feeling comfortable.

'Yeah, yeah, it's fine – where's your watch?' He had noticed her bling-free wrists.

'It's… upstairs in the box.'

'What's the point in spending all that money if you're never gonna wear it?' He was tetchy for some reason. 'I've got mine on.' He pulled the cuff of his shirt up in demonstration, displaying a solid gold Rolex.

'Okay, okay. I'll go and put it on.'

She headed back upstairs in her high heels; he had already criticised her first choice of outfit because it wasn't smart enough. Mark was a label man; if it didn't have a designer name or badge, he wasn't interested.

'I'll wait in the taxi. Make sure you close the door on the way out.'

Yes, sir!

Fastening the gold bracelet around her wrist, she

hurried downstairs and out to the black cab.

Most of the journey was spent listening to a very macho conversation between Mark and the driver discussing football. Mark's phone pinged with messages several times, but he ignored it, which was unusual for him.

It seemed nothing was to Mark's standards that evening. He complained about their table at the restaurant because it was too close to their fellow diners. They were moved to another, which seemed identical to the one they had vacated, but it pleased Mark. He had exerted his authority over the lowly waiter, who probably spat on his dinner before serving it to him with a subservient smile.

Mark ordered too much food and drank too much beer. The food kept him quiet for a while, but the beer fermented his vivacity. His voice became louder, the laughs harder and longer. It was like having a front-row seat at a one-man show.

Lucy got her quiet night out; she hardly said a word. He was hyper. It was rather worrying; there was something missing from Mark, a piece of the puzzle. He knew it too, although whether he knew *what* it was, she didn't know. His testing mood had one benefit; it had allowed her a Joseph Dalton- free night – right up until Mark went to the bathroom. She wondered where Joseph was and who he was with. A man like that would never have to go home alone – that was for sure. The staff roamed around with strained smiles on their faces. They were the last ones left in the restaurant, and it was time to go. Lucy took the liberty of asking for the bill while Mark was absent. She was looking forward to climbing into bed, and closing her eyes on the day.

Mark left a generous tip and drunkenly backslapped and hand shook his way out of there. The moment their feet hit the pavement, Lucy heard the lock turn in the door.

'That was a nice meal, wasn't it? I really enjoyed that.' He looked up and down the street, swaying gently.

'Yeah, it was nice. Have you got a number for a cab, Mark?'

'There's a taxi rank just around the corner,' he said, thumbing to the right. Lucy took his hand and led the way.

'Isn't it a nice night? I love summer evenings,' he stated. It was a lovely evening. The air was warm and clear; despite the darkness it seemed bright. A heavy bassline thundered directionless from a nearby club. Young men and women, couples and singles still strolled the street, despite the fact that one day had become the next.

'It's up here.' Mark stepped ahead while Lucy stopped, stretching their arms apart.

'Up there?' She looked along the long narrow cutting which had a very different atmosphere to the one they were currently standing in. The closeness of the brick buildings shadowed much of the route. A security light flickered intermittently halfway along the passageway. Shivering at the eerie blackness, her eyes caught sight of the traffic- polluted sign that was fixed to the old brown brick: Black Dog Alley.

'Isn't there another way?'

'Yeah, if you want to walk *all* the way round. It's only two minutes, come on.' He let go of her hand and continued to walk into the darkness.

Lucy hesitated for a moment, but Mark obstinately strolled on.

He took his phone from his pocket, and the light from the screen created a glowing halo around his head.

Fucking hell Mark! He was far from angelic that night.

'Wait for me.'

Lucy trotted along after him. The path was uneven. She trod blindly, wobbling on her heels. He didn't comply with her request and continued deeper into the alley, slipping his phone into his back pocket. As her eyes adjusted to the lack of light, she was able to make out that the shadows against the walls were industrial bins, overflowing with bags of rubbish, and more piled against them.

It was a service alley for the bars and restaurants. Skulking doorways reeked with the stench of urine, which combined with the putrid smell of decay from the rat-infested refuse bags. Lucy felt like she'd stepped into the underworld. Her heart raced. She couldn't take two steps forward without looking back. Every square inch of the space seeped with a revolting smell. Even though he was only a few steps ahead, Mark's was no comfort whatsoever.

'I don't even know why we're going home now anyway,' he suddenly blurted out.

'What do you mean?' Lucy asked, confused by his statement.

He stopped and turned to face her. 'The night is young, and so are we. We should be going to a club, not going to bed.' The agitation in his voice wasn't what she wanted to hear.

'Mark, I've had a long day. I'm tired. Can't we just go

home? Please?'

'It's all about you, isn't it?'

'What's that supposed to mean?'

'You know what I mean.' They were halfway along and his anger was revealed in snapshots by the blinking security light.

'What about what I want, eh? Doesn't it matter what I need?' His raised voice volleyed intimidatingly off the brick walls.

'Can we not do this here? I want to go.'

'So I'm supposed to suffer because you want to go to work for no fucking money?' He couldn't help himself. He had been itching all evening for an argument, while Lucy had been walking on eggshells trying to avoid it. She had given in to his childish, selfish ways to please him, and for what?

'What are you talking about? How do you suffer? You go out nearly every night, and I never complain.' It was only their location that stopped her from going at him, all guns blazing.

'Am I meant to be grateful? Well?' He jabbed his head at her, violence in his words. 'Am I? It's all about Lucy *fucking* Eaton. You got the house you wanted, the garden you wanted. Well I want things too!' He beat his chest erratically.

This was a side of him she had never seen before.

'Jesus, Mark, calm down; you're scaring me. Let's go home; it's late,' she implored him with a calmness that was equal to her unease.

'It's not late; it's never too late. I'm going to do what Mark Smith wants for a fucking change.'

Stabbing his finger at Lucy, he marched back the way

they had come.

'Mark! Where are you going?' Lucy chased after him, but her shoes proved to be a hindrance.

'I'm going to a club. You can fucking go home to bed!'

'Don't be bloody stupid. You can't leave me here!'

'Fuck off, will you!' Having issued the vicious insult, he began to run and didn't stop.

The clacking of Lucy's heels ceased. There was no way she could keep up.

She watched with disbelief as he disappeared from view. Left alone, with the ominous silence ringing in her ears, she waited. *Give him a minute. He'll stop around the corner, realise what he's done, and then come back.* Every passing second suffocated that thought. He had abandoned her. Should she go back or carry on? Despair clouded her judgment; she was still in shock at what he had done.

Fear sharpens the senses until you hear and see things that aren't really there. All her reasoning was powerless against the imagination of danger. Having travelled half the distance, she decided to carry on to the taxi rank. She walked as quickly as possible, her head turning left to right, searching the unknown chasm of darkness. Lucy passed their checkpoint. She looked straight into the stuttering security light, instantly regretting it, as pale yellow speckles smeared her vision. She blinked frenziedly, trying to correct her eyesight, hearing the suggestion of footsteps ahead. Lucy stopped her advance. The shadows seemed to separate and the silhouette of a man stepped off the black page. *Just keep your head down and keep walking.* Her back and neck muscles tightened, slouching her frame. The out of range rumble of conversation was now perceptible; the lone silhouette split into two. Her heart rate and blood pressure competed to outdo each other as adrenaline and terror flowed through her body. The figures grew larger and silenced as they neared. It was two men. The taller of the two was bouncing cockily on his toes as he walked. In a futile attempt to conceal her face, Lucy flicked her hair from over her shoulders and hung her blinkered head low.

'Well, hello there,' the taller man said, blocking her path. 'What's a pretty girl like you doing in an ugly place like this?'

'There's a taxi waiting for me, so if you'll excuse me.' She didn't look either of them in the face and side-stepped only to have her action mirrored by the stranger.

'Slow down, girl. What's the rush? We'll take you to your taxi after we've had a little chat.'

Despite the warm night, Lucy was trembling. It hadn't sounded like a genuine offer of assistance. She dared to look up at the face of the man that stood before her. There was a scarcity of light, but she could see he was in his mid-twenties; long, thin, dark eyebrows streaked across the soulless eyes. A stubbled moustache lay closely to the contours of his top lip. He was wearing a long beanie hat, pulled down over his ears and sitting high on his forehead, showing a tuft of black hair. While Lucy examined his face, he had his head tipped to one side, inspecting every inch of her body. His friend was wearing a baseball cap, the flat peak skewed to one side. He was stockier than his taller friend, and moved to stand at Lucy's right side.

The night had drained all colour; everything was black and white. Or in Lucy's case more black. The situation didn't look good.

'You got a man?' the taller man asked, his nose twitching with a sharp sniff.

'Yes, yes... my husband. He... he'll be here any minute.' She pointed over her shoulder. 'He left his wallet in the restaurant.'

'Did he?' The two men exchanged a glance. Lucy was hoping for Mark – or someone, anyone – to come walking down that alley.

She shrieked involuntarily at the coldness of a foreign touch as her hand was snatched up.

'Did you leave your fucking wedding ring there too? Huh?' The men both cackled loudly, secure in the knowledge that no one would hear them. The comedian held out his hand, and his stout friend was quick to step over and slap it, in acknowledgement of his rapier wit. It was clear who the alpha was.

'Oooh, girl, that's a nice watch.' He yanked her hand up closer to his face, jolting her forward. 'A Rollie?' the pencil thin eyebrows arched. 'It's a fake,' she said, knowing that it was a lame attempt.

His stubbled cheeks raised, spreading his beak- like nose. The swirling tattoos that crowded his neck added to the fear of how this meeting would end.

'Oh, it's a fake. Are you sure about that? My man Jay here is an expert on Rolex. Isn't that right, Jay?'

'Fuck yeah,' Jay answered, tittering like a pubescent teenager. The pair of them were a breed that people didn't like to think existed: the kind that preys on the weak and the vulnerable; vultures in human form, only concerned with their own survival, their own selfish, narcissistic needs. Modern day pirates without a ship.

He twisted her wrist around to expose the clasp, the force tipping her upper body over too. With a flick of his nail he released the catch and took the timepiece from her.

It was a relief. It meant that his depraved hand wasn't infecting hers with the corpse-like touch. Jay the sycophant was quickly at his master's heels to take the booty. He had a quick look at it before stuffing the watch into his pocket.

'I think we got ourselves a rich bitch here. Are you a high flying career woman or just fucking someone with money?'

'I'm a teaching assistant.' It was a pathetic reply, but one that she prayed might bring some leniency. 'What, wearing a five grand Rolex? You're a fucking comedian as well, aren't you?'

There was no point screaming: she certainly couldn't outrun them, and she wouldn't have even been able to get the screensaver off her phone before it would be taken from her. The only thing left to do was submit to the fact that she was the victim in this scene. That was the part fate had given her or, rather, that Mark had left her to play.

'You could teach me and my mate a thing or two, I bet. Are those jeans or leggings?' He squinted and hunched over with his hands on his knees to take a closer look. Lucy took half a step back, remaining silent.

'I bet you've got a sweet little ass tucked away in there.'
Jesus, no. Leave me alone. Please God, let them leave me alone.
'Whatcha think, Jay?'

'Damn right. Looks good from here, man.' This was fast becoming a living nightmare. She had to do something.

'Look, please, you've got the watch. Just keep the watch and let me go – I need to go.'

Her head shook from side to side. She knew that she had no bargaining power whatsoever, but a desperate mind will search for hope even when there is none to be found.

'Hey. This here is our playground. We make the fucking rules here, bitch. You do as we say!' The level of aggression had risen alarmingly. This man was unpredictable; it would be prudent not to anger him.

'Is that a designer bag too? Gucci? Prada?'

'No, it was ten pounds from the market.'

'Is that the same place you bought your watch from? Hand it over.'

He snapped his fingers impatiently. She had every intention of giving it to him; it was exactly what she said it was. Lucy unhooked the thin black strap from her shoulder and held it out to him. Feeling that he hadn't taken it, her eyes inched along the length of her outstretched arm, and just off the peninsula of her tremulous hand were the hooded eyes of her future. Would this simply be a callous robbery that would shake her up for a few days, or would it be a life-changing moment – maybe even, life-ending?

His brow lowered and a gold tooth sank into his bottom lip. Lucy's eyes were fixed on the shadows that painted his face, not to show courage, but in order to decipher what intention lay behind the mask. He took a step closer, midnight's effect giving his features a grotesque gargoyle look. He took the bag, flicked the strap over his head and began to rummage through the contents like a dog looking for scraps, tossing away anything that didn't have any value. Jay had moved out of sight behind her.

'What's this, a new iPhone? Sweet. I need a new phone.' It went straight into the pocket of his sweatpants. 'You got any cards? Credit cards?'

'No, there should be 50 quid in the inside zip pocket.'

She volunteered the information for fear of being searched – he was going to find it anyway. The ransacked bag was thrown to the floor next to her make-up and hairbrush. She didn't have anything else except the house key, which was in her jeans pocket. Hopefully he would believe her.

'You've got everything. I'm going to my taxi.'

Before she had even taken one step, his arms splayed out on either side of him.

'Not yet you're not. I'll say when you can fucking go.'

Lucy looked towards the narrow opening at the end of the alley for something to give her hope. What decent, self-respecting person would ever enter such a place? The world had turned its back. She was alone.

Joseph broke the seal of the door and left the stale air of the club. He said goodnight to the doorman and made his way along the paving slabs, the din of the live band fading with each step. His cheeks cooled from the lack of body heat, and his ears whistled like a boiling kettle from the high amplification they had been subjected to. All in all, it had been a good night. He had managed to escape his own thoughts for a few hours, aided by half a bottle of whiskey and the suggestive conversation of a pretty blonde girl, who had jotted her number down on a napkin and stuck it into his shirt pocket. With the haze of alcohol, Joseph strolled along with the inhabitants of the night, who were holding hands, queuing for pizza, laughing with friends. He passed in and out of the lights from the over abundant, never ending, fast food places, scanning for a taxi.

'Spare some change, sir?'

The worn voice caught his attention; it was in stark contrast to the evening that was filled with youth and energy. Joseph looked around for a moment, his vision suffering the side effects of alcohol. Then he saw the man that the words belonged to. He sat in the doorway of an empty shop; his clothes were too dirty to make out any particular colour. Long knotted straggles of hair hung from under an old camouflaged fishing hat. Seeing that he had achieved his objective, he shook the coins in his polystyrene cup.

'Spare some change, sir?'

The wiry grey beard moved, but there was no sign of a mouth hidden beneath it. How could a man have ended up this way? Usually Joseph ignored drunks asking for money, but something was different tonight. Maybe it was the emotional effect of the booze. He stepped over and crouched down in front of the old man.

'I'd be most grateful if you could spare some money for a cup of tea, sir.'

It was easy to criticise and judge others, turning your back on your own faults. Joseph looked into the piercing blue eyes of the old tramp. They were vacant like the shop windows surrounding him. He had lost in the race of life, too far behind to ever catch up. It was then that Joseph realised that he saw something of himself in the broken old face. He knew full well how life could kick you into submission.

Reaching into his back pocket, Joseph took out his wallet and gave the old man his last twenty. His bushy eyebrows bowed and the blue eyes sparkled with moisture. 'Oh, thank you, sir. That's very good of you.' A hand gloved in grime slowly reached out and took it.

'Make sure you get some food with that, you hear?' There was a collection of empty bottles hidden behind the oversized coat he was wearing.

'I will, sir. I will.' Joseph nodded doubtfully.

'Take care, my friend.' At least he had left the man in a happier state.

'Thank you, sir,' he called out. 'Have a good evening.'

Joseph stuck a thumb up, now walking home, having given away his cab money. He didn't mind: his head was beginning to cloud, the exercise would help to clear his mind.

He pulled the napkin from his shirt pocket and read the message that sat above the phone number. Balling it up in his fist, he dumped it in the nearest bin.

There was only room in his life for one girl who could play havoc with his self-control. He wouldn't even allowed himself to say her name but the image of her beauty was irrepressible.

Walk it off, Dalton.

The echo of a voice in distress stole his attention once again. He stood in the mouth of an alleyway, but the source of the voice was nowhere in sight. Focusing as best he could, the spark of a flickering light faintly caught what looked like two figures arguing. He stared hard, but the more he looked the less he saw. 'Drunks,' he groaned, forgetting that he currently fell into that bracket himself. Joseph moved on. He had done his good deed for the night.

'You wearing any jewellery?'

'No.'

He was close enough for her to smell his vile odour of

sweat and cigarettes.

His fingers frisked her ears and neck roughly then stopped when they came into contact with her bra strap.

'What other treasures you got hidden, eh girl?'

Her head hung low, defeated. 'Please… just let me go home.' The tears welled up in her eyes and leapt for freedom from the ends of her lashes. Lucy's pleas went unheeded. Without warning her left breast was groped. At that moment, instinct kicked in and she lashed out. The back of her hand made contact with the side of his face.

Her legs felt weak but she started to run. With only three strides managed, she was yanked backwards by her hair; the searing pain caused a terrified scream to be born from her lungs. Lucy stumbled backwards, only just managing to stay on her feet.

'Shut the fuck up!' She didn't see the blow coming, but it felt like she had been hit across the face with a hammer. The shock of being punched full in the face sent her crashing to the ground. Her central nervous system was stunned, and she lost control of every muscle including her bladder. She didn't know if she was on her back or her head, their voices muffled by the white noise that rang out. Then the pain set in. Jolts and sparks started shooting across her face and around her eye socket, followed by a sensation of heat as blood rushed to the damaged area.

'Get up, bitch.'

She was pulled to her feet by her hair, sobbing.

'This one likes it rough, Jay.'

'Please, don't hurt me,' she begged. A trickle of blood ran down her arm; her elbow was cut from the fall. Shoulders hunched and shaking in abject fear, Lucy was completely at their mercy, or lack of it.

'Whatcha fancy, Jay? A fuck or a blow job?'

The man in question sniggered, rubbing his hands together. He roughly raised her chin towards what scant light there was.

'You've got cock-sucking lips, haven't you?'

Closing her eyes, tears flowed down on to the intrusive hand. He licked her dread from his fingers.

'Mmm, sweet. Does your cunt taste that good too? What's wrong? Lost for words?'

Lucy went limp, her eyes shut tight.

'You will be with my dick in your mouth. Then I'll fuck you raw, girl.' He tilted his head back to his friend. 'Jay, you can have sloppy seconds.' He laughed callously, clearly at ease with the crime he was about to commit.

Like an injured animal, Lucy edged back from the threat.

'Get on your knees, bitch,' he ordered, dropping his sweatpants. Panic bred like rats in the sewer of her mind.

'On your fucking knees, I said!'

Making a futile attempt to save herself, Lucy tried to run.

'Leave me alone!'

He caught her by the throat and squeezed tightly. Lucy's hands clung to his wrists. No match for his strength, she gasped for air while his accomplice sniggered.

'Where the fuck do you think you're going? You know, they say choking increases sexual pleasure. Are you feeling horny?' The grip contracted further still.

Lucy's lips reached out in an attempt to claim a gasp of air. Sparks flashed across her eyes, and she clawed at his hands about to pass out.

'What's that? Speak up, I can't fucking hear you.'

'I think you should fuck her up the arse to teach her a lesson, Taz,' his friend said, joining the sick game.

'Yeah.'

His grip eased, allowing Lucy to take a breath. 'She can give you a blowy at the same time, eh?'

That sparked Jay into action.

'Where do ya wanna do this, Taz?'

'Here's as good a place as any. Take a seat.'

Lucy was thrown into a pile of rubbish bags that were banked up against the building. It was a soft landing, and the contents of the open bags spewed out over her. The stench of rotting, maggot- infested meat was so repulsive that Lucy immediately vomited over herself.

'Fuck me! That stinks man! Jesus!' The two men danced around, holding their faces.

She clambered amongst the toppling bags, trying fruitlessly to escape, her body retching violently.

'I ain't fucking that now. No way, man,' said Jay.

His friend was silenced by the hand over his mouth.

Hearing his words, Lucy stopped her struggling and lay in the relative safety of the rotten waste.

'Come on, Taz. Let's get out of here, man.'

Jay had already begun to distance himself from the smell.

'Yeah, this hoe is fuckin rank.' He pulled up his sweat pants, turned to join his friend and paused. This sudden hesitation caused Lucy's level of fear to peak, her promised freedom held captive by his stilled presence.

'Hold up, Jay.'

He walked back, bent over and removed one of her shoes. Using the light from her iPhone, he looked inside.

'She's wearing rich bitch shoes,' he said, tossing it over

to his friend. 'Jimmy fucking Choo's.'

The remaining shoe was snatched from her foot and thrown to Jay.

'We'll take those, thank you.'

He snorted loudly and hacked up the contents of his nose into his mouth, and spat it out at Lucy.

'You lie in the shit, where you belong.'

Kicking her naked foot, he finally walked away into the darkness.

Trembling, Lucy held her breath, listening to the echoes of their laughter. Once it was gone she sobbed uncontrollably, lying in the cesspool that had ultimately saved her.

CHAPTER TWENTY-FOUR

When he parked up outside Lucy's, Joseph found his father and Adam standing on the drive, deep in conversation, wearing serious expressions. He slipped his cap on and got out of his truck with a heavy head from the night before.

'Morning, guys,' he called out.

Unclipping the cover of his pickup, he noticed the perturbed look on his father's face hadn't budged. Leaving the cover half undone, Joseph wandered over to them, curiosity getting the better of him.

'What's wrong?'

'Morning, son. I'm sorry, I was miles away, thinking about that poor girl.'

'What you talking about?' Joseph asked, confused.

'Lucy. She was mugged last night.'

'Mugged? Where? Is she all right?'

'It happened in town somewhere. The bastards made a right mess of her face. The police are on the way. She rang them while I was with her.' George sighed. 'What's this world coming to?'

'Where was Mark?' Joseph's anger was fast rising. 'Why was she on her own?'

'I don't know, son. She's not in a very talkative mood. I didn't like to push it.'

Joseph rested his hands on his hips, shaking his head.

'Let's give her some space. We're here if she wants us,' George patted his son on the shoulder.

'Adam, can you start taking the gear round, the plants will be arriving any time now.'

Joseph wrestled with himself, while man and boy set about their business. He knew the right thing to do was follow his father's advice, but the thought of anyone laying a hand on that girl made his blood boil.

With his father's eyes diverted, Joseph marched around to the back of the house. The need to know she was okay overrode manners. Sliding the door open, he stepped into the kitchen unannounced. Lucy was sitting at the island, stooped over a glass of water, her hair hanging down, concealing her face. Hearing his entrance, she inched a fraction from her frozen position.

'Lucy, Dad told me what happened. May I come in?' Seeing her nod, he approached, slow and hushed. Joseph stood over her, unsure of his place, and whether he had any right to ask questions.

'What happened?' he asked softly.

Lucy reached out for her drink and took a sip.

'Lucy?' She said nothing. 'Do you want me to leave you alone?'

Her damp hair swayed as she shook her head. His hand hovered over her shoulder, wanting to comfort her but holding back, for both their sakes. He couldn't stand to see her like this.

'Talk to me.'

'We went out for dinner last night, Mark and I. I didn't want to go, as I was tired from work, but he insisted.' Her voice was weak and tremulous.

'We couldn't get a cab, so Mark decided we should take a short-cut to the taxi rank. He said if he flashed the cash we'd get one straight away.'

Her fingers nervously picked at each other as she spoke.

'Then, out of nowhere, he decided he didn't want to go home, he wanted to go to a club. We argued and he stormed off, leaving me in the alley.'

Her final word slapped him in the face. 'What alley?'

'Black something or other. I can't quite remem—'

'Black Dog Alley,' he shot back, speaking more to himself than Lucy.

'That's the one.'

Joseph rocked back on his heels, head tilted back, the voice in his mind screaming at him. It was *Lucy* he had seen last night, and like the pathetic drunk he was, he had left her alone in that shit hole.

'Two guys came along. They took my watch, my money – they even took my shoes, for God's sake.'

Lucy kept her head held low, and Joseph was glad of it; his face was riddled with shame.

'I couldn't care about any of that, apart from my phone.' Her voice splintered. 'I had some lovely pictures of Sam, and now they're all gone.'

Falling tears rippled the surface of her water. Joseph slid his hands over his face as the pain of what he had done seared through his brain. It was all his fault. He could have saved her; he could have stopped it. He was as guilty as the scum who had robbed her.

'They were going to rape me.' Lucy's whisper stuttered out between sobs as her whole body shook; the trauma of crime outliving the act.

Joseph's chin trembled; he felt her pain tenfold. The burden of responsibility weighed heavily on him. Fearing the sight but gladly accepting the pain it would deliver, Joseph reached out and cradled her chin with the tenderness of one who cares. Lifting her concealed face, he slipped the index finger of his other hand under her veil of hair. Carefully, he pulled back the curtain. A faint groan left his lips as he viewed the blunt force trauma.

Lucy's hands clutched at each other for comfort. Releasing her face, his hand blanketed both of hers.

'Tell me who did this.'

'I don't know. They called each other Taz and Jay. Taz was the one that did this to me.'

'And Mark left you there?' he asked the question, which he knew the answer to, still finding it hard to believe that any man would knowingly leave a woman in such a place.

'Where is he?' he rumbled like thunder. A storm was brewing.

'He didn't come back last night.' Remorse repressed the anger that would surely follow. Wrapping his arms around her, he pulled

Lucy close to him. With her face buried in his chest Joseph carefully rested his cheek upon her head, his eyes closed tight. The shock and terror of the night's events bled into his T-shirt. He wanted to tell her it would be all right, shame forbade those words from passing his lips. What right did he have to tell such lies?

A knock on the door ended their embrace.

'Stay there, I'll get that.'

If Mark was on the other side of that door, Joseph was about to be fired. But fortunately for both, it was the police. Joseph invited them in; he wanted to stay, but after enquiring who he was, the officer requested that he gave them some privacy. Leaving the room he left the door open just enough to allow him to listen in. Pressing his back against the warm bricks, Joseph took note of every detail that Lucy relayed. It was painful to hear the despair in her voice, but it was pain he well deserved to feel.

The officers left, issuing promises to do their very best, while being careful to make no promises at all. Mark finally made an appearance, passing them as they drove away.

Hearing his key in the door, Lucy remained motionless in her seat.

'What are the police doing here?' he called out, kicking his shoes off. 'Come to see the *good and decent* gardeners, no doubt.'

Lucy listened to his footsteps. He entered the kitchen without so much as a 'good morning'.

This was often his way: pretend everything was fine, forcing Lucy to instigate an argument. The fridge door opened and she heard the cracking hiss of a Coke being opened, followed by Mark's thirsty glugs.

'Ahh.'

The drained can echoed as he placed it on the granite. He said nothing for a short while, probably wondering how he could play down the drama of the night before.

'Everything all right?'

'No, everything is not all right. I was attacked and

robbed last night.'

'You were what? Where?'

'In the alley – where *you* left me.' She remained calm, although her heart was anything but. Yet another telling silence from Mark.

'Bloody hell. If you'd come with me to the club, none of this would have happened.'

There it was, his specialty, placing the blame on Lucy's shoulders. Indignation was fast outweighing her anxiety.

'Are you hurt? did they take much?'

'They took everything – even my shoes.'

'And your watch?'

She nodded.

'Oh that's just fucking great! Do you know how much that cost? Bastards! And what are the police going to do about it, eh? Fuck all I expect.'

Lucy's head began to bob and her breathing started to gallop as a knot of emotions swelled inside of her. The pressure built, as she thought about how injust it was that she was being accused and blamed. Leaping off the stool, she charged at Mark. He flung his arms up in defence, arching back over the worktop.

'Look at my face!' She pinned her hair back.

'Look what they did to me!'

Mark's eyes were wide in horror as he took in the plum-coloured swollen flesh surrounding her half closed bloodshot eye.

'You're worried about the fucking watch? I thought they were going to rape me!' she screamed, her eye throbbing with the force. 'Do you have any idea how terrifying it was for me?'

The tears came, but she held her stance.

'You bastard, you fucking left me – it's all your fault!'

Her clenched fists hammered down repeatedly on Mark's arms, which were protecting his chest. 'I thought they were going to kill me!'

The blows lost all power as the reality of what could so easily have happened. Sobbing once again she turned from him, wiping her wet face with the palm of her hand.

'Lu – I... I didn't— '

'You didn't think?' She spun around. 'Well, take a good look at the effects of your temper tantrum. You know what? Take your fucking golf clubs and go and see your buddies. I don't care what you do so long as I don't have to see your face or hear your voice.'

Without making any further protest, Mark vacated the room and the house, leaving Lucy to recover from the betrayal, if that was even possible.

Joseph attacked his working day at a rigorous pace; it was the closest thing to punishment that he could inflict upon himself. He drove home with his mind in a cloud of regret and remorse. Hurrying up the steps to his apartment, he slammed the door behind him and tossed his keys onto a small table which held a picture of his mother. Skipping his usual routine of showering first, the kitchen was his next stop.

Reaching under the sink, he took out a full bottle of Jack Daniels along with a glass from the only wall unit the compact space could afford.

Breaking the seal, he removed the cap and carelessly threw it on the floor. The woody aroma instantly hit his nostrils, increasing his thirst to escape himself. Glass clinked against glass; one container was filled while the other was emptied. He held the amber tumbler level with his face, and just as he was about to take a sip he found himself standing back in the mouth of the alleyway.

There she was, being beaten, crying helplessly. It was as real as the glass he was holding. And what had he done? He had watched it; he had let it happen and simply walked away. Why? Because he was too damn drunk, that was fucking why. Just like he was every night.

He focused on the temptation, his shaking hand spilling the contents over his fingers.

Maybe he could take just one sip, to calm him – maybe one glass. But one glass was never enough, and Joseph knew that he wouldn't stop until the very last drop had been consumed.

Even then, the bottles that were hidden would be found and emptied.

Well done, Dalton. You may as well have punched her in the face yourself, you useless drunken shit.

The glass touched his closed mouth, the alcohol kissing his lips coaxingly.

He was falling, just like he did every night. 'Arghhhh!' He spun around, throwing the glass with all his force; it disintegrated against the wall, spraying the room with liquid. Joseph snatched the bottle; turning it upside-down, he shook it into the sink before pulling off his boots and rushing into the bedroom. He threw on a pair of jeans, then took out a clean T-shirt from the wardrobe and stuffed it into the compact rucksack he used for running. Emptying his wallet, he placed some cash into his boots, then put them back on. He moved about his apartment with precision. Ignoring the mess, he filled a water container and placed it into the rucksack. Putting on a lightweight black jacket, he picked up his keys, leaving his phone on the table, then headed out. He threw his bag on the passenger seat and crossed the road to the house opposite, where a garage was being built. Joseph stepped onto the drive, took a handful of sand from one of the open bags and placed it into his jacket pocket. Then he climbed into his pick-up and drove away. It was going to be a long night – possibly a long week.

CHAPTER TWENTY-FIVE

Every woman loves the beauty and elegance of flowers, but they also love to be loved, to feel safe and cared for. Mark had overestimated the power of flora: he seemed to bring Lucy a bouquet every time he returned from a trip out.

Heart-to-hearts were had, meals were cooked and the dishwasher loaded. Mark even promised to enrol in an anger management course. For Lucy, it might have been a promise too late.

Despite Mark pandering to her every need, Lucy returned to school on Monday.

Every night she would return home to find Joseph keeping his distance and George being as kind and considerate as ever.

They were fast approaching the end of their work and the garden was looking incredible.

George was a visionary, with skills that were hard to comprehend, but as much as Lucy now wanted to enjoy his creation, circumstances had prevented it.

Upon hearing of her ordeal, Charles delivered yet more flowers, complete with a sincere card. He also informed her that he was planning to cancel their investment, since she was under enough stress as it was. Lucy managed to convince him that the excitement of their joint endeavour was the one thing keeping her focused.

In response, he invited her to join him on an evening of her choice to finalise the deal. Lucy was relieved that she had managed to secure someone with his expertise.

Wednesday was to be the day that things would finally be set in motion. But when Lucy arrived home that day, she found that George's vehicle was the only one parked outside. She ventured around to the transformed garden to find George leaning on the table, writing on his notepad.

'Hi, George.'

He raised his head, squinting to focus. 'Hello, Lucy. Good day?'

'Yeah, it was actually.'

'How's the eye now?' he asked, pointing to one of his own.

'Getting better, thanks. Still a little tender.'

'Have you had any news from the police?'

'Nooo. I doubt I will. I've just got to put it behind me now. No Joseph today?'

'Yes, he's been in today. He hasn't been gone long actually. Said he's got something to take care of.' He scratched his head with the end of the pen, a troubled look flitting across his face. She knew Joseph was the cause of it.

'Everything okay, George?'

'Kids.' He closed his notepad, slipping it into his top pocket. 'Nothing but a worry from the moment you're born.'

'Is he giving you trouble again?' Her interest ran much deeper than the innocent question implied.

'I don't know, it's probably me worrying about nothing.' His troubled expression gave way to one of contemplation.

'He goes for a run every night, and he always calls round after, without fail – but ever since...' The pen, which had been swirling around to the melody of his words like a conductor's baton, stopped.

'Ever since?' Lucy encouraged.

'Er, well, what I'm trying to say is, I haven't seen him for five days.' He slotted the pen next to its companion in his top pocket. 'He's never done that before.' That didn't sound like strange behaviour to Lucy. After all, they spent every day together, but the look on George's face told her that it most definitely was.

'Maybe he's got a lady friend.'

'Well if he has, she's not making him very happy; he's hardly said a word the last few days.'

It was certainly true that Joseph had gone out of his way to avoid any and all contact with Lucy since the morning after her attack. And even though she knew he could never have a place in her life, Lucy was worried about him too.

George was a very calm and collected man, so there must have been a good reason for his concern.

'Have you asked him, George?'

'He's a closed book sometimes. If he doesn't want to talk, there's no persuading him... Listen to me – as if you haven't got enough to deal with already.'

'Don't be silly, George. I love our little chats.' She

touched his arm reassuringly, which had become her way with him.

'Well, you'll be rid of us by the end of next week.'

Why did her stomach turn when he said that?

'I'll be sorry to see you go, George. You've done an amazing job. Thank you.'

A fatherly smile lit up his face. 'It's been my absolute pleasure, my darlin'. You won't have a chance to miss us anyway. Charles wants us to do his garden when we finish here. So don't worry: you haven't seen the last of us yet.'

'I'm glad to hear that.'

'Lucy,' she heard Mark call.

The smile slipped from her face as she turned to answer him. He was standing in the kitchen doorway.

'Yes?'

'Are you coming in? I've got something I want to discuss with you.'

'Give me a minute,' she said coldly, snapping her head back to George. 'Sorry about that.'

'Not at all, we're going now anyway,' he said, taking out his keys. 'Now, where is that boy hiding?' He peered up the garden.

'I think… I saw him sitting in your pickup when I was parking on the drive.' she said, unable to help feeling like a telltale.

George's eyebrows shot up above his glasses. 'Little bugger. Mind you, I was the same at his age.' He chuckled. 'Have a good evening, Lucy. See you in the morning.'

'You too, George. Take care.'

She watched him go, pondering what it was that Mark wanted to discuss. Lucy walked into the kitchen, which was uncharacteristically clean and tidy. The only cup that was out was the one containing the hot drink Mark handed her as he pulled out a stool for her. *Huh, maybe I should get mugged more often.*

'How's your day been?' He was unusually upbeat, he had been all week.

'Not bad.'

'What do you fancy doing tonight?' Lucy kept her eyes on the chamomile tea.

'You can go out if you want to. I'm not bothered.'

'No, that's not what I mean, Lu.'

All trust had gone; she suspected his every word had an ulterior motive.

Mark sighed taking the seat next to her. 'Lu, I know I fucked up. I can't change that. I swear I'm going to make it up to you.' He rubbed the palm of his hand up and down her back. 'However long it takes.'

But could the trust and respect that had been so badly broken, ever truly be repaired?

Lucy remained silent. There was simply nothing she wanted to say to him.

'So, what do *you* want to do tonight?' She shrugged her shoulders, the repetitive rubbing of his hand against her skin beginning to irritate her.

'You wanna go for a drive? Maybe go for a drink somewhere quiet?'

'I'm not in the mood, Mark.' Lucy sipped her drink, which was cooling fast, like the atmosphere.

'I'm going to see Charles a little later.'

'What for?'

'He's advising the school on how best to raise funds.'

'Funds?'

'Yes, funds.' She turned to look at him. 'For the pool and sensory room?'

'Oh, for the – yeah, I know what you mean now.'

Yet more evidence of what little attention he had ever paid to all of those one-way conversations Lucy had wasted her breath on.

'What time are you going round?'

'7:30.'

Mark hopped off his stool. 'I'll go run you a bath, but before I do, there's something I want to give you.'

He went over to the Nespresso machine and picked up a white envelope which was resting against it. Laying it flat on the island, he pushed it across to Lucy with his index finger. She viewed it, feeling a sense of dread rather than excitement. At least it wasn't more flowers – the house already looked like a bloody greenhouse.

'Go on then, open it,' he encouraged, looking pleased with himself.

Lucy turned the card over and opened the envelope. She removed the card from its sleeve. On the front was a picture of a brown and black puppy with the biggest, saddest eyes imaginable, and a simple message at the bottom: 'Forgive me?'

Her immediate reaction was to be offended. *Do you really think a fucking sorry card is going to make everything okay?*

Keeping her thoughts private, she went through the pretence of being interested and opened it. Two oblong slips of paper fell out and glided along the granite towards her. Lucy speed-read the sickly message on the card and placed it face-down.

'Maybe this is a bit more of what you fancy,' said Mark, as Lucy picked up two first-class airline tickets to

Barcelona. He had put some thought into that one. Barcelona had always been on her list of cities she would love to visit.

'How's that then?' He awaited his praise with a wide grin. Lucy stared at the tickets. He wasn't going to make her feel guilty for being ungrateful.

'Do you think that this will make it all go away?'

'No, but I thought—'

She cut him off. 'What happened that night will stay with me for the rest of my life…' She paused to give him the opportunity to speak. He let it pass.

'I'm scared, Mark. Do you have any idea what that feels like? Scared to be on my own, or to go into my own garden after dark. Every time I catch a stranger looking at me, panic takes over. I feel vulnerable…' Her voice faltered. 'I don't want to live like that.'

Mark leaned against the island, arms locked, head hung in shame.

'Lu, I know this can't fix it, but if I could turn back time, I would.'

He stood up straight, taking Lucy's hands in both of his. 'I know you don't really want to be around me at the moment – and I don't blame you. That's why I've paid for Suzie and Pete to come with us.'

Lucy kept her eyes hooded, not reacting to his caressing hands.

'Then you won't have to be on your own, and you can have some space from me if you wish.'

Was she being sanctimonious? They were both guilty of neglect. Mark had also suffered an injustice. The difference was, he was unaware of it.

'We fly out Friday morning at ten o'clock. I've booked

us into the El Palace Hotel. Five stars – stunning place. We fly back on Monday evening, so we've got a nice long weekend to spoil ourselves.' He ducked his head down, peeking under her fringe. 'How does that sound?'

Lucy had to admit that it sounded great, but she couldn't just set aside what had happened. 'It's very thoughtful of you, but… I'm not sure. I'll have to think about it.'

He let go of her hands, the look of optimism falling from his face.

'I'll… er… I'll go and run you that bath, shall I?'

'Yeah.'

Feeling a little heartless, Lucy called to him before he left the room. 'Mark, I just need some time.' He nodded, giving a half-smile, before heading upstairs.

When she arrived at Charles's that evening, she was relieved to find that Tabitha had ventured out to visit her sister. Apparently that was the one of only two places she would travel to on her own. Lucy was sitting alongside Charles, who had produced a thick and expertly crafted document about the investment. He ran through every single page, using phrases and terminology that baffled Lucy. She was certain about her commitment to the project, although her mind did keep drifting off to the countless questions she had yet to ask.

Charles was very patient, and explained himself multiple times without showing any signs of frustration. He repeatedly emphasised that Lucy had the option to put the whole thing on pause until she was back on her feet, but after some persuasion, he finally conceded.

They both signed the declaration that stated the agreed amount Lucy would be investing, and also Charles's commitment to be guarantor. Lucy stayed longer than she had intended to; Charles was very engaging. It was a welcome respite from her own recent history to listen to someone else's. Increasingly aware of the time, and wanting to avoid an awkward meeting with his wife, Lucy thanked him sincerely before heading home with her very own dossier, another thing that would have to be kept hidden from Mark.

CHAPTER TWENTY-SIX

Joseph took a sip of his water and dropped the bottle back into the bag at his feet.

This was the sixth evening he had spent in the shadows. He was beginning to feel the effects of having only had a couple of hours sleep a night. Even so, he stood firm. Determination kept him awake.

If he had to stand in that alley for the rest of his days he would, waiting to right the wrong. It was deathly quiet and not a single person had travelled the back street the whole time he had been there. No self-respecting person would venture into such a place, which only served to confirm that the two men he waited for were regular users of the passageway.

Rats scurried in and out of the moonlight, seemingly used to Joseph's company by now. At least they provided some entertainment in the stench-filled space, which was like a great wound on the earth's surface, diseased and infected.

He watched as one of the rodents stopped his foraging

to look into the distance, attuned to any and all foreign sounds. In the blink of an eye the little scout disappeared, and the faint sound of voices suggested Joseph was not alone.

Concentrating all his powers of sight, he stared into the inky darkness, waiting for the owners of the voices to come into view. Midnight clouds hurried along obscuring the crescent moon. But then, as if on cue, a clearing appeared; the spotlight was on – showtime. Two figures presented themselves. The taller of the two swaggered, his arrogance clear to see. He had to be Taz. Joseph's senses sharpened, his heart picked up the pace, preparing for whatever was to play out. Keeping a rein on his anger, he assessed the targets. The shorter man was stocky, well-built. From the way his arms were swinging about, it was clear Taz was the one making all the noise, matching Lucy's description. The problem was that Joseph couldn't see their faces; there was still a small chance that they might not be who he thought they were.

The only way to be sure was to face them, which would mean giving them a heads-up on his presence. They were approaching fast, he had to make a decision. It was too risky; he had to be sure.

Joseph stepped out from the doorway, and the two men stopped, falling silent.

'Evening, boys. I was wondering if you could help me.'

'What the fuck is this, man? You're gonna get yourself hurt sneaking up on us like that.' The two men exchanged glances. 'And we ain't no boys either, we're fucking men.'

Joseph had the benefit of the moonlight behind him. Targets confirmed.

'Sorry about that, didn't mean to scare you.'

His eyes darted from man to man, looking for the slightest movement. He was out of striking distance, but one man against two weren't good odds.

Taz laughed, punching his friend on the shoulder.

'We ain't scared, bitch.'

That was true: he wasn't – yet.

'As I was saying, you may be able to help me. A friend of mine lost her phone and a very expensive watch right here about a week ago.'

There were no laughs now. 'You know what, fool? You're gonna lose your fucking life here too, if you don't get the fuck out of my way.' Taz began to take steps towards Joseph, his friend following his lead.

Joseph put his hands into his pockets. 'Does that mean you're not going to help me?'

His heart raced even faster as they closed in on him.

'Yeah, we'll help you alright. We're gonna get you a ride home – in a fucking ambulance!'

Removing his hands from his pockets, Joseph slung a handful of sand into Jay's face. Before he had a chance to raise his guard Joseph took a blow to his right eye. It was a good shot. Taz was stronger than he looked.

He stumbled back, disorientated by the impact. Joseph had no idea where Jay was, but from his screams, the sand had worked. He raised his head to see the blur of another punch coming towards him. His reactions were a second too slow again, and this time he received a right to his jaw.

Joseph was protecting his head, which left his midriff exposed. A trio of jabs folded him, then a fist hammered into the back of his head and he was pulled to the floor by the collar of his jacket.

This was not good. Fall on the floor in a street fight,

and you're as good as dead. Fists were replaced by feet. Joseph curled up into a ball tensing every muscle of his body's armor.

'Who's the fucking boy now?' Another kick. 'Eh?'

Taz paused for a moment, panting from the exertion. 'Yo, Jay, what's wrong, man?'

'The prick threw sand in my eyes,' Jay groaned.

'You're gonna pay for that, boy. I'm gonna beat you like a dog, until you beg for mercy just like your slut friend. She your woman? You need to

keep that bitch on a tight leash, man. I think she came down here looking for cock.'

Taz's provocation was a gift. It gave Joseph time to recover and awoke a side of him that he thought had long been lain to rest.

'You're not good enough for her, bro. Want some advice? You need to man up.'

Joseph attempted to get up, but his attacker responded with another swift kick. It connected, but this time Joseph was ready for it. Putting one hand on Taz's heel and the other on the toe of his trainer, Joseph swiftly twisted his adversary's foot,

sending him tumbling to the ground. Joseph quickly took the opportunity to get back on his feet while Taz was still on all fours.

He rushed over to Jay, who was rocking backwards and forwards holding his eyes. He threw a left hook into Jay's jaw with all the force he could muster; Jay crumpled, knocked clean out.

Looking back over his shoulder, he saw that Taz was up and running towards him, and was almost on him. Joseph snapped back with his right elbow, the hard bone smashing into the nose of his attacker, sending him flying backwards. Blood gushed over Taz's mouth. Wiping it with the sleeve of his hoody, he smeared it across his face.

Joseph removed his jacket and threw it on the floor. He approached Taz, chin tucked in, clenched fists held at the ready. Taz jabbed hitting the top of Joseph's head. It was a powerless strike; he clearly wasn't used to being hit; the shock of it had taken his energy.

Joseph would afford him the same mercy that Taz had shown him. His left fist flew through the air like a cannonball, smashing through his enemy's defences. Then a right, then another left; his opponent was sent flying from side to side.

Each shot delivered a jolt of pain through Joseph's knuckles down to his wrist. It was the sensation of vengeance and it felt good. It made him hit harder, faster. Blows rained down on every part of his enemy's upper body until the criminal had become the victim. Taz collapsed, spitting blood, then, crawling on his hands and knees he cowered against the building.

Joseph took a few deep breaths to calm himself. The victor stood over the bloodied broken body of his conquered foe, who was slumped in a pool of stale urine.

'Wristwatch and phone – where are they?'

'F-fuck you, man. I ain't telling you shit.' Joseph dropped to his haunches and with no warning whatsoever threw a left jab straight onto his mouth. Taz's head was against the wall, he received the full force of the punch.

'Argh! Fuck!' Taz's trembling hands cupped his mouth. 'You broke my fucking tooth!'

'Watch and phone. Where are they?'

'Do you know who you're dealing with? I know people

– you're a fucking dead man.'

He had no option but to surrender, but he was still trying to bluff his way out.

He stabbed a bloodied finger at Joseph. 'You and that slut of yours are gonna get fucked—' Joseph snatched his wrist and held it in a vice- like grip.

'You think I'm worried about you or your bad boy friends? You have no idea what these eyes have seen – I don't fear death. I'm already dead inside.' Joseph's eyebrows were low, teeth clenched, his eyes speared his prey. There were no smart remarks now.

'Watch and phone.'

Taz shook his swelling head with foolish defiance. Joseph reached out to the hand he had captured and snapped Taz's index finger like a twig. Screams of agony punctured the silence. Taz writhed and wriggled, attempting to pull his hand free, but he was no match for his opponent. Not bothering to repeat the question, Joseph prised the middle finger free; it suffered the same fate.

Taz's body contorted, tormented with pain. He sobbed in agony, as tears, snot, blood and saliva dripped from his quivering chin.

'I've got all night, but you've only got so many fingers – you'd better start talking.'

Since the request was being ignored, Joseph wrestled the remaining two fingers out from the palm of his hand.

'NO! Wait! P-please… fuck, don't, don't.' Breathless with panic, his intact hand rushed into the pocket of his sweatpants and he took out Lucy's phone. The offering was held out.

'Put it on the floor, carefully,' Joseph commanded. As

soon as the phone had been set free, he broke the remaining fingers and released his wrist, leaving him rolling around, cradling a disfigured hand.

'Bastard! You bastard!' Taz whimpered. Joseph stood up and put the phone into his pocket.

'I'm just getting started. You've got a whole other hand I haven't touched yet.'

'I haven't got the Rollie, man. I swear.'

'Where is it?'

'I sold it to some geezer for two hundred quid. I don't know who he was.' Joseph knew that Lucy didn't care about the watch. It was the principle that he was thinking about.

'Lie face down on your chest.'

'What are you gonna do? You got what you want, man.'

'Do it!' Joseph warned. He glanced back at the other man. He was still out cold.

Taz rolled gingerly onto his chest, whining in pain. Straddling his legs, Joseph frisked him, taking a wad of cash, house keys and a small bag of cannabis. He sprinkled the drugs on the floor, threw the keys into the darkness and pocketed the cash.

'Get up.'

Losing patience with the injured man's slow reactions, he grabbed his hood and yanked him to his feet. Joseph lifted the lid on the refuse bin.

'Get in,' he said tilting his head towards the stench.

Taz was a broken man in many ways, there was no protest against the request.

'Wait,' said Joseph, 'your trainers. Take them off.'

Complying with the order, Taz kicked them off and like a man three times his age, he feebly tried to clamber into the bin. Joseph crouched down and grabbed his thigh, then hauled him in head-first. The lid slammed down, puffing out a repugnant odour.

'If I see that lid so much as move an inch, it'll be more than just your fingers I'll break.' Walking over to his bag, he took out the bottle of water and quenched his thirst, before washing the blood from his hands and face. He removed his T-shirt, which was speckled with the evidence of violence, put it in his bag and slipped on the clean one. He was keen to get out of there in case the screams had been heard and someone had called the police.

Stepping over to his jacket, he picked it up, gave it a shake and put it on. Jay hadn't made a murmur. He went over to him, squatted down and placed two fingers underneath his jaw. Finding that the unconscious man was still alive, he emptied his pockets, discarding the cigarettes and lighter but keeping the small amount of cash. Joseph hooked his rucksack over his shoulder, picked up the trainers, and headed for the street.

Stepping out of the cold shadows and into the warm glow of the streetlights, he paused for a moment. Now that the distraction of survival was no longer there, the pain certainly was. It didn't matter, he had achieved what he had set out to do and, if nothing else, that was one of his demons exorcised.

He made his way along the street, silently enjoying the euphoria of victory, the pain of his injuries only making him feel stronger. Strangers glanced at his bruised and swollen eye as he passed them, heading in the opposite direction to his home. There was one last thing he wanted to do.

'You still here, my friend?' Joseph said, trying to get the attention of the old tramp, who was indeed still sitting in the empty shop doorway. It took him a second or two before he recognised Joseph.

'Good evening to you, sir.'

He raised his crumpled old hat in acknowledgment.

Crouching down in front of him, Joseph caught sight of the old man's shoes, which were beyond worn. 'Why don't you try these for size?' He handed over the Nike Airs that Taz had very generously donated.

'Thank you, sir, that's very thoughtful of you.' A smile spread, hidden under his shaggy beard.

'Are you all right, sir?' he asked, his, blue eyes passing over Joseph's swollen one.

'I've never been better.' Reaching into his pocket Joseph pulled out the handful of money he had taken. 'Keep this somewhere safe.'

The heavy lids of the old man's eyes rose in surprise. He looked from the folded cash up to the man offering it.

'Take it. It's yours.'

His expression was perplexed, but he took the money and put it into the inside pocket of his grey coat.

'I only want one thing,' asked Joseph. 'Promise me you'll feed yourself with that money.'

He was quick to answer. 'Oh, I will sir, I will. May I ask your name, sir?'

Joseph was touched by his humbleness and held out his hand. 'Joseph Dalton.'

The aged eyes sparkled with moisture. He seemed moved that Joseph wanted to shake his hand. The two men pressed palms.

'Edward Thomson,' the older man said, and they shook

hands in a very civil manner, despite the older man's very uncivilised situation.

'Can I give you something, Joseph?'

'There's no need.'

'It's only words. Words and thoughts are all I have.'

'Sure.'

'Pursue happiness. It doesn't always like to be caught, but never let it out of your sight and never give up on it.' He looked Joseph straight in the eye.

His words were simple but profound; it was as if he had seen inside Joseph's heart.

The younger man rose, uncomfortable with how perceptive the old man had been.

'Take good care of yourself, Edward.'

With that, he turned and began the long walk home.

'May God bless you, Mr Dalton. God bless you, sir.' The old man's kind words chased after him.

'I don't think that's ever going to happen, my friend,' Joseph mumbled to himself, leaving Edward Thomson, no doubt contemplating a life that never was.

CHAPTER TWENTY-SEVEN

Lucy checked her make-up, making sure her bruising was covered up. Closing her compact mirror she was startled by a figure crossing the kitchen window.

It looked like Joseph. The soft knock that followed confirmed her impression. She glanced at her watch, puzzled by why he was so early.

She walked over to the folding doors. There was now nothing but glass between them, and she raised her hand in acknowledgment, his closeness setting off butterflies in her tummy. Lucy unlocked the door and Joseph slid it open.

'Morning. You're early; is everything okay?'

'Yeah, fine. I... er... I couldn't sleep.' His cap was pulled down low, shielding his eyes. 'Come in.' She did her best to act as normal as possible, which was no easy thing. 'I'll make you a coffee.'

'Thank you.' Accepting her invitation, he followed Lucy across the room.

This was only the second time they had been alone together since the summer fete. Would he mention it?

Taking a cup down from the cupboard, she turned around to make general conversation but was rendered speechless by the sight of her iPhone placed in the middle of the island. Without saying a word, she placed the cup down and examined the phone. It was definitely hers. She looked up at Joseph in some confusion, her conversation with George coming to mind. She remembered how he had said that he hadn't seen him for a week. She reached out and slowly raised the cap from his head, revealing exactly what she suspected.

'Oh, dear God. Look at your face. Where did you get this?' she asked, holding up her phone.

'Same place you got that?'

The tips of her fingers softly stroked the evidence of his bravery, and tears welled in her eyes with the knowledge of what he had done. Why had he taken such a risk?

'I don't know if you've still got the pictures of Sam on there.'

'You could've got yourself killed, and all for a phone.'

'No, not for a phone – for you, Lucy. Her hand cupped her mouth, and she fought with all she had not to cry. Why was he doing this to her? Why was he making her want him so badly, when the dream was sure just to be snatched away again?

'You're hurt. Look what they did to you.'

'It doesn't matter,' he muttered.

'But it matters to me, Joseph.' She placed her hand on his swollen knuckles.

Shifting uncomfortably, he put his cap back on, blocking her view. Whenever she attempted to open up, he shut down. Joseph's eyes rose as he heard the sound of the toilet flushing upstairs. Mark was up.

'Have a good day, Lucy. Say hello to Sam for me.'

As he walked to his exit, Lucy listened out for Mark's footsteps. Time was running out.

'He asks about you every day, you know.'

She shot a glance into the hall, making sure no one else had heard. Joseph stopped with his back to her, filling the doorway. He turned his head a fraction, as if to speak. The sound of Mark yawning cut short the opportunity. Joseph stepped out of sight and a moment later, Mark came ambling in, scratching his balls.

'Morning, Lu.'

He had only said two words and already she was pissed off with him. He always slept in late. For the first time in days she had an audience with Joseph, and Mark decided to get up with the birds. Lucy busied herself with nothing at all, rather than sit with Mark listening to his questions about Barcelona. He made several attempts to broach the subject, but Lucy thwarted each one by talking about school news. Her mind was on other things, and another man.

The day was a troubled one for Lucy. She delivered Joseph's greeting to Sam, and was treated to a heartwarming smile, followed by the heartbreaking question: "when will I see Mr Joe again?"

Decisions needed to be made, and not just about Barcelona.

Mark did his utmost to persuade her to go, even enlisting Suzie, who she spent most of her lunch hour on the phone to.

When she returned home from a long confusing day, she was greeted by the sight of Mark's suitcase in the hallway. There was a Post-it note covered with kisses and hearts on the kitchen door. It said that he had forgotten sunscreen and popped out to get some.

It seemed he had also forgotten the abysmal way he had treated her. She dropped the crumpled note in the bin on her way out to the garden, wanting to see George before he left.

'Hi, George. Are you on your way?'

'Hello, Lucy. Yes, my dear. I've got my Dominoes club tonight. Very rock 'n' roll, eh?' He chuckled, folding the camping   chair.

He never failed to make her day brighter.

'Before I forget, have a lovely time in Barcelona, you lucky thing.'

Mark had been making assumptions.

She didn't bother to explain the situation.

'Thank you, George.'

'You go and enjoy yourself. You deserve it after what you've been through.'

She nodded, giving a smile. If only he knew what his son and Mark had done, both to and for her.

He tucked the chair under his arm. 'Have a safe trip, and I'll see you next week, Lucy.'

'Bye, George. Take care, and good luck tonight.'

He waved over his shoulder before closing the gate.

Mark went all out to convince Lucy to go with him, making promises she knew he wouldn't keep. After agonising over what to do, she eventually made the decision to go. Not for Mark, but for herself. She would spend all her time with Suzie, she told herself. It seemed she would only be spiting herself by not going.

Lucy packed her case with none of the excitement that should have been present.

But as soon as she was on the plane next to Suzie, she was sure she would feel fine – she hoped.

For once, Mark was up before Lucy and in full holiday mode, singing and whistling to himself as he pranced around the bedroom, toweling dry his damp hair.

'Come on, Lu. The taxi will be here in 45 minutes.' Lucy sat up, leaning back against the headboard.

'I thought we could all have breakfast together at the airport. What do you think?' he asked, spraying a cloud of deodorant.

'Fine.'

Mark dropped his backside down on the edge of the bed. 'You look tired, babe,' he said, yanking a grey sock onto his foot. 'You need to start going to bed earlier.'

She was tired, and the reason she was tired was because the recurring memories of her attack would start playing the moment she succumbed to sleep.

'I think I'm gonna get myself a new pair of sunnies from duty free.'

Slipping on the remaining sock, he bounced off the bed and raked his fingers through his hair. 'Pete can't wait to visit Camp Nou.'

He opened the wardrobe and flicked through the rows of shirts.

'You know it's the largest football stadium in the world.' Lucy listened to his banal jabbering with ever increasing annoyance.

For Mark, that night ended with the rising of the sun, and now that she was going ahead with his weekend as planned, Lucy knew that he had assumed all had been forgiven and forgotten - not quite. Not only had he put Lucy's life in danger, but he had inadvertently also put Joseph's life at risk too. Seeing the evidence of his bravery, she knew all too well what Joseph had faced. To board that plane with Mark would have been a careless insult to Joseph.

'Have you seen my pink Ralph Lauren shirt?'

'I'm not going, Mark.' There was no easy way to say it. He turned to face her.

'What do you mean, you're not going? You packed a case just last night.'

'I've changed my mind.' Mark stared at her blankly, as if he was waiting for some sort of explanation, there wasn't going to be one.

'I'm not stopping you from going.' He huffed with impatience, biting down on the tip of his tongue.

'What am I supposed to say to Suzie and Pete?'

The selfish irritation in his voice lit the fire in Lucy.

'You can tell them that after you left me alone, I was beaten, robbed, and came within an inch of being raped by two men and that, strangely, I'm still a little traumatised. Will that do – is that good enough do you think?' She shot him down.

'This time, *I am* happy for you to leave me alone, Mark.'

His eyes fell to the floor. He turned to the wardrobe and took out the first shirt his hand landed on, before grabbing a pair of jeans from his chest of drawers. Without uttering a single word, he left the bedroom, closing the door behind him. Lucy felt some relief at having said her piece.

She was so angry with him, with herself. How the hell

had it come to this? On paper they had everything going for them, yet they had never been further apart.

She stayed in bed until the taxi took him away.

It would be nice to have some time alone. She needed time to think things over. Questions that had long begged to be answered would wait no longer.

When George arrived he was surprised to see her still there. Lucy explained it away by saying she had lost her passport. What Joseph had done for her hadn't left her thoughts for one waking moment. Apart from a morning greeting, he kept his distance; Adam was at his side most of the day, leaving her no opportunity to speak with him alone.

In just a few more days he would be gone, and the thought of that hurt her more than any ordeal she had ever gone through. Lucy floated around the house, unable to rest, feeling irritated and anxious. Complications of the head and heart were battling each other, and like in all wars, no one escaped unblemished.

Nearing the end of the day Lucy made one last attempt to try and get a chance to talk to Joseph.

'Can I make you a drink before you go, George?'

He was sat in his camping chair, writing on his little pad.

'I'm fine, thank you, my darling.'

'I'll go and ask Joseph if he would like one,' she said, passing casually by George.

'You've just missed him, Lucy. He's gone.'

'Oh.' Turning away from George, she closed her eyes, fighting back tears of disappointment.

'It must be a popular time for weekends away. Adam's off somewhere with his mates and Joseph's going down to

Rucklestone Bay.' George kept his head down, legs crossed, writing away.

Kimberley. That's who he's spending the weekend with. She wondered if George knew about her.

'Has he gone with friends?'

He stopped writing, but he didn't take his eyes off the pad.

'Joseph doesn't have many friends – well, he has friends,' he added hastily, 'but he's gone on his own. They hold an Ironman competition every year.'

'Ironman competition?' Lucy had a horrible vision of grown men dressed as their favourite comic book characters.

'It's a race basically.' Uncrossing his legs, he propped his glasses on his forehead. 'The competitors have to do a two-mile swim, then a bloody long bicycle ride, finished off with a marathon.'

'Really?' It sounded like a superhuman amount of exercise. 'Is he capable of doing all of that?'

A smile tickled his cheek. 'He won it last year.'

George heaved himself out of his seat. 'I was going to enter myself, but I thought I'd better give the boy a chance.' He winked, and started to fold up his chair. 'Are you going to be all right on your own?'

'Yeah, it will be nice to have some peace and quiet.' She forced a smile.

'I can call in if you like – check that you're okay?'

'I'll be fine, but thank you.'

'You've got my phone number if you need anything. Don't be afraid to call.'

'I won't.' Lucy thought it was very sweet of him to think of her that way. She walked with him to the gate and they chatted for a while about the finishing touches to the garden, before George wished her a good weekend.

He insisted that she locked the gate before he would allow himself to leave. Lucy tried to make light of it, but she did indeed turn the key. Entering the house she closed herself in, and another lock was engaged.

The silence of an empty house seemed lonely now, rather than peaceful. Lucy felt totally pissed off. She had to admit that once she had made the decision not to go away, the possibility of Joseph staying had nudged its way into the back of her mind. But the pleasure of his company would be enjoyed by another. He was hard to figure out. One minute he was giving her all the signals, and the next the cold shoulder.

Maybe he was one of those men who wants the pleasures of a woman, but not the commitment. It was Kimberley that would be getting all the pleasure. *Bitch*. He'd be 'Ironman' all weekend, no doubt.

Bored and lonely, Lucy slouched around the house. There was nothing on TV, she wasn't hungry, and she didn't feel safe going out at night on her own – not that she wanted to go out anyway. She sat on the bed, arms wrapped around her raised knees, locked in her home, a prisoner of her own thoughts. Lucy picked up her phone from her bedside cabinet. Four missed calls from Suzie, and two messages, also from Suzie. Nothing from Mark. She opened the first message:

Lucy, please, please, answer the phone Deleting it she went to the second. *Lu, I'm totally gutted that you haven't come. I know Mark has been a bastard, but he is genuinely sorry. You're right to make him pay, but not at your expense. Sod the men, they can do what they like. Get your arse on a plane and let's go window- shopping. The men here are hot, hot, hot Seriously, babe, it won't be the same without you xxx*

Had she made the decision not to go just to hurt Mark? Sitting all alone, she felt more than a little childish, her ridiculous fantasy of Joseph spending a night or two having backfired.

Fucking men. Wouldn't it be easier to be a lesbian?

Mark was a selfish bastard, and while Joseph was a gorgeous man, he clearly couldn't decide where to settle down – or whether to do it at all.

Neither one seemed very promising at that moment, although for very different reasons. She made her way back downstairs, noticing her suitcase sitting by the door like a faithful dog, ready to go. Lucy poured herself a glass of wine and then sat in the lounge with her laptop. Out of curiosity she looked at the El Palace Hotel website. It was stunning. Every light in the house was on, and all the curtains and blinds were closed. She would be lucky to get any sleep at all. The fear that her two attackers would find out where she lived and come to finish the job terrified and tormented her.

Being stubborn wasn't helping. Lucy searched for flights to Barcelona. She needed to escape. It wouldn't be perfect, but it would be better than the blunt reality of being on her own.

CHAPTER TWENTY-EIGHT

Lucy's eyes flicked from the road to the time on the dashboard. 'Shit!' She had left it until the last minute, then made a snap decision. Her suitcase rolled around on the back seat as the BMW navigated the twists and turns. She arrived with little time to spare, her next challenge was finding a vacant parking space.

Looking left to right, Lucy became increasingly agitated: there were vehicles everywhere. After driving around in circles with little success, she finally spotted a car leaving. With the skill of a stunt driver, she shot into the tight spot. Leaving it parked diagonally across the oblong space, she slammed the door and ran as quickly as her legs would carry her.

It was busier than she had expected. Lucy excused and pardoned her way through the crush of bodies, not sure if she was going to make it on time.

The crowd began to clap and cheer. Through the forest of swaying heads and waving hands, she caught a glimpse of Joseph.

Lucy hadn't followed the satnav; she had followed her heart. As risky as it was, she had to know if there was a chance that he might want her in the same way that she longed for him. Only able to take baby steps, she tried desperately to get to the front, but the crowd became increasingly dense. Standing on her tiptoes, she caught broken glimpses of him. Lucy turned to the man on her left, who was cheering and whistling his encouragement.

'Excuse me. Can you tell me who won?'

'No one yet; he's the first one, love.'

He's winning!

She had to get to the front. He had to know she was there to see him cross the finish line. Suddenly the volume of the crowd's cheers rose. She bobbed her head around the moving bodies, and through a keyhole gap, saw another competitor close behind him. Her heart pounded as the tension rose.

'Go, Joseph, go!' Lucy screamed.

He was almost parallel to where she was. He looked exhausted. Frustration squashed her as everyone leaned and pushed to see the final battle.

'Come on, Joseph! You can do it!' She repeatedly called out his name with all her might, frantically trying to let him know that she was there. Lucy wasn't the only one shouting out; her voice was one of many. An idea came to mind. It was ridiculous, but worth a try.

'Everybody loves Christmas!' she bellowed. Everyone within range turned to look at her.

The embarrassment was soon forgotten as Joseph's face whipped towards the crowd. Unexpectedly, he stopped; chest heaving, eyes searching through the crowd.

Shit!

'No, keep going. Don't stop!' With both her hands on her head, she was filled with utter horror. The crowd's screams became more erratic as his opponent saw the opportunity and picked up the pace. Names were thrown out like stones, but Joseph seemed oblivious to it. Then, through a small aperture he spotted her; their eyes bridging the distance between them.

Lucy held her clenched fists to her mouth, trying to decipher his expression. Had she put him off? Was he angry? Glancing at Joseph with a perplexed expression, his competitor took the lead. The crowd's warnings went unheeded; Joseph didn't bat an eyelid.

The man blocking her view spun around, and said sharply 'well done. I had fifty quid on Dalton winning.' His beady eyes scowled at her from over his hooked nose.

'Shut up, Phil,' said the lady next to him, tugging at the arm of his jacket.

Joseph's breathing steadied; he began a slow walk towards the onlookers.

'He doesn't look like a happy man. You're going to get it now.'

Phil seemed to take great pleasure witnessing Lucy's worried face.

Silently, the masses parted, forming a corridor of bodies that led to Lucy.

Joseph ducked under the rope holding the spectators back, and followed the short path. The surrounding audience listened in as the Ironman himself towered over her. Fearing rejection, she held his stern gaze.

'Joseph, I'm sorry. I didn't mean for you to lose the race. I just wanted you to know I was here.'

Beads of sweat scurried down his face. He dispelled her

fears with the simple touch of his hand on her cheek.

'No, Lucy. I've already won.'

He leaned in and Lucy raised her lips to meet his, the joy of relief so welcome.

A harmonious chorus of sighs emanated from the female observers and she closed her eyes to enjoy the moment in private.

'Yeah, you're right, Phil, she is gonna get it, but you're not. Bloody gambling our money away. Now come on, we're going home.'

Lucy imprinted her smile onto Joseph's mouth. In that moment, all was right in the world. There were many reasons why she shouldn't have been there, but she wanted to be, and that was the only one that mattered.

It was over between her and Mark. She simply didn't love him anymore. There was no point in continuing with the charade any longer. Money could change lives, influence governments, and allow you to set your own agenda. It could acquire just about anything a deviant mind can think of. But matters of the heart were its Achilles heel. The money had only served to distract her from the truth that there was no future for them. She had known it the moment Joseph held her in his arms. Here she was again, but this time she felt no guilt.

'Do you wanna finish the race?' He looked back to the road; a steady flow of runners were now passing by, each one looking more fatigued than the last.

'No, it doesn't matter. It's just a race.'

He offered his hand, and Lucy took it. Hers fitting perfectly in his; like the last piece of the jigsaw that completed the picture.

She walked proudly alongside him. Random strangers

gave their congratulations, patting him on the back as they passed. Free of the rabble, they stood at the edge of the car park.

'What now?' She looked up at him.

'I think I should take a shower,' he joked, shaving the perspiration from his brow with a finger.

'You know what I mean.'

Lucy tugged gently on his hand, half-expecting Kimberley to come bounding over and steal him away from her.

'Where are you staying?' He held her hand a little tighter. 'That is, if you are planning on staying?'

She couldn't believe that there was doubt in his voice. 'There's nowhere else I'd rather be.' Clinging to his arm, she let go of her fears.

'I haven't booked in anywhere yet – I only arrived five minutes ago, to be honest.'

'You'll be lucky to find a vacancy. The Ironman competition is very popular.'

'Oh.' She hadn't driven all that way at break- neck speed to just go back home again. She would sleep in the car if she had to.

'There's room where I'm staying – it's nothing fancy though.' A smile grew along with her excitement. There would be no excuses this time; he was happy for her to be there.

'Sounds great.'

'Where are you parked?' he asked.

'I'm at the bottom of the car park somewhere.'

'My truck's just over there. Follow me in your car – it's not far.'

'Okay.'

Reluctantly, she let go of his hand and walked at double speed back to her BMW, eager to spend every second with him.

Unlocking the car she climbed in and checked her appearance in the rear view mirror – all was good.

Hastily, she clipped her safety belt in and manoeuvred out of the tight space. Joseph was already backed out and waiting. Lucy flashed her lights, and the convoy moved on. She couldn't quite believe it was really happening. She chatted away, telling herself that she would book into a separate room, but secretly hoping she wouldn't have to.

There were lots of problems waiting for her at home, but that was exactly what they could do – wait. Today was going to be problem-free; there was nobody in the whole world but her and Joseph.

On the drive there, all her concentration had been focused on getting to him before the race was over. Now she could relax, the beautiful landscape became her interest rather than just the road. A narrow, steep incline led them away from Rucklestone Bay, passing quaint, whitewashed houses that were nestled into the rugged hillside like roosting birds. Stone walls lined the route, bearded with moss. Once she had climbed out of the bay, the road levelled out; Lucy switched off the air-con and opened the windows. Fresh air burst in, playing with her hair. The simple elegance of nature drew a smile. Bushy hedgerows, rickety old fences and ancient trees were a pleasant, but unfamiliar sight. Breathing it all in, she knew in her heart that it was right, however it might turn out.

They turned onto a dirt road – one car wide, tunnelled with trees. Lucy thought that it seemed a strange entrance for a hotel. They passed an old timber building submerged in the greenery. A collection of wind chimes hung from a corrugated lean-to covering a small deck, and a sign hung on the door handle, which read: 'Welcome! If there's no one here, please feel free to make yourself at home and we'll get round to seeing you eventually!'

'What kind of hotel is this?'

They emerged from the shade of the trees, and the open land ran free, galloping towards the boundaries of its reach, stopping at the cliff face to give way to the deep blue expanse of the ocean.

Looking around, Lucy chuckled to herself. *This will be a first.*

Joseph parked a short distance from the land's end, next to a blue and grey tent. He was out on his own, everyone else on the campsite was keeping a safe distance from the sheer drop. Lucy parked her car alongside him.

'I told you it was nothing fancy,' he said, unzipping the tent and disappearing inside. She heaved her suitcase off the back seat, bumping it over the grass, keen to show him that it didn't bother her one bit, which it didn't. He emerged with a white towel over his shoulder, and a black toiletry bag hooked on his little finger.

'It's perfect.' She tried her best to look convincing, sensing his apprehension.

'Are you sure? It's not a five star hotel in Barcelona, I'm afraid.'

'I don't want that; that's why I'm here.' She adopted a stern tone, punctuating the truth of what she had said.

'Okay?'

He nodded. 'Okay. Make yourself at home, Miss Lucy, while I go and freshen up.' He strolled off to the shower block; she watched and waited for his glance. Only a few steps into his journey, he looked back over his shoulder. They shared a smile before she entered the fabric shelter.

It was larger than she had expected. An airbed occupied one corner with a sleeping bag neatly rolled up on top of it. In the opposite corner was a camping stove with a miniature gas bottle, pots, pans, and various other camping equipment, all neatly organised and laid out.

Lucy put her suitcase down and opened it up, then started to rummage through, trying to get to her sandals. Swapping heels for flats, she took the liberty of borrowing his folding chair and planted herself outside to take in the glorious view.

She had half contemplated stripping off and lying seductively on the bed waiting for his return, but there was always the risk of the owner of the site turning up to say hello. Plus, she knew he must be exhausted after his race.

Whatever he wanted to do was fine with Lucy. She was going to be spending the night literally under the stars with him, and there wasn't another place on Earth she would rather have been at that moment.

She closed her eyes, totally relaxed, which she hadn't expected to be. Everything was perfectly quiet, apart from the distant sound of the ocean pushing back the land with unrelenting wave after wave.

'Relaxing, isn't it?' Joseph's dulcet tones startled Lucy. She sprang upright, bleary-eyed having surrendered to sleep 'What? Oh, yes – sorry.' She wiped her eyes. 'I dozed off, I'm afraid.'

She shuffled around in her seat, finding that Joseph was barefoot and had only a white towel hugging his waist. Now she was awake.

'I got you this from the camp shop.' He handed her a

bottle of white wine.

'Thank you.' She pretended to examine the label while secretly inspecting the hump in the towel. The sun took a break, hiding behind a cloud, he was radiating more than enough heat for both of them.

'I'm no wine connoisseur, I'm afraid. I hope it's okay.'

Dragging her eyes away from the towel, she followed the skyscraper of his height to look up at the face that had the power to stop her heart. His damp hair kinked and curled around his perfect features.

Jesus, does he know the effect he has on me?

'Do you mind if I have a lie down for a while? I'm pretty knackered, and then I'm all yours.'

'Yeah, of course. Please don't worry about me. Is there anything you want me to do?'

'Just be here waiting for me when I wake up.'

Her palm fell flat on her chest. She hadn't been expecting that. Lucy nodded, giving a smile, still caught up with his request. He turned away and Lucy's fanned her face.

'Would you mind hanging this on the truck for me?'

She rose from her seat and stood in the doorway. Joseph was dangling the towel from his outstretched arm.

'Sure.' Stepping inside she happily took the towel, but Joseph turned away before she got a glimpse.

Was he just going to lie there naked? Not wanting to miss any of the show, she flung the towel, lassoing the wing mirror.

'I'll set my alarm clock in case you want to go for a walk. I only need an hour.'

His voice was raised, thinking that she was by the truck hanging out the towel out.

Lucy hadn't moved an inch. She was salaciously examining the body that was made for pleasure.

The span of his muscular back tapered down to the finest set of honed buttocks any girl could wish for. Legs spread, the shadow of his heavy balls hanging low was clearly visible.

How was she expected to wait a whole hour with that sprawled out just a few feet away? It was a cruelty equal to laying out a feast before a starving man and telling him not to eat. Lucy had waited long enough, and she was ravenous.

Moving closer, she rolled her thumbs into his shoulders.

'Mmm… that's so nice,' he mumbled.

'Do you want something to help you sleep?'

'I think I might now. What do you suggest?'

'You're all tense from the physical exertion. You need to release it.'

Once she had touched his skin, that was it: she simply had to have him.

'Do I?'

'Oh, yes. Let me check you over.' Admiring the view, her hands kneaded their way down the magnificent architecture of his body.

Taking one of his buttocks in each hand, she sunk her fingers into the firm flesh with gritted teeth. It was Lucy's turn to groan. Her heart beat faster, her skin prickled and her body clenched.

She was evolving into a sexual creature that he had created. Every code from her senses of sight, touch and smell was converted into one basic carnal need.

No other man had ever held such power over her

body.

She followed the divide in his cheeks, until the weighty sack spilled over her palm. Caressing his balls, she unashamedly fondled the silky skin for her own pleasure.

He hissed like a steam train. 'I think you found all that tension you were looking for.'

'Yes, I have. And now I'm going to rid you of it, Mr Dalton.' Placing her weight on her knees, she scraped her hair back. 'Turn around.'

He did, quickly, his cock swinging like a wrecking ball, semi-hard, long, thick – muscular, even – and like the rest of him, highly capable of what it was designed for.

Joseph peered down at her darkly; his eyes alive with the energy that sexual need delivers.

Lucy's mouth flooded with the anticipation of tasting him for the first time.

Without hesitation, she pasted her lips with a sheen of saliva and held his girth at the base. She circled the foreskin-cloaked head with her moist lips, breathing in his seductive aroma. The hardening flesh made her expand her grip and drew back the veil from the engorged head. With each regression she eased her mouth further along, stretching her mouth to accommodate him. The hot, salty flesh continued to set like concrete in the sun, filling the void. Her squashed tongue squirmed in delight under the confinement.

'Don't tease me,' he growled. It sounded like a warning rather than a request.

Drawing back, her cheeks hollowed, she sucked with everything she had, gliding her wet lips along his delicious dick, daring to take more each time.

'Fuck, that feels good.' Joseph thrust his hips

impatiently. 'More – deeper,' he demanded. Lucy slapped her hand against his abs, already full to capacity.

He wasn't listening. Lucy moaned with each thrust, but it was a turn-on being forced to suck his enormous cock, and within five minutes she had gone from a respectable teacher to a dirty slut that would let him use her any way he wanted.

One hand was still on his abs, restricting his thrusts, and the other released his shaft and wrapped around the soft skin above his balls. She tugged at them, letting him know to ease off. It didn't work, only seeming to spur him on.

'I want to come in your mouth,' he said breathlessly, hitting the back of her throat with another merciless thrust.

Dizzy from lack of oxygen, she pulled away. 'Not yet.' she gasped, wiping the drool from her chin. Grabbing the back of her arms, he lifted her like she was made of air. Lucy's insistence matched his. Taking a fistful of his hair, she pulled his face to hers. Their mouths collided, delivering a taste of his own body.

Her tongue communicated the ferocious need that had built up deep inside of her. Joseph broke their seal and sat upon the bed.

'Lie down,' she said, shoving his shoulders away.

Joseph fell backwards, bouncing on the air-filled bed, his cock slapping down on his abs. Lucy unbuttoned her jeans and cast them aside, knocking over the pots and pans.

She scrambled onto him with no finesse at all and squatted down. Gripping his dick, she eased the bulbous head beyond her soaked lips.

'Fuck, it's tight,' gasped Lucy.

Joseph pulled her T-shirt up over her head. Lucy raised her arms for him; then, losing her balance, she fell down on the tower of hard flesh and screamed out in perverse ecstasy.

'Stop, stop, stop,' she blurted out. 'No deeper.' Her chest heaved in and out; beads of sweat decorated her body.

'You'd better be quick, Eaton. I can't hold this much longer.' Joseph sat up, reaching for her bra strap and withdrawing his cock slightly. He unclipped the lace garment, they were both naked.

Lying back, he pawed her aching breasts, tugging on her taut, dark nipples. Lucy held onto his forearms and bounced up and down, dipping deeper each time, coating him with her excitement with each drop of her bottom.

'It's too big,' Lucy winced, feeling the pressure of his cock on her anus.

'You'd better finish what you started,' he commanded, lacing his fingers behind her neck. Her pussy was soaking his cock, accepting more and more, and the friction eased as he tunnelled deeper and deeper. The airbed helped in exaggerating the height of her bounce, allowing her to travel the full length, enjoying all there was on offer. Feelings of surrender built fast as the relentless shafting continued.

'No one's ever fucked me like this.' Lucy grunted, delirious with gratification, locked out from the world, held captive inside this hypnotic walls of bliss.

'I'm coming – don't stop.' Her arse slapped down on his balls. 'Yes… Oh God, yes.'

She clawed at his arms, temporarily relieved of all self-control. The whisper of climax built to a scream of a thousand people as the bird of ecstasy took flight, and her body broke on his. She pulsed and clenched around the enormous dick buried deep inside her. Joseph's gasp gave warning.

Lucy sprang off, remembering his request.

She missed the first burst, but her mouth fell open just in time to catch the second. Eager to equal the pleasure she had received.

Lucy yanked away, twisting and squeezing to tease out every last drop, snorting greedily as she gulped down his seed.

Joseph roared with the detonation, fists clenched on his forehead, writhing as if in pain, until the storm was replaced by peace and serenity. Satisfied that his request had been fulfilled, Lucy withdrew her mouth.

'Has the tension gone, Mr Dalton?'

'I feel like an empty banana skin,' he mumbled, eyes closed, arms spread, his body painted in a glossy sheen of sweat.

Lucy took hold of his softening penis, which was still bloated, and waggled it.

'Oh, I don't know, there's still a bit of Ironman left in you.'

He bounced on the bed, a deep chuckle rumbling in his chest.

Lucy pushed herself up, the dull pulsing throb of her sex a sure sign that she had been well and truly fucked. Picking up her jeans, she plucked out her knickers that were tangled inside.

'You stay there, mister.'

'Where are you going?' He raised his head, already

halfway to sleep.

'To get you a towel, you're a bit messy.' She twirled her finger over the pearl-coloured pool on his midsection before putting on her jeans and T- shirt.

'Yes, you can clean that mess up, madame. You made it,' he said wearily.

'Cheeky – you did play a part in this, you know.' She smiled down at him admiringly, but he didn't witness it: the lids of his eyes had become too heavy to hold back any longer.

Lucy stepped out from the sexual heat into the refreshing coastal air and almost jumped out of her skin. Only a couple of feet away was an old,

bottle-green and white Volkswagen camper van, with an elderly couple sat in front of it in two deck chairs, enjoying a flask of tea.

'Afternoon,' said the old lady tentatively, her eyebrows raised high above her chunky spectacles.

'Oh, hello...' Frozen to the spot, Lucy held her palm up in greeting, like an Indian chief. *They are so close.*

The elderly man leaned forward from the cover of his wife, plastic cup in hand.

'We were just admiring the view,' he explained, his expression like that of a child caught stealing sweets.

'It's lovely, isn't it?' Lucy's cheeks were not the only things burning.

'We're both 76 you know, our hearing's not that good these days.'

The man's wife elbowed him in the ribs while pretending to settle herself in her seat. Lucy covered her mouth, making a pretence of scratching her face. It wasn't a convincing performance from any of them.

Lucy turned away, cringing and sniggering at the same time. She unhooked the towel from the wing mirror, and they all exchanged awkwardly polite smiles. She stepped back into, what she thought was the privacy of the tent.

Joseph was out for the count, spread out like a starfish. Lucy knelt before him and mopped up the pool of semen that had dribbled from his flaccid penis onto his abs.

'Did I hear voices?' he muttered, rousing.

'Shhhh, it's no one. Bloody hell, doesn't this thing get any smaller?' She kept her voice low, now knowing there were more ears listening.

'You're not moaning, are you, Miss Lucy?' he rambled, intoxicated with sleep.

'Certainly not, Mr Joe,' she whispered.

'You will be... later...' His head fell to one side, unable to hold off his body's need for rest.

Lucy felt alight in his presence – alive. She would be spending the night with the man who had taken her understanding of lust and desire and turned it upside-down. Was this to be the only night she would ever know with him? That question was too painful to contemplate. Whatever the answer to that was, she was determined to make it a night to remember.

Unrolling the sleeping bag, she allowed herself one last viewing, before hiding his physical perfection from her insatiable gaze.

CHAPTER TWENTY-NINE

Joseph's eyes cracked open to find the brightness of the day had faded. Pulling back the sleeping bag, he sat upright, weak from sleep and a multitude of other things. The alarm clock told him that he had been out for more than an hour. Rubbing his face awake, the sound of activity rustled outside.

'Is that you, Lucy?'

'Yes. You're just in time, sleepyhead.'

He pulled out a pair of khaki shorts and a black T-shirt from his backpack and got dressed. He unzipped the opening and was greeted by a kiss before he had even taken a step out. The genuine softness of her plump lips evoked something inside that he hadn't expected, or ever experienced before. Her beautiful face was food for the soul: flawlessly fresh, like a blue sky on a crisp winter morning, and alive with enthusiasm.

'I let you rest a little longer. I hope you don't mind. I couldn't bring myself to wake you.'

'That's fine. It was the best sleep I've had in a long

time.'

'Are you hungry?' she asked, her hand on his chest.

'Starving would be more accurate.'

'Good,' she grinned. 'Then step this way, sir.'

Joseph ducked out into the open air and looked around in wonder. The stove sat on the camping table, responsible for the alluring smell of food tempting his nostrils.

A chequered blanket covered the ground, surrounded by candles which were now coming into their own as the early dusk started to settle. It was perfect, just like Lucy.

'Wow. You've been busy. It looks…'

'Romantic?' Lucy suggested, handing him a plastic cup. A measure of whiskey swirling in the bottom.

He smiled cautiously.

'How does ratatouille with poached eggs and fresh crusty bread sound?'

'Sounds great.'

'I went to the camp shop. It's very well equipped, although I did buy every single candle they had.' She collected her cup of wine from the table and took a sip. 'Will this do?' she asked, looking worried by his silence.

'Will this do?' he repeated, hooking his hand around the back of her neck, drawing her closer to his side. 'Lucy, it's perfect.'

Joseph buried his face in her hair and drew in her sweet smell. 'Just perfect.' He kissed the top of her head.

Lucy wrapped her arm around his waist and held her drink up. 'Here's to the simple pleasures in life.'

Their cups met, making a dull tap, Lucy took a sip from hers.

'I wasn't sure if you wanted Coke,' she said, spotting him peering into his whiskey, looking unsure.

'No, it's fine. I drink it neat.'

'Don't look so worried. I'm not going to get you drunk and take advantage.'

'Really? That's a shame,' he smiled, taking a small sip.

'Let me check on dinner before you get me too distracted, mister.'

'Is there anything you want me to do?'

'No. Just park your bum and look pretty.'

Joseph did as he was told while Lucy busied herself. He sat contemplating whether or not he could control his thirst once he had the taste for alcohol.

Relax. It's just one drink. That's all.

He hadn't touched a drop for over a week. The nights were hard, but the mornings were easier.

Fearing the power the whiskey was already exerting over him, he tossed his drink aside while Lucy's back was turned.

It was time to be a better man, for everyone's sake.

Lucy fed Joseph the last mouthful of cheesecake before settling back down on the blanket. Lying at her side, Joseph spooned her, propped up on his elbow.

With no need for words, they enjoyed their elevated views, watching as the youth of dusk matured into darkness, stealing the view from them. The candles fought bravely, lighting their tiny corner of the world.

Lucy had never been more content in her life. Joseph was the almighty creator of her joy – and her fear. That on the other side of this short weekend her heart would be broken. She cast the thought from her mind. The future was a time her eyes could not see.

'Don't you want to know why I'm here and not in Barcelona?'

'You are here. That's all that matters,' he said, his arm curling around Lucy's waist, pulling her closer.

'Tell me about yourself, Joseph.'

'What do you want to know?'

'Everything.'

His chest ballooned out against her back as he silently took a deep breath.

'There's not much to tell. I'm just an ordinary guy... your average Joe.'

He was avoiding her questions. Was it modesty or did he have something to hide?

'You're selling yourself short. There's nothing average about you at all. You must have some stories about your youth.'

'The stories I have aren't ones you'd want to hear.'

'Try me.'

'Maybe one day,' he said quietly.

'I'll hold you to that.' She placed his hand on her beating heart, holding it there tightly.

Another white light punctured the moonless sky, adding another dot to the great astral map. There were thousands of stars out that night and it seemed that Lucy had an unanswered question for every single one of them.

With the understanding that not all questions hold the answers we are looking for, she turned her thoughts to the one thing she did know. He was hers, and hers alone, if only for that one night.

Joseph nuzzled her hair with his nose, baring the flesh of her neck. Feeling the contact of his mouth, Lucy closed her eyes, purring involuntarily as her body was suddenly charged with electricity. His sleeping hand awoke, seeking out her breasts through the green and white polka-dot dress, causing a flash of goose bumps that puckered and hardened her nipples. Lucy's body answered the call of his magic touch. There was no need for smoke and mirrors. This magician could conjure up powerful feelings and desires that had long been dormant.

'Are you trying to take advantage of me, Mr Dalton? I'm not even drunk.'

'Well, you were good enough to treat me to your culinary skills, so I think it only fair that I repay you with what I'm good at.' His voice melted into her ear while he gently gnawed and tugged at her lobe.

'And what *exactly*... is it that *you're*...good at?' Lucy gasped, her words blurting out uncontrollably as he proved his point, sucking and biting at the junction of her jaw and neck.

'I nurture and encourage...' . . .' the rousing mouth latched onto her shoulder. 'Flowers to bud, bloom . . .' His hand travelled south, massaging the hot, plump little V between her closed thighs. 'And blossom.'

'Show me,' she encouraged.

Pure lust poured through her body and seeped out into her tight white thong.

Encouraging his fingers with her own, they delved deeper into the sodden material, manipulating and teasing the fiery pink bud that lay buried in the hot cleft. The need in her had awakened, stirred by his touch, a temporary madness that would not rest until it had been satisfied. It was completely selfish and unconcerned with circumstances or situations, driven by carnality, desperate to experience the euphoria of release.

She groaned in displeasure while he mauled a chunk of her arse, forcing her knickers into the crevasse of her bottom.

'Hand,' she demanded. 'I want it back.'

Taking hold of Lucy's fingers, he dug deep. 'Pleasure yourself for me.'

'No – you do it,' she protested.

He forced her digits into the slick parting through the barrier of her dress, his index finger shadowing hers, circling her swollen clitoris.

He spun her into a frenzy with rotation after rotation – the hypnotic feeling was irresistibly addictive. It was only until she felt the cheeks of her backside being groped that she realised she was flying solo. By now she didn't care and continued stroking with increasing speed, ascending the ladder of pleasure all on her own, moaning in self-gratification.

'You trying to take my job?' he teased.

'Finish what you started then, Dalton.'

She didn't have to ask twice. Joseph sat up, allowing Lucy to lie on her back before plummeting down and trapping her mouth with his. The partnership of his forceful lips and wicked tongue caused a tidal flood between her thighs. Caged inside the bars of his arms, she submitted to her body's confession, guilty of wanting him in every filthy, indecent way that was imaginable.

Her hands scrambled down between their bodies, which were pinched together, forcing his shorts open in a frenzied attack, desperate to feel his heat in her palm. Joseph eased her legs apart, occupying the space between with his, while Lucy satisfied her addiction, filling her hand with his mighty cock.

Travelling only half the distance of his shaft, she dropped her shoulders in an attempt to extend her reach. Frantically shuffling to please him had the side effects of pleasuring herself yet again. Lucy's arm rubbed and teased between her spread thighs through the fabric of her dress, trapped under his muscular frame. She pressed down harder, desperate for stimulation, becoming more and more fevered and impatient. Joseph retreated, stopping to take a bite of her nipple; the moist heat of his breath cooled her as he moved further down, tightening her skin. She watched from between the valley of her heaving breasts, knowing full well where he was heading.

He looked self-satisfied, aware of his power, in control. Lucy was anything but. She yearned to feel his merciful touch and rid herself of this affliction that was ravaging her body and mind.

His head disappeared, rippling her dress like the dorsal fin of a shark closing in on its prey. He was at the top of the food chain, a machine built for domination of the fairer sex.

A finger delved beneath the intimate material, stretching it to one side, combing the tuft of pubic hair. Lucy laid her head back, closing out the world, readying herself to be sacrificed to pleasure.

His broad shoulders forced her raised legs further apart while his hands curled under her thighs, seizing her by the waist. The tickle of his fervent breath introduced the slippery tongue, beginning its work at the crack in her bottom, sliding up to part the swollen, pouty flesh of her sex, before stroke after stroke sent Lucy's arms flying out in spasms. Bunching up the blanket in her fists, she clung on for dear life while he rocked her world. His tongue lapped her glowing nub ferociously, lapping at the overflowing goblet, bingeing on her body. Out in the open, ringed by candlelight like some circus freak show, he ate her pussy and Lucy didn't give a fuck. Lust poisoned her mind, killing off all prohibitive thoughts and leaving but one single purpose. Resting her legs on the stirrups of his shoulders she clutched at his head, forcing it deeper. Reacting to the urgency of her silent pleas, he sucked her clitoris into the vacuum of his mouth, edging her ever closer to the peak, the pressure engorging the self-destruct button. Lucy thrashed about like a fish out of water, gasping for air, her back arched, the fever taking over. Without warning he pulled away. She grunted selfishly, ignoring the fact that he probably needed oxygen. He rose, lifting the cover of her dress up around her waist. The canopy of his body hung over her supported by a single arm. Lucy dipped into the pool of his eyes, glossed with an unimaginable yearning.

He swiped the searing length between the wings of her pussy, stroking himself before splitting her in two with his red-hot cock. It was slow and steady; long, fat and hard. If gluttony was a deadly sin, then she surely was a sinner. She wanted every single vein-filled inch of him.

'Fuck!' Lucy winced, still tender from earlier. 'Don't you stop,' she insisted, feeling him easing off. 'I want it all.'

Her request was granted. Joseph rutted bullishly, forcing in the last few inches until his balls rested on her bottom. Claws out, Lucy held him there, savouring the pulse of his dick, throbbing like a distress beacon, suffocating in the claustrophobic walls of her sex. His pelvis ground against hers, singling out her tormented clit. The whimpers of a building release sneaked out from him.

Her body was sapping his self-control. It was such a turn-on to know that her effect was equal to his, and her pussy was slowly becoming accustomed to the giant intruder.

She raised her hips encouragingly, and he stared into her eyes, his face strained with concentration. He set the pace with short controlled thrusts, watching her reactions closely. The race had begun.

Lucy bucked her hips.

'Harder.'

She held his salacious gaze defiantly. Competitiveness awoke in her. Who would break first? Accepting the challenge, he broke into a sprint, slamming into her harder and faster, deeper and deeper, drawing almost all the way out then mercilessly lancing her again with his rock-hard cock. He was totally relentless, each lunge sending an unintentional groan of pleasure out into the night sky. His exertion puffed into her face and the sweat dripped from his nose as the blanket ruffled around Lucy's head, his cock unceremoniously shunting her inch by inch across the ground, fucking her as if his life depended on it. Lucy gritted her teeth, feeling the delicious tightening in her tummy. The fuse had been lit, a slow burn that fizzled and sparked with each plunge of his monstrous cock. She clenched down, her pussy milking him, greedily craving his seed.

Joseph's breath hitched, his eyes flickered and the speed of his strokes slowed; growling, he made one more long, deep slice, before exploding with a flood of hot semen, jolting as his body emptied.

Her own journey was also nearing its end, and she drew his face to hers. The touch of his lips was all it took to tip the balance. The soft wetness of his tongue connected them in more than just a physical way, allowing her a window into the desire he felt for her. Spasms racked her body as she imploded into orgasm. Lucy held onto him, the pleasures of flesh opening the doorway to another world. True freedom revealed itself —the reality of time seemed powerless, if only for a brief moment, their bodies and minds becoming one and the same, riding a vortex of ecstasy, between worlds.

Reaching a high that no spaceship could ever hope to, Lucy began the decent. Still shuddering from the shadow of the fading climax, she re-entered the earth's atmosphere, clinging to the vessel that had taken her beyond its limits.

Covered with the blanket of his breathless body, both of them broken, she lay speechless, full to the very limit, as satisfied as any woman could be.

Lucy woke to find herself the only occupant of the bed. The hangover of a deep, peaceful sleep still lingered over her. She turned her cheek into the soft pillow, infused with his heady aroma. Stretching out with a yawn, the mumble of conversation honed her senses. Lucy's elbows subsided into the bed as she tried to prop herself up. She focused on the high-pitched voice.

It was another woman.

Feeling the primal threat of a rival female, she bounced out from under the blankets to grab her dress, quickly wriggling it on over her head. Bending at the waist, she ruffled her hair, flicked it back and tried to smooth out the creases of her dress, having no effect at all.

Lucy stepped out into the morning sun to find Joseph wearing a tight black vest and shorts, leaning against the back of his truck, his companion hidden by his frame. With the grass tickling her feet, she approached apprehensively.

'Good morning,' Lucy chirped, announcing her presence.

Joseph twisted at the waist, his relaxed smile setting her at ease.

'Sorry, am I interrupting?'

'No, no. Come and say hello.' He held his hand out for her.

'Lucy, I'd like you to meet a devilish little minx.'

A hoot of laughter rang out from the lady he was introducing.

'I'm glad I had the protection of your company last night, because she prowls around in the small hours looking for victims.'

'Oh shut up, you.' The stranger slapped him on the forearm. 'I'm Kimberly, my love.' She offered her hand along with a warm smile.

'I'm Lucy. It's very nice to meet you.'

It was very nice indeed. Kimberly wasn't at all the many creations of her imagination. She was tall and slim, in her late fifties or possibly early sixties, with mousy-brown feathery hair and a kind, motherly face. Lucy took to her instantly, and not just because she wasn't a big-titted playgirl.

'He's full of flattery, isn't he? I'll have you know, I'm a very happy singleton. I've had enough of men. Had one for thirty-five years. Pain in the bloody arse.'

Her high, perfectly round cheekbones meant that every word she spoke seemed good-natured, which in this case it was.

'Hey, steady on. You're not doing me any favours here.'

'I'm not talking about you, Joe. You're one of the good ones.'

Kimberly leaned into Lucy. 'So he keeps telling me anyway.' Her cheeks rounded with a grin.

'Kim owns the land. It's her site,' Joseph explained.

'It's a beautiful spot. Have you been here long?'

'We have. It's been in my family for three generations.'

'Three generations? She doesn't look that old does she?' he joked, raising his guard.

'Cheeky sod. Do you want another one of those?' Kimberly scowled playfully, pointing to his bruised eye.

Whatever their connection was, it was a close one.

'Why have you both got a black eye anyway?'

Lucy looked up at Joseph, hoping he would conjure up a story.

'That's how we met. Lucy's a cage fighter. It was a close one, but she knocked me out in round five.'

'You should've been a comedian.'

Kim knotted her arms, rolling her eyes good-humouredly.

'I'm gonna go and see Chris this morning. It's been a while since I last saw him,' Joseph said, steering her in another direction.

'He'll like that. He asked how you did in the Ironman.'

'How's he doing?'

'Good. You know Chris, he's pretty laid-back. He's still having trouble sleeping at night, but other than that he's doing well.' Kimberley's voice had become somewhat less jovial.

There was a short, awkward silence. Lucy couldn't help but think it was her presence that was stopping the flow of conversation.

'Okay,' exclaimed Kim, her brightness returning. 'I'm going to leave you to enjoy your day. Lucy, it was nice meeting you.'

'And you. I hope to see you again.'

Lucy's response was an innocent one, but it did pose an awkward question.

'I'm sure you will.'

Kimberly shot a questioning look at Joseph, as did Lucy.

Giving nothing away, he held his friend by the shoulders and kissed her cheek.

'Don't you leave this time without saying goodbye, you hear me?' She prodded his chest with a long finger. 'Promise?'

'I promise. Scout's honour.' He saluted with two fingers.

'Yes, I know your 'scout's honour'. Keep an eye on this one, Lucy. He doesn't always keep his promises.' It was only a jovial comment, but still, it stung Lucy's insecurity.

'That's enough from you, Nanny McPhee. On your way.' Joseph shooed her off with the back of his hand, the smile that Lucy adored spread over his face.

Today is going to be a good day.

He turned to Lucy, a humorous glint still in his eyes.

'Morning.' A kiss to the forehead accompanied the greeting.

Lucy raised her face, lips parted, needing a reminder of how his mouth felt on hers.

Stepping into the cocoon of his embrace, Joseph's tender lips made themselves known.

The gentle softness of his kiss was in stark contrast to

the hard body underneath her roving hands.

His arms grew around her like vines around a tree, leaving Lucy feeling impervious to all harm, yet more vulnerable than she had ever felt before.

Her eyes fluttered open as he withdrew, their noses still touching.

'Mmm, that was nice,' she purred.

'Nice? I think I deserve a higher rating than that, don't you?'

'Then you'll have to try harder,' she teased.

His eyes pinched with a smile before he took up the challenge with persuasiveness and force. Caressing. Biting. Sucking with sublime expertise.

Lucy's closed eyes had never been more open. A mosaic of feelings, emotions, and desires all burst forth, mixing together like an artist's paint, the broad strokes of his tongue creating a masterpiece of fine detail. A rousing image depicting the conflict between needs and desires.

It was a truly magnificent work of art that would forever hang in the gallery of her mind.

Their flesh parted once more. Lucy's eyes remained closed, savouring the memory of his kiss.

'How did I do that time?'

She looked upon the perfection of his face. 'You were off the chart, Mr Joe – off the chart.'

'A more fitting appraisal I think. Are you hungry?'

'I'm always hungry for what you have to offer.'

That earned her a smile.

'Go and get yourself ready, I'll take you for breakfast.' He patted her on the bottom playfully.

'Let me just have a quick shower.' Rising up onto tiptoes, she pecked him on the lips and patted him on the bottom.

She hurried into the tent, grabbed her things, and quickly made her way to the showers, not wanting to waste a moment of the day.

'Hey, Lucy!'

The call spun her around.

'You can swim, can't you?'

'Yes,' she called back before hurrying on her way. *Looks like we're going for a dip.*

After enjoying breakfast on the sun-soaked terrace of a quirky little cafe set into the hillside, they drove down to the cove that the campsite overlooked.

After parking up, Joseph walked around to open Lucy's door. She was perfectly capable of doing it herself, but she had to admit the special attention was nice. Taking her hand, he helped her out.

'Are we going for a swim?'

'There will be some swimming, yes.' He closed the door and began to unclip the cover on the back of the pick-up.

'Do I need to be worried?' she asked, using her sunglasses as a headband.

'So long as you're with me, there is absolutely nothing to worry about.'

How true those words are.

He removed his vest and dropped his shorts, stepping out of them. His red swimming trunks were like a second skin, and did their best to conceal the heavy bulk lying dormant within. Her insides contracted as totally inappropriate thoughts flashed through her mind.

'So what are you going to do with me today then?' She

admired his sculpted backside while he leaned into the back of the truck, her devious thoughts not easily discouraged.

'Today, Miss Lucy, you are going to experience the closest thing to heaven.'

Huh, I already have. But I'm ready for another trip.

'We, are going surfing.' He pulled out a great white board and stood it next to her. 'If you can hold on to that for me.'

'Surfing? I can't surf.' The early onset of panic began to grow with visions of her being swallowed by a great tidal wave.

'Not yet you can't.'

She did not share his confidence.

He delved into the back of the pickup and took out a blue cool box and a wetsuit.

'There are a couple of beach towels in the back. Can you grab them for me?'

'Why don't I just watch you?' she said nervously, tucking the towels under her arm.

'And what fun will that be?'

Joseph dusted each foot in turn, before sliding his legs into the black spring suit, leaving the body hanging down from his waist.

'We just need to get you suited up.'

He pulled back the cover on the truck and they made their way across the sand-dusted car park and down the worn stone steps towards the beach. Lucy eyed the tempestuous ocean with growing distrust. A wooden walkway started where the steps ended, which they followed to an old timber building. Green, hardy shrubs defiantly sat in the sand at the foot of the gnarled, branchless tree trunks, which held up the gable-ended roof. The rustic appearance suggested it had been built by the first settlers to arrive – or by children.

'The Shack' was crudely carved into what looked like a large piece of driftwood that hung from a short chain above the open double doors.

'This is an old friend's place,' explained Joseph, leaning his board against the white, flaking timber post.

'What does a guy have to do to get any service around here? Are you asleep back there, buddy, or what?'

He winked at Lucy, letting her know it was all light-hearted.

'If you're looking for a fist in the face, you're going about it the right way, mate' came a stern reply from behind a curtain-covered doorway at the back of the shop. He didn't seem to be in on the joke.

The curtain flicked to one side, and out came the owner of the voice.

'Joe! You shit,' said the man, his tanned face suddenly dimpling with a smile, much to Lucy's relief.

'Chris, how are you?'

His friend placed the half-eaten sandwich he had been holding on the counter next to the till, and the two men met with a warm embrace, slapping each other's backs with masculine affection.

'Good to see you again, mate.'

'You too, Chris.'

'I heard you dropped out of the Ironman. What happened?'

'I got distracted.'

Chris's eyes diverted to Lucy. 'So I see.' He patted Joseph on the shoulder and his bare feet stepped in Lucy's direction.

'Chris Lockwood,' A sun-tanned hand reached out.

'Nice to meet you, Chris. I'm Lucy.'

She recognised the perfect cheekbones: he must be Kimberly's son.

'Is he taking you out there today?' His shaved head motioned towards the water.

'That's the plan, but I'm not sure it's such a good idea. I think I might just watch.'

'Nah, you'll be fine. Joe is a total amateur compared to me – in fact, he's more of a novice really – but he'll look after you.' His bronzed face only emphasised the whiteness of his smile.

'Yeah, dream on, Chris. Don't listen to him, Lucy. Too much sun has fried his brain.'

Lucy chastised herself for being so stereotypical. She had expected a blonde, straggly-haired, twenty-something – the kind who said 'dude' after every word.

'You can never have enough sunshine, dude.'

A discreet smile tickled her lips.

Chris made his way back to his sandwich. The baggy board shorts and frayed pink T-shirt he was wearing certainly matched her preconceived images.

He beckoned them into the small space, which was crammed with brightly coloured surfboards, clothes and water sports paraphernalia.

Chris very kindly offered his stool to Lucy, and she sat next to the till while the two friends caught up. He had the good manners to include her in the conversation, asking where she worked and other minor details. She couldn't help noticing that they seemed to talk in code, and that there was a very subtle change in both men's demeanour whenever they did.

'I need a spring suit for Lucy. Got anything available?' asked Joseph.

'A lot of my stuff's hired out at the moment.'

Lucy spotted her chance. 'Don't worry. I'm more than happy to watch.'

'Let me take a look in the back. I'm sure I've got something.' Chris disappeared behind the curtain.

'You're not getting out of it that easily,' said Joseph, squeezing her thigh.

'This may be an inappropriate question to ask a lady, but what size do you need?' Chris called out.

'Perfect,' replied Joseph, grinning at the curtain.

Hidden laughter mixed with the sound of boxes and various unknown objects being thrown around, and eventually Chris appeared with a red suit draped over his forearm.

'Despite his rough appearance, he's really quite smooth, isn't he?' Chris said to Lucy.

'He certainly has a softer side to him,' she answered, holding Joseph's amused gaze.

'There you go, Lucy. That should be fine.'

'Thank you.' She took it from him, not sure what to do with it.

'What do I owe you, Chris?' asked Joseph.

'What? For the suit?' Chris frowned. 'Come on, don't insult me.'

'I wasn't going to give you any money. I was just being polite.'

'Yeah, only 'cause there's a lady around.'

'You know me too well, old friend.'

Joseph took the wetsuit from Lucy and unzipped it.

'Put this on here, so you don't get sand in it.'

'Oh, okay.' She kicked off her sandals and lifted her smoky blue sundress, then dropped both of her legs into the suit.

'I've got to ask: why the hell have you both got black eyes?' Chris asked, folding his arms; a puzzled expression wrinkled his otherwise smooth head.

'Lucy bumped into a door, and a week later, I did the very same thing – didn't I?'

Joseph looked into her eyes as he pulled the suit up over her thighs.

'Yeah. You did, didn't you?' Now they definitely were talking in code.

'What are the odds of that happening?' Chris smirked. 'How's that feel?' he asked, as she wiggled her bum into the snug fit.

'It's a little tight,' she said, running her hands over her hips. The top half of the suit hung down over her legs like Joseph's, and her dress was ruffled over the top.

'It'll loosen up with the water, don't worry – you want a board too?'

'No thanks, Chris. We'll be okay with just mine. I said I'd pop in to see your mum before I pack up tonight. Shall I drop the suit there?'

'Perfect. I close at one today then I'm going to Mum's place later this afternoon, so I'll see you there.'

'Okay,' Joseph nodded. 'Ready, Lucy?'

'Yes.' She slid off the stool and hooked her fingers under the straps of her sandals.

'Thanks again, Chris.'

'Anytime, mate.' They shook hands again and bumped shoulders.

'Nice meeting you, Lucy. Keep an eye on him; he's not as good as he likes to think.'

She replied in kind. She contemplated giving him a kiss on the cheek, but settled in the end for a wave of her hand.

With a towel tucked under each arm, she stood waiting on the coarse decking, while Joseph armed himself with the coolbox and surfboard. Ready When she was ready to go, Lucy's feet immediately sank into the soft sand; it shifted mischievously, giving no traction whatsoever. As they advanced into the warm sea breeze, the waves got larger and the sand firmer.

'This should do us,' Joseph said, dropping the surfboard. Lucy rolled out one of the towels, anchoring it with the coolbox.

'Let me help you with your suit,' he said, lifting her dress over her head, placing it on the towel.

A captivated look cast over his face while he inspected her body, naked from the waist up apart from her white plait bikini top.

'It seems so wrong to cover up such a sight.'

'You wouldn't have to if we just lay on the beach and relaxed,' she pouted.

'Nice try, gorgeous.' He kissed her on the nose. 'Don't look so worried. I won't take you out to the big waves.'

'Promise?'

'Scout's honour.' He gave her his two-fingered salute then sealed her into the corset-tight suit.

After giving her a quick tutorial on dry land, he took Lucy by the hand and led her towards the water, which had lost most of its rage by the time it spilled out onto the sand. Lucy tightened her grip, the shock of the cool water washing over her toes and taking her by surprise as they waded in.

A shudder ran through her, the temperature seeming to lower the deeper they went.

'Once we get moving it will be like a nice warm bath,' Joseph let go of her hand and dived in to acclimatise himself. After a few moments, he re-emerged, looking completely at one with his surroundings.

The rugged but beautiful coastline held a similarity to the man.

She looked back towards the land, embracing the cove in its arms in a semi-circle. The hard, rocky landscape had dared to intrude into the ocean's domain only to be slashed, cut and carved by its inimitable power, leaving huge chunks of stone stranded, separated from the main body.

The powder-blue sky painted the backdrop to the kind of magnificent view that modern society had forgotten. The beach was virtually empty, yet there was no doubt that the shopping malls were packed.

She turned her attention back to another impressive sight, and found him looking out at his fellow surfers riding the big waves. Beads of water glistened in his beard, and his hair was slicked back and shiny like a seal's skin. She could have watched him all day long.

'Why don't you go out there? I don't mind.'

'Because I'd rather be here.'

The perfect answer, fit for a perfect day.

'Are you going to teach me how to ride this thing then, Mr Joe, or what?'

'All right, bossy.' He flicked a palm full of water at her. Lucy shrieked, hunching her shoulders.

'You're going to get a lot wetter than that,' he laughed.

'Promises, promises.'

'Business first, Miss Lucy,' he smiled, wagging a finger at her.

The teacher became the pupil, and with Joseph's help Lucy caught her very first wave, albeit only while lying down on the surfboard. Nevertheless, it was thrilling. The swell raised the back of the board and her stomach turned, thinking she would flip over, but what followed was a weightless glide down the slope of water which took her almost as far as the shoreline.

The playful child inside her had been awakened and all of Lucy's fears and inhibitions drifted away.

Joseph gave her a round of applause then issued her next challenge. 'Now you need to do that standing up.'

'No problem.' She splashed her way back, eager to ride again.

'Good girl, that's what I like to hear.'

Having overestimated her skills, Lucy went on to fall in just about every way that was possible from a surfboard. Forwards, backwards, head-first, bottom-first. Each failure created more determination until finally she learnt to combine balance and composure, and stand on the surfboard on two feet. Joseph hollered out praise from behind her.

'Holy shit! I'm doing it!' She felt like a bird riding on the wind. It was a feeling of total joy, being at one with nature's energy, with the water chasing her towards the beach. She totally got it.

She looked around, trying to see if Joseph was watching, but this broke her equilibrium, and the board shot out from under her feet, sending her plunging once more into the water.

Springing to the surface, she spurted out a mouthful of salt water. Joseph swam over and she opened her eyes to see him beaming down at her. 'That's my girl. You're a natural.'

'That was… awesome!'

He chuckled, 'you're even picking up the lingo.'

Rocking from side to side in the lapping waves, he contemplated her with a searching expression.

'Don't look at me, I look a mess.'

Dropping her head, she peeled the tangled hair off her face.

Joseph raised her chin with his index finger and placed a salty kiss on her lips. 'You look like a beautiful mermaid.' He kept his face close, their noses almost touching. 'One who's downed three bottles of wine and slept on the beach all night, but still…'

Lucy's mouth gaped in fake shock. She squashed his cheeks with both hands.

'You had me onside there for a moment, Dalton. If I wasn't a lady I might give you a slap.'

'Forgive me, my queen.'

'Mmm, just this once.' She returned his kiss.

'Want to go again?'

'I'm knackered to be honest. I think I'm going to retire while I'm on top.'

Just as he had when they went out, Joseph held Lucy's hand and the tide ushered them ashore, where he wrapped her up in a towel. He opened the cool box and took out a small bottle of rosé wine. 'Would the mermaid care for a drink?'

'Yes, she would. Thank you.'

Lucy wrung out her hair while he poured the wine into

a plastic cup. 'I seem to have misplaced the cut crystal, I'm afraid.'

Taking the drink, Lucy tutted. 'I shall overlook it – just this once.'

'That's very kind of you. If you're hungry there's an assortment of crackers, cheeses, fruit, and some other nibbles in the cool box, okay?'

'Sounds lovely.'

'Do you mind if I catch a few waves?' he asked, wiping the drips from his face.

'I was wondering when you were going to show me what you can do.' She sipped her rosé. 'To be honest, I was beginning to think you were all talk.' Lucy peered up at him from under her raised eyebrows.

'Were you really?' He crouched down, attaching the board leash to his ankle. 'I'm not quite at your standard yet, but I hope to be one day.'

'Takes a lot of practice you know,' she teased.

'I'd better make a start then.' He knelt down in the sand and kissed her, his beard wetting her face. 'Won't be long.'

He tucked the sandy board under his arm and strutted off back to the ocean.

'Be careful!' Lucy called out, admiring the perfect shape of his silhouette. The black wetsuit generously favouring him.

Now without distractions, her thoughts turned to where this weekend was heading. He certainly made her feel at ease, but there was no doubt he was holding something back. Was it because of Mark, maybe? Whatever happened, Mark was history; Lucy refused to spend her life in a loveless relationship.

She decided not to confess everything to Joseph for fear of scaring him away. She didn't want him thinking he was the reason for the breakdown in their relationship. It was just a coincidence that he had been around at that time – or was it fate?

Sitting with her knees raised, she pulled the towel around her shoulders. Her gaze travelled out past the breakers to where he was sitting, waiting, patiently. The ferocity of the water began to unnerve her. *Oh my God. Come back in Joseph, it's too rough.*

As if hearing her plea, Joseph stretched out on the board, his arms propelling him forwards. An enormous swell of water began to rise, dwarfing him by comparison. Placing the cup down, she clasped her knees, feeling on edge.

With what looked like no effort at all he sprang to his feet, stretching his arms out as if commanding the mighty ocean to obey his will. He rode above it fearlessly, like King Neptune himself, the white water charging behind him like a herd of wild horses. With a twist of his hips, he sliced diagonally across the thundering water, diving under when his run came to an end and disappearing beneath the surface.

'He's very good isn't he?' Surprised by the stranger's voice Lucy jumped, knocking over her wine.

Twisting her neck around, she squinted up into the bright sky. She saw an elderly lady with a mass of charcoal curls. She was wrinkling her nose and peering out to sea. Even her canine companion sat still for a moment, chest out, ears cocked, admiring Joseph's skills.

Lucy turned back to see that he was setting up for another ride. 'Yes. Yes, he is… very good.

'Oooh, there speaks a woman in love.'

'No, no, we're... just . . . friends.' Lucy stumbled over the words while the stranger looked down upon her with a faint smile.

'I was young once, you know,' said the old lady, wistfully.

Lucy opened her mouth to offer another unconvincing protest but was interrupted.

'Enjoy all your todays, my dear, because before you know it, it's tomorrow.' Her little dog had seen enough. He trotted on, stretching out the lead and drawing his owner away.

Lucy followed her journey for a short while before the tears obscured her view.

She had suspected it, feared it and fought it, but Lucy wasn't falling – she had already fallen, right to the very bottom of the hole. Never in her life had she felt like this; it was a fantasy only seen in Hollywood movies. Yet here she was, every molecule in her body and mind wanting him and needing him, regardless of the consequences.

When he wasn't there she longed for him, and when he was, she longed for him all the more. Her heart ached with a thought that filled her with dread: what if he didn't feel the same? If that were the case, she would surely spend the rest of her life at the bottom of that hole, never to see the light of love again.

Chasing away the thought, she saw that Joseph was making his way back in. Fanning her face with her hand, she set about preparing their picnic.

'I never get tired of that.' He dropped the board and raked his hair back. 'Surf's good today.'

'You didn't have to come back in for me,' Lucy said,

speaking into the cool box, busily emptying it.

'Everything okay?' he asked, his voice concerned.

Tucking her hair behind her ear, she flashed her face at him. 'Yeah, fine.'

'Sure?' Joseph knelt down on his board.

'Sure. There you go.'

He hesitated before taking a bite of the cracker she was offering. His silence provoked her self-consciousness.

'I was just thinking that I may have fallen in love with it too.' She jumped to her feet feeling a temptation to confess, but fearing rejection more. She spun the towel from her shoulders to his like a matador.

'It's very addictive isn't it?' he said, munching on a cracker.

'*Very.*'

Joseph ruffled his hair and removed his wetsuit with professional ease.

'Every time I catch a wave it's like it's my first.'

Patting himself down, he laid the towel out next to Lucy's.

'Here, let me help you out of that.'

'Thank you.' She stood, turning her back to him. 'I did attempt to take it off, but I couldn't get to the zip.' She dragged her hair around onto her chest. 'It's a bit like wearing a straitjacket.'

'That's a little worrying,' he said.

'What is?'

'The fact that you know what a straitjacket feels like.' The zip buzzed down, easing the constraint. 'Is there something you're not telling me, Lucy?'

'I don't have any secrets. Do you?'

The playful question was met with abrupt silence.

Intuition told her to change the subject.

'There's a little wine left if you'd like it?'

'No, thanks. Water's just fine.'

She turned around placing her hands on his cool damp chest. 'Can I have a kiss?'

'With pleasure.'

Their lips shared the biting saltiness of the ocean. Lucy did her best to convey her feelings, mouthing the enslaved words, desperate to set them free. Would it spoil the moment? Shatter the dream?

Joseph drew back. 'Let's get this off. I want to feel your skin.' Lucy wriggled her shoulders while he peeled off the clingy suit. Dropping to his knees he rolled it over her bottom and down to her feet, then tossed it onto the sand next to his.

Rising to his feet, he held his hands high in the air.

'Don't shoot – I surrender.'

'What?'

Lucy puckered her nose with a smile.

Joseph gave a nod to each breast. She looked down to see that both her nipples were fully erect and straining against the white fabric.

'It's my damp bikini,' she laughed, covering them with her fingers,

'Well of course it is – what else could it be?'

'Anyhow, you haven't completed your duties yet, Dalton.'

'Have I not?'

'No you haven't.'

She spun around and stuck out her backside, which had eaten half of her bikini bottoms.

'Would you like me to use my hands or my teeth?' he

asked.

'As we're in a public place I think we'll go for the hands.'

'As you wish.'

A finger slipped under each seam, brushing over her cheeks as he freed the material, letting it snap back. Lucy turned to find him arched back, his eyes slowly scaling up to her face.

'You look... bloody awful in that bikini.'

'Really?' This time Lucy was the one nodding.

Joseph dropped his head, taking a look at his bulging trunks. 'It's because they're damp,' he said, eyebrows raised with a look of total innocence, making Lucy buckle up with laughter.

God, she loved it when he was like this. He made her feel like all was right with the world and that they were just another couple enjoying Sunday on the beach. Preferring this pretence, she closed the door on the mess that awaited her.

Between conversations, they sat feeding each other. Lucy was surprised by the generosity of his openness. He told her about his childhood and about the various scrapes he had got himself into, extending her knowledge of his past no further than his teenage years.

But what touched her the most was that he shared the memories of his mother with her.

Looking anywhere but into her eyes, he spoke fondly of a strong, compassionate, loving, beautiful lady that he so obviously missed. The focus then turned to Lucy. Another surprise was his interest in Sam, and from the context of his questions she knew he was not just being polite.

She did her best to keep things light-hearted, although when it came to Sam things were anything but.

Feeling invigorated from the water and more than content with the company, Lucy carried their wetsuits, wishing that the afternoon could last forever – the memory certainly would.

Joseph tailed behind, her dress hanging over his shoulder. She had intentionally decided not to wear it, and knowing he was watching her every step was a thrill.

'Keep up, Dalton,' she taunted.

'I'm perfectly happy where I am, thanks.'

'I do hope you're not being inappropriate back there.'

'Whatever would have given you that idea?'

Arriving at the beach showers, Joseph placed the coolbox and her dress on the dwarf stone wall that bordered the sand dunes.

'I have to say your bottom is something of a contradiction.'

Lucy's hand hovered over the shower button while she contemplated his statement. 'Is it?'

'Mmm, it is.' He joined her at the adjacent shower. 'On the one hand I want to hold it and caress it tenderly, following its perfect curvature. But, on the other hand, I want to smack it and watch the glorious wobble as your cheeks turn a deeper shade of red with each stroke.'

His tone grew more serious, and his eyes darkened with every word.

Lucy loved the influence she had on him. It was incredibly empowering, not to mention a huge fucking turn-on. Deciding to exercise some of that power, she bent her knees and jutted out the object of his desire.

'Take your best shot.'

His silence didn't prepare her for the thunderbolt that ripped through her body, his hand meeting her outstretched backside with a mighty crack.

'Jesus!' She clawed at the shower pole, and the intense sting slowly subsided, leaving a fever on her skin. For some fucked-up reason Lucy actually found herself wanting another. She had never been spanked before and always thought it the activity of leather clad middle-aged men in gimp masks, yet here she was out in the open air, bent over, her rosy rump eager for another.

'Is that doing it for you, Dalton?' She looked back at him, his fists and teeth were clenched.

'I think the results speak for themselves,' he retorted. His trunks gaping, the curve of his growing manhood embossed onto the strained material.

Such an erotic sight was not lost on her; Lucy's taut nipples weren't down to the damp bikini this time.

'What are you waiting for, permission?'

His eyes rose from her backside, filled with menacing determination. Lucy broke eye contact, preparing for the blow. Enjoying his front-row seat, he made her wait. The anticipation of feeling his big hand against her heightened the sensuality of the scene. Wiggling her bottom with impatience, she was about to administer some encouragement when another crisp slap sounded out, rupturing the air like a popped balloon, quaking her fleshy globes.

Lucy sucked in air through grinding teeth. The heat of the impact poured over her tingling skin like hot wax, reaching deep between the intimate folds of her body. Once again he was master of her emotions. Palpitations left her breathless. The fact that they were outside added to the thrill and knowing he was standing behind her with a cock so big it could barely be contained, gave rise to a sexual appetite that cared nothing for time or place. Taking pleasure in resistance she kept her eyes front, fighting the urge to view what awaited her.

'You know if you ask for it I'm going to give it to you, don't you?' It wasn't an apology; it was a statement of fact. Why should he apologise? She had asked for it.

'Give it to me then.' Despite her being the one at his mercy, the provocation embellished her with authority. Who was the one in control now?

Skin lashed against skin once more. Lucy's back arched, her head thrown back, the initial bite of pain scolding her tanned skin. Her body clenched and contracted, oiling itself in readiness for the welcome intrusion.

Joseph's pure, animal masculinity had shown Lucy what uncontrolled sexual desire was.

Her sex life with Mark had always been entrenched in routine. A quick shower followed by fumbling around under the duvet in pitch-black darkness.

This was about as far from that as you could get, and she loved it. He cuffed her wrist with a firm grip pulling her behind him. Lucy skipped along, trying to keep up with his wide hurried strides. Joseph towed her up and over the sand dunes, between the clumps of long wavy grass, before stopping in the concave of two camel hump-like mounds.

'On all fours,' he demanded.

She dropped like an anchor, hands sinking into the arid sand. He pitilessly tugged down Lucy's bikini over her cooling cheeks. A furnace now burnt inside the swollen pouty lips that peeked between the closed crease of her thighs.

Lowering onto her elbows she spread her knees, making her bikini ride back up. Joseph yanked on the drawstrings and Lucy watched them fly over her head like a stringless kite. His hand was fastened on the shallow of her waist, she felt him drop to his knees, groaning with unadulterated yearning. The whispering grass kept time with the sensuous melody of his harsh breaths, a playful breeze reminding them that they were in the great outdoors.

Lucy's back arched and her bottom yawned open, completely disclosing her feminine treasure for his viewing pleasure.

He parted her outer lips before plunging a finger inside, to feel the heat of her growing arousal. She was ready, her pussy clenching around him. The relative slimness of his finger teased as it delved, leaving her wanting more – much more. A prod from his short, stubby thumb stretched her open a little more, before retreating. Coated in a slick of her desire, it began to roam freely around her clit while his finger continued to gently prod. The fat thumb revolved around the tight, hard little button, encouraging it to flourish.

Sand slipped between her fingers as she dug in, pushing her rear back to increase the depth of his finger, sensations deepened and strengthened with each swirl.

'More.'

In answer to her insistence he delved knuckle deep, shaking his hand like a jackhammer. The intense vibrations rippled her cheeks, obliterating any authority she held over her body sparking a torrent of sexual delectation. Gasping for air, Lucy closed her eyes, flying towards Elysium – its secret energy beckoning her ever closer to the tipping point.

Right at the crucial moment, Joseph removed his hand from the controls, diverting the flight.

'Mmm. Not fair!' she protested, wiggling her derriere.

SLAP!

'Oww!' Lucy screamed, totally unprepared for the strike.

'Did that sting?' he asked.

'Fuck, yes!'

'So will this.' The great mushroom head butted against her tight opening before brutishly barging past her bullied flesh.

She reached back to his hip in an attempt to slow the thrust, but her hand was swatted away.

'You wanted more, you're going to get more.'

With each successive inch that plunged deeper, Lucy thought that had to be it. Yet still his widening girth continued to delve further until their bodies made contact. Somehow the square peg had gone into the round hole.

His hard hands sank into the soft flesh of her hips and the pounding began; the thrusts were short at first, letting her juices ease his passage before building to full, long strokes. The tempo was merciless, each punch of his hips driving her elbows deeper into the sand. She thrust out her bottom to meet the blows.

His heavy balls slapped against her clitoris, each impact driving her closer and closer, pushing elation to its very limit. The tension was cranked up further and further until the line of the cognitive world snapped, momentarily sending Lucy into a hypnotic state where the body overruled the mind, transporting her to new territories, breaking the frontiers of expectation.

Having no self-awareness, she howled, moaned and screamed – the rush of pleasure wreaking havoc with her self restraint.

Joseph harnessed her shoulders pummelling his shaft deeper still, spurred on by the power at his command. Lucy jolted and spasmed, full of cock. Defeated, she waved her hand like a white flag.

'Stop,' she panted. The pace slowed but didn't stop. Regaining her senses she crawled forwards, wincing as his mammoth erection dragged against the tender walls of her battered sex. She turned around and lunged at his chest, knocking him onto his backside.

'I want to watch you come.' Shuffling along on her knees, she shoved his shoulder back with the same force he had used on her.

Allowing the transfer of power to take place, he fell back on his elbows, knees bent, legs spread, cock curved over his abs. Dusting off her hands, she sat on her haunches. The grease of her body oozed between her tightening grasp as she took him in hand.

Lucy tugged him steadily from the base to the bulbous head while he watched her.

'How's that? Fast enough? Hmm?'

He nodded, concentration etched on his brow. The thumbs of both hands massaged slowly up to the great height of the flushed head, squeezing out a dribble of semen, beading at the hilt then trickling down over the great dome.

'Don't hold back now, Dalton.'

'Stop talking and finish me off then.' He bucked his hips insistently, air snorting from his nose, his chest rising and falling like the swell of the ocean.

'All in good time.' Knowing he was at her mercy stirred her arousal; she couldn't get enough of this man. Following the natural curvature of his cock, Lucy's hand ran the full length. His balls bounced with each stroke, leaving pits in the sand. Reaching down with her free hand she circled the loose skin of his sack and gently tugged, straining the swollen balls against their bag. Joseph's head fell back between his shoulders, and his feet dug into the sand.

His head shot back up. 'Argh!' A guttural alert boomed from his chest. 'Don't stop.'

Lucy's grip tightened around the trunk of his engorged shaft. Tugging at his balls, his cock jerked in her yanking hand. A jet of semen reached for the sky, before falling back to its origin, thick fluid coating her hand, lubricating her strokes.

Joseph tensed, his face as red as the swollen tip of his spewing cock. She continued to pump him dry until every last drop had been syphoned off and his flesh began to soften.

Bankrupted of all his body's resources, Joseph fell flat on his back.

'Ten out of ten, Miss Lucy. You get a gold star for that one.'

Shaking webs of cum from her hand she smiled to herself, contented in every way imaginable. 'You weren't too bad yourself, Mr Joe.'

She was just about to clamber on top of him when she froze, glancing over her shoulder. 'Did you hear something then?'

'Hear what?' he croaked, nursing an orgasmic

hangover, eyes closed.

'I thought I heard—'

'Here, Dutch. Come here, boy.'

The stranger's voice found its way to them, floating in from an indeterminable location.

'Oh fuck! There's someone coming!'

'Don't panic.' Joseph lazily tucked himself back into his trunks and rolled onto his stomach 'Just pretend we're sunbathing.'

'I've got no bikini bottoms on. You ripped them off in case you forgot!'

Joseph laid his head onto the pillow of his folded arms, his ribs shaking with silent laughter. 'There are plenty of naturists around here. Just let it all hang out.'

'You shit!' She danced left and right, not knowing which way to turn. A gnarled piece of wood somersaulted through the air, landing a few feet from Lucy.

'Go boy. Go get the stick.' The unknown voice fast approached.

'Bollocks!' Bare-arsed Lucy ran to the nearest dune and planted herself behind a clump of long grass that fanned out between her spread legs. The timing could not have been more perfect. A second later a bald middle-aged man appeared with a shaggy dog which ignored the stick and immediately ran over to Joseph, tail fanning the air like he was an old friend.

'Oh, hello there,' said the man, removing his sunglasses.

'Hello, my friend,' returned Joseph. Lucy flashed a palm from her vantage point.

'He won't hurt you – he's a big softy.'

Joseph ruffled the dog's ears and scratched under his

chin. 'He's lovely. Aren't you, buddy, eh?'

'You'll have a friend for life if you keep doing that.' The stranger chuckled, smiling awkwardly at Lucy.

'Come on then, Dutch.' He picked up the stick and threw it on ahead. 'Enjoy your afternoon folks.' He walked on, whistling encouragement to his dog.

'You too, my friend,' said Joseph.

Filled with the happiness that dogs are blessed with, it bounded towards his master, but stopped en route to sniff the area. Finding Lucy's bikini bottoms, he snapped them up and merrily went on his way.

'Oh, no. Err, doggy, come back. Come – shit.'

Joseph sat with his knees raised, arms wrapped around his legs, his whole body jumping with repressed laughter.

'The little sod,' said Lucy.'

'I know, I wanted to keep those.'

Although she was trying her best not to smile, one burst out anyway. 'It's not funny.'

Joseph let go, rolling onto his back in fits of laughter.

'You're in trouble, Dalton. That was a brand-new bikini.'

'Don't blame me, the dog stole it.'

He climbed to his feet, knocking sand from his bottom.

'And who ripped them off me? You're going to cost me a fortune in clothes at this rate.'

'That's what you do to me.' He stood at the base of her throne; for once, she was higher than him. 'You're like a savage, aren't you? I'm going to have to teach you some manners.'

'Yes, I need taking in hand.'

'I thought I just did?'

Stealing his persona for a moment, she saluted him

with two fingers.

Joseph shook his head, a smile emerging from his beard. 'I'm not sure who is the bad influence here, me or you.'

'I think I know the answer to that one, Mr Dalton. Now I know you are lacking any gentlemanly qualities, but could you please get my dress for me?' she requested, doing her best Mrs Shoesmith impression.

'Right away, my queen.' He took a bow, then left to execute her wishes. Lucy ogled the sandy perfection of his arse as it swaggered out of sight.

What a perfect day. Mark had only occupied her thoughts for the briefest of moments; it was as if he was a figment of her imagination. Lucy felt so far removed from the reality of her everyday life that the thought of returning to it seemed like a fantasy in itself.

Returning with the dress, he climbed up to her. Once he had helped her into it, he threw a screaming Lucy over his shoulder, slapping her bottom playfully.

'You were the one that said I was a savage.'

Having sand just about everywhere a girl didn't want sand, Lucy showered while Joseph screened her with a towel. Then they returned to Joseph's truck, leaving drips of fresh water trailing behind them.

Once they had got all the equipment on board, they drove back to the campsite in a weary but contented silence.

After a late lunch overlooking the cove, Joseph set about hanging out their wetsuits and one half of Lucy's bikini. He was wearing only his shorts, and his hair swirled and kinked, styled by the water.

She couldn't take her eyes off him. There was only one

thing that spoilt her sense of contentment – his tattoo. It was the only mark on his skin, and Lucy envied the lady he held in such high regard. Tying her hair up, she rose from the folding chair and sauntered over to him. She circled his back with her fingers, craving attention. He placed the camp table into the back of his truck and turned to face her.

'Kiss,' she requested, lips open.

Lowering his face, Joseph obliged.

'Thank you for today. I can't remember when I last enjoyed a weekend so much.'

'My pleasure.' He encased her with his arms.

Looking up into his handsome face, her hands glided into his chest hair. 'Can I ask you a question, Joseph?'

'Sure.'

Twirling a finger in the short curls, Lucy decided to take advantage of his openness.

'Who was she – Aashna?' The embers of his smile died out with the mention of the name. His head raised above Lucy's.

'Did she break your heart?'

he shook his head, eyes cast far out into the past.

'What happened…? Joseph?'

Breaking his hold, she watched the shutters fall. He moved and stepped ahead of her.

Lucy turned, realising that she might have taken a step too far. But she wanted so much to give herself to him completely, and if she was going to do that, he would have to surrender himself to her as well.

Looking at his back she could see his hand caressing the spot where her name rested.

'You can tell me anything, you know – how bad can it

be?'

He spun around, the stern look on his face startling her. He looked scared, confused, and angry. At that moment, she felt her grip on him slip and she watched the man standing before her fall beyond reach. 'Joseph I'm sorry, I–'

'You've got a long drive home.'

She suffered a direct hit, and, Jesus, didn't it knock her off her feet. Walking away, he grabbed his T-shirt from the back of the camp chair and put it on. All emotion and personality had been wrung from him.

'I promised I'd see Kimberley before I go.'

Joseph Dalton had already gone, and the man before her was a stranger.

'Drive carefully.' His words were lifeless and cold.

'Is that it?' Lucy hung out for the slightest bit of hope – a look, a word, a kiss goodbye.

His face weighed down with gravity, he gave her his answer. 'What else is there?'

She had allowed herself to be stripped of all her armour and when the strike came she was defenceless.

'Go back to your home – to Mark.'

Taking her wetsuit from the bonnet of the truck, Joseph walked away, leaving her shell-shocked. Lucy tried to call out to him, but the words knotted and snagged on each other. Her legs trembled and tears fell; a mortal wound had been inflicted.

She didn't move, waiting for him to turn around to give her something – anything.

The heavy foliage of the trees closed in on his distant figure. That *was* it.

With her case once again on the back seat, Lucy drove away, hoping maybe to see him on the way out. It was one hope too many.

Somehow the car managed to navigate itself around the country roads while Lucy spiralled down into her thoughts. What had she said? What had she done? He was like a Rubik's cube: whichever way she turned, the puzzle was still incomplete. Was he a man that enjoyed women physically but preferred his own company?

She would have given the world to make her dream come true, but it wasn't hers to give. All she had to offer was her all, and it had been rejected.

Love is no fairy-tale white knight that sweeps you off your feet. It's more like a black knight on a black steed. It will charge into your life, honouring you with its presence or smiting you with its parting. No backwards glances, no mercy.

CHAPTER THIRTY

An all-too-short weekend gave way to a long night and a very early morning. Lucy sat in the kitchen until the sun drove away the darkness and shone gloriously on her now-beautiful garden.

It was everything she had dreamed it would be, and yet its manicured perfection failed to raise any emotion in her at all. It had been expertly created by hand, and she knew full well what those hands could do, how they felt on her skin. A touch so right it would never be forgotten.

His callous dismissal occupied her every waking moment. She felt foolish for admitting that she loved him, and angry that he had made her feel the way she did. Above all else, she was angry with him for making her want him. Angry with him for being funny and handsome, for being sexy, charming, and for dissolving every single thing in her world until all that was left was Joseph Dalton.

She was infected with an incurable disease that was making her head and heart sick, and the prognosis wasn't good.

Now their work was at an end, and in a day or two, he would drive away, leaving Lucy to torture herself thinking about where he was and who he was with.

The thought of going to work was not an agreeable one, but she needed a hiding place.

Sending George a text message to explain where she had hidden the key, Lucy deserted the house.

As she had expected, Monday lived up to its reputation but she trudged through it, not helped by the fact that Sam was absent and no one knew why. This only added to the weight of her worries: Sam *never* missed school. His father was only too happy to make sure he was on that bus every morning.

She was thankful when the end of the day finally came, but felt reluctant to go home for fear of seeing Joseph. Collecting her things, she walked down the corridor and exited through the battered old door. She crossed the car park and heard the distinct tone of Mrs Shoesmith calling her name.

'Lucy, can I have a word with you, please?' she asked, propping the door open.

'Of course.'

Mrs Shoesmith made no effort to leave her kingdom, making Lucy retrace her steps.

'It's about Samuel,' she said, inviting Lucy back in the building with her open palm.

'Is he okay?' Lucy asked, beginning to worry.

'Yes, yes, he's fine.' The old hinges of the door grumbled as it closed behind them. 'Nothing to worry about. However, I'm afraid he will no longer be a pupil at this school.'

'What? Why not?'

'Because Samuel and his father are moving some twenty miles away. After the summer holidays, he will be attending Drury Special School.'

Lucy clasped her hand to her mouth as her world imploded. Her biggest fear had become a reality.

'Of course it's not to our standards, but it will suffice for the boy.'

'This can't happen – it's not right. He can't do this.'

'I'm sure you don't need reminding, Ms Eaton, but he *is* the boy's father and can do whatever he wishes,'

Still on duty, she clasped her hands with unsympathetic indifference.

Lucy paced up and down in front of the emotionally vacant woman, wringing her hands with worry.

'I know you have a fondness for the boy, which I don't condone, but I also know your intentions are good. That is why I'm extending you this courtesy.'

'So why isn't he at school today? Why wasn't he here?' The frustration in her voice was irrepressible and the distinct lack of compassion antagonising.

'The move takes place in two weeks, and his father has deemed it suitable for the boy to be desensitised before the change.'

'That's bullshit.'

'Ms Eaton, take control of yourself!'

'I'm sorry, but his father is doing this deliberately so Sam won't get to say goodbye to his friends, to Mrs Timpson – to me!' Lucy said, folding her arms and gnawing at her thumbnail, her shock now turning to anger.

'It's not all about you, Ms Eaton—'

'No. No, it's not. It's about a child who is being robbed

of his potential – his happiness – by that sick bastard.'

'Ms Eaton, that is enough! I suggest you take yourself home and spend a day or two collecting your thoughts. I have notified the authorities that he is being withheld from school, and as far as I'm concerned, the matter is closed.' Having made sure she had the last word, Mrs Shoesmith marched off down her corridor of power, leaving Lucy seething.

This was all because of the summer fete, the new clothes, the toys. That bastard couldn't stand Sam having any love or attention and he knew Lucy was watching him, waiting for him to slip up.

He was going to make sure that Sam didn't have a single friend in the world.

Lucy's kindness had only inflicted more pain on him. Bursting through the doors, she ran to her car. Fuelled by rage, she drove to the squalid streets, parking outside Sam's home.

The moment she raised her eyes to the broken window, the anger bowed down to pity. This was a so-called civilised society, and yet here was a child living in Dickensian conditions.

Thanks to red tape, Sam was a prisoner of the very laws that had been created to protect. Powerless, she sobbed for the poor boy. Attacking his father would only result in hurting Sam further. Reluctant to leave, she allowed the pain to flow out of her, before eventually starting her car and driving away, feeling that she was deserting him.

When she arrived back, she threw her bag onto the stairs and saw that George had left a note. Going to the kitchen, she opened one of the many bottles of wine left over from the barbecue. She wasn't doing so to enjoy herself, but simply to numb the fucking din in her head. Taking a large gulp of red, she unfolded the note.

'Sorry I missed you Lucy. You'll be glad to hear that we have finally finished! I have to say, this has been one of the most rewarding jobs I've ever done, partly because you have been such a wonderful client – I hope you will allow me to call you a friend as well. I'll pop round tomorrow evening with the final invoice, if that's okay. Have a good evening and enjoy your garden. You deserve it.

George.

Yet more bad news. Someone else she cared about would soon be gone from her life forever.

She emptied the glass, before filling it to the brim and going upstairs to run a bath.

It was getting late when she heard the front door close, signalling the end of her peace and quiet. Lucy was lying on the bed in her dressing gown and considered pretending to be asleep.

'Lucy? It's me,' Mark called, announcing the obvious. 'You awake?'

'Yeah.' There seemed to be no benefit in postponing the inevitable.

'Want me to bring you a drink up?'

'No, thank you.'

He was offering an olive branch. Lucy wasn't sure if that was a good thing or not – Honesty often came more naturally in the heat of an argument. Listening to him clattering about downstairs, she removed her robe and slipped into bed.

Mark came in holding a can of Coke and wearing a sheepish smile. 'All right?' he asked, his finger tapping nervously on the can.

'Fine.'

'Bloody flight was delayed.' Placing the drink down, Mark turned around to empty his pockets onto the chest of drawers. 'No explanation, of course. I'm sure they think none of us have anything better to do than swan around the airport for hours on end.'

He pulled off his polo shirt, and it was immediately clear from the colour of his skin that the pool had been more tempting than architecture or culture. He kicked off his shorts, collected his Coke and shuffled into bed. There was so much to discuss, yet nothing she wanted to talk about, not with Mark anyway.

'We didn't see much of Suzie. I think she spent most of the time hitting the shops.' He slurped down the remainder of his drink. 'She missed you though… I know I did.'

Placing the empty can on the bedside table, Mark returned to staring in front of him, as did Lucy, like two strangers on a train. She was fully aware that he was waiting for a reply to his endearing comment. Unfortunately for him, he was well down on the list of things that occupied her thoughts.

'Did you do anything nice?' he asked.

She needed no encouragement, and the memories of the weekend danced out to the tune of Joseph's voice calling her name.

'I went for a little drive, went swimming.'

'Cool,' he nodded repeatedly, rocking the bed. 'Lucy… I—'

'It's late, Mark. Let's get some sleep. We can talk tomorrow.'

Now wasn't the time for a heart-to-heart; in fact there would never be a time. His absence had clarified what she already knew: there was no future for them.

'Yeah, you're right.' Turning out the bedside lamp, Mark slipped down into the bed and pulled the duvet up over his shoulders.

'There's nothing like sleeping in your own bed is there?'

Lucy didn't reply. Someone else's bed is where she would rather have been.

'Good night, Lu.'

Goodbye, Mark.

CHAPTER THIRTY-ONE

The next few days were like a double whammy of having no school and no George was sobering. Lucy wasn't quite sure what to do with herself. She felt like a stranger in someone else's dream. Her home was now just a house and the garden was a bitter reminder of the very reason that Joseph and Lucy's paths had crossed in the first place. The thought of the impending conversation with Mark was at the forefront of her mind from the moment her lids had drawn back. Her stomach churned, unsure how he would react to being told of the death of their relationship.

Mark was still in bed, and waiting to speak to him was like waiting for a heart bypass; she didn't want to go through it, but knew it was essential for her future.

Having only managed two bites of toast at breakfast, Lucy decided to call on Charles for a progress report. That would take her mind off things for a while, and hopefully Mark would be up when she came back. Closing the door softly, she walked around to next door.

Disappointment struck as she saw that both cars were absent. A man in a grey suit was standing at the front door, holding some paperwork, looking up at the flaking paint of the first floor windows. She assumed he must have been a surveyor of some kind, come to give them a quote on renovations; the house was in need of repair.

'I'm afraid they're out,' said Lucy.

The man turned on his heels.

'No cars.' She offered a weak smile and turned to head back to raise Mark from the dead.

'Excuse me, Miss!' the man called out stopping her. 'Do you have any idea when they'll be back?'

'I'm sorry, I don't. Mrs St Clair is usually always home.'

'Mrs St Clair is in France,' returned the man, looking puzzled.

'Oh, I didn't know,' said Lucy.

'So is Mr St Clair,' he added.

'Is he? He never said that they were going?'

The man approached Lucy, concern playing over his face. 'As far as I'm aware, Mr and Mrs St Clair haven't been to the UK for over a year now.'

'I'm sorry, Mr…?'

'Newton.'

'Mr Newton, you're mistaken. I saw Charles only a few days ago.'

'I think it is you who is mistaken, Ms…?'

'Eaton.'

'Ms Eaton, Charles St Clair is a retired surgeon and has lived in France for some ten years with his wife, Tabitha. This is one of several homes they own and rent out.'

Her throat dried, unease rising.

'I'm the letting agent. The current tenants are behind

435

with their rent, three months behind now.' He continued talking but Lucy's brain crashed, struggling to decipher the conflicting information it had just received.

'Are you sure you have the right address?' she blurted out, interrupting him.

He squinted at her with a smirk before answering 'I have been managing all five of Mr St Clair's properties for ten years, ever since his retirement. I have a set of keys to this very house.'

This can't be happening. Charles would never lie to me. This has to be a mix-up of some kind. 'Did you say you have a set of keys?'

'Yes I did. Although I'm not allowed—'

'We have to go inside,' Lucy demanded, hand on forehead.

'I'm afraid I—'

'Mr Newton, I have to see inside that house!'

He seemed wary of her insistent tone and looked back at the property, as if asking its permission.

'The lady that lives here suffers from poor health. She may have had a fall. Now, come to think of it, I haven't seen her for a while.'

'But I thought you said—'

'Quickly, Mr Newton.' Lucy interrupted, hurrying on towards the house. 'Every minute could be crucial.'

Untangling the keys from his pocket, Mr Newton quickly strode over to Lucy.

'I suppose we have a duty to make sure all is well.'

The moment he turned the key in the lock, Lucy rushed in ahead of him. Her hand trembled hesitantly on the lounge doorknob. *Please, please let this be a mistake.*

The heavy door silently swung open. At first glance,

everything appeared as she had remembered it. The old lounge suites sat facing each other, but once her panicked eyes had settled, the evidence was plain to see. The bookcase that had once strained under its load was now empty. The repetitive tick of the carriage clock could no longer be heard. Its stencilled footprint in the dust by the fireplace was the only proof that it had ever existed.

Not one single bottle or glass was still resident in the drinks cabinet.

Denial is always first in the queue when disaster strikes. Lucy ran upstairs, ignoring Mr Newton's calls. It simply couldn't be true.

She burst into one of the bedrooms, and her fears were confirmed.

A single mattress with a dishevelled blanket lay on the bare floorboards. Next to it were a couple of empty beer cans and a saucer full of cigarette ends, which tinged the stale air with the smell of ash. In a state of shock, she frantically opened all the doors, finding every room empty apart from the last one, the contents of which again comprised of a lone mattress, a lamp and a scattering of newspapers.

Separate rooms. They weren't even husband and wife.

'Is everything all right up there?' Mr Newton called out from the bottom of the stairs.

'There's no one here. They've gone.'

Lucy clung to the handrail, her legs weakened from the results of being a trusting, kind-hearted person.

'I think Mr St Clair can kiss goodbye to his rent.'

That was loose change compared to what Lucy had willingly given.

Mr Newton guided her out while waffling on, unaware

of the personal crisis she was suffering from. He handed her his business card in case they came back, he wished Lucy good day, locked the empty house then hurried back to his car.

Lucy's phone rang in her pocket. She took it out to cancel the call, but then saw that it was the school and decided to answer, in case it was news about Sam.

'Hello?'

'Hi, Lucy. It's Penny, the school secretary. I'm sorry to bother you at home, but it's come to my attention that the cheque you gave us – from your neighbour, was it?'

'Yes.'

'Well I'm afraid it didn't cash. I'm sure it's just a silly mistake, but I thought I'd let you know. I hope everything's okay?'

'Everything's fine, Penny,' said Lucy, void of any emotion.

'Great. I'll leave that with you then. See you in the week.'

It wasn't a silly mistake. It had been a very deliberate, calculated plan to exploit her passion and commitment to the kids of Tall Trees. How fucking heartless could a person be?

Standing on the pavement in between the two houses, she felt sick to her stomach, desolated by the betrayal. She didn't know what to do or where to go.

She certainly couldn't face Mark. He would spot there was something wrong and think it was all about him. Feeling that she needed somewhere to go and someone to confide in, she decided to try Suzie, hoping that she'd be at home.

Her conversations with Charles replayed in her head

while she filed along in the morning traffic.

He had been so convincing, kind, considerate, and caring, but it had all been an act, an act of incredible cruelty. It seemed that Charles, or whatever his real name was, was the very opposite of everything he had pretended to be.

The sight of Suzie's car parked outside her house was a very welcome one. Lucy knocked at the door, unsure where to begin. When the door opened Lucy began with tears, breaking down in the arms of her friend.

Suzie automatically thought Mark was the cause of her distress. She led Lucy, sobbing, into the lounge where she sat and recounted the whole saga. Without the proof of how convincing Charles was, the story sounded like an obvious con. Lucy wept into the palms of her hands. She had lost all her money, and Joseph and little Sam had been stolen from her life.

'God, Suzie, how could I have been so stupid? What am I going to do?'

Suzie knelt down in front of Lucy, rubbing her thighs, wearing a sympathetic expression.

'Now that you've let it all out, let's get you calmed down. Then we're going to drive straight to the police and you're going to tell them everything you've just told me. Okay?'

'Yeah,' Lucy sniffed. She pointed at her face, mustering a smile. 'I'd better sort this out first, hadn't I?'

'You're still gorgeous, even with red puffy eyes,' Suzie wrapping her arms around Lucy.

'I've been such a fool.'

'No, Lu. You were your usual big-hearted self, and this evil bastard took advantage of that.' Suzie gripped her by the wrists. 'Don't you go blaming yourself, you hear me?'

Lucy nodded, attempting a smile. 'Can I use your bathroom, Suzie?'

'Of course you can. Excuse the mess though. I haven't got around to doing any housework. I'm still in holiday mode.'

'How was Barcelona? Sorry, I forgot to ask.'

'Don't apologise, I think you've got enough to think about. I enjoyed it, but I would have enjoyed it more with you there.' Suzie stood up and pulled Lucy to her feet. 'You go and get cleaned up and I'll put the kettle on.'

'Sounds good.'

Lucy trudged upstairs, and entering the bathroom, stepping over discarded knickers and jeans. Sighing at the sight of her bedraggled reflection, she leant on the sink and looked deep into her bloodshot eyes. All her relationships with men seemed to be disastrous. Mark, Charles, Joseph – not to mention Sebastian. Thank God for Suzie. She was always there for her, good times or bad. Pooling cold water in her hands, she bathed her face for a moment. She saw that there were no towels in the bathroom, so called down to her friend.

'Suzie. Have you got any towels?'

'In the cupboard next to my room.'

'Okay.'

With her hand catching the drips, Lucy opened the narrow cupboard door and took a clean towel off the pile. It hung from her hand while beads of water trickled down her face and dropped onto her blouse.

Lucy stood perfectly still, her eyes arrested by something she had seen hidden behind the pile of laundry.

The self-preserving voice in her head told her it was

nothing. Just close the door, go downstairs and drink your tea. But despite this, she reached out for the bright orange bag. She pulled it out, her heart pounded.

Dress To Impress: Fancy Dress For All Occasions'

Lucy dropped the towel. Hoping against hope, she opened the bag, then closed her eyes tight shut at the sight of a white naval officer's uniform.

The familiar smell of Mark's cologne filled the air incriminatingly. The discovery was utterly crushing. Not because Mark was having an affair, she wasn't such a hypocrite. Lucy had already suspected that he was playing more than just golf, but with her best friend? Suzie's betrayal was the one that cut the deepest. It burned and twisted inside her chest, stealing her oxygen and recasting a friendship that had travelled from pigtails to perfume as nothing more than a fantasy that had never truly existed.

'You okay up there, Lu?'

'I'm coming down now.'

She took the stairs cautiously, numbed by the shock.

'All right, babe?' asked Suzie, bent over, tidying her copies of *Vogue*.

'Not really.'

Suzie's enquiring look was met by the orange bag slamming into her face. Reacting too late, she lost her balance and fell onto the couch. Wide-eyed with horror, Suzie looked down at the uniform protruding out from the bag.

'How could you? I thought you were my friend.'

Her eyes downcast, Suzie clutched the magazines to her chest like a shield.

'I've shared secrets with you, told you things that I haven't told anyone else. And I did that because I trusted you. I never doubted your friendship – not for a moment.' Her resolve not to cry faltered. 'I bet you've both been laughing at me behind my back, haven't you?'

Suzie didn't raise her eyes above knee level.

'It's a powerful aphrodisiac, isn't it, Suzie? All that money. Well you're fucking welcome to him. I don't need him, I don't want him and I don't love him. Fucking look at me when I'm talking to you!' Lucy panted, the indignation bleeding into her temperament.

Forlorn, Suzie's rueful stare met the watery fire of Lucy's.

'I don't want to see your face again – ever. Good luck. You'll fucking need it.'

Lucy snatched herself around and stomped to the door.

'Lucy, wait! I can explain!' Suzie tossed the magazines aside and sprang up from the couch.

'Let me guess: you never meant for this to happen, but ever since he won the lottery you've found him wildly attractive.'

Lucy flung the door open and made her way down the path, car keys in hand.

'I think we need to talk.'

'We just did,' said Lucy, opening her car door.

'It's Pete…'

Lucy stalled, one foot in the car.

'Mark's been seeing my brother.'

Lucy whipped her head round.

'I swear it's true. Like I said, we need to talk.'

Feeling concussed by the brutal blows of the last few days, Lucy sat and listened in disbelief.

Suzie recounted that when she was in Barcelona one particularly hot afternoon had proved to be too much for her. She decided to cut her sight-seeing trip short in favour of the hotel pool. Returning earlier than planned to her room, she heard noises coming from Pete's. Thinking that Mark and Pete were out visiting the Camp Nou Football stadium, she opened the adjoining door to their rooms to investigate and caught them in the act. Initially, Mark tried to deny it, but since she had found him naked in bed with her brother, he was left with no valid explanation. He made her swear not to tell Lucy, but not happy with deceiving her friend, Suzie promised that she would only remain silent for one week, insisting that Mark confess the moment he got home.

She had long had suspicions about her brother. He would often go out to see nameless girlfriends that Suzie never got to meet, but never had she imagined that it was Mark he was seeing. Lucy quizzed her as to how long this had been going on, but Suzie knew very little. Pete had refused to discuss the matter, despite his sister's support and understanding. He seemed embarrassed about his sexuality, or maybe it was more by the circumstances under which it was revealed.

The two friends shared a long embrace. Suzie re-affirmed her devotion as a true friend, while Lucy apologised for jumping to what had seemed like the obvious conclusion.

Declining her friend's offer to accompany her to the police station, Lucy kissed Suzie goodbye and drove away feeling more alone than ever.

CHAPTER THIRTY-TWO

Waiting to be seen, Lucy spent her time in a nervous state, trying to think of ways to make the truth sound more convincing. She spoke to one of the older officers; he must have vast experience dealing with this sort of thing, she thought to herself.

He listened sympathetically, which was a relief, and took detailed notes. But when he actually spoke, his words held no relief at all. He told Lucy it was highly unlikely that any of the money would ever be seen again.

If it hadn't have been gambled away or used to pay off heavy debts, then it almost certainly would have been hidden overseas. But he promised that every effort would be made to apprehend the two individuals responsible.

She drove home knowing there was no hope: she was a victim of crime and even if the perpetrators were caught, she would still be a victim.

Lucy parked on the empty drive and exited the car with a huff. Sliding the key into the lock, the thundering sound of brake horsepower caught her attention.

Expecting Mark, Sebastian's Porsche was no consolation. With her feet remaining on the bristled doormat, she removed the key. If he was allowed in, there was no telling how long it would take to get rid of him.

'Hey, sexy,' he called out, the lights of his car winking as he locked it.

'Sebastian, it's not a good time.'

'Why not?' he asked, swaggering towards her. 'It's always a good time when Seb's around.'

'Please, I'm being serious.'

'What the fuck have you done to your eye?' His lascivious gaze had finally made it up to her face.

'What?' Her fingers brushed over the fading bruises, the day's revelations at the forefront of her mind. 'I was attacked.'

'Today?'

'No, a while ago.'

'Why don't you let me cheer you up? I'm sure I can put the smile back on your face.' He rolled up his sleeves, having exhausted the extent of his concern.

Lucy pitied him. To be so engrossed in one's self was surely a disability.

'So are you going to let me in?'

Her mental defences were too low at that moment to deal with Sebastian's buoyant ego. 'What have you come round for? What do you want?'

'You know the answers to both of those questions. Now be a good girl and open that bloody door; we've got unfinished business.'

'I think you should go.'

'You know the more you fight it, the more you'll enjoy it. Now let's fuck and get this over with, shall we?'

'Joseph will – I mean, Mark will be here any minute.' Wishful thinking divulged her heart's true longing. Sebastian knotted his arms, his eyes fidgeting between hers, scrutinising her restless demeanour.

A hissing snigger shook his chest. 'Well, what do you know? Lucy has a thing for the gardener.'

There was no point denying the truth any longer. He slipped his hands into his pockets, the tapping of his black patent shoe playing a petty tune of annoyance.

'You need to set your sights higher, Lucy. A fucking gardener?'

His parochial opinions, those of a man who couldn't see past the bonnet of his Porsche grated on Lucy.

'His job doesn't define who he is. Just as yours doesn't define you.'

'Very philosophical. Where did you get that from, a fortune cookie?'

The glib remark awoke Lucy's egalitarian convictions.

'No, it's an observation: you wear designer clothes, drive an expensive car and you're a self-infatuated arsehole.'

He glanced at his watch, looking uninterested.

'Joseph wears old clothes and drives a battered truck, but he's a good man. Decent, hard-working, honourable. Twice the man you can ever hope to be.' Although Joseph had discarded Lucy, she believed with all her heart that what she said was true.

'Is he now?' He nodded, his eyebrow cocked insolently. 'You missed one thing from that truly glowing endorsement.' Putting his hands back in pockets he leaned in, his nostrils flared. 'Murderer.' Rocking back on his heels he wallowed in self-gratification, clearly enjoying the puzzled then disturbed expression on Lucy's face.

'And.' He held a finger in the air. 'He is a murderer of the very worst kind.'

'Liar,' spat Lucy.

'Ask him.'

'I will,' she said, head held high. 'And I'll be sure to tell Joseph the question came from *you.*'

Sebastian's lower lids twitched, his arrogance faltering. 'You are quite right, Lucy. We are two very different men. I have standards. Without them we are no better than animals. My only crime is enjoying life to the full.'

'Well fuck off and enjoy it somewhere else.' With that, she put her key to good use, slamming the door behind her.

'*Bastard!*' Lucy ran upstairs and peeked through the bedroom window, waiting for him to go.

Why would he say such a thing? He had to have the last poisonous word.

His car had now gone, and she sat on the end of the unmade bed, her head whirling with thoughts of Joseph, Mark, Charles, the money and poor Sam. It seemed like the world had turned against her in just a few days.

The reality was that deception had been conspiring against her for some time. All lies and deceit had an expiry date. The truth would live forever and it was about to have its day.

Fired up by Sebastian, Lucy was keen to get her discussion with Mark over and done with. She paced the lounge, restlessly awaiting his arrival. After an hour she gave in to the fatigue of her thoughts.

There were many questions she wanted answers to, but

the one for Joseph was the most pressing. Everyone else's secrets and lies had been exposed, but he remained mysterious. There was a part of him that he kept hidden, locked away.

The words of Sebastian still prowling around her mind, Lucy settled on asking the one man she still believed in: his father.

If George turned out to be a charlatan as well, then surely she couldn't have any faith in anyone.

When Mark finally arrived home, he carried on like everything was fine and set about making himself a sandwich. Lucy listened to his idle chat, waiting for him to broach what was surely looming, amazed at how *normal* he seemed, even though things were anything but. He ventured onto the subject of the new bathroom, she knew he was willing to spend yet another day of his life, or maybe even the rest of his life, in denial. It was Mark's prerogative to live as he wished, but Lucy had no desire to lead an artificial existence.

She rubbed her clammy palms together, the pulse in her neck throbbing. What she was about to say would change both their lives irrevocably.

Mark had his back to her, chopping lettuce.

Lucy licked her parched lips, drew breath then held it for a moment, unsure of how to begin the end.

'I know about you and Pete.'

The knife stopped, his bowed head raised. There was no denial, only silence.

'All those times you were playing golf or out with your friends, is that where you really were?' Her voice was emotionless; she knew she had no right to lecture him.

'Some of the time.' He kept his back turned. 'Suzie

promised me a week's grace.'

'I think this has already gone on too long, don't you?'

He nodded. 'I tried, Lucy. I fought it with all I had until it almost tore me apart. I couldn't get away from it: what I am, what I felt. Do you know what it's like to be ashamed and disgusted with yourself?

'Pretending to be someone that you're not, but wanting to be that person so bad, the person everyone knows and loves. But really you're just a...' His voice cracked. 'A gay boy. A fucking faggot.' Mark's shoulders began to shudder with his outpouring of regret.

Lucy had a different perspective; she couldn't be angry with him, far from it. It was quite clear the mental torture he had been going through. That would have explained his irritability and mood swings as he wrestled with what society expected and what his heart needed.

Lucy approached him. Taking his knotted hands in hers, she turned him to face her.

'It turned me into a monster, making me say nasty things out of my own frustration. I'm so sorry, Lucy. I never meant to hurt you.' He breathed in stutters between sobs. 'I got so low I even considered taking my own life.'

Mark closed his eyes; the burden of his secret falling onto their conjoined hands, soft as raindrops. Now was not the time for blame. They were both responsible, for living a life of pretence.

'I do love you, Lucy – just not the way a man is meant to love a woman. And now everything I've worked so hard to hide is about to be blown wide open. I'll be a laughing stock: 'have you heard? Mark and Pete are fucking each other.'

'No one will say that.' Lucy tightened her grip.

'What, you mean no one will talk about us?' He shook his head in defeat.

'Of course they will, but soon it will be old news and then you can both live your lives as they were meant to be. Mark, you don't have to run from who you are anymore.'

Lucy shook his hands like the reins of a horse, encouraging him to pick up the pace. The race wasn't over. It was just the beginning, for both of them. 'It's not a crime to fall in love.'

He let go of her fingers and wiped his eyes with the heel of his hand.

'The times we split before... was that because of Pete?'

He gave a faint nod. 'I've never put you at risk. There's only ever been Pete.'

Now that the mask had been removed, Lucy didn't altogether recognise the man she had spent so much time with.

'Aren't you going to shout and scream at me? God knows I deserve it.'

'I think we've done enough of that, haven't we?'

'Yeah.' His eyes glistened above a broken smile. They held each other, silently saying goodbye to the two people they used to be.

Mark packed a bag and left to find a hotel despite Lucy insisting that it wasn't necessary. It was a relief that it was finally over, and in a strange way, so much easier than she had anticipated.

Scraping the unused salad into the bin, Lucy wept silently. There was a finality in tidying up after Mark for what would be the very last time.

CHAPTER THIRTY-THREE

The empty silence allowed Lucy to ruminate about the changes to her life that had already begun. The house would certainly have to be sold; no doubt Mark would give her the option of buying him out, which, thanks to the neighbours, was no option at all. She had left herself a year's salary, but the rest of her money had been invested in something she thought was a very worthy cause.

It was approaching early evening when a familiar drumming at the door interrupted the monastic silence.

George.

Lucy hung all her hopes on the fact that Joseph might be accompanying his father, seeing as this was their final visit.

In anticipation she had changed into a plain but pretty dress, disguising her distress with a confidence-boosting application of make-up. To see his handsome face would surely bring some sunshine to an otherwise very dark day.

She opened the door, and quickly found that her optimism was not justified.

'Hello, Lucy,' said George, an envelope tucked under his arm.

'Hello, George. On your own?' she asked, glancing longingly behind him.

'Yes, just little old me. I'm not interrupting anything, am I?'

'No, no. Please come in.' Lucy mustered a smile, trying to hide her disappointment.

'Is Mark not at home?' George wiped his feet on the mat before crossing the threshold.

'No. He's catching up with an old friend.'

'Ah. Do you mind if we go into the garden? We altered some of the planting, and I wanted to run through what we've changed.'

'No, of course not.' Lucy didn't have the heart to tell him all of his hard work would soon be only for the pleasure of someone else's eyes.

The garden was now a beautiful oasis, and apart from the infancy of the plants, it looked as though it had been that way for many years. George spoke with the same passion she had so admired when they first met. Lucy felt terrible for having to fake hers. It wasn't that she didn't appreciate the beauty of it – she certainly did. But the thought that it was no longer really hers had raised an emotional barrier against it. If only the same could be applied to people.

'Is Mark happy with everything?'

'Yeah – I think so,' she nodded, looking around, uneasy in her own presence. It wasn't the plants she wanted to talk about.

'He's not much of a gardener is he, Mark? Likes his cars and sport.'

'Mmm.' She folded her arms, offering a tight-lipped smile.

'He's a man's man isn't he?'

'You're right there, George. He's definitely a man's man.'

'Lucy, is there something you're not happy with?' George's fingers ran over his mouth, doubt creasing his forehead. 'You know you can tell me, my darlin'. Whatever it is, I'll put it right.'

Turning to face him with a sigh, Lucy reached for his hand. 'Oh God, George, no. Please don't think that. I love everything you've done. It's perfect. I've had a bad couple of days, so I'm sorry if I don't seem myself.'

'Want to talk about it? I'm a good listener.' There was no shortage of subjects to talk about. But Sebastian's accusation was easily the one at the forefront of her mind.

'Actually there was something I wanted to ask you.'

'Fire away. Although I'm afraid I can't reveal the secret of my youthful, dashing good looks.'

The smile Lucy shared with George quickly dissolved. The awkward question waited in the wings.

'I'm not quite sure how to put this. Has Joseph ever... been in trouble?'

George blinked down at the ground with a frown. 'What do you mean, trouble?' The subtle change in his demeanour implied a truth being hidden.

Despite the defamatory nature of the question she simply had to ask it.

'Has he ever... taken a life?'

The hand she held fell limp from hers. 'Who have you been talking to?'

'Someone – no one of any importance.'

George removed his glasses, pinching the bridge of his nose.

'I wouldn't have asked, but if I'm honest, it has been worrying me.'

'Worrying you? What else have you been told?'

'Nothing at all.' For the first time there was awkwardness between them.

'Lucy.' George looked straight into her eyes with all the sincerity that she knew he possessed.

'At no time have you *ever* been in danger. Quite the opposite.'

'George,' she sighed, ashamed of causing his jaded appearance. 'I know that, I absolutely do. It's just that what this person said to me was such a shock; I can't get it out of my head.'

'And what exactly did they tell you?' he asked, fear swimming in his eyes.

'They said that… Joseph was a murderer.'

George turned his face away. The pain of her words broke the proud man's posture. As if winded, his chest rose and fell, and he laboured for air.

Shocked by his reaction, Lucy placed her hand on his shoulder.

'Let's go and sit down shall we?'

George simply nodded. To show her unity, Lucy slipped her arm under his and walked him towards the house.

Joseph didn't want anything from her, and they would probably never see each other again. Yet there was a part of Lucy that wouldn't, couldn't, let go. There was so much she still didn't know about Joseph – but maybe there was a good reason for that.

They sat in the dying sunshine, occupying a corner of the garden table. George gently placed his glasses down. His anguished face cruelly displayed the decay that age brings. He looked a very different man. It upset her to see him like this and she felt guilty for being the cause of it.

'George, I'm sorry. I have no right to question you. I shouldn't have said anything.'

'No, Lucy. I want to tell you,' George began, fixing his gaze on the tabletop. 'My son isn't really a gardener. Well, he is, but it was never his heart's desire. When he left school I persuaded him to come and work for me, hoping he would lose interest in what he really wanted to do. It was selfish of me. I wanted to keep him under my wing. He's my boy.' George shrugged, the tabletop receiving his full attention. 'Not long after his seventeenth birthday he left home to pursue his ambition. Broke his mother's heart.' He paused, opening and closing the arms of his glasses. 'And mine.' His voice weakened.

Clearing his throat, George continued, 'But 32 weeks later my wife and I went down to see him. It was one of the proudest days of my life, and one of the worst. My boy was now a man. A Royal Marine Commando.'

Lucy had known there was something more to Joseph: he had an inexplicable capability about him. She was totally engaged in George's narrative but also somewhat apprehensive, hearing the sorrow in his voice.

'Why do you say it was one of your worst days, George?'

'Because, I knew my son would one day go to war. That he would suffer the brutal unfiltered surroundings of combat, things that would scar his mind and change him forever. When you have a child, Lucy, that is what they always are to you. It doesn't matter how big and strong they grow. Joseph is my child, and it's my duty as his father to protect him. When you simply can't do that, it leaves a hole in your existence. We would pray for letters. They gave us the thinnest connection possible, but still it was like Christmas when the postman answered our prayers. He was a professional soldier in every sense of the word. One of the best.' George raised his head in a moment of pride. His eyes flickered from left to right and he came back down like a deflated balloon.

'On his third tour of Afghanistan he lost four of his friends. They died right at his feet – killed by a sniper.' Lucy's eagerness at finally getting to know about Joseph's past was becoming more uncomfortable as she watched the colour bleed from George's face.

'He was out on patrol in Sangin with Chris, one of his mates. He's the only one Joseph keeps in touch with. He goes to see him every year. He's got a surf shop down south – good guy.'

Lucy wanted to tell George that she knew who he was talking about, that she had met him. But she couldn't.

'Joseph and Chris were passing through a cluster of shanty houses, most of them derelict. Tensions were high. An eighteen-year-old from the Rifles Regiment had lost both his legs that morning from a roadside bomb.

Chris lost his footing on the rough terrain, twisted his ankle and took a fall. Joseph was walking back to give him a hand up when Chris started shouting out, "man-on. Ten o'clock, ten o'clock!"

Joseph spun around, his weapon raised, to see the barrel of a rifle poking through the old shutters of a window.

He fired two rounds, one after the other. By that time Chris was on his feet and he ran over to the building. Joseph joined him, kicked the door in, and they both entered the house.' George's slight pauses were becoming longer. 'There was no one living in there. They entered the room looking for the gunman.' George moistened his lips, his eyes needing no such help. 'And they found... an eight year-old boy.'

Lucy fell back in her chair, hands clasped to her mouth. 'Oh my God,' she whispered into her fingers.

George turned his reddened, sorrow-filled eyes on Lucy.

'It wasn't a gun he had; it was just a bit of old pipe. He had tied it to a piece of timber to make a toy rifle.' He shook his head repeatedly. 'Joseph knew him. He loved the British troops because they paid attention to him – especially Joseph. He would often play football with him when he wasn't on patrol. He sent us a letter saying he'd met this kid who wanted to be a soldier like him. He said he felt sorry for him because he had absolutely nothing and asked us if we would send a shoe box full of toys for him. Rose posted ten.'

George ran his fingers over the deep trenches in his forehead. 'Joseph sent us a photo of him with the little boy – such a good-looking kid. Big dark eyes and a smile far too beautiful for such an ugly place,' he sighed, his head resting on his hand.

'He held the boy in his arms and watched him die in the dust.' A single tear wove its way down the side of George's nose. 'His name was Aashna.'

The revelation hit Lucy like a bullet; she remembered the tattoo over his heart. A flash of images and thoughts flooded her brain: Joseph's sad eyes calling to her; the humble, defeated tone in his voice, which seemed so at odds with the man himself. It all made sense now: that was why he'd pushed her away at the campsite.

Even though Lucy was only just getting to know the real Joseph, at that moment she had never felt closer to him, and there had never been a man she had wanted, ached for more.

Lucy took George's hand. They both looked at each other through a veil of tears.

'My son's not a murderer, Lucy. He's a casualty of the futility of war.'

'George, I never—'

'I know, I know.' He squeezed her fingers. 'That's why I'm telling you this, Lucy, because I can see what you are. Joseph needs more people like you in his life. He's isolated himself. He was cleared of any wrongdoing whatsoever, but I can tell you, there is not a court in this land that could punish a man more than my son has punished himself.

He left the Marines after that. When he came out he was a very different man from the one who had gone in twelve years earlier. He had a few counselling sessions, then stopped going. When I asked him why, he said he didn't want them to make him think that what he had done was okay.'

Lucy listened with a heavy heart, captivated by the revealing nature of the story. It gave her the slightest glimmer of hope. Maybe there was still a chance for her to love him.

'In some ways I'm glad that my wife didn't get to see him suffer like this. But she always knew what to do. I'm sure she could have made things right.'

'George, don't doubt yourself. I think you're a wonderful father. He thinks the world of you, that's clear to see.'

He nodded with an attempt at a smile. 'He loved his mum – so did I. I'd give all the time I have left on this earth for just one minute with her.'

Lucy couldn't help but shed tears at his sincerity. She too wanted to be loved in such a way.

'You know what really worries me, Lucy? After Rose died, I started going to church every Sunday. She believed in God and the afterlife so strongly that it made me think: what if it's true, and we do live on after death? I began to believe it too. So much so that at one point I actually wanted to die so I could be with her once again.' Crystal beads sailed down into the grooves on each side of his mouth.

'Oh, George.' Lucy held on to him tightly.

'I've seen that look on my son's face. A serene, careless, vacant expression. I know it well because I saw it in the mirror every morning. He goes out late at night, I don't know where. When I ask, he tells me it's some woman he's seeing. Yet his phone never rings and he never mentions anyone. I know this sounds crazy, but I sometimes wonder if he's out looking for an honourable death. He used to say he wished he'd stayed in Afghanistan and taken a bullet.' George leaned back and searched the answerless sky.

'I'm so worried about him. I don't know what to do.' The exhaustion of his long exhale sank him deeper into the chair.

'Tell him that you've told me.' Lucy rose from her slumped posture, feeling the need for action.

A spark of interest roused George.

'I'll go and talk to him. Sometimes it's easier to talk to an outsider,' she suggested, blinking away the haze of tears.

'You don't have to do that, Lucy.'

'I want to. I want to help you both. Please let me.'

The relief on George's face was answer enough. 'You know he's been a different man since coming here. That's why I was so disappointed when it was over.'

'It's not over, George. It's only just beginning. We're friends now, and friends help each other.'

He rose from his chair, leaned over and his arms expressed the gratitude he felt.

'Thank you, my darlin'. You're a good girl, Lucy.' The misshaped words whispered through the emotion, infecting Lucy with their power. She desperately wanted to tell him that she loved his son, that she would have walked through the fires of hell for him and that she would never give up, no matter what. But she couldn't. In George's eyes she was attached and she didn't want to risk destroying his opinion of her.

He sat down looking more himself. 'He's coming around tonight after his run. I'll have a talk to him then.' He tapped the table with his finger, enthused. 'I'll call you in the morning to tell you how I got on.'

'Or you can call me tonight,' she suggested, not caring how desperate it may have sounded.

'If it's not too late, I will.' He put his glasses back on, along with his smile. 'I'll not take up anymore of your evening.' Using the arms of his chair he pushed himself to his feet.

'You're not at all, George. Stay as long as you like.'

'No. I'll go now, just in case Joseph calls earlier than

usual.'

'Well promise me you'll come back tomorrow, and I'll make us dinner.'

'I would be honoured. That's very kind of you.'

Lucy walked him back to his pick-up, her arm through his, hope in both their hearts.

Climbing in, George closed the door and opened the window. 'You know my wife would have loved you.'

'I'm sure I would have loved her too. How long were you married for?'

'50 years,' he said proudly.

'That's quite an achievement.'

'Mind you, it wasn't all sunshine and rainbows. But when you find someone special you have to fight for it, Lucy, don't you?'

She wasn't sure if the knowing look he was giving her was coincidence, or was he trying to tell her that he knew of her feelings for his son?

She leaned through the open window and kissed him on the cheek. 'Yes, you do. Drive carefully and don't you worry, George. It will all work out in the end.'

The engine rumbled into action.

'You know, I think you're right.' He smiled. 'Bye, sweetheart.'

Lucy stood in the road, waving until he was gone.

CHAPTER THIRTY-FOUR

It was dark by the time Joseph arrived at his father's. Suspecting that he would be asleep, Joseph used his key to open the door.

'Dad, it's me,' he called out, closing the door.

He walked through the hall and into the living room. George was flat out in his La-Z-Boy chair. His crossword and glasses on his lap, the TV was providing the only light in the room.

'You're getting too old for this game, Dad.' Joseph wandered into the kitchen and opened the fridge to get himself a beer. He paused, taking in a photo of his mother. His father kept an image of her in every room.

The photo had captured her beauty and warmth in a split-second. The kind eyes and gentle smile, so real it was as torturous as it was heart-warming to look into the face of yesterday. Feeling the pain of her parting beginning to grow, he diverted his eyes, grabbed a chilled bottle and went back to join his father.

Weary from his run, Joseph collapsed down on the

couch. Sipping his beer, the narrator of a nature program provided one-way conversation while the antics of an orangutan family kept him entertained. He watched the child-like animals with a smile as they showed remarkable affection for one another. For just a few short minutes his mind was distracted from its constantly rotating thoughts.

He glanced over to his father, the dancing images of the TV illuminating his face. On the little table next to his chair was his diary, open at the day's page, along with a beer and the TV remote.

His father had kept a diary for as long as he could remember. He wrote about trivial things mostly, but it had become a routine of his. Curiosity got the better of him and he rose from the couch and leaned over George to take a look. It read as most days did. What time he woke, what he ate for breakfast, what the weather had been like. Joseph skimmed over the page until the mention of Lucy hooked his eye. He stooped down, eyes squinting, to read the compact writing.

I visited Lucy this evening to give her my final invoice. We sat in the garden and had a nice long chat.

I felt so much better for it. She's such a lovely girl.

I always told Joseph never to tread on another man's toes when it comes to women, but I have to say, I'm tempted to tell him otherwise when it comes to Lucy.

There aren't many gentle souls out there such as hers. I know in my bones she'd be good for that boy of mine, and I suspect she has some affection for Joseph, too. If only circumstances were different.

Joseph stood up straight. He had allowed himself to get too close to Lucy. He didn't deserve her. What could a man like him offer her anyway? Nothing.

Losing the taste for his beer, he placed the bottle next

to George's and closed the diary.

'Let's get you to bed, Dad. Dad… Dad?'

A flash of panic seared through him and he shook George's shoulder. His father's head flopped onto his chest.

'Dad! No, no, no! Dad, please.' Joseph fell to his knees and held his father's cold face in both hands, lifting his lifeless head.

'Dad, I'm not ready.'

His tremulous hands shook the old man's cheeks, and he pleaded and begged for the impossible. Joseph dropped his head onto the silent chest, fruitlessly searching for signs of life. Desperation taking over, he clutched at his father's wrist, then sank his fingers under the old man's jawline, fighting in vain against the indefatigable force. Realising his worst fear had come true, he looked up above him, sorrow washing down his face. 'I'm not fucking ready!' Joseph screamed. 'He's all I've got. Please don't take him from me . . . anything but this.'

His relinquishing sobs came from a heart beaten and crippled by loss. Death wasn't something to be bartered with. George had lived and died. – No amount of pleading could change that. The pain of death was suffered not by the deceased, but by the living, those left behind with nothing but memories and a thirst that would never be quenched. George Dalton's time on earth was now over, and with his parting went the love and support that kept his son's head above water. Now there was nothing, and no one, who could save him from the undercurrent that forever threatened to drag him down.

Joseph buried his face in the soft white hair, the comforting smell one he prayed he would never forget. He held on to his father all night long, and the grown man wept like the boy he had once been.

CHAPTER THIRTY-FIVE

That night Lucy didn't move more than a few feet without taking her phone. It was the start of a new calendar day before she finally conceded that George wasn't going to call.

When the call finally came late the next afternoon, her heart felt as if it had taken flight with apprehensive excitement. Its flight of fancy was a fated one. The momentary joy of hearing Joseph's voice speak her name soon turned into misery.

The message was short, cold and to the point. Shock captured her words and empathy set her tears free. By the time Lucy's stifled sympathy stuttered out, the line was dead.

Somehow, her legs carried her out into the garden where George always was. Evidence of him was everywhere. The chair where he had sat just the day before was still in the position in which he had left it. The flowerbeds he had carefully planned and planted swayed in unison to the silent sigh of the wind. His ghost was already present. Trying to comprehend the blunt truth, Lucy grieved for George and his son. Now she knew Joseph's history, it broke her heart to think that he was now all alone, with nothing but the torment of the past and the pain of dealing with the end of a life so crucial to his own. With an enlightened perspective, Lucy remembered the moments she had witnessed between father and son. She thought of George's tender smile, kindness and patience; he was the kind of man that was sadly an endangered species. George was a true gentleman in every sense of the word. Taking deep sighing breaths, Lucy walked through the garden to the bench that George had helped her carry. Under the parted green curtains of a weeping willow she sat and remembered. Letting the tears fall, Lucy contemplated the confused fragility of life. When their lottery numbers had come up she had thought that everything would be a breeze from that point on, and yet she was more confused than ever. There didn't seem to be any rhyme or reason to the world. Vanity, selfishness, and deceit walked brazenly through life, and goodness and innocence were trampled under its feet. The evolution of time was leaving her evermore jaded.

Everything that she had known and loved was slowly being taken away from her. Like a jealous child, life was spitefully snatching the things closest to her heart. And now George had been added to the growing list. Lucy couldn't believe that she would never see his face or hear his voice ever again. Their final conversation played out in her mind to the percussion of raindrops. The solemn grey sky watered the earth and droplets fell like tears from the leaves and bowed heads of the flowers, as if the very garden he had created was now grieving for the man who had loved it so dearly.

The rest of that week, like the preceding few, was a test. A 'For Sale' sign now stood where the 'Sold' sign once was, but this time the name 'Kingsfellow Estates' was *not* on the board.

Lucy wasn't ready to face a classroom with no Sam, but spending the week at home proved to be just as painful, as she showed a series of happy couples around the house. Each one were a carbon copy of the last, and all asked the same questions: 'Who did the garden?' 'Why are you selling such a beautiful house?'

She did actually tell one particularly annoying couple the unvarnished truth, but it seemed so ridiculous to them that they burst out laughing, thinking it a joke.

Her repeated phone calls to Joseph went unanswered. All she wanted to know was when George's funeral would be. To her surprise she did receive a reply to her first text message, albeit a terse one.

Funeral is this Tuesday 10 a.m. St Francis Church.

It was as good as an invitation. Lucy would be there to say hello to one man and goodbye to another.

Once again the house was full of boxes. Mark had decided that he and Pete would continue the pretence of being good friends, but once the house sale was completed, they would move to Spain. They had plans to buy a bar there and start a new life together.

Along with prospective buyers, the investigating fraud officer paid Lucy a visit. They had identified what she thought was Mr and Mrs St Clair from the CCTV of the rental agent's office. Reggie Sloan and Agnes Webb were their real names.

Officer Lawson's assurance that those two were

professional scumbags with a very sophisticated plan was meagre consolation for Lucy.

Agnes was the investment banker, and a convicted one at that. It seemed fraud was a temptation that not even the prospect of two years' incarceration could discourage. She had an obsessive, geeky love of all things fiscal was a gift that rendered her uneasy in the company of anything other than a spreadsheet.

That was where Reggie came in. A failed actor, he possessed the skill to take on another persona. The two of them together were a perfect combination: Agnes had the know-how and Reggie had the ability to gain Lucy's confidence.

Their plot was so finely executed that even the investment plan had been genuine, so if Lucy had sought a second financial opinion, it would have come back fine. They had covered all bases, the officer told her, a hint of admiration seeming to ride on the officer's voice.

Slurping his tea, he reassured her that Bonnie and Clyde would eventually be caught, but when it came to her money, he was less optimistic. Having proved his investigative skills, Officer Lawson left Lucy to the company of her boxes, asking, as he stepped out of the front door, why she was selling such a lovely house.

Rolling her eyes, she gave her stock answer.

'I'm moving on to bigger and better things.' Lucy certainly was moving, but to what was unknown.

The sky was bluer than ever and the sun shone brightly. The birds sang a joyous tune while people chatted in the street, and others walked their dogs. Cars raced to beat red lights, in a rush to get to their destination. All was well in the world, and no one gave a fuck.

Joseph felt invisible behind the tinted glass of the funeral car. For him, the world had stopped revolving.

He was no longer second in command. There was no one above him, no one to turn to for advice. To be bereft of both parents left him with the sombre sense that he had finally become a man.

The car eventually stopped outside the church, and Joseph saw Father Brian standing at the gate, a doleful countenance hung heavy on his face. He greeted Joseph compassionately, caressing Joseph's hand with both of his own.

'On our last meeting you said I wouldn't be seeing your face here again.'

Joseph nodded.

'This is not how I wanted that promise to be broken, Joseph.'

Not trusting his voice, he answered with another nod, unable to make eye contact.

The hearse doors opened, and with the help of the other pallbearers, Joseph raised his section of the coffin onto his shoulder.

He headed the procession. The slight incline leading up to the stone building felt like a mountain, his breath labouring under the strain of the day.

If the outside world had seemed oblivious to the loss of one of its citizens, it was a very different scene inside the church. Not a single empty seat remained. People even stood around the fringes, shoulder to shoulder. The humbling sight of his father's popularity broke him.

The coffin was placed on the bier below the effigy of Christ hung above, which cast his merciful gaze down upon the casket.

Joseph took his seat and the service began. Father Brian spoke reverently and with great admiration of George, his composure only faltering at the mention of his devotion to his wife and son – a reminder perhaps of the losses he had experienced in his own life.

Joseph's consciousness drifted back to random times he had spent with his father, like his eleventh birthday, when he had woken up to find the bike his parents had been telling him was too expensive placed at the bottom of his bed; or the camping trips to France, when the sun never seemed to sleep and the days were simple, but happy.

The first time he ever saw his father cry was when Joseph had received his green beret. Joseph was a lucky man to have had such loving parents, and he knew it. Yet he felt cheated. A nameless, faceless force had taken the one person that truly knew him, truly loved him. His father, his friend.

With the service over, the hum of discussion and shuffling of feet filled the lofty space as people exited.

Joseph remained seated, fearing the end. When silence returned he stood up and laid his hand on the grainy timber. This was the closest he would ever get to him now. Closing his eyes tight, he wished with all his heart for this to be just another one of his bad dreams.

'Love you, Dad,' His voice was unable to rise above a whisper. 'Go to Mum now. She's waiting for you.'

Removing his hand from the polished timber was the hardest thing. It really did mean letting go.

Half-remembered faces gave their condolences along with a eulogy of their own. Joseph did his best to remain civil, their kind words drowned out by his own internal cries. When the last few sympathisers had gone, one face remained that he could not forget. Standing at the back of the church, dabbing away streaks of mascara from her blotchy skin, Lucy clutched a single white rose, its pure luminous beauty in stark contrast to her midnight clothes.

Joseph walked towards her between the empty pews. He managed to gain some control over himself until he saw his own grief mirrored by her pained face.

'Joseph, I'm so sorry. I really am.'

Her breath hitched as fresh tears ran down the well-travelled route. He looked down at her, his eyes stinging, heart aching, and words failed him. Lucy stepped closer, her unsure hand taking its chance to hold his.

'Mr Dalton.' A gentle touch to the small of his back interrupted the moment. 'We're ready when you are,' said the undertaker softly. In the fast-paced world of today even death was on the clock. Joseph leaned in and kissed her damp cheek. She clasped his arm like a helpless swimmer clinging to the rocks. She offered the rose to Joseph, her hand shaking.

'This is for your Da…'

Her lips pressed together and tears rolled down the perfect contours of her face. Joseph nodded, unable to thank her, choked by Lucy's grief as much as his own.

With the final conclusion to his father's life yet to complete, he broke away towards the shaft of light pouring in through the open doors.

As the car slowly pulled away, Joseph looked across to see Lucy, framed in the stone archway like a lost angel, wingless and stranded. The departing car took her image from his sight, but not his memory.

His thoughts travelled over the incidents in his life, which had long gone. Yet still they refused to slumber in the bed we call the past.

His heart thumped as the car turned into the wide mouth of the long drive and past the imposing cast-iron gates, into the city of the dead.

Row after row of grey and black stones appeared to sprout from the lush grass. Some bore fresh flowers of those still remembered, while others were decorated with the withered stems of those long forgotten.

With the car parked, they trod the spongy sward towards the stone that bore his mother's name. Joseph broke out into a cold sweat, seeing the gaping mouth that had opened in the ground before him.

George had spent so much of his life in the earth: digging, planting, feeding and caring for it, and now he was to spend the rest of eternity buried beneath it.

Through a fog of tears, Joseph laid the rose onto the coffin. Disbelief still refused to concede to reality, even as the coffin made its descent from the light into darkness. Shuddering sobs shook the tears from his lashes while Father Brian solemnly read the committal.

'We therefore commit George Dalton's body to the ground; earth to earth, ashes to ashes, dust to dust, in the sure and certain hope of the resurrection to eternal life.'

Goodbye, Dad.

CHAPTER THIRTY-SIX

The beautifully landscaped gardens no doubt had a hand in acquiring the *SOLD* banner that was diagonally stuck to the board outside. A young couple, undoubtedly in love, viewed the house, exchanging telling glances and give-away smiles. Their generous offer reflected their desire to make Lucy's home their own.

Lucy envied them. Beginning a journey in life with love on board was the best start possible, rather than hoping to pick it up along the way.

Mark came to collect his things. He wanted very little from the house, only a few photographs and his coffee machine. She made him a drink while he took his souvenirs of their time together out to his Ferrari.

For the final time they sat in the kitchen with a reticent silence between them. Their recent history was such a tangle of lies and deceit that they were left with almost nothing to talk about. Lucy had kept the story of the fraudulent neighbours to herself. Exhausted by it, she saw no point in going over what she already had, a hundred times or more.

By way of something to say, Mark offered an invitation to come and visit him in his, as yet, non-existent home in Spain. With his coffee cup empty and small talk all used up, Mark made his excuses for having to leave so soon. Relieved that he hadn't drawn out their strained meeting any longer, Lucy followed him to the door. Breaking through the barrier, they stood and held each other, both of them shedding tears, returning momentarily to their old selves as they said goodbye.

Lucy closed the door and collapsed on the couch, all cried out, the huge TV staring blankly at her.

Ebay.

Examining the hairline cracks in the ceiling, the uncertainty of her future gave rise to speculation. Her half of the house sale would be more than enough to buy another, more modest home.

She would have to return to paid work. Whether Mrs Shoesmith would accommodate her remained to be seen. Ruminating over what was and what would be, the exhaustion of the last few days began to tell on her. Lucy's thoughts melted into dreams, as her semi-conscious mind conjured up an alternative reality where things had played out very differently indeed.

the moments between sleep and waking, all problems seemed magnified while the brain recalibrated itself from the limitless imagination of sleep.

In her dreams George was alive and well, Sam was happy and healthy and Joseph loved her.

She closed her eyes, hoping to return to that imaginary place for a little while longer, but it was beyond reach – gone.

Hauling herself up, she stumbled into the kitchen and gulped down a glass of water. Spotting the car keys next to her handbag she snatched them up, needing to escape the silence of the house.

The pale yellow paper of George's invoice caught her eye amidst the receipts and general junk in her bag.

She plucked it out and stared at the neatly folded square for a moment before heading out of the door.

Number 2, Bluebell Court was the address on the invoice.

It made her smile. She thought it a very fitting address for a gardener. Curious to see where George had lived, she tapped the information into her satnav and the strange, nondescript accent directed her as she began the 25-minute drive to Bluebell Court.

Only five houses occupied the secluded crescent shaped spot. Lucy rolled slowly along, peering out the open window at the picturesque properties.

The heavy shade of the trees made the evening seem darker than it was. Her foot hit the brake when she saw Joseph's pick-up parked on the drive of what was obviously George's home. It had been a couple of days since the funeral and she had agonised over whether or not to call him. Fearing rejection and not entirely sure what to say, she had chosen the protection of refraining. But now he was just a few short steps away – no need to dream.

The desire to see his face and hear his voice burned inside of her. This was her chance. She parked, and without giving doubt time to surface, walked up the path with a confident step, although her heart was anything but.

The beautiful cottage garden was unmistakably George. Mature plants brimmed each side of the curved route, which led to a white half-glazed door, overhung by an abundance of scarlet roses whose subtle fragrance sweetened the air. Lucy raised the brass fox-head door knocker then let it fall.

Her breath quickened as she saw his figure approach in the patterned glass. The door opened and there he stood, surprise in his eyes.

'Hi. I was driving by and I saw your pickup. I thought I'd come and see how you are.'

He had a look of uncertainty for a second or two, then stood aside and said 'come in.'

God, it was good to see him. Such a face was made to be looked at day and night. Lucy stepped into the hallway and noticed the shadowy borders on the walls, where pictures had once hung.

'How are you feeling?' Lucy asked as he closed the door.

'Oh, you know.'

Joseph massaged the back of his neck. He looked tired.

'How did you find this place?'

'The invoice your dad gave me.'

He nodded, eyes dropping to the floor. The dead silence and his clear unease cancelled out all the things she had imagined telling him.

'It's a lovely spot, you'd never know it was here.' A pitiful smile followed the trivial comment, unseen by his still downcast eyes.

A cardboard box sat next to the front door, filled carelessly with a jumble of photographs.

'What's this?'

She knelt down and pinched the corner of a black and white picture, pulling it free.

'I'm sorting a few things out.'

Lucy looked over at a yellowing photo of a young couple descending the steps of a church. It showed a beautiful blonde lady holding the arm of her handsome new husband, their blissful smiles captured behind a scattering of confetti.

'Is this your mum and dad?' she asked, looking up from the picture.

'Yeah.'

'You're not getting rid of these, are you?'

'I've got enough ghosts.'

She rose to her feet. 'Joseph, you can't throw these away.'

'I can't look at them either.' He took the photo from her fingers and dropped it back on the pile.

'But they're memories. Very special ones, I'm sure.'

'That is a box full of pain. It's a reminder of a life and people that I yearn for.' He looked at her for the first time, vulnerability widening his red eyes. 'You wouldn't understand.'

'I understand better than you know.' Lucy rubbed her clammy hands together and ran her tongue over her lips. It was cards on the table time.

'I know about Afghanistan... what happened. Your dad told me everything.'

Joseph ran his hands through his dishevelled hair. He turned away puffing into the air.

'He was worried about you – I'm worried about you.'

His arms fell limply to his sides.

'You've got to stop punishing yourself, Joseph. It was an accident.'

He spun around; the lids of his eyes drawing closer.

'An accident?' he snapped.

'I didn't–'

'An accident is when you spill your coffee or tread on someone's toes. Not when you fire a bullet into the chest of an eight-year-old boy. That's not a fucking accident.' His face flushed, and the veins in his temples bulged.

'I'm sorry. I didn't mean to trivialise it. I'm trying to help.'

'There is no help.' He slashed the air with a flat palm. 'None. All the talking in the world can't undo what I've done. I wake up in the morning and he's sitting at the end of the bed. I drive to work and he comes with me. When I look in the mirror, I see his blood-splattered face, coughing, choking for air, for life.'

His voice gave out, his face hardening under the strain.

'I wake in the night feeling his fingers clawing at me.' He scratched erratically in imitation, where the tattoo sat. 'His terrified eyes, begging me to help him.' He paused for breath, almost panting, his eyes shimmering at the memory. 'What did I do? Nothing. I watched him die.'

The anger in his voice didn't scare Lucy – quite the opposite; it wasn't aimed at her. To witness his suffering wrenched at her heart and only drew her nearer to him.

'You can't keep blaming yourself. Like it or not, it *was* an accident. How were you supposed to know it wasn't a sniper?'

He shook his bowed head.

'You're tearing yourself apart, and I'm not going to let you do that.' She stood in front of him, her hand softly lifting his face to hers. 'You're a good man – don't ever forget that.'

'You're just seeing what you want to.'

'No,' she replied defiantly.

'I can cover 30 miles carrying 32 pounds on my back. I can take a man out from over a mile away with a single bullet. I'm an expert in death and destruction. What good am I to anyone?'

'Joseph, listen to me. You did your duty and served your country, but your past does not have to be your future. You can't change what is done. You've punished yourself enough.'

'That's easy for you to say. I'd trade my life for his in a heartbeat.' His fingers snapped in front of her face. He sat down on the stairs, his head in his hands.

'What do you want, Lucy?' he murmured.

She knelt down in front of him, placing her hands on his knees. 'I want to be here for you… more than anything I've ever wanted in my life.'

'Won't Mark be wondering where you are?' The heat of his voice turned cold.

'Mark and I are finished and the house is sold.' His eye line rose briefly at the news.

'I never really loved him. I thought I did.' She paused nervously. She had gone this far, it was time to close her eyes and take the leap of faith. 'Until… I saw you.'

Joseph kept his face hidden. With no way of gauging his reaction, she continued, blindly.

'I tried to fight it at first, but the more time we spent together the deeper you took me. I think you feel the same.'

An agitated hand passed back and forth across his forehead, concealing the truth in his eyes.

'Tell me I'm wrong.'

'I'll drag you down,' he whispered.

'I'll pull us back up.'

'You deserve better.'

'I'll be the judge of that. Let me in, Joseph. Please,' she implored.

'Go home, Lucy. You've got a good life. Forget about me.'

'That's just the thing. I can't get you out of my mind and unless you tell me that you don't want me, I'm not going anywhere.'

Lucy started to feel that his barriers might be about to fall.

He lowered a hand to the hard line of his mouth. Lucy watched helplessly. He was caught in a vortex of blame and guilt. It constantly tore through his mind leaving him no rest, no hiding place. It was an ever-present force that would only cease when he drew his last breath. Lucy was his shelter, if only he would let her be.

His long lashes raised, the blue eyes boring into hers as she waited for his verdict.

'I don't want you.'

Lucy fell a hundred feet, impaled by his sharp reply. Her devastated face softened his flinty stare. His image blurred and she shook her head repeatedly until she was able to speak.

'I don't believe you.' The doubt in her voice said otherwise. 'You're just saying that to protect me.'

Joseph pulled himself up by the handrail and stepped to one side of her. She heard the door unlatch, and the scent of the roses told her it was time to go. This was not what she had imagined, but it was what she had feared.

'If you don't mind, Lucy, I've got things to do.'

On her knees in more ways than one, she mustered the

strength to stand. She showed him her wet, red face one last time, he chose to ignore it. Lucy nodded to herself and glanced at the box of photos.

'I'd like to have these if you don't mind.' She picked them up without waiting for permission. 'I'll keep them for you. I'm sure you'll want them back one day.' Stepping into the dim light of the evening, she fought to keep her composure.

'Lucy, it's for the best,' he uttered.

'Is it? I don't see that it is.'

'You'll thank me in the long run.'

'No, Joseph, no. Just as Aashna haunts your life, you will haunt mine.' Her voice broke along with her spirits and she spun around, feeling an emotional collapse threatening. Brushing past the groping flowers, she came to a halt as she heard the gunshot sound of a door closing. He wasn't coming after her like in the movies. It was over.

She knew his resolve would not bend or break for anyone. It was the result of a life of discipline, learning to live with difficult decisions and completing uncomfortable tasks for the greater good. He was an expert at it, a professional. Lucy had no doubt that he would stay true to his beliefs no matter what the personal cost to him might be.

Dropping the box on the passenger seat she started the car and waited, praying that the door would open and he would run out to claim her love. A light in an upstairs window extinguished the most delicate of hopes.

She drove away, feeling rejected and embarrassed. Turning the corner of Bluebell Court she pulled over, the road a blurred watery image. Her nails sank into the steering wheel and she screamed until her throat felt like it was tearing.

Why was everything falling apart? What had she done to deserve this?

The feeling of powerless frustration racked her body and mind. Her lifeline had been severed. The dreams that were unrestricted by day or night were now nightmares that held the same power.

In making what he thought was a merciful decision, he had convicted her to his own fate. A life forever wondering what would have happened if another decision had been taken the moment the grain of sand fell through the hourglass.

I don't want you. A simple statement, but one that held the power of an ocean; there was no other force in nature equal to it. Joseph was a tempest and Lucy was just a raft, hoping to ride out the storm and see the calm of the other side. How foolish to think she could have survived on such a flimsy vessel.

Fishing around in the compartment of the car door she found a few scrunched up tissues, wiped her streaming nose and dabbed her eyes. She looked at the box of jumbled pictures. Turning on the courtesy light, Lucy took a lucky dip and pulled one out.

Despite her tears, a smile spread across her face as she looked at the slightly blurred picture of a blue-eyed little boy, no more than two, peering up at the camera in surprise, having been caught drinking from his father's cup in the garden. The window into the past made her delve further, wanting to find more.

Another showed a ten to twelve year old Joseph, all teeth and ears, wearing a Michael Jackson T-shirt, cheek to cheek with a beautiful blonde lady who had his eyes: his mother.

The next picture commanded tears in an instant. It was of a clean-shaven Joseph in full combat gear, grinning broadly and holding his rifle diagonally across his chest – the very rifle that had killed the little boy standing right next to him.

Joseph had his hand affectionately on the boy's shoulder. Beautiful was a word rarely used to describe men or boys, but he was truly deserving of such praise. He had butterscotch skin, jet black hair and deep brown eyes that could melt the sun. The boy looked so happy and Joseph so proud.

Somehow the picture made it all very real. Lucy recollected George's telling of the story with the moving images of those pictured. *Dear God. What he must have gone through.* Running out of tissues, she placed the photo back in the box, face-down.

Her hand reached up to the light when the corner of a pale green card caught her eye. Curious, she tugged it free from the packed photos. It was a small booklet with the crest of the Royal Marines embossed on the cover. She opened it up and flicked over the general information.

Then she was hit by a sight that was surely impossible, the shock of it ripped the breath from her lungs. Lucy's head shot back against the cushion of the headrest.

She glared through the windscreen, seeing nothing but the image – an image that was beyond the bounds of possibility. She was almost too scared to look again in case she had been mistaken.

Shaking, Lucy held the booklet in front of her, the palpitations leaving her breathless. She read slowly, carefully.

Royal Marine Commando Joseph Dalton, 3… 2… 9…
7… 4… 6… 1… 5… *Oh. My. God.*

Lady Lavinia's numbers. There was no need to check,
she knew them by heart, having compared them to just
about everything that had a set of numbers of any kind.
She thought back to her reading, bullet points screaming
out at her.

Troubled heart. Great sorrow. A battle lies ahead. Feeling like
she had been hit with a sledgehammer, her hands hung
onto her hair. 'What the hell am I doing sitting here?'

Turning the light out, she smashed the accelerator
down and wrestled the steering wheel to full lock,
bumping up the curb.

The engine screamed out as she redlined it back to
George's house, then screeched to a halt. Continuing the
race on foot, she ran up to the door and started to hammer
it with her fists like a crazed woman.

Joseph flung the door open. 'What the hell's going
on?'

Before he could say any more Lucy charged, shoving
him back against the wall, both her hands flat on his chest.

'You think the marines were tough? Well I'm tough
too. I am not going to let you punish yourself any longer. I
won't give up. No matter how many times you slam that
door in my face,

as sure as the sun rises I *will* return, every day, without
fail until my very last breath if I have to. How dare you
presume to tell me what is for the best?' She slapped him
on the chest. 'Is a broken heart, sleepless nights and a deep
yearning that is fucking relentlessly eating away at my soul
good for me?'

The muffled chimes of his phone tactlessly interrupted

her. Taking it out, he cancelled the call.

'You're hurting, I know. And now that you've lost your dad it's even worse. But I loved him too.' Her voice fractured. Determined to finish she spoke on. 'I promised him on the day he died that I would look after you.' She fingered away her tears defiantly. 'I will keep that promise – do you hear me?'

His phone rang once again. 'Jesus, will you answer that bloody phone?'

He Looked at the screen again, cancelled the call and slipped the phone back into his pocket.

'I didn't know you could be so bossy.' The soft tone of his voice was a relief.

'I'm like you, Joseph. I'm willing to fight for what I believe in.'

'Don't cry, Lucy – please.' His finger swept a teardrop from her cheek.

'Don't make me cry then,' she sniffled.

'I don't deserve this.'

'Why do you say that? Everyone deserves someone to love them. So here I am. And whether you let me or not, I will – I do.'

She gave a sigh of exhaustion and her hold on Joseph slackened. He rested his forehead on Lucy's, his arms taking the fear from her soul.

'I hope you know what you're letting yourself in for.'

She slid her hands up to his broad shoulders. 'I'd follow you to Hell and back.'

'I may just take you there.'

'As long as you let me stand by your side, I'm ready to face anything.' She laid her head on his chest, listening to the heart that hers beat for.

The door to Utopia had opened. This was home, not bricks and mortar but the simple embrace of the one man to whom she had given her all. Lady Lavinia's prophecy had been fulfilled. He was meant to be hers and she would forever be his.

Determined to ruin the moment, Joseph's phone interrupted again.

'Whoever it is, they're persistent,' muttered Lucy.

It rang on. Joseph made no attempt to answer.

'You'd better see who it is.'

'They can wait.'

'It might be important.'

Frowning at the screen he answered abruptly 'Yes…? Sam?'

Lucy looked up at Joseph.

'How did you get this number?'

Somewhat confused, she mouthed 'my Sam?'He nodded.

'You got it from my picture card? You mean the business card – the one with the lawn mower on it?'

She stepped back, watching Joseph's face closely.

'Is everything okay, Sam…? You're a bit worried? What about…?' Joseph's confusion hardened into deep concern, worrying Lucy.

'What? What's wrong?'She asked.

Joseph began to look around patting his pockets with his free hand. 'There's smoke coming from under the living room door.'

Lucy held her hand to her mouth, worry now turning to panic. Joseph bolted upstairs and ran back down clutching his keys.

'Where's your dad…?'

'In the lounge and the door's locked,' he said, repeating Sam's answer for Lucy's benefit. He looked at her gravely and started to usher her out of the door.

'Sam, you've been a very good boy calling me. Now, get out of the house, go into the street, knock on someone's door and ask for help, okay…? You can't get out? That door's locked too.'

They both climbed into Joseph's pickup.

'Go to your bedroom, close the door and put a pillow or a blanket at the bottom of the door. Do you understand, Sam?' Reversing off the drive, they spun around. 'What's that beeping, Sam? Sam? Sam! Fuck, his battery must've died. Do you know where he lives?'

'Yes – oh my God, is he okay?' Lucy sank into her seat as they sped off.

'I think there's a fire. Call the fire service and put your seatbelt on.'

Lucy made the call while being flung from side to side. His slow, steady driving style was gone. The outside world became a melted blur as he worked the old pickup to the limit, running red lights and screaming around corners.

Apart from giving directions, they didn't speak. Joseph was focused on driving and Lucy was hoping it was all a silly mistake. But when they turned into Eden Row it became very clear there was no mistake. Black and grey smoke was escaping from one of the first floor windows, twisting and swirling like a ghostly apparition.

'Oh, dear God, no!'

Joseph unclipped his belt. Parting the gathered crowd with his horn, he screeched to a stop, overshooting the building. Orange flames licked at the brickwork like the tongue of a great dragon, growing more ferocious every second.

'Where the fuck is the fire brigade?' said Lucy, throwing the door open. Joseph was already out. She ran behind, catching up as his pace slowed to a halt and his shoulders sagged at the sight of the noxious fog bellowing from under the main entrance doors. The more the monster devoured, the bigger it grew, climbing with its forked stabs.

Motionless, Lucy stared at the unstoppable force. She knew what Joseph was thinking, because she was thinking it too. She began patrolling backwards and forwards, repeatedly questioning the absence of the fire brigade, half hysterical with helplessness, the heat burning her face even though they were some feet away.

Joseph turned his back on the flames and calmed her, his hand caressing her cheek with the whisper of a touch. The strange picture of calm, innocent serenity gracing his face puzzled her for a moment.

Tears bravely defied the heat, drying before reaching their journey's end. She knew the expression: George had described it to her perfectly. It was the face of acceptance.

'Lucy.' He took in all of her beauty for a moment. 'Thank you for saving me.'

She held onto his wrist with what little strength she had, paralysed and choking with fear at what he was about to do.

'I love you.'

He spoke with the clear honesty of a man at the end of his days, and in that instant he snatched himself away, leaving Lucy clinging to the heated railings, screaming his name helplessly as she watched him charge down the path in a futile attempt to save the boy. He was quickly swallowed up in the black smoke.

She stumbled backwards, the heat too much to bear, Lucy pressed her palms together offering her soul to save their lives. But she knew Joseph was aware of his fate. He had found his honourable death.

A large crowd watched with a sickening amusement reminiscent of the ignorance of the middle ages, their phones held high to capture the action.

The raging demon snapped and crackled as it crunched on the bones of its poor victims, the bitter smell of melted paint and scorched wood poisoned the air. The sound of approaching sirens ignited the flames of hope, the square-faced truck a blaze of blue lights, a vision for desperate eyes.

Lucy ran over to the army of men that spilled out from the vehicle and grabbed on to the closest.

'Please hurry. There's a six-year-old boy in there and two men.' The fire officer turned around and she recognised the big ginger moustache.

'Do you remember me – from the school fete?'

'I remember, you were with the little boy with the cap and the man with the beard.'

'Yes! They're both in there. You've got to get them out!' Lucy tugged at his arm.

The face of experience viewed the task ahead while his team rushed around rolling out hoses. The look in his eyes held no promise at all. 'We will do our best ma'am.'

He rushed into action leaving Lucy bereft of any faith. Helplessly, she watched life plot another course. The firemen hurriedly set up their equipment yet everything seemed to take an age.

She stumbled back towards the end of her world,

getting as close as the heat would allow, ignoring the instructions to move back. Her hopes, desires and dreams were now nothing but ashes.

'You get back out here, soldier,' she sobbed quietly. 'Go save Sam and come back to me. Please... please come back to me.' Crushed, her head dropped.

Another fire engine arrived. More organised chaos ensued. The blaze continued to roar out its dominance; firemen called instructions to one another, against a background of constant flashes from pictures being taken by the viewing public blinked out. Overwhelmed, Lucy felt her sanity and consciousness slipping away from her. The unmistakable sound of shattering glass dragged her fading senses back to life. An old TV flew out of the first-floor window, crashing onto the bonnet of the battered Honda below. Injected with adrenalin, Lucy fixed her eyes on the plume of smoke spewing out.

The hoses were now ready to go, and the firemen began to move in. Then, as if her pleas had been answered, Joseph shot out of the blackness, curled up like a cannonball, the flames chasing after him. He crashed onto the roof of the Honda, the impact shattering its windows.

Lifeless, he laid on his side, his back to her. Lucy's heart stopped. Standing on the edge of sanity, the ground beneath her feet began to crumble with each second that passed. She willed him to move, to give her a sign that he was okay. He had spent a long time in the belly of the beast and now he lay at its feet, either victim or victor. Firemen rushed to his aid. Joseph rolled onto his back, his arm flopping over the edge of the crumpled car, and there, tucked against his chest, clutching his beloved teddy bear, was Sam. Joseph's baseball cap was pulled down over his face.

'Oh my God, he's got Sam!' Lucy sprang into action, running towards them, but was tackled by a fireman. Despite her protests, he carried Lucy, wriggling, to a safe distance while his colleagues moved in to help the two of them.

As soon as she was set free Lucy ran straight back to them. Sam was taken away from his saviour, carried by a fire-fighter who delivered him to a waiting paramedic.

Unsure of which way to turn, she ran to Joseph first and leapt into his arms. 'I thought I'd lost you both.' She held onto him, the horror of her imagination still lingering.

The *what if,* slowly seeping from her eyes into the smoky T-shirt of a man that was surely above all others. The best feeling in the world was the way in which he clung to her, desperate with need and in that gruesome setting, Lucy felt truly blessed.

'You can't get rid of me that easily,' he coughed. 'You're stuck with me now.' Joseph stroked her hair with his face. 'Go to Sam, Lucy.'

She nodded, not wanting to let go. 'Go to him; he'll be scared.'

'Come with me.' She looked up into his smoke-polluted face.

'I will – I just need a minute.' He kissed her on the lips savouring the taste like a starving man would his first meal. 'Go – go,' he breathed.

Tearing herself away, she dodged through the mass of people, looking for Sam.

Joseph stumbled forward a few steps, coughing, as the night air chased the poison out of him. Exhausted, he turned to face what he had believed would be the place of his death. The whole building was now a ball of fire, casting great shadows that stretched out across the ground, clawing at his feet like the hands of the devil.

He fell to his knees, the relief of saving a child's life was as powerful as the grief of taking one. He turned his face up to the starless sky. The purity of a single tear cut a track down his black face.

'Thank you.' The whispered words floated away on the warm air. He did not know whom he was thanking – it was beyond his understanding. Whatever label you cared to give it, luck, a guardian angel… God. Joseph submitted to it gladly.

Sitting in the ambulance, Lucy shielded Sam's face from the glaring lights, cradling him in her arms. The paramedic said it was a miracle that he had survived unscathed, but he had, and that was all that mattered.

Her body tense with unease, Lucy kept her gaze fixed on the disarray beyond the open doors. The horror of the evening would not be dispelled until he was by her side.

Backlit by the flames, Joseph's silhouette appeared. Sam sank down on Lucy's bosom as pent-up anguish escaped from her lips. towards them he was stopped by the fire chief who shook his hand, no doubt showering him with the praise he so richly deserved. Even though she could see he was safe, her impatience began to set in. She was desperate to look into his eyes and feel his hand in hers, she jealously watched the fire chief, who was delaying a moment she had long dreamed of. Finally, giving Joseph a pat on the shoulder, he set him free.

'Look who's here, Sam.' He peeped from under the peak of his cap and came to life on seeing his rescuer. Climbing down from Lucy's lap, Sam leapt out of the ambulance and ran into the open arms of Joseph, crouched down to greet him with a bright smile.

'Thank you for saving me, Mr Joe.'

'No, Sam. It was you who saved me.'

Lucy exchanged a tearful look with Joseph. She understood him completely and loved him unconditionally. Joseph groaned in pain as he stood with Sam in his arms.

'It's time for you to get checked out,' said Lucy, placing her hand on his cheek.

'No, I'm fine.' He kissed her fingers and looked back at the great jets of water which were coming from all directions but having little effect.

'We've got to move now.' Holding Sam with one arm, he reached out and took Lucy's hand, leading her across the street and into the gathered crowds.

'Joseph, the police are going to want to talk to us.'

'It can wait until tomorrow,' he said, weaving between the strangers.

'But what about Sam? We can't just…'

He stopped at the edge of their cover, twenty feet from his pickup. 'I know. Just for tonight we can. You trust me?'

Squeezing his hand, she looked up at him. 'With my life.'

'Stay close to my side. Sam, keep your head down, little man, okay?'

He nodded, his head resting on Joseph's chest. Boldly, they walked out to the pickup.

Expecting someone to call after them, Lucy looked back over her shoulder.

One police officer was with the fire chief and the other was talking on his radio. Lucy climbed in and Joseph handed Sam over to her, then closed the door. She scrutinised the reflections in the wing mirror, fearful that they wouldn't get away and Sam would be taken from them to spend the night with total strangers who didn't understand him – didn't love him.

The engine started before Joseph had closed the door. He drove Sam away from the nightmare of his little life for the last time, never to return again.

The quiet comfort of the cab rocked Lucy and Sam. It was a therapeutic refuge from the bombardment they had all experienced.

'Where are we going?' asked Lucy, placing her hand on his thigh. Joseph laid his eyes on Sam for a moment. 'To keep a promise.'

The night was calm and so was their unhurried journey back to George's house. Sam clung to Joseph's neck as his rescuer carried him through the sweet smell of the garden and upstairs to the place that been his bedroom when he was just a boy himself.

Lucy undressed Sam, exposing the marks of his father's fists across the boy's fragile back. Fighting back the tears, Lucy looked up at Joseph. Pity welled in his eyes and anger strained in his taut fists.

Wrapped in one of Joseph's T-shirts, Sam lay down in a clean bed for the very first time in his short life. Lucy leaned over and kissed him on the forehead. Sam reached out and held onto her tightly, his embrace conveying what he could not. Wiping her tears from the boy's face, she wished him sweet dreams.

Joseph turned out the lamp and knelt beside the bed, intending to make good on his promise. He told Sam a bedtime story filled with all the things that the boy had only ever dreamt of: love, laughter, kindness, and a happily-ever-after. Brushing the boy's hair with his fingers, he tucked him in.

'Mr Joe?' Sam asked eyes half open. 'Can I live here now, with you and Miss Lucy?'

Joseph looked over at her.

'I don't want to go back home.'

Lucy's hands covered her face. His naive simplicity tugged at her heartstrings.

Joseph laid his hand on the boy's cheek. 'Sam, this is your home now, with me and Lucy. You may have to stay with another family – just for a short while until we've got a few things sorted. But you know I'm going to come and get you. I always keep my promises, Sam – always. So don't you worry, everything is going to be just fine, okay?' Sam nodded before tiredness took him.

'That's a big promise you've just made to that little boy,' she whispered.

He stood and held both her hands tightly. 'I'm a soldier, soldiers fight, and we're going to fight for him. As I live and breathe, that child will suffer no more.' His teeth gritted. 'No more. This will be our home – mine, yours and Sam's.'

Lucy's arms belted his waist with no feelings of guilt or shame. No more wanting and wishing; he was hers, as she had been his from the moment his face became known to her eyes.

'Do you know what you've done to me, Joseph? I love you so much I'm almost scared to think that this is real.'

'Lucy, look at me.' His hands softly caressed her face. 'You are the one chance I never thought I'd get. I'm tired of being scared. Love me, because I love you with everything and all that I am. No more tears.' His thumbs brushed aside the pear-shaped drops. 'Let's start living.'

Their lips met, not in lust or the heat of passion, but in a complete and utter covenant to each other; the kiss of truth.

They decided to sleep in Sam's room in case he woke in the night. Joseph made a makeshift bed for them with pillows and cushions, and Lucy lay propped up on her elbow stroking his hair until he drifted into sleep.

Despite the shadow of the hour, Lucy gazed at his face, her hands seeing what her eyes could not. There were a few people in this world who had a light about them, and Joseph was one of them. He was oblivious to it, of course, but to everyone else it was plain to see.

He was brave, honest, decent and kind. Qualities that shouldn't be so rare in the modern world, but sadly were. He had risked his own life with nothing but the tiniest speck of a chance that he might save another.

There simply was no higher level of selflessness.

EPILOGUE

After five months of fostering, endless paperwork and interviews, the adoption was finalised.

Sam was legally theirs.

The investigation into the fire concluded that his father had fallen asleep with a cigarette, having become drowsy after coming down from a heroin-induced high. Evidence was found alongside his remains to support this theory.

Joseph was awarded the George Medal for his act of outstanding bravery. It hung above Sam's bed, Joseph had humbly declared that he was the real hero.

Lucy returned to school full-time and watched Sam rise to the top of the class, free of the persecution and fear that had weighed him down. He was finally allowed to flourish into the boy he was meant to be.

Mark and Pete bought a bar in Spain and continued to live under the pretence they were friends. Mark's initial influx of emails slowly decreased to nothing, until it was left to Suzie to give her the odd update on how they were.

Suzie had, yet again risked her heart to Andre, the rock

climber, despite Lucy's diplomatic warnings. He was a man that could never love another more than he loved himself.

Charles, or Reggie Sloan as he was really known, walked into a police station in Dover to turn himself in, claiming a guilty conscience. Lucy suspected revenge was the motivating factor.

His partner-in-crime had used him as a pawn in her masterplan. Now that he was penniless, he was only too happy to help with the investigation.

Lucy didn't care about the money; financially, they were secure. Her half of the house sale amounted to over half a million.

More importantly, she was emotionally secure and that brought her more happiness than any amount of money could.

Lucy poured hot milk into the three mugs. As she mixed in the chocolate powder she enjoyed her view from the window, beautiful as it was in many ways.

A heavy covering of snow had turned all sharp angles and edges into soft curves. Joseph and Sam were rolling along a great snowball, leaving the green track of the underlying grass behind them. She watched with a smile as Joseph pretended to struggle to lift the snowman's head, Sam's rosy-cheeked giggles warmed her heart.

Joseph still had his demons, but this time around he had Lucy to help him fight them. When he woke in a cold sweat she would soothe him back to sleep.

On dark nights when darker thoughts came, he would sit in Sam's room and watch over him. He had found redemption in the innocent adulation of a child.

Both boy and man had their disabilities, but each filled

in the gaps that the other was missing. Sam would always have his problems, but with love on his side anything was possible.

Stuffing a carrot into her pocket, she wriggled her hands back into her gloves and collected their drinks.

She stopped to look at Joseph's Service Record, which was now framed and proudly hung on the kitchen wall.

Every single day, without fail, she read it.

'Royal Marine Commando Joseph Dalton. 3 2 9 7 4 6 1 5.'

They certainly were her lucky numbers.

ACKNOWLEDGEMENTS

Lucky Numbers has taken far longer to complete than I ever imagined or intended.

Life has thrown many obstacles in my way, and there are a few people I'd like to thank that have helped to clear my path to the finish line.

First on that list are my girls, Carver's Cuties. You are all truly amazing. Thank you so much for your unwavering encouragement and support. I want to say a special thank you to Nicola Rhead from

Nicola Rhead Editing and Proofreading Services, and Kerry Callaway. Ladies, your generosity and love astounds me. Thank you for keeping the wheels turning.

To Elena Cruz, Paula Radell, Jen Lassalle Edwards, Maggie 'Nana' Smith, Claire Ridley, Laura Nelson and Jude Prendergast. Thank you for your advice and guidance It means so much to me.

Thanks also to Neil Badland for spending endless hours reading my manuscript both forwards and backwards.

To Veronika Fabisiak, my friend. When technology conspires against me, she is always there to save the day - and she brings me bread and milk. The dream would be impossible without you.

Thank you to my amazing wife, Sarah, and our three beautiful children. You are the very reason my heart beats.

To my best friend Carver Jnr. The one who never judges me. When I am talking away to myself he always listens to my nonsense and makes me smile every single time I see his big brown eyes. My nights would be very lonely without him by my side.

Many thanks to all the wonderful ladies of Facebook. I'm truly grateful for your support.

And of course to you, the reader. Thank you so much for allowing me into your life. I hope your journey with me was an enjoyable one. Until next time...

ABOUT THE AUTHOR

Born in the heart of England to two devoted parents he enjoyed a happy, loving childhood. Not long after completing his further education he set off on a worldwide adventure visiting various places around the globe, but it was New Zealand that stole his heart. It was here that he discovered his creative side with amateur dramatics, and he made several brief appearances in national soap operas.

After 5 years he returned to England and discovered his passion for writing. He wrote several unpublished children's books, but had a vision for a book that would take him on an exciting journey.

He also lives with his close companion Carver Jnr his cuddly pup that features in many of his humorous Facebook updates. He enjoys keeping fit, long walks in the fresh air and spending time with close family and friends.

Stay in touch with the author via:
Facebook: facebook.com/ggcarver/
Twitter: twitter.com/ggcarver

If you liked Lucky Numbers, please post a review at Amazon, and let your friends know about Lucky Numbers and Whiter than White

Printed in Poland
by Amazon Fulfillment
Poland Sp. z o.o., Wrocław